CURSE
OF
SHADOWS
AND
THORNS

By: LJ Andrews

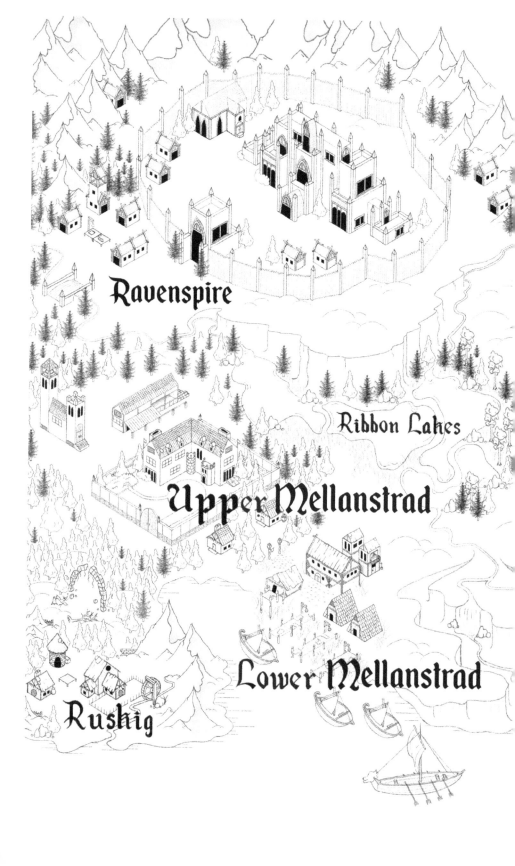

Ravenspire

Ribbon Lakes

Upper Mellanstrad

Lower Mellanstrad

Rushig

To those who pretend to cheer for the hero,
but really love the villain.

AUTHOR NOTE

Hello beautiful readers. For those who follow along with an audiobook, since the audiobook's recording there are some passages in a few chapters that have been changed slightly in the ebook and print book. The meaning will be the same, but it could read differently. But I know you'll enjoy Legion Grey however you read.

CHAPTER ONE

I'D DIE if I stayed much longer.

My father warned me if he caught me sneaking into the game hall again, my name would be blotted out from the royal house, and I'd be tossed into the quarries to rot alongside the king's captured fae.

My uncle was the king, and if I shamed our family, I had no doubt he'd be the first to bind me in chains.

But I couldn't leave. Not yet. This was my time to pretend I was someone else, someone with a life beyond the controls and demands of the royal house.

I startled when a heavy body thudded onto the greasy floorboards. A few grunts preceded the roar of curses to the gods, as if his drunkenness had been their fault. A grin curled over my mouth, one I promptly hid behind my cards. No sense in drawing attention to myself when I was the only one in the game hall breaking the law.

Korman, the nightwatchman, had knocked out his front

tooth when he landed onto the floor of the bawdy game hall. Spiced red spilled from the ewer over Korman's woolen gambeson, pasting his hand of cards to his chest like badges of honor. He dabbed his mouth, bemused. At the sight of blood on his dirty fingertips, he cursed more than once, then followed it with an eruption of laughter.

I scooted over as Halvar, a stable hand from the estate, leaned over to clasp Korman's hand.

"Up you go," Halvar said, and clapped the shaky nightwatchman on the back.

Korman fumbled back into his seat at the table. An eel fisherman slammed a new horn of spiced red in front of the man, then barked a laugh as Korman drained it so quickly the drops dribbled down his russet beard onto the table.

"Had enough?" Halvar asked.

"Carry on," Korman said, words slurred, lips pink with blood.

The game went on as though nothing had delayed it to begin with.

Halvar lifted his eyes to my side of the table. The deep brown reminded me of roasted chestnuts, and sometimes the flash of unusual light in his gaze left me wondering if he might have a bit of Night Folk fae in his blood. He didn't have the pronounced point to his ear, but according to fae lore, some could conceal their true natures with their fury, the magic of the earth and of illusion.

I hoped Halvar wasn't fae. I liked him too much, and Night Folk were known to be ruthless.

Unless my uncle found them, forced them into submission in his quarries, or sent them to the executioner, of course.

Part of me did not believe Night Folk existed anymore, and Zyben simply told pretty tales of his power over the fae folk to seem more ruthless than he already was.

I tugged on the brim of my napless cap and dragged my hand to the back of my neck to ensure my braid remained tucked underneath. I was a little discomposed by the way Halvar's gaze lingered too long.

No, he didn't recognize me. Why would he? As the second daughter, of the second royal family, I was of little importance at the royal estate.

Halvar's sun-toasted skin still had smudges from the day's work, but every man in the game hall smelled of unwashed skin, old fish, and topped with a bit of brine from being so near the Fate's Ocean. The exact reason I'd patted my moonlight pale cheeks in soil before sneaking into the game hall.

"Boy," Halvar said, looking at me. "Play or be played."

My grip tightened around my playing cards. The two missing fingertips on my left hand made them harder to hold, but I didn't let on as I fanned out each card.

Unskilled as I was at the game, I'd watched enough monte tricks and gambles in town to know I had a decent hand. Shoulders slouched, barred away from the men at the table, I played three golden axes painted on the bent, yellowed cards.

The eel fisherman groaned and cursed the trickster god as he tossed his hand down.

Korman had already become lost in his cups again and didn't notice.

A financier at the trade docks balked and countered my play with two gold axes and three black wolvyn.

Halvar chuckled. "Piss poor luck, boy."

My heart thumped in my chest. Don't play it. Don't draw attention.

"Wait," I said in the deepest voice I could manage. It sounded ridiculous. Never was I more grateful for the amount of ale passed around, since no one seemed to notice in their haze. Call it pride, but I couldn't resist and slammed down the card I'd hoarded all evening. The battling crowns: one blood red, one black as a starless sky. "Crowns trump wolvyn."

Before my hand left the pile of cards, once more, Korman found himself on his back when the table erupted in shouts of counting cards, of tricks and schemes and cheats.

Halvar's eyes brightened as he burst out of his seat, his fist colliding with a tradesman in a boisterously patterned suit, though, the man had nothing to do with our game.

The stable hand laughed as if he'd waited all night for this moment, then leapt into a tussle between the eel fisherman, the financier, and a bulky brute from the docks.

I dropped the last of my cards and ducked beneath the tables, scurrying toward the back of the game hall.

Glass shattered. Wood on wood scraped over the floors as chairs and tables were tossed. Cracks of knuckles on jaws. Laughter—always laughter—as the warrior and raider blood of these people burst into yet another fight.

The first of the evening, but surely not the last.

As I crept past the ale counter, the aleman took in the scuffle. His shoulders slumped and I thought I heard him mutter, "Here we go," under his breath before he grabbed a wooden rod and lunged into the tangle of fists.

How dull life would be without respite eve at the dock

shanties, the once-a-week night when serfs were afforded a few hours of fun.

With chaos at my back, I used my shoulder to shove through the door, but smashed into another body.

I squeaked my surprise, then quickly remembered I was meant to be a sturdy boy indentured at the local blacksmith. Rough and unafraid. My eyes raised enough to note the polished boots and merchant's belt meant I'd collided with a wealthier man.

"Apologies, *Herr*," I muttered deep and low.

"No apologies," he returned, pausing for a breath. "*De hän.*"

I froze. He'd addressed me as female.

My hand whipped to my neck again, but the plaits of my braid were still tucked beneath my cap. He leaned forward, his skin like the spice of the forest.

"Not to worry," he whispered. "I'm good with secrets."

I fumbled for the coin purse tucked deep in the trousers I'd stolen from the uniform closet back home. The man placed a hand on my arm. A shudder danced down my spine. I didn't look up; afraid he'd piece together my face beneath the dirt and oil smudges over my nose.

"Are you paying for my silence?"

I swallowed the scratch in my throat. "Doesn't everyone in Mellanstrad?"

He chuckled, a sound I felt to my bones. "True. Even still, keep your *shim* for another day, *de hän.*"

With that, he strode toward the debauchery of the game hall. I stole a glance over my shoulder. My throat tightened at the sight of him. Three hells I was a fool. Legion Grey.

The face I'd hoped to see all night, and now he'd caught me.

Would he recognize me? Tell my father? All gods, would he tell the king?

The dark gold of his hair, the broad shape of his shoulders, hands that looked too rough to be a merchant, all of Legion had become the most recognizable attributes in Lower Mellanstrad township.

Rumors filtered through high society about Legion—most suspected him to be the son of some noble family from one of the exotic kingdoms beyond the horizon. Others thought him to be half Timoran and half Ettan.

I favored the theory.

His hair was paler like Timorans, my people. But his skin and eyes glimmered with the unique dark shade of Ettans, the people mine had defeated during the raids.

Legion Grey had made a mark among veteran merchants for his ability to negotiate financials for the wealthy, but more so among desperate mothers aiming to convince the handsome stranger to take on one, or even two, of their daughters.

He was intriguing. Nothing more. And I had no desire to *speak* to the man. Doubtless, I'd be as invisible to him as I was to everyone else.

Before he let the door shut, Legion looked back at me. A curl tugged at the corner of his mouth, then he disappeared into the game hall.

When my heart stopped racing, I adjusted my cap and turned down a narrow alley.

Mellanstrad docks were always coated in a fine layer of brine and sea grass. It reeked of oysters, eel, and exotic fish caught in the precarious reefs far out to sea. The dock shanties were made of tenements and old shacks that leaned from turns of sea storms. Here the lampposts were chipped and rusted. Mud pooled over cracked cobblestones. Here folk spent their miserly incomes at game halls, alehouses, and brothels.

Here, I was free.

I ducked into an arcade when a trio of Ravenspire guards rounded onto the street. Castle Ravenspire often sent more patrols after the midnight tolls, likely looking for Ettan folk to indenture.

In the shadows, I shot a quick prayer to the war gods for Halvar to find his way home safely. Though he said little to me, I knew the stable hand was a favorite among the other serfs at the estate, and he'd only been indentured for half a turn.

After the patrol passed, I sprinted down the back roads until I found the loose board in the wooden gate separating the lower shanties from Upper Mellanstrad.

Snake grass and wild roses snagged my tattered jacket as I climbed the slope to the villas and overseeing estates.

When my legs had been poked and prodded, scraped, and mangled by the brambles, I arrived at the iron gate of the Lysander estate. Trimmed lawns and quaint wood and wattle longhouses dotted the surrounding knolls near the white, center manor. Made of pearlstone, the estate sang of prestige, of royalty.

I ducked into the hedgerow and carefully inched toward the back cellar.

Along the curve of the brick drive, fine hansom cabs and cabriolets with velvet curtains parked at the main entrance. Lyres and lutes sang out a sweet melody from inside.

The closest unit of raven guards was at least thirty paces away. The regal blue, black, and white paint on their faces gleamed in the lanternlight. A way to look more like the warriors of the gods. Runes hung from talismans on thick beards and battle axes on their belts.

The guards looked ready for war, not protectors of a wealthy fete.

When the guards turned about-face in the opposite direction, I darted across the soft lawn.

I fumbled with the key a bit before the lock to the cellar clicked and the door groaned on old hinges. My teeth clenched as I carefully ducked inside, desperate not to draw attention to myself, and closed the heavy door at my back.

The cellar was murky, and the pungent scent of damp soil and starch burned my nostrils. Boxes lined the arched stone walls, and only the light of the pale moon burst in blue shadows through the windows.

I'd done it. Well, halfway. I still needed to slip into the main halls without being seen.

It was a fool's dream.

Before I'd finished standing, fingernails dug into the meat of my arms and dragged me out from behind my crate.

I stumbled, nearly falling forward. Two figures blocked my way. Sharp, narrowed eyes met mine, but the most worrisome was the knife at my throat.

"*Kvinna* Elise," the girl holding the knife grumbled. "We've been looking for you."

CHAPTER TWO

"THREE HELLS, Siverie! Put that bleeding knife down." The second girl swatted the blade off my throat. She was the tallest of us, the thickest, and had a constant furrow of worry over her brow.

"Siv," I said, eyes wide. "I agree with Mavie. I don't particularly like knives at my throat."

To see a smile on Siv's face was rarer than blossoms in winter. Constantly looking over her shoulder, blades hidden in her aprons or in her boots. A serf with a history. I didn't know what always put her on edge, but most Ettans had not lived a peaceful life. Perhaps I never asked why she wanted to slit everything that moved because I was too afraid to learn the horrors of her life.

Siv pinched her lips and tucked the knife into her apron pocket. "Where have you been?"

I let out a nervous chuckle and held out my hands. "I know you both are probably angry—"

"Angry?" Siv said. "Angry at what? That the *Kvinna* was missing, or that you left without us?"

"Enough with the *Kvinna*," I said, more because I hated when my title followed me everywhere. Somehow it left me feeling dirty and grimy.

"You're the king's niece. Especially tonight," Mavie said, smoothing the front of her serf frock. "We're going to call you *Kvinna*."

She held out the silver wrist band with two forward facing raven heads on the ends. Then Siv handed over a rowan berry tiara I'd tuck in my braids soon enough.

I rolled my eyes and took them. Being a *Kvinna*, a royal daughter, meant my mother practically pasted the title to my skin. Not that I'd need it. Even being an insignificant member of my family line, the wrist band would give me away at first glance. Everyone knew the Lysanders.

How could you not know the family of the king?

Sometimes I wished I could live like the Ettan serfs, or the townsfolk in the shanties. The desire said a great deal because there was something mightily wrong with how the Ettan people lived.

New Timoran had been built from what was once the country of Etta. This land was lush, green, and once filled with abundant forests and glassy rivers. Two centuries ago, Timorans had raided for the resources, since beyond the North Cliffs the old Timoran was tundra. Cold, hard. Unforgiving.

I tugged off the cap and let my frosty braid fall over my shoulder. A color so pale it almost looked blue. Timoran to the bone by looks, but more Ettan by heart.

"You keep causing a stir around here and who's to say what

King Zyben might do to you," Mavie insisted and snatched the cap from my hand, returning it to a peg near the door. "Take it from me, enjoy the wine and the parties. The lower side isn't as glamorous as we make it seem."

"Zyben has too much affection for my mother to do anything drastic," I lied. Somewhere along the way my uncle had left his heart behind. He held no affection for me, for I had no purpose in his court. Only my sister, Runa, had necessity. But one step out of line, and I did risk him withdrawing his much-needed graces regarding my father.

As a second family we did not have mediks, the healers of Castle Ravenspire. If anyone in the kingdom had fae fury, the mediks of Castle Ravenspire did. I did not understand how they kept my father's blood infection from spreading.

Without the king's mercy, without our compliance, my father would be left for the Otherworld.

The king knew it, and used it to exert power over our house. Over me.

The cellar door clanged open and Siv huffed, gesturing for us to move out of the dank room.

I tried to lighten the tension with a chuckle. "Being a little loud tonight, Siv."

The gilded brown of her eyes flashed in something like anger—or amusement—with Siv it was hard to tell. "You left *without* me! Without us."

Siv kept her glossy black hair tied in a long tail at the base of her neck. She had nicks and marks from fights in her past. I thought she had a wild beauty that had drawn more than one eye—even from Timorans.

"I'm sorry," I said as I secured the wrist band. "I needed to get out, just for a moment. I couldn't find you."

"Next time, I expect to be found before you leave," Siv said.

Mavie nodded. "Me too."

Siv stood in front, while Mavie ushered me forward from the back. I had no choice but to move. Out in the corridor, Siv opened a thick door in the wall, and waved us inside. "There are too many Ravens wandering about now. We'll take the serf passages."

Raven was the nickname for Ravenspire patrols, and if anyone else but Mavie and me heard Siv use the slang she'd be lashed on the post at the edge of the thicket.

"Why are there so many?"

"Because the Blood Wraith and his Guild of Shade attacked the slaver caravans in the southern foothills," Mavie grumbled.

A sharp heat struck me in the chest until I coughed to simply catch a breath.

"W-what?" I leaned against the mossy river stone walls. "The Blood Wraith?"

At the mention of his name, I rubbed my two missing fingertips.

Mavie made a noise of disgust. "Bleeding killers. Can't be human if you ask me. Not the way he slaughters."

The Blood Wraith had hunted the lands of New Timoran for as long as I could remember. Said to be the kind of Night Folk with dark fury and a fondness for blood and bone.

Timoran was made of guilds, and the Wraith was no different.

The guild who followed him killed as well as him. I'd had

the misfortune of facing the Blood Wraith—but not even Siv and Mavie knew.

He was a ghost who seemed to step from one shadow to the next.

I agreed with Mavie. The heat in the Wraith's eyes, burned so red it was like flames. The way his guild wrangled the Wraith away from slitting my throat the night he took my fingers—he couldn't be human.

But this was the first I'd heard of any sightings in nearly half a turn.

"All right?" Siv asked, her expression softer.

"Fine."

"I wouldn't fret over the Guild of Shade. Folk blame them for any killings. Could be someone else. But what I wish you'd consider, *Kvinna*, are Agitators," Mavie said. "They're becoming bolder."

"Cursed gods, does the trouble never end?" Agitators were a thorn in my side, in the entire royal line's side. Zealots that took pleasure attacking any Timoran with a drop of noble blood, insisting we were imposters.

I supposed in a way we were, being that Timoran overtook former Etta, removed their royals, and took the crown for ourselves. But Agitators wanted to take back the throne, and when Zyben abdicated to my cousin, his heir apparent, the passing of the crown would create a temporary weakness the Agitators could exploit by destroying an inexperienced ruler.

"Things to think about, is all," Mavie went on. "You put your neck on the line tonight, and we're here to remind you of it."

"My neck was not on any line," I insisted. "I went to a game hall. Besides, I know how to use a blade."

"Yes, but I'm better with one," Siv said."

"True."

Siv tilted her head. "Plus, I always enjoy a good night of rebellion."

"A game hall," I said. "How rebellious."

"Yes," Mavie said and began fiddling with my braid, smoothing the plaits until I batted her away. "Since women are not welcome at the game tables it is a bit rebellious."

"Honestly, for you, everything beyond dreaming of a husband is rebellious," Siv said.

By the gods, she grinned. Kind of.

I snorted a laugh because it was true, sad as it was.

My sole purpose would be to carry on the royal line and be silent about it. I'd have gone mad this last turn with all the chatter about my future match if not for Mavie and Siv. They were my only real friends and lamented over the unfairness of our lives with me.

"I have maybe one turn left before the king barters me away like a prized hog. Let me live a little without reprimands."

Siv lifted a brow. "Live a little? Is that what you call it? Funny since we all know why you sneak off to that particular game hall."

My cheeks heated. "Your pardon?"

"Oh, don't be so prickly," Mavie said, simply to irritate me, no doubt. "We know *Herr* Legion frequents the place. Did you finally speak to him?"

I quickened my steps. "It's illegal for me to even be there. Why would I draw the attention of anyone of position?"

"So, you did see him."

I rolled my eyes. Curses to me for admitting I found the face of Legion Grey handsome. Ever since, Siv and Mavie have been determined to weasel a way for us to speak. "If you must know, yes, we spoke tonight. In passing."

I never imagined Siv's face could show such expression, but her eyes widened like dark orbs, and Mavie forgot herself, squealing loud enough someone in the main house must have heard. "You did! Don't keep it there. What happened?"

There was no reason to lie, they'd force the truth out soon enough. In one breath I repeated the brief interaction, omitting my clumsier moments of colliding into him.

"Honestly, I don't know why it excites you," I said with a touch of bitterness. "I will be matched with someone of the king's choosing, and without Timoran nobility in him, Legion Grey will not be in the running."

"I still think he'd make a delightful face to fantasize about." Mavie grinned. "I know you're against taking vows, and trust me, I've always found it strange how second or third Timoran daughters receive a lottery of potential husbands. Allow yourself to dream of Legion's lips on yours, instead of—"

"An old fool who smokes too much?" I proffered dryly. "At least Runa knows who she'll take vows with."

My sister had the responsibility as the eldest to ensure our delicate royal blood remained secure. She was already betrothed to our cousin, Calder. A blithesome man who had eyes for everyone but Runa. Perhaps, I was the more fortunate one.

"Well, blame your uncle," Siv snapped. "Who, by the way, has been here for nearly an hour. Pick up the pace."

My stomach lurched. It was required to greet the king, and if I never showed, even my absence would be noticed. As we walked, I stripped my coat and the heavy leather belt around my waist. I'd need to be washed and dressed before the next hour, so no sense waiting to undress until my room.

Siv paused at a divot in the wall marked with a blue sash. With a firm nudge of her shoulder, the wall gave way to a large sitting room made of satin chaise lounges, endless shelves of books, pewter tea trays, and bear-fur rugs next to an open hearth.

"Welcome home, *Kvinna* Elise."

I jumped at the voice and shot my gaze to the door leading to my bed chamber. Bevan, the steward of the house, hunched in the shadows, smiling. I guessed him to be a few turns older than my father. His hair had thinned on top, but his skin had only started to sag a bit.

"Bevan," I said, casting furtive glances at Siv and Mavie.

The steward took in the two serfs at my back. "Siverie, Mavie, I'd advise veils and to hurry back to the kitchens before Cook resorts to the switch."

Siv frowned, but I guessed it was more at the command to place the netted veil over her face. A requirement in royal households. Mavie paled, but for her, it was because of Cook. The old woman was terse and took her frustrations out with willow branches.

"We'll speak soon," Siv murmured under her breath.

Together my friends abandoned me to the stillness of my chambers.

"*Kvinna* Elise," Bevan said after a stretched silence. "It's not my business where you spend your time, but I will beg of you, whatever you are doing, please never do so beneath the night sky again. What if you were injured, or mistaken for an Ettan? Could take weeks to sort out such a mess."

"Bevan, what about me screams Ettan?" True enough. My skin was freckled, pale as paper, dry as an onion. Not the smooth, tanned complexion as most Ettans, with their chestnut, or raven-wing black hair.

"All the same, I hope you'll hurry. A bath has been drawn. I'll wait for you downstairs." Bevan gestured to the washroom and left me with a nod to his head.

A gown sprawled across my goose-down mattress. My fingers traced the cold beads sewn into the indigo fabric, the swooping neckline that would show too much flesh.

In the washroom, the water had gone tepid from my tardiness, but was still fragrant with lavender, mint, and rose. I scrubbed the dirt with the bristled brush, scrubbed my fingernails, my hair, until I was pink and raw.

Cleaned and dressed, I once more braided my hair with the rowan tiara. Black lace gloves rested on the edge of a chest of drawers. My frown deepened. Doubtless, my mother had put the gloves out. I wished she hadn't. Was it such a shame to have survived an attack with a scar?

Before leaving my chamber, I practiced walking in the new heeled shoes, and curtsied in the mirror. Satisfied I would not tumble on my face, I gave my reflection a lazy salute, and left with a healthy reluctance toward the fete all together.

At the thick ballroom doors, Bevan waited.

He wore a grim sort of smile. "Lovely, *Kvinna.*"

"Thank you, Bevan," I said.

"I am told congratulations will be in order after your meet with the king."

I paused; my brow furrowed. "Congratulations?"

Bevan's bronze skin paled. "Never mind."

"No, no, Bevan," I scolded. "What do you mean?"

His granite eyes locked on me. "Forgive me, but the talk, uh, the talk in the serf corridors is that *Kvin* Lysander . . . he . . ."

"Bevan! What is it?" My heart lodged in the back of my throat. My stomach turned in sick.

Bevan licked his chapped lips. "Seems at the king's behest, your father has agreed for his majesty to open the bid for your hand, *Kvinna*. You're to be matched."

CHAPTER THREE

My hands wouldn't stop shaking. Married? Matched? Forced to become my mother, an ornament on the arm of a man.

I'd avoided this moment, but with my twentieth turn on the horizon, it was only a matter of time. What men would bid once the king opened the dowry barter?

A distant cousin from the west cliffs had no less than twenty potential matches. It took nearly two months to narrow it down to her husband, a man twenty-seven turns her senior who refused to give up his favorite consort for the marriage.

Timoran culture was archaic. Dowry barters reminded me of some primal competition on who had the most wealth and strength.

No doubt the king would select someone haughty and pompous. Most dowry barters were overseen by fathers, but my father could hardly leave his bed chamber most days. It had been known for some time Zyben would oversee the Lysander daughters.

Doubtless the man who purchased my hand would be someone who would not take kindly to his wife spending her waking hours lost in books on Night Folk lore or wandering in the slums.

"It will be all right, *Kvinna*," Bevan whispered.

His tone was rife with pity. Bevan knew as well as I that life would not be the same. In fact, everything would change. Timoran wives were given purses to spend at their leisure, they turned heads when their husbands took mistresses, kept silent over matters of state. A voice? No, thinking was better left to the men.

I closed my eyes, clenched my fists, and took a deep breath before I strolled into the ballroom.

Three crystal chandeliers lined the gold filigree on the ceilings. Noblemen, women of the High court, high ranking military, and business brokers were drunk with spiced liquors and freshly squeezed juices from the orchards in the back of the manor.

All along the walls were serfs. Masked in black netting. Nameless. Forgotten. Some bore the tattooed raven on a wrist, or a throat. Artistic, as if the bird were flying, but a symbol of servitude to the Ravenspire empire.

I shook my head and allowed myself to be swallowed by the dancing. My mother, Mara, stood at the head of the room, glamorous, condescending. On a velvet chair, my father, pallid with heavy circles beneath his weary eyes, drank one of his pungent tonics. Unaware of his surroundings. Such a proud man once, Leif Lysander had been fading for four turns.

Over his drinking horn his sharp blue eyes caught mine. We shared the same color, but his cut through me. Ill as he was, it seemed my father tried to glare me into compliance for what was to come.

Lifting my chin, I crossed the room to the dais where the king was seated above the rest of us. Zyben only mingled with the loyal families, and an alliance with his sister's daughter and his second son was reason enough for him to make appearances.

Zyben stared down his bent nose, his knife-sharp cheekbones raised when he sneered. His blond hair was braided down the center of his skull, the sides shaved close. Runes tattooed the sides of his scalp, and a silver briar circlet adorned his head. Beneath a black mantle of heavy pelts, Zyben wore chains of silver and gold and jade.

I lowered to my knee, then pressed a kiss to the sharply cut onyx ring on his finger.

"Well wishes, niece," he said, voice like gossamer silk. Soft. Memorable.

I wished to spend as little time as possible with the king.

His presence brought a tight pressure in the center of my chest, one that left me constantly looking over my shoulder as though he might be watching. But I played the doting niece, smiled, and bowed my head.

"I ask you to stay close. You will want to hear me speak," Zyben said. "You understand?"

My mouth tightened. "I believe I do."

Zyben wore a cruel grin. He leaned over one elbow onto his knee, voice low. "I am not a fool, niece. I see how troubled you are. But refuse and—" His gaze turned to the seat of my father. A hacking sound came from my father's throat; his body shuddered. A medik, dressed in royal blue, quietly tended to him while the room wholly ignored the master of the house.

I swallowed past the tight knot in my throat. "I understand, My King."

Zyben slouched back in his seat and waved me on with a flick of his fingers.

I hurried down the line of dignitaries and ended my greetings on two of Zyben's consorts who paid me little attention. I paused to greet a girl donned in a shimmering red gown, hidden beneath a wrap of fox fur. A silver satin cloth shrouded her face, but by her height and figure, I assumed she was young. Possibly still a child. I settled on a simple curtsy.

"A good heart," her soft voice flowed from behind the veil. I was certain now, she was young. "Interesting."

"Excuse me?" I'd heard rumor of Zyben's interest in seers and witches. Not exactly Night Folk, but if books were to be believed, more than fae carried fury in their blood.

"Your heart does not live here," she whispered.

"I don't know what you're talking about."

"There isn't much time." A desperate plea was buried underneath the soft hum of her voice. Pulse racing, palms sweaty, I bent closer. "Don't fear the past, trust those undeserving of it—"

"*Kvinna,*" a guard grumbled. I'd begun to stall the procession of guests greeting the king and his household.

I took a step to the side, reluctant to leave a child who seemed distressed. A gasp escaped my throat when the masked girl gripped my wrist. A hum of warmth bled from her fingers. "When you see the beast within, let him in to let him go."

"Cursed gods," I breathed out as the warmth transformed

into something needle-sharp before fading and the child released me. Who was this girl? Before I had a chance to press, two of Zyben's guards stepped between us, silently nudging me to move on. I lowered my eyes and stepped away from the dais to be swallowed by the gowns and doublets.

"Elise!" Runa bounded across the ballroom.

My sister was a beauty. Blonde curls, pink lips, a pale blue gown. She giggled when she embraced me. For show, of course. We were not the sort of sisters who spoke regularly.

I almost forgot Calder was at her back, stirring his drink as he cast judgment on everyone in the room. My cousin looked more like his mother, the third consort to the king, with emerald eyes, auburn hair, and teeth too big for his mouth.

"I told you, Calder," Runa said. "She wouldn't miss our party."

More like I couldn't.

Runa sipped from a delicate flute of wine. "Calder said you'd found something more important than us."

My sister laughed, her words slurred from drink, but my stare fell to Calder. He returned the smirk with equal intensity. A wretched man who loathed everyone except himself.

"I would never find anything more important than you, Runa," I said.

My cousin clicked his tongue and swigged more of the clear drink with a counterfeit smile. "Lovely Elise, I only spoke in jest." He sneered at Runa before turning his eyes back to me. "It's so good to see you."

"And you." My voice was flat and uninterested.

All at once, Runa urged me away, a shimmer of thrill in her eyes. "Eli, have you heard?"

My stomach clenched. "I have an inkling that the king is going to make an announcement, yes."

Runa squealed. "But have you not noticed who is in attendance?" Her eyes traveled through the many spinning couples to a tall captain. Dark curls, a marble chiseled face. My throat went dry. My fingertips numb.

"Jarl Magnus," Runa whispered. "He's come all this way from the Eastern Kingdom."

Zyben had great influence, even reaching across the Fate's Ocean to foreign dignitaries. The most I understood from eavesdropping on my father's conversations with traders was when the ships left our docks, they returned with new foods, new coin. New Night Folk to use or kill. Strange kinds with different fury, different accents.

The Eastern Kingdom, according to maps, was made of four regions surrounding a smaller sea. With four regions in one kingdom, I had no doubt they were a diverse kind of folk. I'd always wanted to visit, but a woman traveling—unheard of.

"Are you listening?" Runa tapped my cheek.

"Sorry. Yes, I'm listening."

"Well, what do you think?"

My mouth parted. "Wait, Jarl is—"

Runa clenched her fists and squealed. "Do act surprised, won't you? Oh, can you imagine if he makes a bid? Think if he wins, the places you'll go. Skies, you'll dine at the king's table."

Jarl Magnus had climbed to a formidable station in the Timoran military. He came from a noble family, had a face carved of stone, and more than one lady had pined for his attention. No, I could not imagine a more prestigious match.

Jarl was young and not a harsh man. He had always spoken kindly and had the right amount of wit.

"Jarl was just telling us how interesting it is to handle the Eastern Kingdom's Night Folk," Runa barreled on, "and how different the lands are. He suspects it won't be long until there is an alliance made with Timoran. Skies, do you think one of their princes or princesses might become consort to the king? Gods know how many he has."

Heat flooded my cheeks at the idea. I didn't know much about the royals of the different kingdoms, but I imagined I'd rather be a sovereign of my own land than consort to the King of Timoran. Last I knew, Zyben had at least ten lovers to take at his leisure. I didn't dwell long on the thought before Runa wrenched me across the room toward the handsome captain in his leather officer's coat.

"Jarl, look who I've found," Runa announced.

I swallowed a lump in my throat when Jarl faced me. Half his mouth quirked into a handsome grin. My breath hitched as he kissed the top of my glove.

"Elise," he said, his voice a deep timbre. "A pleasure to see you again."

"What an unexpected surprise," I replied, hoping he understood my meaning.

"I hope it is not a disappointing surprise."

He knew what I meant, and I didn't know what to say. But no matter, my king was watching and took the opportunity to gather the attention of the crowd. With a wave, Zyben silenced the music and all eyes turned to the front of the room.

"You honor my sister's house," he said, "on this special

night to celebrate the upcoming vows of my eldest niece, *Kvinna* Runa Lysander and your future king, Calder."

A polite applause rippled through the crowd, and Runa was beside herself. She fanned her pink cheeks and clung to horridly stupid Calder's arm like he was the only real thing in the room.

The king went on, his nose in the air. "Our family has more than one reason to celebrate. As king, and overseer of the second royal house, I have opened up dowry negotiations for my youngest niece, *Kvinna* Elise."

Gasps, more applause, and congratulatory smiles found me like a thorn amongst roses. I stiffened until Runa dug her elbow into my ribs, then I forced a flush as if this moment were the sweetest. Zyben raised a glass, offering his approval.

"Furthermore," my uncle went on when the voices quieted. "As *Kvin* Lysander's weak disposition will prevent him from selecting suitors, and such tasks are beneath the duties of a king, it is my honor to introduce an overseer of the dowry. No doubt his expertise will call for an interesting bidding. The honor falls to the young, *Herr* Legion Grey."

CHAPTER FOUR

MORE THAN WITH the announcement of open dowry, gasps bounced from wall to wall, women fanned their faces, and all eyes pointed to the back of the room.

My blood went cold. I didn't turn around, didn't dare meet his eye. Legion Grey was . . . my dowry negotiator?

He'd be the man who held my future in his hands, the man who would spend most waking hours with me, scrutinizing me, matching me, setting what I was *worth* as a wife until he handed me over.

I knew he worked in trade negotiations, but this was something else entirely.

My uncle grinned, rather pleased with himself. "No doubt his reputation in foreign affairs will serve my family well."

"I live to serve, My King."

His voice, Legion's voice, prickled up the back of my neck. The soft, mischievous tone from earlier. *I'm good with secrets.*

I'd opened my bleeding mouth and spoken to him. Would he recognize me now?

"Elise," Runa hissed at me. "Acknowledge him. It's expected."

I hadn't realized everyone was staring until a lady of the high court lifted her nose in disgust. I bit my nerves into my bottom lip and slowly faced the back of the room.

Three hells, in the light of the ballroom his eyes were hot coals. He must've stopped at the game hall for only a moment before coming here, still dressed in the dark waistcoat that caused his unique golden hair to look more like copper. His jaw had sharp corners, and the slightest layer of stubble darkened his bronze skin.

Legion lifted his wooden drinking horn. He tipped the drink to his mouth, eyes never leaving mine.

The smirk on his lips sent a rush of anger over my skin. So much for being the face I'd imagine when I vowed with another. Now Legion was simply another man who cared little for me, my heart, or my future. For his position, the one who would give the final say, truth be told, he was the worst of everyone.

With all eyes on me, I wanted very much for the ground to open and swallow me whole until a hand took mine.

Jarl pressed his lips to the back of my glove again, startling me. "Elise, I would like you to know, I plan to enter the negotiations. I hope this isn't displeasing to you."

What to say? This whole thing displeased me. Jarl was a good match, and I couldn't very well hope to stay under my parents' roof for all time. But Jarl bled for Timoran. I doubted he'd ever accept my involvement with Ettan folk.

I had no words, but forced a smile

Jarl seemed appeased. "Would you dance with me?"

"You do not want to speak to *Herr* Legion?" I asked. A quick glance at the back of the ballroom told me the negotiator was already surrounded by three men. My insides cinched.

Jarl tugged on my hand. "I'd rather dance with you."

Surrounded by other couples, with the warmth of Jarl's hand on the small of my back, I almost forgot my life would never be the same. For three dances, Jarl spun me around, until we laughed and caught our breath.

"I'm afraid I've been rather inappropriate keeping you on your feet this long. Shall we take a pause?"

I followed him to the edge of the ballroom where Runa and Calder drank wine. I recognized Arabella, one of our serfs, even under her netted veil as she placed honey cakes and flaky tarts on a silver platter.

"Arabella," I whispered and handed her a tart, "take it for Ellis." Her son had been ill with a rising fever for the last two days. Herbal remedies were starting to help, but I imagined the boy would appreciate a sweet, too. Arabella slyly slipped the tart into the pocket of her smock and bowed away.

"So, you do speak to gutter rats."

I glanced over my shoulder and fought the urge to groan at Calder. "To a woman, you mean?"

Calder clucked like an arrogant cock and sipped his wine loudly. "I must say she did smell. I would think her better suited to labor in the high court quarries. Out of sight."

To my distaste, Jarl chuckled, but Runa simply stared at her glass of wine. I held a bit of pride she didn't engage in the cruel banter, but she didn't shut her intended up, either. I could not stay so tight lipped.

"She's a lovely woman, actually," I said.

Jarl looked at me with a bemused expression.

Calder scoffed, his beady eyes narrowing. "I'd send all Ettan blood to the quarries if they did not prove so useful cleaning out our chamber pots. *Rotter* scum belongs in the dirt, Elise"

Runa rolled her eyes. "Skies, must we continue this sort of talk? The quarries are dreadful places and I'd rather speak of pleasanter things."

"Yes, we have that choice, Runa," I said. "The Ettans do not."

Jarl cleared his throat. "The quarries are dangerous for Timorans, and Ettans without fury. Only Night Folk are sent to the quarries."

"I'm not sure that is any better," I said, trying to keep my composure. The quarries were dangerous and brutal. As mischievous and dangerous as fae were, I pitied them all the same.

"Why are we talking about this at my engagement party?" Runa whined, drawing me back to the moment.

"It seems your sister is hells-bent on difficult conversations tonight, my love," Calder said.

"Sorry," I said. "You're right. We should be celebrating."

Jarl's smile returned, and I wondered if he might be regretting his courtship arrangement to a vocal conspiracy theorist, but I supposed if we were to be vowed, he ought to know the real me.

"Forgive me, I must take a leave for a moment. I have military business to attend to." Jarl faced me. "Perhaps I could take another dance later, *Kvinna*."

I bowed my head as a reply. Runa left with Calder, and I was glad to be rid of him. I had no desire to make idle chat with anyone in the room and took my leave outside on the balcony.

The cool night brushed against my skin, raising the hair on my arms. I breathed deeply, wondering if Mavie and Siv would congratulate me, or if they would know taking vows would change our friendship. Or perhaps Jarl would be the sort of husband who didn't mind a charitable wife.

Could I love Jarl? Or any potential suitors?

My parents showed little affection to each other, even before my father's illness. But I had seen many romantic couples to know love was possible.

I wanted to be loved like that, but knew it was too rare to hope for. If I did not take a position as a wife, odds are I would end up like the faceless princesses of the distant kingdoms— vying to be a consort to some powerful man. Even further from the idea of love, and more a body to be used for pleasure.

"I need to do more before I can do nothing. Something great," I said to the breeze.

"I'm interested to know what great things you have planned."

I wheeled around, gripping the balcony. Legion rose from the wicker chair in the shadows. In his black waistcoat, without the lanternlight, he might've remained invisible. A red band around his wrist marked him as an important guest of the Lysander manor, and the flash of mischief in his gaze sent a trill running through my insides.

This close I could make out the bits of gold swirled with the black of his eyes. There was a seductive darkness in him, as if he might laugh or cut my throat at any moment. Another man stood behind Legion's shoulder; his slate eyes narrowed as he tipped back a horn of ale.

"*Herr* Legion, I didn't see you."

"I noticed." His lips tilted into a half grin, as if he knew all my secrets but refused to admit to anything. He bowed his head. "*Kvinna*, an honor to meet you. This is Tor, he'll be assisting with the negotiations."

Tor was Ettan. His dark hair curled over a hooded brow, and his eyes were like a moonless night. A flicker of disappointment tightened my chest. Legion hadn't seemed the type to indenture serfs. Then again, Tor was dressed as fine as Legion. Perhaps he was one of the rare freeman Ettans permitted to roam the streets without cause to look over their shoulder.

Whoever Legion's companion was, he had no desire to acknowledge my existence, and turned away into the shadows once more.

Whatever etiquette was required between a dowry negotiator and the woman he served, I didn't know it. I had no idea what to say.

Legion took a step closer, voice rough. "If I had to guess, I'd say I make you nervous, *Kvinna*."

What little admiration I felt for the man quickly dissolved into raw defensiveness. I straightened my shoulders, refusing to allow Legion Grey to witness my discontent. "*Herr*, I assure you I am not nervous. I'm sure we will find many things to discuss soon enough as you learn the *lengths* I will go to keep honor in my family's name."

I expected Legion to frown, maybe lock me in one of his

hot-coal stares, but he grinned. "I look forward to learning a great many things, *Kvinna*."

"Forgive me, but I thought you bartered trade with merchants."

"You're right," he said and leaned one elbow against the rail. "But vow negotiations are prestigious work. I have prepared for this for some time. I assure you, *Kvinna*, you are in capable hands."

"The only hands I consider capable are my own."

Legion lifted one brow, a playful gleam in his eyes. "Ah, but you have never experienced what mine can do."

My insides backflipped. The grin, the lull of his voice, would ruin me. I'd never need to fret over taking vows because I would not survive Legion Grey.

CHAPTER FIVE

Five. By the second day after my father's announcement, five official bids for my hand were placed. Jarl being the only man I knew.

If I thought my stomach toiled at the first announcement, now it turned over like a violent wave. The only bright spot was I had seen little of Legion. Assessing the bids kept him busy enough. There were times he'd simply be there, though. A silent shadow, peeling back my skin without my permission to gauge what was inside.

I'd become a hostage in my own home.

Moments were slipping through my fingers like water in a sieve, and I was powerless to stop it.

Better to not think of it at all.

Outside I stood between Mavie and Siv, now officially named as my personal serfs who'd attend me as a married woman. They were free of their veils since I set the terms, and the veils were burned straightaway. Whenever bids closed, I would be allowed to take some serfs with me to my new home. It wasn't a question who I asked to join me.

In the heat of the noon sun, the black wool of my dress clung to my skin like a new layer, but at my father's command I was to accept a new gift from a potential match. Bjorn Svart, a wealthy shipping merchant who drank spiced red ale so much his teeth were forever stained. Svart didn't want me for love, he wanted me to tend to his nine children since his wife died last turn.

Accepting anything from the man raised the hair on the back of my neck.

"His youngest is a pleasant child," Mavie said at my back.

"Because the brat can't speak yet," Siv retorted. "The Svart boys are demons and have a love for toads. We'd all need to check our sheets by the hour."

"At least he's sending gifts," Mavie said.

My hands started to sweat beneath the thin blue gloves hiding my fingers. I fiddled with the hem of one and didn't join the conversation. Whatever the gift, it wasn't worth taking vows with the man.

Too soon, one of our cabriolets entered the gates; a cloud of dust wrapped the wheels as it rambled down the drive. I took a deep breath and stepped off the last step.

Halvar pulled back on the reins, drawing the cab to a halt. How different he was as a serf than when he laughed and gambled at the game hall. The dark waves of his hair were covered by a brimmed cap, his clothes demure and black. But the blue fire still danced in his eyes when he faced me.

"*Kvinna*," he greeted. Playful as the stable hand was, there were times I didn't know if he cared much for me. Perhaps his distaste was for Timorans in general. Still, from Siv and Mavie's reports, Halvar was kind and had chased off more than one thief from taking our mares.

"Halvar, I'm told you've brought something."

The cab shifted as the passengers abandoned the bench beneath the cover. My shoulders slumped. Legion met my gaze, winked, then disembarked from the seat. I allowed myself to gawk at his handsomeness for half a breath, then promptly remembered my silent vow to dislike the man.

"All at once the day is made lovelier with you in it, *Kvinna* Elise," Legion said.

I scoffed. "Careful *Herr*, I might mistake you for being earnest and fall all over myself from your flattery when I am to be chained to another soon enough."

Mavie muffled a laugh behind her hand and Siv seemed ready to slit Legion from navel to nose should he try to retaliate for my disrespect. He didn't. Truth be told, he seemed delighted.

"I am fascinated by your sharp tongue, *Kvinna*. So unusual."

"That's Elise for you," another voice said.

I beamed when a tall man made of lean muscles and dark stubble materialized from the opposite side of the cab.

"Mattis." I hurried past Legion, stopping a pace away from my friend. "It's been too long since we've spoken."

"I know," he said. "No one has laughed at one of my jokes in ages."

"Because they're not good," Siv blurted out. She dipped her head as if recalling she was a serf and Legion Grey was present.

Mattis was undeterred and seemed wholly satisfied she'd spoken. A bit of desire gleamed in his eyes when he focused on her. "Lovely Siverie, the way you had tears in your eyes from laughter at our last encounter, I would humbly disagree."

I bit the inside of my cheek to keep my own amusement tapered when Siv balled her fists, jaw tight. The woman wanted to retort, but her status demanded she hold her tongue. Legion watched the exchange, amused, and I hated it. These were moments I treasured, when my friends—no matter their station—forgot I was a *Kvinna* and we laughed together. He wasn't welcome.

Resting a hand on Mattis's arm, I urged him to stand a few steps from Legion's stare. "What brings you here?"

Mattis held out a wrapped box. "I come bearing gifts from *Herr* Svart, along with my congratulations. We all know how you have longed, and longed, and *longed* for this—" I swung a fist to hit his arm, which Mattis dodged with a laugh. "Perhaps I should offer condolences."

I snatched the box from his hands, glaring. "I could demand your tongue be removed, you know."

"Oh, please try. I yearn for a bit of excitement. But remember, *Kvinna* Elise, Siverie would miss my jokes." Siv grumbled under her breath and turned away. Mattis used his chin to point at the box in my hands. "You going to open it?"

I tore into the waxy parchment to find a polished jewelry box. The gloves were troublesome, but in a few moments the paper fell away. Delicate purple blossoms wrapped around a golden dagger were painted on the lid. Plush velvet lined the inside. I traced the intricate lines of the blossoms, in awe. "Mattis, you made this?"

He grinned with pride. "I was told to create something that spoke of your qualities. I'm not sure *Herr* Svart knew any of your qualities to be more specific, so I took a few artistic liberties."

"A dagger?" Legion's deep voice spurred me from the moment.

"Seemed fitting. Kindness on the outside." Mattis touched one of the blossoms, dragging his finger to the hilt of the dagger. "A warrior on the inside."

There was a bit of satisfaction from being acknowledged as something more than an ornament. "Thank you, Mattis. I vow to forget who commissioned this and take it as a gift from a friend who actually knows me."

"*Herr* Svart is a promising match," Legion said.

I shot my annoyance in his direction. "Perhaps you should pursue him, *Herr*. I'm sure you two could make each other quite happy."

Legion took several steps over the space between us, drawing Mattis to inch half in front of me. As a carpenter, Mattis did not have status, but bore the fire of an outspoken. He wouldn't stand by if Legion retaliated.

But Legion still wore his amusement in his frustratingly attractive smirk. "You are determined to make these negotiations difficult, aren't you *Kvinna*?"

"You mistake difficulty with having a voice, *Herr* Legion."

"I don't mind your voice," he said. "But understand I must pick someone eventually. If you detest everyone, you have officially made my task difficult."

"Apologies, but that is not my problem." I turned to Mattis once more. "Thank you again. It's lovely."

Mattis cast wary eyes at Legion, but when the negotiator said nothing, he relaxed. "I have brought you one other thing.

This one truly from me." He dug into his pocket and removed a tattered leather-bound book. "Held my attention well into the night.

Delight sped through me. For most of our friendship, Mattis and I had exchanged books. Usually, the opposite of what the other found interesting; a kind of challenge to see who would refuse to read first.

"*Love in Thorns,*" I read from the faded title. "More Night Folk tales, I see."

"Well, we all know your prejudice against the fae, so."

I slugged Mattis in the arm, undignified and inappropriate. I hardly cared. "I am not prejudiced against fae. A healthy dose of reservation toward fury is not prejudiced. And don't pretend you aren't leery yourself."

"I am not. If a fae tossed my mind into an illusion, I wouldn't know any better. What's to be leery about?"

"Shouldn't talk about Night Folk," Mavie muttered. "The earth speaks to them. They'll know and call your bluff."

Out of all of us, Mavie was the most superstitious. Mattis rolled his eyes and lowered his voice. "Says an Ettan, a people once ruled by Night Folk queens and kings."

"Centuries ago," Mavie snapped. "I can hear you, carpenter."

All during the exchange I kept Legion in my sights. He watched with a bemused sort of expression. As if he didn't understand any of it and expected this all at once. Most men of even half his station would demand serfs and lower merchants like Mattis to hold their tongues. They'd certainly find a crass *Kvinna* intolerable. Yet, he listened. He watched.

I had a sudden desire to know everything he thought.

"I should be getting back," Mattis admitted. "I'll expect to hear—no doubt—your numerous opinions on the book when we meet next."

I waved as Halvar drove Mattis off the grounds, sensing Legion's eyes pouring into the back of my head.

"Join me inside."

I let out a startled cry. Legion had been at least five paces away, then in a single heartbeat at my side. "By the hells, you move like a ghost."

"I've been called a wraith more than once." He flashed his white smile. "Will you join me inside?"

When had he gotten so close? If I adjusted a hairsbreadth, our shoulders would brush. My tongue swiped over the dryness of my bottom lip; my eyes danced between his. "I'm sure with so many formal offers, you have more to do than spend time with me."

"Tor will handle the suitors today." He paused, then brushed my braid off my shoulder, gently. His fingertips grazed my collarbone, sending a trill across my skin as Legion lowered his voice. "I wish to know *you*."

I blinked as through a fog and nodded before I could think better of it. "As you say." Bleeding hells, what was I saying?

Legion stepped back, grinning. "Lead the way, then. Wherever you'd like to go, I am at your service."

Whatever spell he'd cast over me by such a meaningless touch faded, and a heady reluctance weighed down over my shoulders. I looked to Siv and Mavie for help, for some excuse.

"Oh, um, Bevan, he needed our help," Mavie said.

My eyes widened. Traitor.

She nudged Siv in the ribs and Siv shoved right back. With a sigh, Mavie grabbed Siv's elbow and went on in her betrayal. "We will find you . . . shortly, *Kvinna*."

Then, they disappeared into the manor.

Silence grew too much, too suffocating. Legion cleared his throat, and I jolted as if the sound burned me. I was a bleeding fool, allowing him to have such an influence on me. But I couldn't avoid him forever, either. The sooner we spoke the sooner he'd be out of my life.

The sooner I'd be matched.

I resisted the urge to groan. Even if I resented Legion Grey for his role in my marriage match, I could admit he was far better company than some pretentious suitor who had no interest in my thoughts. Including Jarl. A new ache tightened in my chest as frustration grew. I'd known most of my life one day this all would happen, I'd be given to another household to build an alliance, to strengthen loyalty to the crown through vows, only now the moment had arrived, I could not stop resisting every step of the way. Ettans and Night Folk were not the only prisoners in New Timoran.

"I await your first step," Legion said lightly. "If you're in need of suggestions, I am told your library is much cooler than here in the sun. Besides, you have your bawdy new book."

"Bawdy? What do you mean by that?" I traced the faded letters of the title burned into the leather.

Legion chuckled. "*Love in Thorns*? It is a common adage for old Night Folk love spells. Quite seductive, actually. I heard it describes the outcomes in great erotic details."

A proper lady might flush or turn away embarrassed. I was neither proper nor a lady. I was a second daughter who gambled in game halls and spent my days with a mouthy carpenter and opinionated serfs. I laughed and took on a new understanding for Mattis's desire to leave this book. Doubtless he was still grinning over his joke.

Book tucked in my arm, limbs relaxed, I faced Legion. "Fine. If you must interrupt my day," I said with a sigh, "then, follow me."

CHAPTER SIX

I soon learned Legion's way of knowing me, meant being near me. Whatever it was I wanted to do, he assured me he would be a willing participant.

Stunned, all I could think was taking his suggestion and visiting the manor's library.

Now, soft hair on my arms raised. I knew he was looking at me, but I kept my attention schooled on the birch parchment pages.

"You know, *Herr*, staring is considered rude by most standards," I said and flipped the page.

The book he held slapped closed. Legion leaned onto the arm of the chaise, chin propped on his fist. "I must confess, I'm surprised, *Kvinna*. I stare because I find myself on edge, wondering what you might say or do next. I thought one thing before coming here, and as I said, now I find myself rather unsettled."

A mutual feeling. I'd not expected a vow negotiator to

spend hours reading with me in silence. My mother said I spent too much time with the written word instead of honing more valuable skills. Runa teased me, saying my books caused my head to spin with too many foolish ideas. But Legion, he'd settled across from me, asked a few questions about the sorts of tales I enjoyed most, then faded into whatever reality lived between the bindings in his hand.

I closed the pages on a tonic used for fae and mortal consorts to increase desire and pleasure. Strange as it was, the spells were fascinating. "Dare I ask what you expected to find?"

"A woman with long lists of requirements about her future husband's purse size, being one."

"Rather condescending, *Herr*."

"But not exactly wrong," he said. "From my experience, women at your station would live for fetes like your sister's betrothal ball, not escape to the balcony. Certainly, they would not befriend serfs, prefer books to conversation, or sneak into game halls on respite eve."

My stomach twisted violently. Blood drained from my face as I met his gaze with wide eyes. "*Herr* Legion, I—"

He held up a hand. "I told you, I'm good with secrets."

His assurance didn't settle the race of my pulse. Any moment I feared my heart would snap a rib and burst out of my chest. The things he could use against me were too numerous for comfort, and I needed to know what he intended. Terrible as it might be. I lifted my chin and forced my voice to steady. "And what must I do to ensure you keep certain secrets?"

A look of bewilderment shadowed his face. "You think I would use it to gain an advantage over you?"

"Am I to believe you have no intentions of telling anyone you saw me?"

"Yes," he said with a touch of exasperation. "The thought never even crossed my mind."

"Doubtful. Ambitious men like you are always looking for a bit of leverage. What is better than holding lawlessness over a member of the royal household?"

"I might be more wicked if I viewed what you did to be lawless."

I hesitated. "Women are not allowed in game halls."

"Perhaps, but would you agree it's a rather ridiculous rule? Ridiculous rules are truly asking to be broken."

He was teasing me, but the carefree way he said it, drew a cautious smile over my lips. I fiddled with a bit of torn leather on the corner of my book. "To be fair, you are not exactly what I expected from a vow negotiator, either."

"What were the expectations I've failed to meet?"

"A man with skin falling off his bones for one."

"In due time, *Kvinna*. I have no doubt I won't age well."

"I wouldn't be so sure." *Three hells.* I shook away the thoughts of his attractive face, and prayed to the gods, who should never have given me the gift of speech, that I wouldn't make a fool of myself by admitting as much. Before he could comment on my slip, I barreled on. "I expected someone who was more interested in impressing my father, or the king, than spending time with me. A man who critiqued all the ways I'll make a poor wife."

"That would make for awkward conversation," he said, but his smile faded. "Do you think you'll make a poor wife?"

"I make a poor royal, so yes, a Timoran wife will be another of my failures." I closed my eyes. "I don't know why I said that to you."

The flicker of candles brightened the rich darkness of his eyes as he stared—scrutinized was more like it. Only when the quiet grew thick enough it caused the room to shrink did he speak. "I am sympathetic to your situation, and your reluctance to this vow does not escape my notice. But at least we can agree we are both unconventional in our positions. Perhaps fate has a plan with all this after all."

I opened my mouth to reply my lack of faith that the Fates cared for me at all, but stopped when Bevan shoved into the library, rolling a silver tea cart.

"Forgive the interruption, *Kvinna*," Bevan said. "Your sister wanted to ensure you were still breathing in here, and if you were, I was asked to supply you with food."

I rolled my eyes. "Runa is just being nosy and maybe jealous she can't be locked away with an unfamiliar man for hours."

The bridges of Bevan's cheeks reddened, but Legion laughed. At least someone thought my inappropriateness was entertaining.

"It is a custom I've always found interesting in New Timoran. First daughters like your sister have their virtue guarded like it is the survival of the people, but second daughters . . ."

"Can dally as we please."

"*Kvinna*," Bevan warned under his breath.

"No," Legion told the old serf. "I appreciate *Kvinna* Elise's proclivity to speak her mind. And I'm interested to understand, not being Timoran myself. No one has even given us a second look being in here unaccompanied. What is the difference between you and your sister?"

I accepted a cup of tea, ignoring Bevan's look of disapproval. "It's to protect the bloodlines. There can be no question Runa produces heirs only of Calder's line. For me, who will never ascend the throne, a few watered-down littles aren't cause for concern."

In truth, I'd never given the differences between my sister and I much thought. Runa had never been alone with a man for . . . forever. And if she were to be, at this point, it could only be with Calder.

"If bloodlines matter so much, then why do the royal households take mistresses and consorts?"

"Because they . . ." I paused, not truly knowing the answer. "You know, I've never really thought of it. Calder is the heir apparent, but his mother is the third consort, not even the queen." My own father had taken mistresses during his healthy turns. Traipsed them through the corridors of the manor, and no one would dare gainsay *Kvin* Lysander. If my mother took a lover, it was done in the shadows. "Seems the law rests in the favor of the menfolk."

Legion lifted a brow knowingly and drank from his own cup. Bevan looked utterly discomposed at this sort of talk.

"Of course, now that my dowry negotiations are open," I went on. "It would be rather scandalous if I were seen with a man. Other than you, of course. Because you would never attempt to seduce me as negotiator."

"Oh, I wouldn't say that," Legion said with a sly grin.

I snickered and admitted I enjoyed his irony. Always tossing out a bit of wit, and it made an unbearable situation bearable.

"Bevan, thank you for the tea," I said gently. "But you really don't need to stand there if you'd like to leave."

He cleared his throat, eyes straight ahead. "I have a message still to give, *Kvinna*. *Herr* Mattis sent word he'd like to discuss your new book at the bell tower." Bevan frowned. "I can only assume you understand whatever it is that feckless man means."

I absolutely understood what Mattis's message meant, and a bit of fun could not have come at a better time. With such dreary recent days, a rendezvous at the bell tower was needed more than I could say. I didn't say, of course, didn't lead on any hidden meaning was buried in the message.

"You don't approve of the carpenter?" Legion asked.

I firmed my jaw, then leaned into whisper. "Mattis is Bevan's great-nephew."

"A shame, really," Bevan said wryly.

"Say what you like, Bevan, but I know you secretly think highly of dear Mattis." The old man grunted and positioned the tea tray nearer for us to reach. "And all he is asking is for a stroll around town center after worship meet in two days."

"The boy would do well to *attend* worship meet."

"I'm sure you're right." Truth be told, if I were not required to attend, I would not go to worship meet and listen to a pious sermon where the old clergy rambled on about how favored Timorans were of the gods. Being half Ettan, Mattis had more status than Bevan, but I think the carpenter favored the Ettan way of worship more than even his great-uncle. Through personal reflection of the gods' purposes, through war, or through fury.

When Bevan left us alone, Legion opened his book again, but closed it soon after. "I've found today to be interesting."

"Have you? Reading in silence with me?"

"Yes, it's been shockingly enjoyable. I don't recall the last time I stayed still for so long."

I sighed and leaned back into the cushion of the embroidered sofa, covering a yawn with the back of my hand. "This is my refuge. Books are my windows to another world, another life. Being a woman, you must know I'm not permitted to travel."

"A pity. There is much more to see beyond the borders of New Timoran."

I shouldn't ask, shouldn't even care to, but I'd never been one to listen to even my own intuition when curiosity was at play. "Forgive me, but you mentioned not being Timoran, and I've been curious—I mean I *am* curious, not that I've been thinking about you or anything of the kind."

"*Kvinna*, what is it you want to ask?" Legion pressed with a laugh.

Somewhere, my warrior ancestors were cursing in the Otherworld at their blithering namesake. "I was simply wondering where your people are from?"

He took another slow drink. "What is your guess?"

Oh, the theories on Legion Grey. He was clever, no doubt he knew the gossip in town was heavy with questions of him. "Well, I've heard you are nobility, but from a different kingdom."

"Is that what people say?"

"That is the hope. Many a mother would happily toss their daughters at your feet."

"Wouldn't work, I'm afraid. I prefer my women off their knees, upright, and standing on their own."

"At your back?"

"At my side."

Heat bloomed inside my middle. A visceral, unexpected reaction I hoped Legion didn't notice. "I see," was all I managed as a reply.

Small muscles in Legion's jaw pulsed for half a breath before he spoke again. "The truth? I am no one, not really. I do not know my family, or my people. The story told in the waif house where I was raised, was I'd arrived on one of the many passenger ships, then was promptly abandoned. There you have it, *Kvinna*, the glamorous truth. I'm not new to this land. I've walked these shores for turns but was merely invisible until I wasn't."

Legion turned his gaze to the window as the last skeins of golden light faded over the ocean. I didn't know what to say. Waifs roamed the streets throughout all corners of Timoran. Boys and girls who ate scraps from compost bins, who lit the gas lamps for a bit of coin, or delivered royal missives. Unclaimed, unloved. Most were Ettan orphans, either losing their parents to the quarries or illness, but there were some who'd stowed away or had been traded from distant lands. A slice of sympathy cut through me imagining the charismatic Legion dirty, hungry, and alone.

"How did you—" I gestured to his person. The fine suit, polished shoes. Healthy teeth.

"Gain such a prosperous reputation?" He crossed one ankle over his knee, face as stone. "I think that is a tale for another day."

"You don't trust me?"

"Would you trust me with something you've never told anyone?"

"You've never told anyone your story?"

"Only two others have ever been close enough for me to open the past."

My eyes dropped to my gloved hands. I understood the hesitance of allowing others to see the darker pieces.

"I hope I haven't offended you," he said with sincerity.

"No. Not at all. Trust is earned, is it not *Herr* Grey?"

The corner of his mouth twitched. He returned a deep nod. "It is, *Kvinna*." Legion rose from the chaise, returning to the shelf the book he'd read. "I should leave you to get some rest. Tomorrow, you get the opportunity to meet with some of the suitors."

I let out a sort of growl. "Must I?"

He scoffed. "At some point I must observe you with some of them. Or I might place you with an utter bore, then I'd feel terrible."

"You know," I said, adjusting on the sofa, so I could rest my elbows over the back, my chin propped on my arms. "I think you might like having this sort of control."

"A touch," he admitted with a grin. "Though, I feel more pressure to get it right, than anything. But that will be our secret, *Kvinna*."

"Our second secret."

"Of many more, I'm sure." Legion tipped his chin. "Goodnight, Elise."

He closed the door, the weight of my name from his lips hanging in the silence. Almost like we'd stepped over a threshold into something . . . friendly? It brought a bit of relief knowing Legion took this task seriously, took my wants and hopes into account. I'd known of enough vow negotiations where the bride was simply an afterthought.

At this rate, I might even trust him someday.

But not today.

When I was sure Legion would be far from my chamber, I swung my legs off the sofa and hurried to my bed chamber. I stripped the gloves from my hands, stripped my gown, donned rough-knit breeches and a loose tunic, then strapped an heirloom silver dagger to the inside of my thigh. A broad, brimmed hat covered the sheen of my hair, and I tied a black cloak lined in bear pelts over my shoulders.

At the window, I twisted the latch until it clicked. Turns ago, I'd discovered my manor had enough jutting stones in the walls, I could scale to the ground easily enough.

Once my boots touched the loamy soil beneath my window, I ducked behind the wild roses, waiting for any patrols to step into the moonlight.

I was met with silence.

Securing the brim of my hat low on my brow, I aimed for the thicket, and disappeared into the night.

CHAPTER SEVEN

FROM THE MAIN THICKET, the road broke away into two narrower paths, both carving up the hedgerow like snakes in the grass.

One led to Ruskig, a shanty settlement made of free Ettans, rumored to be warded by fury. Though I'd never been, Ruskig lay in the heart of old Night Folk territory. The shanties were supposedly more ruins of palaces and fae fortresses than wooden huts and hovels. A perfect refuge for Ettans and the criminally inclined to avoid the Ravenspire patrols.

If there were any chance the true fae existed with a desire to claim Timoran territory, they would reside in Ruskig.

Zyben never crossed over, unwilling to tempt his fate by catching the attention of rogue Night Folk. Brutal as my uncle was, he believed the tales of vengeful faeries were still out there, enraged at the death of their royals during the Timoran raids.

I didn't know if any of it was true.

Ruskig was not my intended path, anyway. At a dead aspen

tree, I padded around until my fingers dug into a knot with a makeshift cork plugging a hollowed opening. Inside, rodents had packed away sap-soaked needles, nuts, and leaves for the coming snows, but buried underneath, the small lantern remained untouched. Pleased my flint and steel was still dry, I ignited the wick, hurrying into the deeper trees. When Mattis mentioned the bell tower it didn't mean the great iron bell in town.

Heavy brush and thorns devoured the end of the path.

My skin prickled at the sound of snapping twigs.

My lantern raised, I scanned the pitch of the trees. Nothing. It was nothing. A squirrel, a fox.

Anyone who ventured this deep into the forest would turn at this point, seeing no way forward. Exactly how we intended. On hands and knees, the handle of the lantern between my teeth, I slipped through an unassuming hole in the briars, entering a hidden grove on the other side. In the center was a tall pine, greater than all the others—the bell tower.

Soft laughter broke the night until my flame cast shadows over the dry grass.

"Elise," Mavie sang, freer out here than anywhere. "I was beginning to worry you hadn't gotten the message."

Mavie had stripped her frock and apron, replacing them with trousers and an open-back top that showed the raven tattooed between her shoulders. She bent over to help me from the ground. On her waist were twin knives with gold stripes down the blades. Siv stepped out from the tree line, never satisfied we were secure enough. Like Mavie, Siv rested her hands over the hilts of two knives, but added to her leg was a dagger like mine. Her hair was secured in a tight knot, and her scowl deepened as a flutter of pigeons escaped the treetops.

I withdrew my dagger and added my lantern to the others nearer the bell tower. "My discussion went longer than planned."

Seated on a boulder at the edge of the grove, Mattis snorted. "With the negotiator? I'm certain you had heaps to talk about."

Mattis dragged a whetstone across a narrow short blade, grinning. I folded my arms over my chest. "If you're asking, we did not say a great deal. He enjoys reading as much as I."

Siv balked. "You read. All this time?"

"Why the tone of surprise? Yes, we read. Asked a few questions of each other, too." I bit my tongue before I spilled out Legion's tragic history. He did not come from the pedestal by which the whole of Timoran placed him, and I suspected my friends might trust him a great deal more if they knew.

But it was not my story to tell.

Mattis hopped off the boulder, his smile widening. "And? What did you think of my book?"

My heart raced simply thinking of the intimate descriptions of the fury spells. But Mattis was fishing for satisfaction that he'd produced the winning book enjoyed by us both. I did love to irritate him, so I shrugged. "Written well enough, but highly unbelievable."

His mouth dropped. "Unbelievable? It's history! True accounts of the richest form of fury."

"Lore, Mattis. It's lore," I insisted, and reveled a bit in his obvious frustration.

Mattis waved me away, shaking his head. "I can't speak to you when you're irrational. Let's spar."

A moment later, I blocked a jab from his blade with my dagger.

What began as a jest with branches a few turns ago, had grown into a kind of weekly meet to fight, to be as our people— Timoran and Ettan alike—once were. Warriors.

When Siv joined, our skill increased. Still closed-lipped on how she learned how to fight, she'd taught me the proper way to hold a dagger, helped me learn to dodge a backward strike. Mattis knew how to scan the surroundings in one sweep. Mavie and I learned, we sparred. We gained bruises and scrapes and knots on our heads.

For a moment, in our secret grove, we were all equal.

Mattis slammed his elbow into my shoulder, forcing me to retreat. "What do you think of your negotiator, really?" he asked, rolling the sword once in his grip.

"You rode with him," I said through a grunt as I sliced the dagger at his chest. Mattis dodged easily. "I could ask the same thing."

When I reeled back to strike, being the dirty fighter he was, Mattis kicked my knee out, so I dropped. I was forced to roll to avoid a mock killing blow.

"Getting fast, *Kvinna*," he said, pleased. Locking hands, he helped me back to my feet and we reset. Mattis prowled like a fox to a hare, a quizzical furrow between his eyes. "I found *Herr* Grey to be . . . unique. He asked about my shop, seemed interested."

"Yes," I said louder than intended. "Yes, he does that. Just today he admitted he wanted to ensure my desires if a match were met."

From the corner of my eye, I caught the tail end of Siv tossing Mavie over her shoulder, landing Mavie flat on her back, coughing.

Siv dragged a long breath through her nose and looked to us. "Be cautious." She rested her hands on her hips, gathering air, and wholly ignoring Mavie as she fumbled back to her feet. "Personally, I don't trust him. I think he flatters to gain trust."

"*Kvinna*, I'm aghast," Mattis said, a hand to his chest. "Our dear Siverie does not *trust* someone."

"Odd, indeed," I added, laughing as Siv spun a threatening knife in her grip, eyes on Mattis like she might stab him—or kiss him—I could never tell with Siv and the carpenter. Her words stuck to me, though. It could be possible Legion knew how to read people, how to say the things they wanted to hear.

"All I'm saying is to be on guard," Siv said. "There could be reasons he wants folk to think highly of him."

"Couldn't possibly be because he's decent," Mavie muttered.

Siv narrowed her eyes. "Could be, but it's called caution. By the gods, do any of you have a survival instinct?"

At that we laughed and raised our weapons again. This time I slashed at Mavie. She towered over me, and had a talent for snatching weapons out of grip. Not entirely fair, while my left hand was my dominant, she knew its grip was not as sure. But as Mattis often reminded me, a fight in New Timoran was rarely fair.

Mavie swung. Gripped my wrist. Twisted a few sly twists.

My blade fell, and she tossed it ten paces away near the edge of the grove.

My shoulders slumped. Lungs burned for deeper breaths.

"Go on," she commanded. "I won't fight you unarmed."

If my mother heard a maid speak to me in such a way, she'd flay Mavie in the center of the yard. I hardly noticed. My back to the grove, I trudged over to retrieve my dagger. The point had pierced the soil near a tree with tangled roots that reminded me of sea snakes digging up and down in the earth.

I bent to retrieve the dagger, and as I straightened, the whistle of steel and air sliced past my head, followed by a thud. A knife made of black steel stuck into bark. The point narrowly missed the side of my head.

Panic seized my chest. For a breath, the grove silenced in stun. No one breathed, as if none of us could get our minds to consider the next move.

"Never turn your back on your opponent." The evenness of his voice set my nerves on edge, and at ease in the same breath.

From the shadows Legion appeared, but he wasn't alone. His trade companion, Tor, and . . . Halvar. The stable hand stood at Legion's shoulder, a smirk on his mouth.

When Mavie realized we were not alone, that she'd been seen throwing knives at the *Kvinna*, she clasped her hands in front of her body and prayed. Tearful prayers to gods who cared little for matters of mortals. Siv had a flash of the same fear but gripped her knife as if she might plunge it into Legion's chest. Mattis simply tracked the three men as they strode into the grove.

As the leading power here, my friends would be mine to

defend. Should Legion tell anyone, their necks would be in my hands. A tingle of hot pressure weighed over my shoulders.

"*Herr* Grey," I said with a touch of suspicion. In the moment, I hoped the sincere man I'd spent the day with was the true side of Legion Grey, and not an ambitious pariah as Siv suspected. "What are you doing here?"

Legion tilted his head. "My duty."

My fists clenched and unclenched. "What duty?"

"You, *Kvinna*. My task is looking out for you. By a happy coincidence, Tor here, noticed someone sneaking off into the thicket. Naturally, we can't have lurkers about, so we followed. I admit I'm rather pleased with what we've found." He gestured at the towering evergreen in the center. "The bell tower, I presume."

I stole a worried glance at Mattis. He ignored me, nervously rolling his sword in hand, eyes on Legion and the others. Legion didn't seem upset or disgusted, hadn't mentioned anything about reporting the truth.

He'd said nothing threatening at all.

I lifted my chin as a kind of challenge. "There is nothing wrong with wanting my maids and me to know how to defend ourselves. Mattis has been teaching us, so if you plan on telling my father—"

"I have no plans of telling anyone," Legion said, the irritating smirk tugging at his lips. "Why would I upend yet another interesting thing about you?" He faced Tor and Halvar. "Who would have known a Timoran royal could be so entertaining?"

My limbs relaxed when the other two men laughed. Legion approached the tree. He'd lost the fine waistcoat, and wore black trousers and a dark tunic, laces over his chest undone so a peek of his strong chest caught my eye.

I shook my head, anxious not to let my thoughts think any longer on his skin or—three hells—his bare chest.

Doubtless it would be a pleasant train of thought.

Legion maneuvered the knife until it broke free. "You turned your back on your opponent," he said, holding the knife like it was made for his grip. Then again, if he truly grew up as a street waif, I had few doubts Legion Grey knew how to handle a weapon. He circled me. "You turn your back, and it gives opportunity for an unseen strike. No one fights fair, I assure you."

Tor withdrew a stiletto dagger from inside his woolen jacket, and Halvar rested a hand on a small axe clipped to his belt.

"What are you doing?" I asked.

"May we not join you?"

Mavie had stopped praying, and Siv shook her head. Mattis grinned.

"Well, uh . . ." I didn't know what to say. This was highly unusual. First, to have a royal woman sparring with servants, but even more, to have a vow negotiator encourage it. "I wouldn't mind if you stayed."

The truth, and I'd say it again for the thrill in Halvar's eyes, as he let out a pleased cry, and gripped the handle of his axe. Tor said little, and truth be told, he looked uneasy. I nearly snorted a laugh—Tor was Legion's Siv.

Strange as the setting was, not long and I was laughing, head tossed back, with the others as we set up an awkward circle and watched two opponents at a time. Mattis stood against Halvar, but the carpenter cried out in shock when the stable hand dropped to his knees and took a cheap strike at Mattis's knees.

Legion grinned, pleased when Mattis's retreat landed him facedown, Halvar straddling his back, the axe at his throat. "Halvar does not lose, I should warn you all."

The stable hand flicked his brows, then helped Mattis from the ground.

"How do you know him?" I asked as Siv and Tor took the center, both scowling at the other. Tor wasn't as broad or tall as Legion, but the shadows in his eyes, the hold of his dagger, told me he could fight as well, perhaps even bloodier.

"We needed a ride here. Couldn't risk my feet getting tired, not as important as I am."

"And humble."

Legion grinned, turning back to the sparring match. "I've known Halvar for some time."

"Oh, respite eve." Of course, Legion would know Halvar since they both attended each week.

Legion didn't confirm it, but instead, watched as Siv took the upper hand on Tor. She pulled her signature move of locking one leg around the back of her opponent's knee, knocking them to the ground, then thrusting the point of her knife at the soft space just below the hinge of the jaw. Not the throat—she said it was too messy, too obvious.

It said something about Tor's skill when he managed to shake her away before she could finish. They were back on their feet in an instant, lining up for a rematch.

"She's frightening, right?" I whispered. Legion hadn't stopped staring at my friend.

"How long has she served you?"

"Nearly a turn."

That drew his eyes to me. "Only that long?" I nodded. Legion's jaw pulsed as he studied the footwork of Tor and Siv. "You're fortunate to find such loyalty from a servant in so short a time."

A new husk in his voice sent a chill up my arms. Like Siv, I detected a hint of mistrust in his tone. Before I could question him on it, Tor wrapped an arm around Siv's neck, drawing her against his chest, and held his dagger over her heart.

Siv shoved away and cursed under her breath. Even if he won, Tor seemed as angry that the defeat had been such a challenge.

"Elise," Mattis said. "You and the negotiator! Let's see how our *Kvinna* fares."

Legion opened an arm up, inviting me to take a step ahead of him. I walked backward, eyes on him as I stepped into the circle. "Never turn your back."

Legion tossed his knife between his hands, a gleam in his eyes. "A quick learner."

In the center, I crouched, legs burning as if I'd been running all night.

Legion struck, fierce and swift. I imagined he'd offer a few moments to prepare, so I stumbled back. Legion knew more than his way around a blade, it was as if the steel bent to his will. Jaw tight, I crashed my dagger against the black blade of his. We sparred back and forth. I dodged, he stabbed. I dropped to my knees, rolled to one side; his strike met me there.

"Your fingers, Kvinna," he said, breathlessly. "How did you lose them?"

An embarrassed flush filled my cheeks. I had forgotten my gloves were at home. I wasn't about to confess I'd faced the Blood Wraith, not when so many believed the Guild of Shade to be nothing but a terrifying children's story.

"An accident," I said. "One I keep close. Surely you understand."

He bowed his head as he prepared to set up again. "I do. Perhaps one day you'll tell me."

Perhaps.

Legion fought brutally. Clearly, he was a man who'd seen too many skirmishes and knew how to end them. My arms powered with heat, but I couldn't draw in a deep enough breath. I made a clumsy jab, fumbled over my feet, then ended wrapped in Legion's arm, my back to his chest, his breath on my neck. My elbows swung, aimed at his ribs, but he locked one leg around mine, and dragged us both to the ground. We were a tangle of arms, steel, and legs, breathing heavily.

Legion's knife tucked against the empty space in my lower ribs. My body still pressed to his, I shuddered when he drew his mouth against my ear. "Congratulations. Yet again, you leave me surprised. You fight well, Elise."

One of his arms was curled around my waist, and slowly, his thumb drew small circles over the peak of my hip. I'm not sure he noticed, but I held my breath, a bright spark of heat overpowering the need for air.

"I lost, *Herr*," I whispered.

"Barely. I'm not sure I can stand, now," he returned. "I defeat Tor faster than this."

"Untrue!" Tor shouted, one of the first words the somber man spoke.

Legion laughed and with him so close, I felt it to my bones. We unraveled from each other. The way we'd all fought, the aches would set in before dawn, but I couldn't remember a time when I'd been this light and at ease.

"I openly welcome you to our unofficial sparring guild," Mattis said when the first morning birds sang in the treetops. He was bleeding from his lip, but something feral lived in his eyes. Siv nursed a jammed knuckle, I rubbed the tips of my missing fingers, pleased to see Legion with sweat on his brow, too.

"Shall I walk you back, *Kvinna?*" Halvar asked.

"No," I said as I sheathed my dagger. Dawn was fast approaching, and we all needed to return separately. The risk of being found out was too great if we tromped through the trees in one group. "Thank you. I've gotten skilled at sneaking into my bedroom."

Halvar smiled, revealing a scar over the dimple in his cheek. I'd never been close enough to notice. "As you say."

Legion volunteered to stay back with Tor and Halvar to make sure the grove went unseen and undisturbed. They would venture back to the manor the way they had left, unassuming, out for an early correspondence, or some other excuse. I waited until Mavie and Mattis disappeared, then I, too, faded into the trees.

Twenty paces in, though, I realized I'd left my lantern and in the thickest part of the wood I'd be walking blind.

Back at the grove, I paused. Legion, Tor, and Halvar remained. They were speaking in low, deep voices. Why had they drawn their weapons? I'd watched them all sheath their blades. Now each man gripped his without mercy.

I ducked behind a fallen tree when whoever had been speaking stopped and the group broke apart. My pulse thudded in my skull as Siv, eyes wide, face pale, ran from the center. As if she'd escaped an ambush, and the fierce way the men stood, I didn't think an ambush was too ridiculous a thought.

Siv darted into the night. Never had I seen terror on my friend's face, but undeniable fear alighted her eyes tonight. Legion signaled to Tor and Halvar, as if they'd not terrified a woman, and together they were lost into the trees.

I leaned back against the fallen tree, heart racing.

Whatever gentility I had seen in Legion tonight, I'd been wrong. It would take anything but gentleness to draw out pallid fear from Siverie.

There was more to him than I realized.

A motive for being here I had yet to uncover.

For Siv, for Mavie, I wholly intended to find out everything there was to know about Legion Grey.

CHAPTER EIGHT

My PLANS TO assert my status and command on Legion Grey faded by noonday.

All morning I'd sought him out. An attempt to test him, see if he admitted he'd cornered Siv. If he confessed, well then, I'd certainly have something to say about it.

What, I didn't know, but I would say something important, surely.

Grand imaginings of intimidation played in my head, the things I'd say, the tone I'd take. And by the time I arrived at the arched doorway of the wood and wattle cottage he'd occupied, I'd convinced myself Legion Grey would soon tremble beneath my ferociousness.

With learned influence, I gave a heavy-handed knock at the door.

The cottage was not large. Enough to house a washroom, a bed for two, and a pantry of sorts with a table to eat small meals. The knock would be heard at all corners of the cottage, and it would take even less time to reach the door.

Stillness returned my summons.

I knocked again with more frustration behind it. There were qualities of being raised in a royal household that reared up on occasion. Being kept waiting too long was one of them. I didn't like it, and grew rather ill-tempered when I was ignored.

"*Herr* Grey," I demanded.

Nothing.

"*Kvinna*, the negotiator is not in." At my back, the old man removed his woven cap off his stark white hair. His thread-bare tunic had once been white. Now, with yellowed sweat soaked into the fabric, a musty wake typically announced Viggo before his voice. Skin like leather after turns in the sun, he leaned on the handle of a rusted garden spade and lit an herb roll. The folds of his rough skin stretched as he puffed out a plume of smoke.

"Where has he gone, Viggo?"

"Parts of his agreement, last I heard. Gets every last moon off."

The last moon came every twenty-two nights, but I'd never heard of the agreement. Quite the opposite, I'd always been told negotiators rarely left the side of their charge.

"Why?" I asked, though why would a servant know?

It was foolish to underestimate a gossip like Viggo. The old man jabbed the spade into the small flower berm around Legion's cottage, teasing the soil. He puffed dark smoke as he worked and talked. "Hal's the one who mentioned it. Went with him, and all. Don't know where to."

"Halvar is with him? How long will they be gone?"

Another shrug, another dig with the spade. "Packed for a'least a night. Him, Hal, and the stern fellow. I saws them leave right after the sun rose. If I can say, your negotiator looked like he'd stumbled outta one of the hells. Red-eyed, staggering. Didn't look well's all I'm saying."

Legion was ill? When I was meant to be angry at him, a pang of worry pierced my heart instead.

Viggo started to hum as he turned the soil. I thanked him and strode up the path to the manor. My confrontation would be turned to Siv, I supposed. She'd tell me what happened, and then when Legion recovered, I'd make him wish he was ill again.

But how does one plan an illness?

Viggo said he planned to take every last moon off. Was it coincidence he'd simply woken on his assigned day ill? Or was this ailment recurring, so Legion knew to expect it?

My reluctant worry deepened.

At the stoop of the house, my father claimed the steps, leaning over a wooden cane, a deep, unforgiving frown curling his lips. A prince consort through marriage, but in this moment, my father looked every bit as formidable as any king.

"*Mon Kvin.* You look well today." I bowed my head. Proper greetings seemed prudent in this moment. He was angry or agitated at something. My first thoughts ran to the idea that he might know about our sparring nights. I prayed to every deity I could name that he didn't.

"Daughter," my father said airily. "Glad to see you up and about. I thought you might sleep until the moon."

I'd hardly slept past dawn, but my father expected a punctual, early-to-rise household, as if without our presence the day would be utterly wasted. "Forgive me, I overslept."

"There are some who seem to think you abandoned your chambers last night." My father leaned his ruddy face close to mine. "Red eyes, pallid skin—"

"Daj, I—"

"Do not speak, Elise," he hissed through his teeth, but it only caused a long cough. He cleared his throat when it passed, voice hoarse. "A woman in the throes of betrothal." He sniffed me. My face heated in fierce embarrassment when he pulled back, disgusted. "Did you bed someone?"

My eyes widened. "No! No, of course not."

"You are a wretched, selfish girl. I'd be surprised if any more offers are made. We ask little of you. If you wish me dead, then continue being the selfish child you are."

"Daj—"

"Get inside." He clicked his tongue, snarling. "*Herr* Grey is absent for the day and tonight. You are not to be unaccompanied now that your hand is for bid, so you will remain with your sister until otherwise told."

My heart sank. How would I get the truth out of Siv with Runa around? I knew enough not to argue, though. Head down, I hurried past my father and into the manor.

He called me selfish. It broke my heart and angered my soul all at once. How could he say such a thing when I made no protest simply for the sake of his healing? This vow was in honor of him, for his life. And it was all he cared about.

The main hall bustled with servants behind netted veils. Spices and roasting meat wafted through the corridors for the midmeal. An ever-present hint of mulled, spiced red and sweat heated beneath the high sun. Smells of the home I'd soon leave behind. With the knowledge my negotiator may not be as kindly as thought; that my friend and servant might have secrets; that I was to meet with suitors without the looming presence of Legion (even if I held some resentment toward him, I could not deny his intimidating figure put me at ease around pompous nobles)—all of it struck me in the chest. Hard and unrelenting. This would end sooner than later. I'd leave this behind and be forced to learn a new kind of life.

Hot tears sprang to my eyes—a collision of anger and hopelessness as I climbed the steps, desperate to hide away in my chamber until I was forced to emerge.

A giggle stopped me halfway up the wide-set staircase.

"Eli." I leaned over the polished banister and looked at Runa. My sister winked. "What were you thinking?"

Being vowed to Calder, Runa had her own maids, but they were of a different station. They were of Ravenspire servitude now and were not masked. In fact, their frocks were hemmed in silver and gold and emerald thread. Their dark hair braided in satin ribbons. They were the maids of the future queen, after all, and lifted their noses in the air as well as any royal.

I suspected Runa didn't laugh well into the night with her maids, though. I doubt they spoke much at all.

With a stiff wave, I urged my sister to join me on the stairs, out of earshot of anyone listening. She glanced over her shoulder and obeyed, stifling a laugh as she did.

"Eli, did you truly sneak out? Why the risk?"

Her remarks answered two lingering questions: no one knew I'd gone to spar last night, and someone had spied my escape and had a rather big mouth. Runa linked her elbow with mine and walked with me up the remaining steps.

"Well?" she pressed when I didn't answer.

"I needed air," I lied. "It's suffocating in here."

"What a bleeding weakling you are, sister. So like our father." Runa snorted, a bit like the hogs kept in the pens outside. But then, Runa's voice often came through her nose rather than her throat. In truth, I think she did it on purpose, as though the higher pitch made her sound more important, smoother around the edges, unlike folk in the townships. I thought it made her more like someone always trying to draw in breath, but never succeeding. The nasally, whistled pitch heightened as my sister went on. "You feel suffocated because men are seeking your hand, because you are the bright star for the moment. Cursed gods, what more can be done for you?"

"I expect nothing to be done for me, but to be allowed to live as I wish." We turned down the upper corridor, in the direction of Runa's chambers. I didn't argue, even when her maids whispered about my unkempt braid. Her chambers were larger and more secluded. "Did you truly have every desire to vow with Calder? Or was there ever a thought that perhaps someone else might make you happy? Might love you?"

Runa lifted a brow like I'd suggested pure insanity. She didn't answer right away, and opened the door to her personal study, or tearoom mostly. My sister had a taste for exotic teas, and would surely cost Calder a small fortune importing the dark herbs and sweet flowers from the distant kingdoms.

Dismissing her maids to sit in the corner, she lifted a silver bowl to her nose and inhaled. Adding a few leaves to a cup, she sat on an upholstered chair with a sigh. "Eli, I have no idea what you expect me to say. Calder is the finest match in the kingdom. The *future* king. What could possibly be better?"

"But you don't love him."

She balked and added a touch of honey to her cup. "What good is love in a monarchy? We fuel each other's ambition. The drive to rule Timoran better than the generations before us is alive in our match."

I sat on the twin chair across from my sister, choosing to nibble at one of the saffron cakes on the tray rather than take the pungent tea. "Zyben will rule for turns to come. I see more benefit in an affectionate match than one fed by ambition to take the throne, when the day won't come to pass until your face is drooping."

I knew how to get under my sister's skin, and I took a bit of pride in the glare she cut at me. Mention of her youth and beauty dying someday always gave Runa a puckered look. "How little you know. Your lack of interest in the growth of our kingdom is disappointing. You'd rather spend your days in books of fairy tales, or laughing with maids who are friendly to you out of fear you'll slit their gullet if they are not."

She might as well have slapped me. I looked at the half-eaten roll in my hand, worried she might be partly right. Would Mavie and Siv ever be their true selves with me? Or was it partly because of my status and they felt obligated to be courteous?

Runa groaned. She returned her teacup to the tray. "I'm sorry, Eli, but you and I were not meant to have friends or romantic love. We're made to lead Timoran into glory, into power. Like the gods battled before us."

There was no sense in arguing with her. I lifted my gaze to

the table near her hearth. Scrolls of vellum and parchment were pinned back by books and ceramic carvings of the goddesses of fate. "What are you studying over here?"

Runa brightened. "Oh, you might find this interesting. Since I am to move into the palace after my wedding, I thought it would be wise to fully understand the history of Ravenspire. However, the palace goes far beyond our family. I'm learning of the cursed royals, the last Ettan bloodline our great-grandfather destroyed."

"Really." She wasn't wrong. I was intrigued to learn more of the Ettan royalty. I knew a little of the rulers before us, but after nearly a hundred turns, some stories had become more like lore than fact.

"Have a look."

A grin played at my lips. I set the roll back on the tray, gathered my skirts in hand, and leaned over the fading histories. One parchment was painted in names of Zyben's line, each marked with a rune of their attributes. The line ended at Zyben, with a few marks acknowledging he had children and a sister. My name had been whittled down to a tick mark that someone —be it a son or daughter—existed in the king's sister's household. My mark on history was less than impressive.

My fingers danced across the names of my grandfather, a man I never met, and my grandmother, his second consort. Then onto King Eli, my namesake. The king who led the raids on Etta and destroyed one country to claim it as his own.

Before him, when Timorans still lived in the tundra and icy cliffs, the family units were tighter. One king, one queen in a match. One or two children. Not until Eli did Timorans think so highly of themselves that they claimed everyone they desired in the slightest. The first king of New Timoran having no less than eighty consorts and five wives.

How would my great-grandfather even remember the names of such a harem?

My attention focused on the scroll beside the Timoran lines. Former Etta. The runes were similar, but the edges of the yellowed parchment were filigreed in thorny vines, some with the sketch of roses or wild rowan. The royal crest was a crescent moon, a crossed dagger and axe, wrapped by Jörmungandr, the sea serpent encircling the whole of the earth. I smiled sadly, tracing the sharp lines of the snake's jaw. Once, Ettans had believed much like Timorans. Why had King Eli not united the people? Why crush their heads at all? Wouldn't this kingdom be stronger if Ettan folk stood with Timorans?

The family lines of the Ettan royal bloodline went back generations. Most marked with a moon and the rune for fury —*magi*. Night Folk blood raged through the royal lines of Etta. It was strange how a healthy dose of fear for the fae hovered around modern Ettans. Mattis teased Mavie for her reservation to the fae, and for good reason. According to this history, I'd be surprised if Mavie was without a touch of fae blood. Nearly all but a few of the royals across twelve generations had the mark of fury.

"The way I understand it," Runa said, interrupting my thoughts and pointing to the last three generations of royal Ettans, "royalty began uniting with common folk—possibly Timoran lines. See here, the queen two generations before the last Ferus bloodline; her prince consort had no fury. And then you see it only passed to two of their nine children. Calder believes the dying fury gave our folk the opportunity to seize the land."

Where I ought to feel pride for the cunning and strategy of my ancient family, I felt a twinge of guilt. To me, this looked as if Etta had reached a hand of peace to the tundra warriors across the peaks. Took vows with them, loved them.

The stark difference between the Ettan families and Timorans—one actual vow. The spells in my passionate book spoke of numerous causes for dalliances, but when I thought on it, most writings of fae royalty spoke of loyalty to consorts. Only taking new lovers after the last passed to the Otherworld. Though some mortal consorts did complete *förändra*—the Change. Since Night Folk outlived mortals by hundreds of turns, there were tales of fae granting their mortal loves the gift of life fury, so they'd live long, many lifetimes. I didn't know if *förändra* was even real or possible. But it made for good stories.

"The last royals, King Arvad and his queen, Lilianna, were the final Ferus bloodline," Runa said with a hunger in her voice. "Lilianna was Timoran, did you know? There are writings of her—the paleness of her hair, her eyes."

"So then, King Eli must've known her when he raided."

"I believe Lilianna was a friend of King Eli. But she chose to marry a fae." Runa pointed at the markings by Arvad's name. I knew a few bloody tales of the last fae king of Etta. Ones that made me shudder. I wondered if Lilianna even had a choice.

"Did King Eli invade because of her?"

Runa shrugged. "That is one theory. Out of anger."

"Or maybe he loved her."

"Love is not a motivation for war."

I bit the inside of my cheek to keep from laughing. In all the books I'd read, love turned even the sanest people mad. Love gave plenty of motivation for war, but what was the point of trying to convince Runa otherwise? If a loveless match satisfied her, fine. At times I wished I could be the same.

Names had been scorched away from Arvad Ferus's line. His children. As if King Eli had wished to burn away any proof a Timoran woman had mated with Night Folk.

"They couldn't scrape the symbols," Runa said. She gestured at the blackened marks, but true enough, next to the missing names were the symbols of their titles. A rune for the sun, of beauty, and of darkness.

Though the names were burned from history, there were enough writings on the Ettan royal family most Timorans had guessed the three names of Arvad's heirs. The heir apparent, the sun prince—Sol. Second born, a daughter. A book on warriors had mentioned Queen Lilianna had named her first daughter Herja, a name for a beautiful warrior maiden of the All Father.

"The Night Prince," Runa muttered bitterly. "You know the idea of him being alive is what spurs the bleeding Agitators."

My eyes fell to the last smudge. Histories wrote of the third heir, Valen Ferus, most. Probably because he was believed to be the only fae child of the last king. The Agitators worshipped the idea of their night prince, insisting he'd not been killed because of fury. They believed the land would never thrive and would die like Old Timoran if the rightful heir did not take the throne. If that were true, where was he? Why wait? Besides, if the Night Prince survived due to his power, how had Arvad been killed? The last king had strong fury, undeniable by his gruesome acts during the raids.

A knock came to the door. Siv stepped inside and my breath caught. I'd been so lost in the parchment I'd nearly forgotten my friend had been threatened—or so it looked—last night. I needed to speak with her.

"*Kvinna* Elise," she said properly. "*Herr* Gurst has arrived and wishes to speak with you."

Runa chuckled. "So it begins, sister. The parades of menfolk looking to woo you. Come, I've been looking forward to this since father placed you as my charge."

I groaned and followed behind Runa and her maids. At Siv's side I whispered, "How are you?"

"Fine," she whispered back, her familiar scowl in place.

"Siv, I need to speak to you about last night."

Her eyes snapped to mine, but only for a moment. "I'm sure we can speak later. Right now, you have one thing to worry about."

"What's that?"

Siv paused at the door to one of the front parlors. "You ought to know, Gurst has made clear his unyielding desire to take vows with you. But be warned—the man has no teeth, and smells like he was swallowed by a whale, then vomited back out. Shall we?"

A little paler, a little more nauseous, I followed her into the parlor.

CHAPTER NINE

"THERE IS MORE where this comes from, dear girl," Willem Gurst crooned. For the fifth time the bulbous man pointed to his russet cabriolet, the wheels painted in real gold, as he put it. "My estates claim two-hundred square lengths of the Ribbon Lakes region; a household any woman would be proud to claim as her own."

I smiled, but was certain it came more as a grimace as I fanned my face with a white handkerchief, desperate to keep the cloying scent of mildew and rot from my nose.

"Then there is the fishery . . . Did I tell you I have no less than ninety folk in my employ? That goes without mention of the many serfs in the estates and—"

"Yes," I interjected. "Yes, *Herr* Gurst. You've mentioned it all. Quite impressive." Bleeding hells, does the man roll in the innards and blood at his fishery? Does he not wash? I didn't understand how a human could be so unaware of their odor.

Gurst offered a gummy smile, took my gloved hand, and

pressed a kiss to the top. "Ah, then, I've given you a great deal to lust over tonight. I hope to call upon you tomorrow, *Kvinna*."

"Uh," I looked to Siv and now Mavie who stood on the steps.

It was Runa who snickered, then cleared her throat. "Apologies, *Herr*," my sister said. "But *Kvinna* Elise will be asked to meet with others. You understand."

Gurst didn't seem pleased, but how could he argue the glorious tradition of bidding on a royal bride like chattel? "Of course. I assure you, my dear, I will call upon you again at the first opportunity."

Please, by the gods, please do not.

Once Gurst was in his coach, I allowed my shoulders to slump, but grinned up at Runa. "I could kiss you, sister."

She chuckled and waved me away. "Please. My dismissal was purely selfish. I would be forced to cut you off should *Herr* Grey select such a pungent man as that. I'd never allow him to step foot inside Ravenspire."

Since Gurst's visit lasted until the haze of twilight curled around the trees, Runa took her leave of me, entrusting me to the care of my maids to settle for the night. Finally, I'd get the chance to speak with Siv. I stole a glance toward Legion's cottage and frowned. The windows remained shadowed, and no hint of life existed. I hated how part of me felt a pang of worry about his condition, whatever it was.

The other was still furious with the man.

"Bleeding skies," Mavie swore as she closed the door to my chamber. "I thought he'd never leave."

"Speak for yourself," Siv grumbled. "I was downwind."

"You both had it easy. I, on the other hand, endured a kiss

to the cheek. The *cheek*." My skin still prickled as if a thousand creeping things had burrowed beneath my face.

Mavie laughed, turning down the furs over my bed. "Be sure to inform *Herr* Grey when he returns, Gurst is not the match."

At the mention of Legion, I flicked my gaze to Siv, looking for any kind of reaction. Perhaps it was because I'd been looking, but I was certain I saw her flinch.

"Do you think he was hurt last night and didn't say?" Mavie asked and turned the flame in a lantern by the bed.

"I don't," I said too briskly. "Sometimes I think Legion Grey is not who we think. I'm sure he has secrets."

Mavie furrowed her brow but shrugged it off. "I'll go draw a bath. No doubt you'd like to wash the day away."

"You read my mind." I really wanted a moment alone with Siv. When Mavie disappeared into the washroom, I chased away the space between us before I lost the opportunity. "Siv, I saw you speaking with Legion last night. I saw how he threatened you. Will you tell me what it was about?"

Her eyes went wide. "You saw—" Siv shook her head and acted busy with the pillows on the bed. "No, you misunderstood. It was nothing. He didn't threaten me."

"I saw your face. They had weapons drawn. If he has harmed you, I swear—"

"Elise, he didn't," she said abruptly and faced me. "At first he was . . . suspicious of me is all."

"Suspicious, why?"

"Said I fought too well for a serf. Truly, he was concerned for you, what with us being so close. Once he realized the mistake, we, uh, left it at that."

I pinched my lips into a bloodless line. "So you told him where you learned to fight?" A bit of jealousy bloomed in my gut. Siv never opened her past.

With a tilt to her head, she sighed. "It isn't some grand story. I was taught as a child by my father before I was a serf."

An itch in the back of my head put me on edge. A sense that I wasn't seeing something right in front of my eyes. But Siv wouldn't lie. As powerful as he might be in the world of trade, I still outranked Legion Grey. With him absent, this would be the opportunity to admit to any threat, for the Lysander estate to rid itself of a man who turned on its serfs. She wouldn't lie. I had to trust she wouldn't. If I did not trust Mavie and Siv and Mattis, then I trusted no one.

"If you promise you're all right—"

"I promise," Siv said, even rested a hand on my arm. "Legion Grey is . . . not a threat."

As I mulled over our conversation once Mavie and Siv left me to their own beds, I couldn't shake the toil in my stomach. The way Siv had bristled during the conversation, the fear in her eyes. The way she'd said the word "threat" through her teeth.

Legion burdened my thoughts well into the night. He'd been arrogant, but gentle. Haughty, but unassuming. Perhaps I was so desperate to find more goodness outside of my narrow circle of friends, I'd trusted too easily.

But the idea that Legion Grey couldn't be trusted, I didn't understand. It left my heart heavy until my mind could think no more, and I drifted to sleep.

Not so many hours later, rough hands shook me awake. The

blur of my dim room took a moment to come into focus, but when my eyes adjusted, Mavie hovered over me.

Her eyes were wide, filled with terror. "Elise, wake up. Quickly. We must hurry!"

"What's wrong?" I tossed back the fox fur comforter off my legs.

"Shh," Mavie held a finger to her lips. She froze.

My pulse pounded in my skull. In the distance, voices rose over the quiet night. Screams. My blood drained from my face as I scurried across the room to my window.

Over the knolls, at the border of our gates, the yard patrols rushed toward thick clouds of black smoke. The bloody glow of flames over the hills ignited the midnight sky in a battle of flame and shadow. Serfs screamed as they raced through our gardens, aimed at the main manor cellars. They looked as if they ran for their lives.

"Mavie," I said, breathless. "What's going on?"

She wrung her tattered nightdress between her fingers, tears in her eyes. "Agitators . . . they're taking lower Mellanstrad. Folk say they're coming here!"

"What?"

"Elise some of the . . . some of the serfs said they saw in the trees . . . a man in a red mask."

No. The floor tilted. "The Blood Wraith?"

Mavie ignored me and gathered the cloak still dropped in a heap on my floor. "We must get you to the cellars. There is no reason to risk waiting in the open in case anyone breaches the gates."

Thoughts of facing the demon of my nightmares faded.

Panic rose in my throat, but of a different kind. "The cellars? No! We need to help."

"Elise," Mavie said. "You are a *Kvinna*."

I narrowed my eyes and pulled out a wooden chest from beneath my bed. "Yes. And I bleed the same as others."

Mavie fidgeted, wringing her fingers in front of her body. I lifted the lid of the chest. My mother would shriek her disappointment if she knew I kept a trunk of weapons beneath my bed. No doubt Runa never had need to handle a blade, but as for me, I'd rather draw a bit of blood before anyone slit my throat.

The door slammed open and Siv filled the doorway as I fastened a slight bow over my shoulder and five arrows, more reminiscent of bolts than anything.

"Why are you still here?" Siv snapped. "Do you think your mother will wait to lock the cellars if you are not there?"

"Exactly. If I am of no importance, we might as well make a difference for those who cannot fight for themselves." I wheeled on Mavie and Siv. "I am going to the old chantry. The tower has the best vantage point of the lower neighborhoods."

"Elise," Mavie warned.

"Stay here," I said. "Hide, and do not come out until you know it's safe."

Siv snorted her disgust. "Tell me to stand back one more time, *Kvinna*. I dare you."

I fought a grin. "Fine. We'll be shooting, Siverie. Take up a bow." I gestured at my open trunk but kept my gaze on Mavie. "Mavs? Focus."

Mavie trembled, eyes wide. She shook her head. "I-I-I want to stay with you."

There wasn't time to argue. Our fates belonged to our own choices tonight. I gave her a quick nod, handed her a knife, then took to the corridors. Siv and I with bows, Mavie, a blade against a beast who could slaughter us in one blow.

The manor was silent. Tension grew the dim light, the quiet of the bedrooms, but danger spun the house in a way that seemed at every corner a knife might jut out and slit our throats where we stood.

On the lower level my father's guards took to each window, each doorway. Others marched in tight units toward the gates. They wore formidable, wiry, black belts over their shoulders. Sheaths of knives, of axes, on their chests. It was a sight to see some top their skulls with heads of deer or slaughtered bears. Like the warriors of my great-grandfather, King Eli.

If we were not placing our lives at risk, I might stop and revel in a bit of pride at the warrior blood showing through tonight.

"This way." I gestured toward the narrow corridor that would lead through the kitchens and to the trellises on the east side. We kept low, kept quiet. Outside, the cold air struck my face, raising my skin. Smoke from tower fires warned upper Mellanstrad of a threat, and added a burning layer in the air.

Serfs darted from the cottages. Guards went for the gates. Shouts broke the peace of the night and added chaos. I couldn't tell where the voices rose from, couldn't see Agitators. But if we were the royals of this region, then we ought to stand for our people. Not hide in a damp cellar while the innocent were left alone.

All my nights sneaking into the surrounding forest quickly became of use.

I took to the trees on instinct, Siv and Mavie close at my back. Damp from the shore hung in the air. My hair clung to my brow. Each step trembled, but I didn't slow my pace. In the trees, smoke darkened the path, but it wasn't long before we arrived at the gray rock wall of the old worship chantry on the grounds.

The bell tower rose above the walls of upper Mellanstrad, giving sight to the narrow alleys between the tenements, but also a good view of our grounds. The old chantry was built against the edge of the forest. Shadows from the trees twisted my insides. Hair on the back of my neck rose on end, as if unseen eyes drank us in.

I shoved away the apprehension and tugged open the heavy, wooden door.

My father's guards took to the walls and their towers to protect our precious royal blood, but the bell tower was left unguarded. Good. I didn't need to worry over sneaking past patrols who believed me to be something breakable like glass.

"Hurry," I said, and held the door open for my friends.

Siv notched an arrow in the larger bow and stepped into the shadows of the chantry. Mavie followed.

I turned to follow but was stopped.

I must've screamed, my throat grew raw, but it drowned beneath the thud of blood in my head.

Before I knew what was happening, a strong hand curled around my arm, and wrenched me away from the door and into the night.

CHAPTER TEN

I SWUNG THE BOLT, aiming for whoever had grabbed onto my arm. My frenzied attack was blocked. I reeled back again. I jabbed, sliced, tried to break free.

"*Kvinna*! Stop. *Elise!*"

I blinked through my stun, the bolt raised above my head. Halvar gripped my wrist, keeping the point from slicing his throat. He breathed heavily and held up a hand as if to guard against another swing.

"Halvar . . . what are you—"

"I came to make sure you were safe," he said. "I saw you running. This way, *Kvinna*. They've locked the cellars, but there is a hatch in the stables that—"

"I'm not running to safety, Halvar," I said, holding up the bolt again. "I'm fighting."

The stable hand lifted a brow. A muscle pulsed in his jaw. "I was asked to keep you safe."

"By Legion? Where is he?" I turned over one shoulder as if

he might appear. "I heard he'd taken ill, and you'd left with him."

"Yes," Halvar said, drawing an axe from his belt when the trees echoed with shouts. "He is recovering in town."

"He is at risk then." My throat tightened. "They are coming from town!"

Halvar studied me for a breath, but slowly, a grin curled over his mouth. "I assure you, Legion Grey knows how to survive, *Kvinna*. Are you truly planning to use that?"

I followed his gaze to the bow in my hand. "I did not bring it as an accessory, Halvar."

The stable hand chuckled and rolled his axe in hand. "With all respect, *Kvinna*, you are strange."

I smirked at him, then rushed into the chantry. The place was never used anymore. My family made it a point to worship in town, in the spotlight. Where they'd be adored and worshipped in their own way.

Hints of old, dusty parchment perfumed the air, and the cushions of the benches were tattered and worn.

We ran for the staircase behind the gods' altar that wound up to the bell tower.

Halvar surprised me. He moved lithely, as if he were born for battle. Not feeding mares and repairing battered carriages. I made a note to wonder about his past later, for now I was grateful he knew how to handle the axe in his hand. What had Legion said during the sparring match? Halvar didn't lose.

At the top of the stairs Siv met us. She glared at Halvar. He glared at her.

Like a fist to my chest, I recalled that I had yet to confront Legion on his behavior toward my friend. It hardly seemed important now. I hated that I worried for him. Hated how I wished he were here with us, so I'd know he was alive and unharmed. Then, once it was over, I'd shout at him.

Next to the chipped iron bell the patrols were easier to see. All the attention had moved toward the north side of the manor where the forest grew thickest, and the peaks cut through the treetops. Lanterns had been doused at the house. The lawns were free of fleeing serfs now. All I could hope for was they found a place for refuge.

I opened my mouth to ask Halvar what he knew, but startled back when below us the gates groaned and cracked. Guards roared commands. I fumbled with my bow, loading a bolt, then lifting the weapon.

"Great gods," Mavie said under her breath.

The gates shuddered, split, and soon the guards were overpowered. A swarm of darkly dressed people rushed into the lawns. They swung at the patrols with jagged swords, with crudely carved rods and clubs. Agitators, perhaps, but they behaved more like rabid dogs.

Mavie screamed as a man leapt onto one of the guards and bit the guard's neck. My insides coiled hard and angry when the Agitator finished the guard with a blade, but his chin dribbled in blood from the ravenous bite.

Siv's eyes widened in horror. "What is wrong with them?"

I lifted the bow, my hand against my cheek. My pulse raced, but on the outside I steadied. This was my duty to protect this land. These people. "I don't know what is wrong, but they do not belong here."

I let the bolt fly.

The point sank deep into the Agitator's arm. I would not sit idly back while others fought, but it didn't mean I was the best shot. I handled a blade well enough, but Mattis had only started teaching me how to maneuver with a bow. Siv made up for my poor aim. Her arrow dug deep into the man's skull.

The trouble with firing on the siege, it drew attention to our position. Mavie dragged in a deep breath, holding it too long, as a few Agitators rushed the chantry. Their movements were strangely disjointed and stiff. Still, they moved swift enough.

"Dammit," Halvar said through his teeth. "Keep them back if you can. I'll take the door."

My hands trembled as I took aim once more. I had four bolts left. I had to make them count. An Agitator dressed in a dark bearskin glared at the top of the bell tower. Light from the warning flames cast his face in a bloody glow. He sneered. His lips and teeth were stained in a filmy black. But his eyes were dark as pitch. Not even the flames reflected in them.

Siv stared at him, aghast.

I licked my lips and aimed my bow, desperate to ignore the crashes of bookshelves and glass inside the chantry. Desperate to ignore the worry over Halvar.

"I-I-I need to help him," Mavie stammered.

"No Mavs," I shouted back. "Don't go. Defend yourself only."

"I can spar too!" Mavie rolled her shoulders back and lunged back down the winding steps away from the bells and into the chapel.

"Bleeding hells." I forced myself to turn away from the empty space that swallowed Mavie and aimed at the climbing Agitators.

Arrows whipped through the air from Siv's bow. More

Agitators fell. One of my bolts hit a woman in the thigh. She fell in a sick thud. Did I kill her? My stomach turned. I didn't have time to dwell on it before a man curled over the ledge.

Siv screamed my name. I stumbled to the ground. Raised my final bolt. The Agitator's chin was soaked in black spittle. His eyes wild. Perhaps his mind was lost, but he still raised his carved spear well enough. The point of the wooden rod lowered. I rolled onto my shoulder, narrowly avoiding the strike. He slammed it down again.

I slashed the point of the bolt over his thigh. When he staggered back, I kicked at his knee. The Agitator fell, but managed to curl his hand around my ankle. I tried to kick him off, but his hold was unrelenting.

He said something—more gurgled it—before he rammed the point of the wooden rod into the side of my foot. I screamed through the pain. Black dotted my sight. I held my breath, gritted my teeth, and tried to focus enough to fight back. I cut the bolt across my body. The Agitator stumbled.

My head spun. Hot, blinding light filled my head when he yanked the rod out of my foot. Bile burned the back of my throat. I wouldn't die this way. Not with so many unknowns I had yet to unravel. Against the ache in my foot, I scooted back. Pain spread like fire in my veins.

The Agitator raised his killing blow. I closed my eyes against what would happen.

All at once the Agitator coughed. His breaths grew raspy, strangled. My eyes flashed open in time to see him fall to his knees. The man convulsed. More blackness spilled over his lips. His eyes rolled back into his head. Dark veins cut across his skin.

I dragged myself away from him. Heavy footsteps echoed up the staircase until Halvar and Mavie materialized. Both breathless. Halvar was covered in dark blood. Mavie trembled, but gripped her knife well. We watched in horror as the Agitator struggled to breathe. In another rattling breath he went still. A puddle of black pooled beneath him. As if his sweat and blood turned to ink.

"What the hells?" Siv's voice drew me to look over the edge of the bell tower window. The Agitators below us, the ones fighting my father's guards, fell to the ground.

I didn't understand. My eyes scanned the surrounding trees, searching for answers.

I found one.

My body froze. For a moment, hardly longer than two heartbeats, in the trees a blood-red mask stared out from the darkness. At this distance I couldn't see his eyes beneath the dark cowl, but the shine of the flames caught the fabric over his mouth and nose; it caught the gleam of the black axes.

"By the gods and hells," Siv said in a gasp. "Is that . . ."

The Blood Wraith was gone on second glance.

He'd returned. To my land. For me.

Now that the guards were free of the Agitators, they reinforced the wall. They must've given the Blood Wraith pause to scurry back to the hell he escaped from.

"*Kvinna*," Halvar said, voice rough.

His hand touched my shoulder and I startled. My body wouldn't stop trembling. "Did you see him?"

Halvar's eyes turned to the spot where the Blood Wraith had disappeared. He didn't need to answer. His glance was response enough, but he did all the same. "A lookalike. To frighten folk."

I knew better. Doubtless no one survived the Blood Wraith. All these turns later, he'd come to finish the job. But no one knew that. What was worse—if the Blood Wraith wanted me dead, then everyone around me would be at risk.

"Elise," Halvar said my name softly. "You're wounded."

My eyes flicked to my foot. My boot was soaked in blood, but I didn't feel the pain anymore. "I'll survive."

"Even still," Halvar said with a cautious smile as he helped me to my feet, "we should treat it. There are a few . . . suspicious ointments we store away in the stables."

I grinned to keep tears at bay. "Suspicious as in forbidden."

"As in illegal. I'm trusting you to keep your mouth shut."

"Don't speak to the *Kvinna* like that," Mavie said.

"Mavs, we all nearly died. Let's drop titles for a moment," I said and hooked my arm around Halvar's shoulders. He helped me stagger down the steps. "Halvar," I whispered when we were alone. "I saw the Blood Wraith. I think . . . I think he came for me."

I don't know why I said it. Perhaps I needed to confide in someone. Halvar was quiet, but he'd come to stand with us. He was as trustworthy as anyone right now.

His jaw tightened. "The Blood Wraith comes for no one in particular."

"So, you do think it was him?"

"No," he said quickly. "No. I don't. But out of curiosity, why do you think he'd come for you?"

I pinched my lips tight, wincing as I limped off the final step. I shook my head. "Doesn't matter."

Halvar hesitated. His grip around my waist tightened. "I swear to you, *Kvinna* Elise, we would not let him bring you harm. No one will."

"We?"

"You understand what I mean."

I smiled. Legion.

Mad as I was at the man, even ill, he'd sent Halvar to defend me. I could chalk it up to him protecting his investments, but if I had to take a guess, I think Legion was more a decent sort and genuinely cared.

The moment of affection passed as the weight of what happened here tonight crushed my shoulders. Had the Wraith done something to the Agitators? Why did they behave so . . . strangely? What was the blackness bleeding from their bodies? Like a blight in their blood.

"How did they die, Halvar? The Agitators. They all died at once."

Halvar met my gaze but didn't speak. I swallowed past the knot in my throat and shuddered. Fury.

Did the Blood Wraith have fury? Was he the one who'd slaughtered the Agitators? Hells, were those who'd attacked even Agitators at all?

One thing was clear, if fury was rising—tonight would not be the last time blood spilled.

CHAPTER ELEVEN

DAWN BROUGHT GLOOMY CLOUDS, a sea wind, and a haze that added to my sour mood. My foot ached, but Halvar's concoction had already sealed the wound. The paste tingled. It tugged on the threads of my split flesh like a needle and thread.

I didn't ask, but if the paste was illegal, doubtless it had a bit of fury. Maybe herbs from the king's peaks where common folk were forbidden.

Before dawn, a pyre was lit on the back lawn. My father demanded Runa and I remain inside. According to his missive, we need not worry ourselves over the death of a guard. My fists clenched as I leaned my forehead against the bubbled glass of my window, watching the flames lick toward the sky.

The guard defended this house with his life. He deserved to be set to the sea with his pyre. Not on a haphazard bonfire in the corner of the grounds.

A bit of guilt twisted my gut. I wished not a single life had been lost, but at our latest count, the guard who'd been bitten was the only one who'd fallen besides dozens of Agitators. My family had holed up in the cellars. The serfs in the hatch in the stables, in the trees, beneath beds. Our guards proved themselves, and a royal courier had already sent word from Castle Ravenspire that those who'd fought to defend the king's sister would be honored at a fete at the castle in the coming weeks.

I wanted to hide beneath my furs and quilts and stay there at least another week.

No one seemed out of sorts that our household had fallen under attack. Already my father's trade council was making light of it. I overheard two bulbous men laughing that they'd expected such an attack much earlier than this.

The serfs went about their duties. Bevan hardly mentioned what happened, but fear lived in his eyes. Fear he wouldn't talk about.

I tried.

Runa was more perturbed her sleep had been interrupted. I didn't understand any of it. I'd thought of nothing else. The black spittle. The way the Agitators moved. I thought of the Blood Wraith. But by the evening after the attack, all the Lysander household worried over—once again—was my betrothal.

Two suitors had been allowed to call. Neither inquired about the attack.

Herr Svart came to call and asked how I appreciated the craftsmanship of the wooden box. In the end, his visit turned more into praising his—how did he put it—his astuteness in comprehending the intricate needs of women. Then, the fool proceeded to ask me questions I had no idea how to answer regarding the rearing of littles.

My response that all littles should be sent to waif houses didn't appease him.

"You know Ellis heard you," Mavie whispered after Svart had stormed out of the manor in a frenzy of disbelief and a desire to tame the wildness inside his future bride.

After that, I'd hurried to the kitchens where Arabella worked with Cook and gave the boy two fruit tarts with a dozen promises *Kvinna* Elise fibbed to stupid men quite often. I'd only been satisfied when the boy gave me his toothy grin and offered some of his lingonberries from off the top of the sweet.

The second caller was a young shipping merchant who'd inherited his fortune from his father. Wilder Kage was fine enough, but had a reputation of bedding anyone who glanced his way, then leaving them battered the next morning.

Even my father seemed thrilled when his visit ended.

The moment the door slammed shut at his back, I slumped into the padded chair, skirts wrinkled over my knees, and legs spread in a way that would fluster my mother.

I'd been alone for a few blissful moments when the sitting room door opened and Runa stepped inside, flanked by her maids.

"Eli, you have a visitor."

The groan slipped out before I could stop it. "No more, I beg of you."

"Apologies, *Kvinna*. I can return another time."

I dropped my skirts back around my ankles and wheeled around in my chair. "Jarl," I said, heat in my cheeks. "Forgive me, it has been . . . a busy day."

Jarl stalked into the room, holding no trinket of affection, nothing to impress me with. He wore his black military gambeson over crimson fatigues. His eyes held a bright spark of amusement when he sat across from me.

"So I've heard. Forgive me, but I had to see you were well. I heard of the breach at the gates."

I nodded. "Yes. It was frightening, but we live on."

"Were you injured?"

I shook my head, having no energy to explain my foot, nor how it healed so quickly. "I'm fine."

Jarl grinned softly as he sat beside me. "I'm sure you're tired, and I know two more suitors have stopped by. Truth be told, I almost wondered if I should come or not, knowing you've likely entertained several callers by now."

"But you came."

A bit of color tinted Jarl's cheeks. "If I told you it was because I wanted to see you were well with my own eyes, and talk as we used to, would you believe me?"

I studied Jarl for a stretched pause. I didn't know how to answer his question, so instead, I stood. "Walk with me outside? It's always pleasant right before a storm."

Jarl held out his arm. I gripped his elbow, and together we entered the back rose garden. My mother had paved walking paths with white river stone and allowed the wild roses to grow in natural tangles. She always said they appeared to be more formidable that way. Salt and flowers perfumed the air, and the chill of the sea felt calming against my skin.

Death and blood stained the grass not hours before, but at my mother's insistence the gardens had quickly been returned to their natural beauty. Only a few dark marks on the stones hinted anything amiss went on here at all.

"This is a lovely garden," Jarl started, his eyes darting to the various bushes.

"Jarl, I know you didn't come here to speak of roses." I stopped walking. "I wonder if you would speak plainly with me."

"I have no intentions of speaking any other way. Ask me anything and I'll tell you."

"Why are you seeking my hand?" I didn't hesitate, and I wanted to know. From him, most of all, because out of all the suitors I'd been tasked with visiting, Jarl seemed the least likely to make me miserable, and I him.

I didn't understand why Legion's face entered my mind at the same moment, but there would be time later to peel back potential reasons, no doubt frustration the man had yet to appear was partly to blame.

The way Jarl shifted on his feet, I assumed he was taking my question rather serious, and considering the answer.

"We have known each other for turns," Jarl said. "I admire you, and always have. You are not afraid of thinking for yourself."

"I don't know if most would find that attractive in a wife."

Jarl grinned and rubbed his thumb over a velvet rose petal. "Perhaps not, but there are changes happening in Timoran, and I think a wife who looks beyond what is expected, who adapts to change, is exactly the sort I want. That she is not ugly also helps."

Jarl winked and for the first time since dawn, I smiled. "Ah, a man such as yourself would never suit a homely woman, even if she were the most brilliant."

"Not when my face is also quite handsome."

"Naturally. What a sin it would be to taint such a face as yours."

"It would. Terribly unfortunate." Tension lessened in my chest, and when Jarl faced me, my hands in his, I was nearly at ease. "All teasing aside, I think we would make a fine pair, Elise. As Timoran strengthens, evolves, I plan to be part of it, and I think you have similar ambitions."

My smile faded. That word again—ambition. Runa was the same. I slid my hands free from his grip and turned toward a wild shrub, nearly as tall as me. My fingertips gently tapped the tops of the thorns, as if daring the point to draw blood. "What changes do you foresee in Timoran?"

Jarl came to my side, his hands clasped behind his back. "A new dawning. A Timoran unafraid of the fury in this earth. One that uses the powers the gods intended to be used, not destroyed or kept hidden."

I pointed my confusion at him. "You mean Night Folk?"

"Among other things. There is power in this land that is being concealed out of fear of losing it. Left to our dark enemies to use instead."

I thought of the darkness of last night. Were dark fae returning fury to this land with such violence?

"Timorans were not blessed with fury, though," I said. "Ettans were. Fae were. How could someone without their magic even dream of controlling it should fury be unleashed?"

"The Agitators are gaining strength, Elise," he said. "They worship fury, and the only way to crush them, is to use what they worship to satiate them. Some of the journeys I've completed to neighboring kingdoms have garnered a better understanding of fury. It isn't all the same. There are many powers out there. Think of it." Jarl took my hands again, eyes bright. "If we could join fury with the strength of Timoran people, our kingdom could perhaps find peace. It does nothing to try to destroy what was gods-given to this land."

I blinked as through a fog. "You disagree with the king and his quarries?"

Jarl's jaw tightened. "I find some practices are based in fear. Prince Calder believes, and I agree, if we're to ever claim our position as the strongest of the kingdoms, we cannot act in fear by trapping Night Folk and locking them away. We must use the power to our benefit."

"Like . . . unity?" A unified Timoran where Night Folk, where Ettans, could walk freely—I almost dared not hope.

"This land resists us, and I believe it is because we do not accept the natural blessings—fury. Do you not grow tired of the constant bloodshed from Agitators? Just last night they tried to reach you." Jarl shook his head as his passion tinted the curve of his ears crimson. "Change would not happen immediately, but under Prince Calder's vision if we're to live amongst each other, then Timorans must find a way to connect with fury, too. Not run from it."

I agreed. I wanted peace, wanted attacks to cease, wanted Siv and Mavie to be free women, to live as they wished. At the very least, be paid for their work in our household. The only trouble with Jarl's vision was Calder had no power and wouldn't for turns to come. Zyben was not terribly old, and kings ruled until they aged to the point of weary bones and poor health.

A voice cleared across the garden. Mavie stood beneath a

rose archway. "Excuse the interruption, *Kvinna*, but you asked to be informed if . . . the lights in the cottage returned."

My stomach flipped. A bit pathetic how fiercely the response came, and even though I'd enjoyed the conversation with Jarl, I faced him without a thought and said, "I apologize, but I must go. Thank you for this, Jarl."

He bowed his head, a flash of disappointment in his eyes, but he would never speak it. "I hope to call again soon."

I rested a hand on his forearm. "I hope you do."

With the hurried farewell, I rushed to Mavie. There were questions I needed to ask *Herr* Legion Grey.

CHAPTER TWELVE

"WHEN DID HE RETURN?" I added a bit of speed to my step as we darted through the rose gardens.

"I haven't seen *Herr* Grey," Mavie said. "Only the lights, but Tor has returned. Poor man seems ready to sleep for days. If he helped tend to *Herr* Grey, the man must've been terribly ill."

Two days. What sort of illness came so violently, then ended as quickly?

At the bend, I came to an abrupt stop. The flicker of an oil lamp in the window sent my heart racing. This draw to speak to Legion Grey was irritating. Anger and frustration, worry and desire, all boiled in my brain until I hardly knew which emotion to pick. I drew in a breath, holding it in place, and slowly made my way to the door. My knock went unanswered, though there was movement inside.

"*Herr* Grey," I said as firmly as possible. Even still, there was a shudder in my voice and I hated it.

Footsteps shuffled across the floorboards. The scrape of a

chair, the wheeze of strained breath. Then, the door clicked and opened just enough to see his shadowed expression. Hair tousled, shirt undone at the top, Legion seemed half put together. The dim light at his back added a grim, sunken look to his dark eyes. Red and irritated lines bloodied the whites of his gaze and added to his pallid expression.

"*Kvinna*," Legion said, his voice stronger than he looked. "A pleasant surprise."

"No need for pretenses, *Herr* Grey," I said. "You're ill. Sit."

"I'm not ill. I'm afraid this is simply what I look like," he said with a grim smile.

I rolled my eyes. "Mavie, why do men refuse to show weakness? Legion Grey, sit. Clearly you aren't well enough to be up and about. I'm quite skilled at herbs and remedies, you know."

His shoulders slouched, but the sly smirk I'd come to admire found its place in the corner of his mouth. Stubble had grown on his chin. Mismatched from his dark golden hair, but the shadow added to the strength of his jaw and sharp lines of his face. "Always the surprise, *Kvinna* Elise. A gambler, a woman of study, a swordswoman, and now a healer. Is there anything you don't do?"

"Yes, lose arguments," I said and took a deliberate step inside the cottage. "Mavie would you mind sneaking some of the dandelion tea from Cook and bringing it to me?"

Mavie's mouth parted. "You realize what you're asking?"

"I promise my spiced cakes to you the rest of the week."

It took a moment, but soon Mavie offered a curt nod and left us alone.

Legion took a step closer. "Elise, Halvar told me what happened. Forgive me for not being here."

Nerves coiled hard in my stomach. "We survived."

"I heard it was a close call."

"Halvar lies. There was never a moment when I worried." I dropped my eyes to the floorboards. The way he grinned stirred unrequited heat in my center. "I am glad you were not here, not if you were ill. You'd have been too vulnerable. Now, I'll say again. Sit."

"You wound my pride, *Kvinna*." Legion pulled a chair from the table and sat with a long sigh. As he leaned against the back, he winced, and I caught a glimpse of an angry red mark trailing down his neck until it disappeared beneath his shirt.

"Hells, are *you* injured?" Before I could think better of it, I was at his side.

"No," he said and jerked away.

"I'm not a fool. I can see the welts."

"They will fade by tonight." I propped my hands on my hips, glaring. Legion lifted a tentative gaze and the decorum between us died—he rolled his bleeding eyes at me. "Elise, you need not worry. I've survived this many times before."

I took the chair at his side, leaning in until he met my gaze. "Survived *what*?"

One fist curled over his knee. "An affliction that comes every few weeks."

"What kind of affliction? You can hardly stand."

He dragged his fingers through his hair. "I grow weak, become quite unlike my normal handsomeness."

"You think too highly of yourself."

Weary lines were written in his face when he smiled. "The welts are a mark of the ailment and fade in time."

"How do you manage with such a thing?"

"I adapt, *Kvinna*. This will in no way hinder my ability to serve as your negotiator, I assure you."

"Legion," I said softly. "I wasn't worried about your duty. I was worried for *you*."

The way he studied me, I guessed he was as surprised as me at the sincerity in my tone. True enough, despite needing to question him—perhaps threaten—regarding Siv, I didn't cherish the thought of Legion Grey suffering to the point of being unable to stand, unable to even think.

Mavie returned before either of us found anything more to say. Ruffled, she handed me the dried stems and flowers. "That woman is mad. Literally mad, Elise. Don't bother returning these, you'll likely disappear into her stock pot if you do."

I dragged my bottom lip between my teeth, grinning. "Thank you. I'll request icing on any cakes. I won't be long here."

"Am I not staying with you?" Mavie wrinkled her brow.

"*Herr* Grey and I have much to discuss, unfortunately. I'd rather not force you to sit and listen when now is the perfect time to escape to my chambers before Runa or my mother find something frivolous for you to do."

"As you say, but I know when I'm intentionally being sent away." She winked and had this all wrong. Yes, I wanted to be alone with Legion, but to question him not . . . anything else.

She turned away, a knowing grin on her face, and left me again in the quiet of the cottage. Legion had his gaze trained on the table when I returned and asked for a kettle. He said little as I brewed the dried flowers, and there were moments I'd turn and catch him staring. As if he were seeing me for the first time.

Some of the redness had faded in his eyes, and Legion sat

straighter by the time I set a cup of murky tea in front of him. What a strange thing, a sickness that faded moment by moment. He inspected the tea with a curl of disgust on his lip, but sipped without complaint.

More silent heartbeats passed, until Legion tugged at the collar of his shirt, skin damp with sweat. "Gods, I'll never understand how Timorans wear this bleeding garb."

I scoffed. "What would you rather wear? Being a man of trade and finance, I assumed you'd be rather used to waistcoats and trousers."

He shifted in his seat. "All I'm saying is if there were another attack, I'd get my arms cut off for being unable to move."

"Planning on a siege in the cottage, are you?"

"One must always be on guard," he said. "As we've learned."

My knee started to bounce. Nightmares would come, no doubt from last night. I buried the fear, unwilling to show my own vulnerability to Legion Grey.

"Let's not talk of last night. Besides, you're just griping because you're not well. Drink your tea, by the way." I nudged the cup he'd slyly inched away from him back in front of his reach.

With a grumble, he took another sip. "I'm fine. In fact, you should feel no obligation to stay."

"Someone must force you to drink." I tapped the cup, eyes narrowed. "And I assumed we would need to speak again at some point, being that you are here to violate my privacy and control my life."

"True. I do look forward to uncovering every private

thought." He hesitated. "So, if we're not talking about last night—how were the suitors?"

"Awful, if you must know. The only tolerable one was Jarl, I suppose. But I expect it's because we've known each other since childhood."

"Ah," Legion said, spinning his cup. "Do I detect a bit of admiration?"

"No, you detect the absence of disgust."

"Same thing." Legion leaned back in his chair again. "If it makes you feel the slightest bit better, my turn to meet with the fools begins tomorrow."

"I do pity you, since, ultimately, you are the one they must impress. I expect you could get them to follow you on hands and knees around the gardens and they'd do it if you promised to choose them."

"I'll try to remember that one for tomorrow."

The rasp of his voice turned playful and irritated on a whim. I admitted never knowing what Legion might say was enjoyable. When he called me *Kvinna* it wasn't the same as others. He said it like he was bored of using my name and wanted to say something else. Or like a jest because he knew I was nothing like typical *Kvinnas*.

Legion lived the life of a wealthy man, yet sparred like a street urchin over a copper shim. But the mystery of him added to the ripple of unease always present on the back of my neck.

Legion took another sip of the tea, grimaced, and shoved the cup away. "Though, I appreciate the effort, I'd rather be ill than drink another bit of that." He rose from his seat, much of the weariness faded from his step as he reached for a silver ewer on a narrow countertop. "This is what heals the fastest.

But I'm not certain you'd be up to such a drink. Hard to stomach for most."

"I am not fragile." I puffed my chest, as if proving my point.

Legion stared at me—peeled back my skin was more like it —for at least ten heartbeats. "In that case, I think you deserve a drink."

I let out a long breath as Legion poured the amber drink into two drinking horns, handing me one when he returned to the table. "From the Eastern Kingdom. They call it brän, I think."

"All hells," I swore. "I don't think I'll ever not be envious you've traveled to distant kingdoms."

He shrugged, grinning. "Sometimes it feels like I've traveled there more in dreams. Someday you should go see them."

Women didn't travel, I wanted to remind him. But why? It didn't matter. I tipped the horn to my mouth and a bold tang hit my nose. Unappealing, but I wasn't about to be rude and refuse a foreign drink. Truth be told, it was exciting. The liquid touched my lips, trickled down my throat.

Three hells it burned.

I coughed twice. The taste was sharp, a little woodsy, but once it settled into my tongue, it softened.

"Good?" Legion asked, hardly blinking as he drank.

"Interesting."

"Good enough for me. Drink up, then."

"Bleeding skies, I already feel the haze in my head." I snickered and took another sip. "This is likely not appropriate. What will folk say if I stumble out of here?"

"We'll tell them we spent a memorable moment together."

I kicked his shin underneath the table, feigning embarrassment. "You are inappropriate, Legion Grey."

"Don't be ashamed, *Kvinna*. Not many can stomach the Eastern Kingdom's ale. You look flushed. What did you think I meant?"

"Inappropriate and infuriating," I muttered and took another drink, then relinquished my horn.

Any more and I *would* be stumbling out of his cottage. What tolerance folk in the Eastern Kingdom must have for such a potent, slightly foul drink. I rubbed my missing fingertips, watching Legion finish off the last of his brän. I enjoyed his company, but had a pressing question that needed to be asked. With the haze in my brain, there didn't seem to be a better moment. "*Herr* Grey—"

"Would it be too much to ask that we forget the *Herr*? Legion will do fine. *Herr* sounds too stupidly pious, and I'm about to lose my wits from brän. I'm hardly deserving of proper titles."

I snorted a laugh. "Fine, if you cease with *Kvinna*. Tell me a moment when I behaved as a proper royal."

Legion gestured at the cup of tea growing cold. "Then. Right then when you demanded I drink that gods awful stuff."

Fair enough. "All right, then. Legion, I think you ought to know . . . I know you threatened Siverie."

The horn paused halfway to his mouth. A shadow darkened his eyes more. "She told you I threatened—"

"No," I hurried to correct. My palms grew sweaty as nerves gathered in the pit of my stomach. "I saw you, Halvar, and Tor surrounding her. Then, you were gone, and I never was able to ask you."

109

He set down the drinking horn. "And what did your maid tell you I said?"

"She gave one story." I wanted to know if Siv covered for him—if Legion was dangerous. "I'd like to know your side."

He considered me for a long moment, the blackness in his eyes sending a trill down my spine. When it felt as if the walls might cave in on me if he didn't speak soon, Legion cleared his throat and leaned over the table. "I mistook her for someone else. As waifs, there was an older boy who tried to kill Tor once. He had a sister. The way Siv sparred . . . anyway, I'm ashamed to say, what you saw was a bit of childhood vengeance. I discovered the error; she was not related to him, and we left it at that."

More detail than Siv provided, but the stories aligned well enough. Although, for Siv, I needed to see it never happened again. "Understand, Siv and Mavie are more than maids. They are closer to me than my own sister—"

"I understand," he said. "I made the error. Had I been here, I would've apologized again. You have my word I mean them no harm, Elise. As long as they never mean *you* harm, that is."

I nodded and tangled my fingers in my lap. "Good. I don't mind your company, Legion Grey. I'd hate to find a reason to start. Although, I didn't realize Tor was in the waif house with you."

He laughed softly and took a drink of his horn. "Halvar, too."

"What?" My eyes widened. "You said—"

"I said I've known him for some time. You did not ask how long."

"But Halvar ended as a serf."

"Partly his choice," Legion said. "Halvar has a gift with seduction, be it man or woman, and he soon learned consorts of noblemen in the south shores ought to be left alone."

I shouldn't have laughed, but I covered my mouth, a shudder running down my back. True enough, those who wanted to save themselves pain on the rack or death could offer their servitude. A sad tale, but the way Halvar kept a bit of mischief, I had yet to see serfdom squelch his spirit. And it was entirely entertaining imagining a poor rake like Halvar leaping out of fine manors, angry lovers at his back, after bedding folk levels above his station.

I composed myself by clearing my throat. "Fortunate he ended here, then."

Legion looked away, amused. "I might have pulled in my own favors."

My mouth parted. "Legion Grey, I'm stunned. It would seem you have your own tricks and schemes to get what you want. You know, the same can be said for thieves."

"But what is the point of power if you do not call upon its benefits sometimes? I see only benefit in this case. I am close to Halvar still, and your father has gained another skilled serf who knows his way around a blade."

I groaned and slumped back. "By the skies, you are infuriating and have, no doubt, won everyone over with your pretty words and petitions. You have even found ways to manipulate serfs. Should you turn into some sort of cur, no one will ever side with me."

"No, I don't think that's right. You're too kind for your own good and have more serfs who value you than any royal I've ever met. I'd be sorely outnumbered."

I flushed under his praise, took another harsh drink simply because I didn't know what to say.

"To make my point, today you came here with the assumption I'd hurt your friend, you survived a terrible ordeal, but first you jumped to help me instead of scold me." Legion shook his head. "Always the surprise."

If a bit of kindness surprised Legion, I hated to think what sort of life he'd known. I stood and gathered the cups of tea and Legion rose with me, clearly unsettled by being served.

"Elise, you shouldn't do this. It's beneath you."

I let out a long sigh as I placed the cups in the wash basin. "Who shall, then? A serf? Perhaps Tor can be summoned." Turning back to the sink, I started scrubbing. "I wish I knew why you were here sometimes. There are moments when you seem bent on embracing my oddities, like this—" I gestured at the cups and the soap suds. "Other times you treat me the same as others. Like a royal who is above the rest, as if I look down at others and . . . mistreat them like so many of my people do."

I didn't know how to stop the outburst, nor where it came from exactly. Such a simple statement unbottled a thousand unsaid frustrations with my station, with my life, and truth be told, I'm not sure why I abandoned them onto Legion Grey.

I scrubbed the cup harder, but shuddered, forgetting how to breathe when a firm hand tugged on my arm. Legion hadn't truly touched me before. I'd hardly call sparring an affectionate sort of touch. But his palm slid down the length of my arm, drawing me close enough I could see the hint of gold in the depth of his dark eyes. My heart pounded, ready to snap a rib as he drank me in, unblinking. He stepped closer. My world tilted.

Legion used the knuckle of one finger to lift my chin, so I had no choice but to look at him.

"Elise," he said my name like a summer breeze, soft and gentle. "I am here to learn about you. To keep you safe until our business is concluded. And what you call oddities, I call qualities. You are unlike the *Kvinna* I expected to meet, but I swear to you, I've not had an ounce of disappointment since that day."

I swallowed with effort; his gaze traveled with it, down the slope of my neck. A hot spark of desire flashed through my chest, and I wouldn't mind if he touched me in a different way.

Legion's grin returned. "You are not made of weak bones. Not glass like I expected."

Cursed gods. I held my breath, frozen as his thumb brushed over a scrape on my chin, still visible from the other night. My fingers curled around the folds of his shirt. Maybe it was the brän, but I'd lost my bleeding mind, allowing such a moment, embracing this kind of closeness. I didn't move away, didn't even try. Legion's eyes traveled to the shell of my ear, fingertips following, where another divot had been cut out from one of my first sparring matches. As if he found all my imperfections, studied them, memorized them, then embraced them.

"What began as a profitable position," he went on. "I now feel . . . honored to know you."

My gaze dropped to his mouth. When had we gotten so close?

The moment would not last long. A single, swift knock sounded the alarm we were no longer alone, then the door burst open, and Tor shoved into the cottage. "Legion, another attack has—" Tor said little most days, and when he realized Legion was not alone, his mouth snapped shut.

I took three, long steps back. Even Legion cleared his throat, dragging his fingers through his hair. We'd stood chest to chest, hands on each other, and as for me, I'd never been so calm and out of control in the same breath.

"Later, Tor," Legion snapped.

"No," I insisted. "What attack?"

Tor looked to Legion, whose jaw had gone taut. Even still, Legion faced me and said, "I was asked not to mention it, but there have been more Agitators acting out."

"Since last night?"

Legion shared a quick glance with Tor before looking at me. "I'm not convinced those were Agitators."

"Who, then?"

He shook his head. "I don't know, but we're working with the guards to find out."

"These true Agitators have burned several coastal farms in the east," Tor said, ignoring a sharp look from Legion.

"Why? I thought they hated royalty, not the people."

Legion frowned. "They're making a new kind of mark, turning the people to the true heirs of Etta, as they put it."

"It's nonsense, *Kvinna*," Legion told me. "They believe some, or all, of King Arvad's children live on and are coming to reclaim the throne."

"Yes, but they are stirring up a following among the people because they insist the Guild of Shade is on their side," Tor said, glowering.

Legion scoffed. "Fools. Agitators are bleeding sloppy with their carnage. When the Guild of Shade attacks, it's purposeful."

My knees buckled, enough I grabbed the edge of the chair. Tor reached out a hand. *"Kvinna?"*

I waved him away, ignoring Legion's curious glance. "You say they . . . might've joined with the Blood Wraith?" My voice croaked and cracked. Dark memories stirred and my pulse quickened until my insides went sour.

"No," Tor said. "It's what they claim. Are you all right, *Kvinna* Elise?"

"I'm fine. I think . . . I think I saw him last night."

The room settled into a dreary silence. Tor was the one who cleared his throat. "Then, you would be dead."

"I know what I saw. He seemed to look straight at me."

"A lookalike. Much like the Agitators are claiming, many rogue groups claim the Guild of Shade is with them."

My hands wouldn't stop shaking. I skirted around Legion who pierced his stare at me, as though he might see inside my thoughts. "I should be going. Tor, make sure Legion drinks another cup of dandelion tea, even if he threatens you."

I tried to laugh off my brisk retreat, but neither man bought any of it. Legion's eyes darkened, and Tor watched me like I'd lost my wits. But I needed to leave. The walls grew too small, too cramped. Outside, I pressed a hand to my chest.

Fear tightened in my veins. A hot tear dripped from the corner of my eye. Somehow, I knew—through intuition or instinct—the Wraith would destroy everything.

He'd make sure the world burned.

CHAPTER THIRTEEN

"THAT WAS STUPID YESTERDAY." In the library, Mavie stoked the fire in the stone hearth. "Locking yourself in there with him. What if you caught his ailment? What if he'd gone mad and lunged at you?"

I didn't look up from the pages of my book, but grinned. "Lunged at me? Has *Herr* Grey ever given you the notion he'd be one to lunge at a woman?"

"All I'm saying is it happens. Folk get infections in their minds and go mad. Happened to my grandfather turns ago. Stark, raving mad."

"Mavs," I said. "You worry too much. I had a dagger on me should Legion turn into a beast and tear me limb from limb."

She blew out her lips. "Right, a dainty little blade buried beneath layers of stiff wool. I doubt a man of his stature and . . . physique would be able to lay a hand on you."

I snorted a laugh. "Do tell me more of this physique."

Mavie wiped her palms over her apron and glared at me.

"Don't pretend you haven't noticed *Herr* Legion looks more like he breaks trees for amusement rather than indulging in spiced red and cakes."

I laughed at that. But Mavie wasn't wrong about Legion. When he touched my face, his hands were as iron. Strong. Capable. His stone sharp jaw pulsed with taut muscles. But the storm in his midnight eyes gave away the potential violence inside. I knew his capability to fight, and knew Legion Grey could cause a fair bit of damage if he ever had the urge.

The door opened and Siv entered, bringing with her the warmth of baked bread. She placed a covered basket on a table and smoothed out a traveling cloak over the back of a chair. "The cab is waiting, Elise."

"Thank you," I said, lifting my gaze off my pages. "Any word on who met with *Herr* Grey this morning?"

I'd hidden away in the library for most of the day, desperate not to see *Herrs* Svart or Gurst again. I had to trust Legion had the brains (and sense of smell) not to consider such matches, but what did I truly know about the process of this? Could Legion be bought? I didn't think so, but when it came to ambition, it was impossible to really know.

"Gurst left with his nose in the air," Siv said, brushing her braid off her shoulder. "Jarl Magnus spoke with him, too."

"And?" I pressed when she didn't go on.

"I don't know. Jarl left as he came in, haughty, handsome, and in a rush. Though, *Herr* Grey seemed unsettled, almost angry."

Mavie waved her hands in the air. "All of this causes my blood to boil. If your match is of such little consequence, why the trouble of all this? Why not let you choose?"

I bit my own frustration into the inside of my cheek, while drifting back to the gentle moment in Legion's cottage—when his fingers brushed my cheek, when his body had been so close. My heart stirred. Foolish of me to hold any kind of affection for my negotiator. Especially when I knew so little about him. But I couldn't help but be envious of my own experience. Would I be matched with a man who'd be as gentle, as wanting of my thoughts, my desires?

I secured the cloak around my shoulders and ran my fingers through my hair. Already the loose waves had gone wild around my shoulders. "Tradition, I suppose."

Siv handed me the basket. A savory hint of saffron teased my nose. The basket was bundled in fresh rolls, sour goat cheeses, and sliced blood pears. Legion requested we meet in the thicket, and if he had plans of keeping me out all afternoon, the least I demanded was we be well fed.

"You sure you don't want us to join you?" Siv asked.

"I would love for you both to join us, but according to my sister, a negotiator is to give feedback privately. Honestly, I feel like everyone is making up rules as they go."

Mavie grinned and opened the door. "At least *Herr* Grey is doing this off the grounds, more fun. More private."

I rammed my elbow into her ribs, but didn't miss the amused expression on Siv's face, too. Doubtless they had discussed my private moments with Legion alone in his cottage. They mistook me. I simply found him bearable. And I repeated my own lie all the way through the corridors until I reached the front drive.

Outside, a storm from the shoreline painted the sky in a haze of gray, but the air was warm and wet. The grounds were busy with serfs tending to the stables, bringing supplies, or trimming my mother's wild roses. Velvet petals of deep, blood red and patent leather black tangled in thorny webs along the drive where a glossy hansom cab waited.

I stopped and studied the back of Legion Grey as he spoke to Halvar. He was dressed in a fine waistcoat, even if he cursed them yesterday. He stood straight, and if I'd not seen him so weary, I'd never guess the man had ever been ill a day in his life. I could play coy, could lie to myself, but I noticed a great deal more than Legion's strength. True, he had broad shoulders, dark golden hair, and Ettan black eyes that always seemed to be filled with secrets, but there was something about the way his mouth set—as if he always had words on the tip of his tongue, but he held them back. Intriguing was the smirk in the corner of his mouth, the way he spoke to me, the way he'd whispered my name.

All the things I'd noticed reeled in my head with each heartbeat.

I didn't know how to stop it. Only a fool would fancy a vow negotiator, and today I was a fool.

"Good morning, *Herr* Grey," I said, a shudder in my voice.

"Elise," Legion said as he turned over his shoulder. "I thought we had agreed you would not call me *Herr*."

"Pretenses," I said, airily and gathered my skirts.

Legion took my hand, helping me onto the step of the cab, but drew close. "Where we're going there will be no need for pretenses."

I blinked my gaze forward, unable, or perhaps unwilling to understand his meaning. In the cab, Legion's shoulder brushed against me as he sat by my side. The spice from his skin reminded me of the thicket—a rugged smell. Fitting for a man named Legion.

With a word, he gave the command to drive, and the hansom cab jolted down the drive toward town.

Mellanstrad was one of the larger townships. Not the size of Lyx and the manors around Ravenspire, but one of the busier trade hubs in New Timoran. The hansom wove through crowds of morning hawkers shouting out prices of precious metals, exotic fruits and grains, some bartering serfs.

"Ah, there is your nefarious companion," Legion muttered on the edge of town.

Mattis waved, a gleam in his eyes, and a wooden board balanced over one shoulder. No doubt the carpenter admired Legion Grey for his rebellious night at the bell tower. Everyone seemed taken with Legion, like he attracted the trust and respect of all classes.

Halvar brought the cab to a stop beside Mattis. The carpenter dropped the board off his shoulder with a grunt, then leaned a casual elbow over the edge of the cab.

"Lovely morning for a ride," he said and wiped the grime on his forehead. "Glad to see you back in our *Kvinna's* graces, *Herr* Grey."

"Well, it is such an enjoyable place to be."

I flushed, pinching my lips into a line. "You both should be so lucky to be in my graces."

Mattis chuckled. "Where are you off to today? Still avoiding suitors?"

"The both of us now," Legion said. "I thought a visit to the Ribbon Lakes would be far enough to hide most of the day."

I grinned. The lakes were secluded and peaceful. Perhaps

Legion could read minds and sensed my desire to flee from the eyes of . . . everyone.

"I promise to misdirect anyone who might be looking for you," Mattis said, then looked at me. "By the by, have you finished the book, Elise?"

I'd nearly forgotten I'd read every word of his bawdy Night Folk book. To hide the heat blooming over my face, I studied the opposite walk where a woman haggled with a jeweler over a bangle made of bone. "I might have."

Mattis clapped the door of the cab, laughing. "Ah, I knew you'd be taken with the prowess of the fae."

I groaned. "Don't you have some work to be doing?"

Mattis winked and took up the board once more. "That I do. Good luck, *Herr* Grey. I imagine our dear *Kvinna* is no average match to negotiate."

"No," Legion said with intention, his eyes locked on me. "She certainly is not."

Halvar clicked his tongue and set the two charges in motion. Mattis turned with a wave and strode toward his shop, whistling a folk tune.

I swallowed to soothe the dry scratch in my throat when Legion settled back so our knees knocked. What was I doing? Every word he said I read as some sort of meaning. Odds were, Legion Grey was simply polite and knew how to speak to the ego of royalty.

It was simply aggravating how much I enjoyed the words he spoke.

The ride was smooth. Uneventful. But Legion grinned with a touch of satisfaction when the smile spread over my lips once the towns faded, and the evergreens rose so high the tops blotted out the sun.

"You enjoy the wood?" he said.

I drew in a long breath through my nose. The spice of pine, the musk of bark and soil filled my lungs. No hint of unwashed skin or mildew on old linens from town lived here. I sighed and let my fingertips drag across the pine needles as we passed by. "I'm free in these trees."

"Careful," he said. "I might think you have a bit of Night Folk in your blood. They connect with the earth, you know."

My chest tightened. "Where do you suppose they've all gone? I haven't seen any fae since I was a child. A lot of folk say they live among Agitators. I think fury was involved in the attack at the gates."

"Perhaps. Agitators are nothing but zealots who worship the old bloodlines of Night Folk." Legion licked his lips, eyes at the sun. "I think most fae have moved on. Gone to other kingdoms. In the south there are lush isles said to be their homeland. Maybe some went there."

"How do you know so much about the other kingdoms?"

"I enjoy reading. If anyone should understand, it's you, *Kvinna*."

One of the qualities I liked most about him. I smiled and plucked a blossom off a tall wildflower on the side of the road. "I wonder why the Night Folk favored Ettans. As far as I know, only Ettan folk and true fae have fury."

"I have theories. The people of this land connected to it much like the fae. I believe they simply coexisted peacefully."

I picked a few petals from the blossom and slouched. "And my people, we destroy the earth. Like we ruined Old Timoran."

Legion cupped my hand with the blossom and lifted it between us, the sweet scent wafting in the air. "Not all Timorans ruin the earth. And not all Ettans tend it. We choose who we become, Elise."

I met his gaze. My body tensed with a strange desire. I adjusted, so I somewhat leaned into Legion. He looked astonished I'd come so close but didn't move away. Even draped his arm around the back of my seat. We didn't say much more until the lakes came into view and were content to simply be.

The Ribbon Lakes were narrow, some with bits of ice from the frosted mountain rivers. The banks bent and curved like serpents in the grass. But they were private, surrounded with lush white aspen forests, and the hip-high grass of the wildflower meadow. One could disappear for hours.

Once we had the cab unloaded, Legion sent Halvar away, and settled on the bank near the largest of the four lakes. With the cloudy day, the water glistened in blue so dark it looked like black glass. I placed the basket atop a boulder, settled in the long grass, and hugged my knees to my chest.

"Well?" I stretched out onto my back, closing my eyes, and crossing my ankles. "What do we do now?"

"We're supposed to talk about suitors."

"Then talking shall be left to you to begin. It is my least favorite subject."

"So demanding, *Kvinna*."

"It is what we royals do best."

Legion grinned. "Very well. I'm interested to know of your preferences first."

A man like you. I clenched my fists at the rogue thought. "Do you want honesty, or what I am supposed to say?"

"Always honesty." Legion laid back, rolled onto one side, and propped onto his elbow.

I turned his way. "I don't want any of them. At least not yet. How am I supposed to know if a man will make a good companion after speaking for a few clock tolls? But then, I'm not supposed to worry about a good companion. I'm supposed to be silent."

Legion dropped his gaze and picked at the grass. "The world would be darker should you be silent." He'd said it so softly I wasn't certain I'd heard correctly. A bit of red colored the tips of his ears and he cleared his throat. "I do promise I will not match you with that pungent fellow—Gurst, I believe. Three hells, you'd suffocate from holding your breath."

I laughed, a true, deep laugh. Legion flashed his white teeth, and it seemed wholly unfair I was not fated to have such an easy relationship with the man I was destined to wed.

Legion's fingers coiled around the end of my braid. I rolled onto my shoulder, so our bodies were aligned. His gaze shimmered with a dark heat. "What do you expect from a marriage match, Elise?"

"I don't think my expectations matter," I whispered.

"Shouldn't they?"

"Royal vows are made for alliances between men. I am but the pawn in the middle."

He looked at the water. "True. Most cultures embrace strength and security over happiness. Although, before Timorans raided Etta, Ettans made alliances from respect and affection."

"I doubt their royalty took vows for love," I said.

"I think they often did." He released my braid and the

whisper of his fingertips on my shoulder quickened my pulse. "The idea behind happy alliances was to create a deeper conviction to their people and their families. Night Folk are similar. Once they find their consort, they hold to them fiercely. Another reason Ettans and Night Folk existed as one so well, perhaps."

"Yet they lost their land."

"Ah, but the royal family fought to the bitter end for one another."

"Yes, they fought for one another. Killed for one another even more."

Legion held a bemused expression. "What do you mean?"

The mysterious Ferus royals of Etta fascinated me. I sat up, hugged my legs to my body, and rested my chin on the tops of my knees. A mute grin crossed my lips. "When my great-grand-father began the first of his raids, to deter him, King Arvad ordered an execution of a neutral township. One filled with Timoran farmers and their families. He left no survivors. I'm convinced all folk, from our kingdom to those across the Fate's Ocean, have the capacity for brutality."

Legion considered me for a long moment. "But you're leaving out the rest."

"The rest?"

"The story. True, the village had been owned by farmers, but during the raids, Ettan war journals described it as a secret Timoran military base. The children of the Ettan gentry had been kidnapped and held hostage. And it wasn't King Arvad who led the raid, it was commanded by his queen. Though, no one knows how she accomplished it since she was held in the tower, a prisoner of King Eli."

I blew out my lips, unconvinced. "I've never read such a thing."

"I have some old journals I've acquired over the turns if you'd like to see."

He chuckled when my smile widened. Reading true Ettan journals—such a thing was practically forbidden. At the very least reserved for Zyben or Calder.

Legion rolled onto his back staring at the slate clouds overhead. "You aren't wrong, though. The Ettans showed their savagery, killing so many, so viciously, but I digress back to their fierce devotion for their families. I imagine should those I care most about come under attack, there is nothing I wouldn't do to protect them."

"Oh," I said with new interest. "And tell me, who does Legion Grey care so much about that he would cut off the heads of men? A lover?"

"No," he said immediately. "A rolling stone is often unsatisfactory for women."

"But if you found the right one—"

"Then, she would need to be interesting. Perhaps a little rebellious." He flicked his eyes to me, and my stomach backflipped. Legion looked away, grinning. "But we're not here to talk about me. Tell me about the young man—the Ravenspire captain who has made his bid for you."

I rolled my eyes. "You make me sound like a hog to be sold."

"A fine goat, perhaps, but never a hog, *Kvinna*."

A laugh broke free. I let out a long sigh as I opened the basket, aiming for the rolls and spiced butter spread. "You are strange, Legion Grey."

"I've been called worse."

"Jarl Magnus. I've known him since childhood," I explained as I picked at the roll. "He isn't a bad man, and recently he did tell me of his desire to unify New Timoran, to break the divide between Ettans and any Night Folk."

Legion moved into sitting, a pinched look on his face. "Unify? Are you sure that's what he meant?"

"Yes," I said through a mouthful of bread. "He told me New Timoran should embrace fury."

"Yes, he mentioned something similar, but I took his meaning quite differently."

My brow furrowed. "How?"

"Elise, I asked because I wanted to warn you about him," Legion said, a rough strain in his tone. "I got the feeling he has little loyalty to your king, or your family."

"No, he said Calder has the desire—"

"Yes," Legion interrupted. "The prince has plans, not the king."

No. He misunderstood. Jarl and Calder wouldn't plot anything against King Zyben. He had too much power, too much influence. Besides, Calder was pretentious enough to never risk his ascension to the throne.

"I think you may have misunderstood him," I said, but my voice came smaller than before.

"It's been known to happen." The shadow in his eyes hinted he didn't believe it. "May I ask you something?"

"You usually do, even without permission."

He grinned. "Why such a resistance to this negotiation? Was it so unexpected?"

I sighed and shook my head. "No. Not unexpected."

"But you despise it all the same?"

"I despise it because I am utterly forced to grin and bear it all. If I protest, or speak out against it, my father dies."

"I don't understand."

My throat tightened as a hot rush of anger settled there. "Four turns ago, my father's illness came. The king has little affection for the prince consort, you see, so he hardly cared. But I suppose he has some kind thought for my mother, and offered his healers and expensive medicines, in exchange for being the overseer of our estate and his two nieces. The king owns my life. I refuse this, he withdraws the healers."

I was not particularly close with my father, but he was still my father. I didn't wish him dead, and certainly not because of me.

Legion remained quiet for a long moment. His eyes shimmered a darker shade when he looked at me. "Do you want to ask me not to choose one of the potential suitors? Besides Gurst, of course, we've already established him."

I shook my head, while inside I screamed the truth. "As I said, I wouldn't interfere."

Legion drew closer and heat from his body warmed the skin on my arms. Fire scorched my insides when his finger traced the divots of my knuckles.

"You could, you know," he whispered. "What kind of match do you want, Elise?"

His eyes peeled back the layers, and I feared he could see into my thoughts. The shocking ones. Ones that suggested I'd want a match like . . . him. A man unafraid to speak to me plainly. To tease me without hesitation because of titles and status.

Foolish of me. I forced my gaze from him, forced myself to forget how close his long body had come.

"A gentle match," I finally said.

"Then you shall have it." I held my breath as he lifted my knuckles to his lips, kissed me there, then grinned. A grin rife with secrets he wouldn't say out loud.

A shadow of movement drew my attention to a tangle of evergreen trees. "Has Halvar returned?"

Legion looked over his shoulder. His body went rigid. "No," he said, hand reaching into his waistcoat, returning with a dagger I never knew was there. "Elise, stay here."

Not again. My throat tightened.

In a breath, Legion was on his feet, once more demanding I not move as he ran off to meet the shadow. I wouldn't get the chance to obey or not.

From behind, a hand wrapped around my face, covering my mouth. I let out a cry but choked on the sound when a hooded man scrambled over the top of me. His legs straddled my hips.

I didn't try to make out his face.

All I knew was the bite of a knife point pressed to my neck, just below my jaw.

CHAPTER FOURTEEN

"You poison this land!" the man bellowed. "Hail the Night Prince!"

An Agitator's cry. They often shouted praises to the Night Prince. This man was without the blackness in his eyes, but had as much hatred as those from a few nights ago.

The blade pierced the sensitive skin under my jaw. Any deeper, he'd ram the tip to my brain; cleaner than slitting my throat. It was a similar strike to what Siv had taught—brutal and would kill good enough.

Either I fought or I died.

The Agitator teased me, played with my fear, and in the interim my fingers curled around a broken stone. I slammed the edge against the man's head. With a grunt, he lost control of his blade, his body crumbled over me. I jutted my knee against the soft upper part of his thigh. He groaned and rolled off me, snatching his knife.

I scrambled to my feet, drawing the kitchen knife from my boot, raising my weapon as he raised his once more.

"You poison this land," he said through a wheeze. "Hail—"

"Yes, you said that already," I snarled. With the point of my blade aimed at the grass, I lunged.

The man parried with more skill than me. The edge of his knife nicked my wrist, swift and deep. Heat from my blood dripped from beneath my lace gloves. I slashed at him again. In my head I replayed each step Mattis and Siv had shown me over the turns. Lunge, parry, dip, jab. Behind me, the grass rustled, and men grunted and cursed. Legion must've taken the assailant from the trees.

"Elise!" he shouted. "Run!"

At that, the man in front of me chased the space between us. I cut my knife at his chest.

"Can't!" I screamed back.

The man dodged my blow, but a swing with his hand caught my jaw. He gripped my wrist as I stumbled, and he dragged me against his body. In a few swift motions, he had the knife free from my hand and tossed five paces away. With teeth bared, he laughed the more I struggled.

"Death to imposters."

Bile scraped the back of my throat. *This*? This is how I'd die. The point of his blade jabbed into the space above my hip. I gasped at the pain. Sharp and icy hot. He'd take me slowly, savoring the way blood soaked my dress, the way his blade carved my flesh.

The hate in his eyes darkened.

His sneer curled like a wolf.

A breath of swift air came, followed by a wet cough, and a splatter of something hot on my cheek.

My eyes widened. Below the lump of his throat, an arrow, dark with blood, pointed out from his neck. The man choked and spluttered. His knife dug a little more. Somewhere in the haze I found the strength to shove him away. I fumbled back as he fell to the ground, his last breath gone before he hit the dirt.

At the line of the trees, Halvar lowered a bow. My palm curled around the hilt of the knife still buried above my hip. I cried out as I yanked it from my body. Not terribly deep, but enough I'd either made a fatal mistake and I'd bleed out, or at the least I'd need a good stitch.

The struggle at my back grew louder.

My fingertips went numb when I watched the second hooded man lash at Legion.

"You do not want to see what becomes of you if I make you bleed," Legion said in a low snarl, eyes like fiery coals.

The attacker moved like a wraith. The next step drew a frenzied curse from Legion. A long gash cut across his thigh. He staggered away to regroup, but the hooded man already had his knife aimed for a killing blow.

I gathered my lost knife and ran.

A fog built in my skull. Movement became rote, almost an instinct. Legion rolled his dagger in hand, ready to fight. To kill or die. The deep gash in his leg hinted at the latter. I didn't know the best place to land a blow, only that in this moment it was a choice between a good man living and a brutal stranger dying.

One pace from the hooded man, I stabbed my knife through the meat of his back. He roared his pain. He crumbled over his knees. Legion's eyes were ablaze, but they locked on me, wild with astonishment.

Another breath and he came to his senses and finished knocking the hooded man to his back, using his dagger to pin the man's hand to the ground. His cries would become the sound of nightmares.

"Who are you!" Legion shouted.

"Agitators," Halvar said, breathlessly.

"Kill me in service of the Night Prince and I will be a thing of legend." Blood glistened on the grass from the knife in the man's back. His skin grew pallid. Legion dug his knife deeper into the man's palm, but it seemed the attacker had gone numb. He didn't cry out.

Halvar nudged Legion's arm. "Enough," he said more like a command. My escort didn't move, he remained fixated on carving at the small bones of the attacker's palm, a flash of red in his eyes, rage on his face as more blood flowed. Halvar shoved Legion now. "I said enough!"

As through a trance, Legion blinked. He shook his head and released the blade, hurrying away from the hooded man. I wanted to reach for him, ask if he was injured terribly, but I was as stone, cold and still.

A shuddering breath, one flutter of his eyes, and the last of our attackers faded to the hells. I trembled. Blood stained my hands that was not my own.

I'd killed him, *killed a man.*

"Elise."

The gentle thrum of my name hit my senses as though underwater.

"Elise." Legion. He was speaking. I raised my gaze. He tilted his head and stepped next to me, hand covering mine, unafraid of the slick blood. "Are you injured?"

Was I? Yes. I'd been stabbed, but the pain of the steel in my side was nothing to this burning knot in my chest.

"I . . . killed him." I had wanted to kill the man. A frenzy of desire to see him bleed at my feet had come so abruptly I hadn't noticed until now. And I'd done it. I'd taken a life. A life someone, somewhere out there cared for. I'd ripped it from existence.

"He left you no choice," Legion said. Gently, he ran his fingers over the gash above my hips. At the sight of it, my knees buckled. His arms curled around my waist, holding me up. "I've got you. Halvar," he faced the driver, "a little help."

Halvar slung my arm over his shoulder and helped Legion limp me back to the hansom.

Through tears, I glanced at Legion's bloodied leg. "You . . . need help."

"I'll survive," he said. "I always do."

How had the smirk returned to his face so quickly? I doubted I'd smile again.

In the cab, Legion drew me against his side. I was grateful. Now that my heart had settled back in my chest, I couldn't stop shivering. My head reeled through each moment. All I saw was red in the corner of my eyes.

Did this mean I was a murderer? How could Legion sit so near me. I tried to scoot away, but his strong arm held me against the warmth of his side.

"Your body is going into a stun," he whispered. "Staying warm will help."

Battle stun. I'd heard of warriors falling into an illness from loss of blood that sometimes finished them off before the wound.

"You drew blood, and the sun is setting," Halvar hissed.

"Then hurry," Legion clipped back.

The stable hand mounted the driver's bench, the cab swaying under his weight. "I told you she fights back."

"Yes," Legion agreed. I wanted to shout at both men that I was bred of warriors and was not some damsel they needed to pander to. Legion tightened his hold on my shoulders, drawing me close to his body. "Why do they flock to me?"

Who? The Agitators?

I lifted my head to ask him, but Legion rested on warm palm against my face. "Elise, sleep now."

How could I sleep when my body was alive with nerves? "You . . . need help."

Legion tightened his hold on my face, his thumb tracing the line of my jaw. I hoped he'd never stop. "I need you to sleep."

Exhaustion draped over me in heavy, palpable waves. Fear, too. "I won't wake up." My voice came soft and haggard.

"You will." Legion's voice trembled through my body, I felt it to my bones. "Today is not the day you die."

My head drooped onto his shoulder and my mind faded into thick, syrupy black.

A KNIFE PIERCED MY SKULL. No question, someone was carving through my bones. My lashes stuck as I cracked my eyes. Abysmal light burned. I winced.

I was bleeding over the soft, fur coverlets on my own bed.

At my side, Mavie washed the blood from my fingers, tears on her cheeks. I had many things I wanted to say, but my mind fought me.

Again, I closed my eyes and embraced the oblivion.

When I woke again, the room was lighted by an oil lantern on a table with a bowl of stew. Hand on my head, I sat up. The skin around my middle tightened. Through the thin chemise I wore, a new linen bandage wrapped my hip bone.

"Mavie sewed you up."

I lifted my gaze. Runa closed a book and rose from the sitting chair. Her hair was loose about her shoulders and reminded me of pale silk. "Mother and father have both visited, as well. And Ravenspire has vowed to hold no mercy for any Agitator. In your name, our uncle has vowed, they will die."

I didn't want to know how much more blood would spill because of this. There had already been enough. I wanted to know one thing. "Legion," I croaked out. "How is he?"

"He insisted his wound needed the attention of the healer in town. I saw no wound and have not seen him since. Honestly, I think daj is furious he left in such haste. It sent him into another fit of coughing and he has ranted deliriously about his need to be informed on the details ever since."

My brow furrowed. "Legion was wounded. I saw it. His wounds were greater than mine."

Runa shrugged and sat on the side of my bed. She brushed

my hair off my brow. "As you say. I'm sure he's still resting, then."

How could she have missed the blood on Legion's leg? "How long has he been gone?"

"Elise, I don't know—all night. As long as you've been sleeping." A new day. The faintest hint of gray dawn broke the black sky. I dropped my legs off the side of the bed, but Runa placed her hands on my shoulders. "No, stay down. You'll get dizzy again. You've been muttering all night."

The door opened and Mavie entered with a carafe and wooden cups. With a touch of reluctance, Runa took the cups from Mavie so she could kneel beside the bed. Mavie's eyes were wet as she took my hand. "The way he carried you in . . . I thought for sure you were dead."

"Legion?"

Mavie nodded. "He brought you in, gave instructions to your care like a bleeding king, then left with Halvar and Tor. Siv was sent after them, too. To help, I suppose."

Siv? A flash of anxiety clenched my chest. Both Legion and Siverie had explained nothing malicious was between them. Siv could help Legion heal. They would both return without trouble. I couldn't accept another option.

Runa snorted a laugh and poured some water. "Honestly, maybe that's why daj is so upset. Another man making demands in his household."

"I want to know he's all right."

"Later," Runa insisted. She handed me the water. "What happened out there?"

I took a sip; the coolness soothed the burn in my throat. "I don't know. We were alone, then the Agitators came from the trees."

"Those bastards don't know when to stop."

I closed my eyes against the memory of killing the man. The tears were relentless, though, and came anyway.

I dropped my legs off the side of the bed. "I've rested enough."

Mavie seemed ready to protest, but Runa interrupted. "Very well. Mavie, would you draw a bath? No doubt, our parents will be needing to speak to Elise anyway."

Mavie dipped her head, offered a final glance my way, and disappeared into the washroom.

I cared little about repeating the details to my parents. I didn't want to relive it. I wanted—needed—to find out what had become of Legion Grey.

CHAPTER FIFTEEN

MY PARENTS DIDN'T REALLY WANT the details of my wellbeing, more the gory bits, so my father could rant about tearing the township down looking for anyone talking about the Night Prince, or anyone who even looked like they might be an Agitator. Not out of concern for his second daughter, but for his own livelihood. If there was a threat to Zyben's throne, it wouldn't bode well for the Lysander estate.

I applied two coats of a pungent paste Mavie brought from the healer. An herbal remedy that numbed skin beautifully. With it, I could sit upright without the sharp bite of pain from the gash over my hip.

Alone in the library, I hid behind a few stacks of books on the family lines of royalty. There were few writings on the Ettan lines. But then, most Timorans would like to pretend our people had not invaded and overthrown this land. They'd rather believe we always stood at the head.

A brief knock drew my attention from the droll pages. Bevan poked his head in the door. I grinned. "Bevan, come in."

The slope of his shoulders was the only hint of his age. There was a youthfulness in his eyes. He held another two books in his hands. "*Kvinna*, I have been asked to deliver these to you, for your entertainment as you recover."

I took the books, then laughed. "*Bloodiest Ettan Battles.*" I shook my head. "Mattis is aware I nearly died, right?"

Bevan tried not to smile but failed. "I believe that feckless nephew of mine sent these books intentionally. To be inappropriate."

I scoffed. Only Mattis would hear I'd been stabbed, then supply me with writings of blood and battle. Still, I tucked the books in the stack of genealogy. "Thank him for me."

Bevan nodded his head, a shadow passing his features. "How are you, *Kvinna*?"

I sighed. "Physically? I'm healing. But I'm worried for *Herr* Legion. I don't know which healer he went to see, and I've not heard anything from him."

All day, I expected to hear word on Legion's health, but no one seemed to know where he'd gone. Now, I feared he might have succumbed to his wounds. Or ran for his life. Clearly, I was a risk no negotiator in their right mind would care to take on.

"I'm sure he will return soon," Bevan said. "As I understand it, the departure had less to do with his health and more to do with discovering how Agitators came so close to you."

"He was wounded."

"When I saw him, he walked straight and steady. You mustn't worry for him."

I shook my head and muttered, "Not an easy thing."

Bevan patted my shoulder and smiled. "You are beginning to trust him, I see."

"Is there any reason I shouldn't?"

"No," said the old man. "Of anyone, I believe *Herr* Grey can be trusted."

"He's unusual," I blurted out. "When I thought of a negotiator, I imagined a man who'd revel in the power he held over me. Sometimes it feels like he cares more about my future than an advantageous match that would surely line his own pocket."

Bevan clasped his hands behind his back and nodded. "I believe *Herr* Grey has a keen interest in your wellbeing and destiny."

I wasn't sure about all that, but it was a relief to know I wasn't the only one in the household who believed Legion had a decent heart, decent intentions.

"Bevan," I said, eyeing the way he shifted on his feet. "Is there something bothering you?"

"No, *Kvinna*," he said. "But I'm afraid more than delivering the books, I've come to tell you, you have a visitor. Captain Magnus. I tried to tell him you were not well enough, but he grew insistent."

I wouldn't be permitted to refuse, not when I'd been walking about all day. To feign illness or too much pain for visitors wouldn't work. I gave a curt nod. "I'll be along shortly."

Once a clean set of gloves hid away the missing tips of my fingers, I traipsed the stairs slower than necessary. Jarl stood next to an open window in the main gathering room. Dressed in the patent black gambeson with boiled leather belt securing a narrow sword to his waist, Jarl Magnus was the sort of man that brought pride to the power of Timoran. But I did not want to see him. And I didn't care, not now, how foolish it made me to want to see Legion over anyone.

I took a heavy step to catch his attention, the heel of my shoe thudding on the wood floor. Jarl lifted his gaze, an obvious furrow gathering between his eyes.

"Elise," he said a little breathlessly. He erased the space between us, hands on my elbows. "I heard of the attack only this morning. Forgive me for not coming sooner."

I forced a smile. "There is nothing to forgive. Had you come yesterday I would not have been on my feet to greet you."

His eyes roamed my body, searching for the wound. "How are you? Runa informed me you were struck."

"Yes," I said and patted the place above my hip bone. "I'm afraid it felt much deeper than it was."

Jarl tangled his fingers with mine and led me to one of the sitting chairs as though I might break any moment. "By the gods, too much freedom has been given to those Agitator bastards. They ought to be done away with. But we will, Elise. The moment I heard of what happened—again—I sent the best trackers in my unit to find anything. If Agitators are being so bold, then they, and anyone associated with them, will die."

"Tried," I corrected. "I hope the law will still be abided, and they will be granted a trial."

"It will be short, I assure you." Jarl said through his teeth, missing my point entirely.

When most might find a bit of gladness at Jarl's vow, a shudder ran through me instead. More blood, more division, more hatred. Where one Agitator died, another would come again. Until we understood what they believed, what they wanted, death would be the only language we spoke to one another.

I settled against the chair, the pain mounting in my side again, as Jarl went on about his plans to see justice through. Somewhere through the conversation, he made a lot of vows that blood would spill in my name. Much like my father. I didn't want anything more staining my hands. A haze built in my head. Jarl paid no notice and went on. And on.

The request for him to leave so I may rest hovered on the tip of my tongue.

"I will speak with *Herr* Grey about more security for you. Thank the gods the king had the insight to place a negotiator who knows a blade in his employ."

I wanted to tell him I fought alongside Legion, but I would relive the moment I stabbed the Agitator, and my head was too heavy to even think of it.

Jarl was interrupted by a knock at the sitting room door. A veiled serf rushed to answer, and as if he were summoned by our conversation, there in the doorway, Legion Grey stood surrounded by Tor, Siv, and Mavie.

CHAPTER SIXTEEN

LEGION WAS DRESSED in a fine suit coat, straight-backed as though nothing happened just yesterday. His expression mute, but for the brief hint of light in his eyes. Mavie and Siv didn't wait for an invitation to enter the room, but then, they didn't need one. Tor remained somber and silent, assessing the whole of the room in one sweep of his eyes. Even the sight of him (though, I knew so little) brought a breath of relief.

My fingers twitched. I wanted to leap into the arms of everyone in the doorway. Would Tor accept an embrace, or would his knees buckle, and his hackles rise in disgust? Now wasn't the moment to find out.

Looking at Legion, the elation in my chest pierced me, swift and sharp. I fought the urge to touch him by clenching my fists at my side.

Jarl hesitated for nothing. "*Herr* Grey, you've returned. I have a great many things to discuss with you about the security of *Kvinna* Lysander and would—"

"Elise," Legion interrupted. "Walk with me."

His voice was clipped, but gentle. It left little room for refusal.

Jarl stepped next to me. "Is she well enough?"

He didn't ask me. In fact, spoke as if I were not standing there. Legion raised his dark brows. "I suppose you might ask her, but if she is not, it's rather inconsiderate of you to keep her on her feet, isn't it?"

Jarl flushed and bowed his head with a taut jaw.

"I'm well enough to walk," I said, going to Legion's side.

"We'll see *Herr* Magnus out," Mavie whispered.

I simply nodded, uninterested how or when Jarl found his way to his coach. Legion offered his arm, so I stood close to his side as we climbed the stairs to my chambers. Tor followed at our backs, his stern gaze bolting side to side as though another attack was imminent.

"You walk so steady," I said, embarrassed how I kept a slow step with the shallow wound in my hip.

"I wasn't stuck badly."

"The amount of blood would beg to differ."

"I assure you it looked worse than it was," he said, glancing at me sideways. "Your uncle sent several declarations, and seems to wish I turn my attentions from negotiations to hunting Agitators."

I shook my head. "If you were unharmed. why did Siv go with you?"

"Your maid is knowledgeable about the upper cliffs. I understand she once lived there, so she offered her services to provide insight where clans might be hiding."

"Ah," I said, envious for a moment he had learned something about Siv's past I didn't know. I shook the envy away and tightened my grip on his arm. Hunting. Killing. It all spun my head. "I need to speak with you. Out of the open."

Legion looked surprised but gestured at the door to the sitting room in my chamber. "Tor, keep an eye out, would you?"

"Always." Tor positioned himself at the doorjamb like a sentinel at a gate.

Legion led me into the open chamber. Tor closed the door at our backs and the rest of the world was cut off. Warmth from the stove brought a sense of home, and woodsmoke in the air chased away the numbness I'd had since yesterday. I turned to the window. How was I to do this? To speak of what happened? Had Legion ever killed a person? Did he remember what I did, or think there must've been another option, another way?

My hands trembled. My body swayed, unsteady.

A touch went to my hair, so gentle it might be mistaken for the breeze. "Elise . . ."

Such a simple word, but my name from his lips, after what had taken place, had power to break down every wall, every hint of propriety. All the worries of the night, of him, burst to the surface as I whipped around, my body to his.

I trapped Legion's face between my palms, breaths heavy. "I thought . . . I didn't know what happened to you."

If he'd been surprised by my reaction, or the way my fingers teased his hair, Legion let it fade immediately. The calluses of his hand were rough on my cheek as he cupped one side, his thumb brushing away a tear. "You cannot be rid of me so easily, *Kvinna*."

I didn't want to be rid of him. Embarrassed at my boldness,

I let my hands fall away from him and clasped them in front of my body. "Where were you?"

Legion's palm traveled down my shoulder, my arm, until he too released his hold on me. "We needed to learn what we could of the Agitators. *Kvin* Lysander and the king wanted to waste no time."

"And did you?" I asked. "Find the Agitators, I mean."

He looked away and I had my answer. Anger carved his features as he nodded. "I can't take credit, Castle Ravenspire found the crew before us. We simply saw what was left of them."

I winced. "Jarl said he'd sent trackers."

"They succeeded. This morning three men were taken to the stocks in town. They're to be executed at Castle Ravenspire."

I closed my eyes. As insignificant as I was to King Zyben, my uncle would shoot fear into the hearts of the people for any attack on his bloodline. The Agitators were brutal, cruel, they were villains in my life, but still, a discomfort spread in my stomach at the thought of more blood and bone spilling.

"I have done my share of killing, Elise," Legion said after a pause. "I've known blood, but the Agitator camp the patrols raided was filled with families. Don't mistake me, when I saw the Agitator attack you, I'm not sure I've ever been so angry, so filled with bloodlust. I surprised even myself. But after seeing the carnage left behind this morning, sometimes I'm not sure who is in the right and who is the monster."

"Me!" A sob broke free. "I am a monster. I murdered the Agitator, and I *wanted* to. You say you felt bloodlust, but I acted upon it." My breaths came too rapid, too jagged. "How am I better than the Ravenspire patrols? I wanted that man to die, so I made sure he did."

Before I could say another word, Legion had his arms around me, my face curled into his chest. Tears stained onto the softness of his jacket.

"Elise, stop," he commanded. "You are *not* a murderer. Without you, I might not be standing now. The bloodlust you think you had, was nothing more than instinct. I assure you—I have seen, have *embraced* bloodlust. You defended the both of us. Nothing more."

"I see it," I said against his chest. "When I close my eyes, I see his face, see the blood, see him take his last breath."

Legion tightened his hold around me. "To kill another is not something anyone soon forgets. I wish what happened had not, but do you think less of Halvar?"

"Halvar?"

"Yes. He killed the man who attacked you. Do you view Halvar as a murderer?"

Truth be told, I'd forgotten Halvar had shot the Agitator who'd taken me. All I saw was my fatal blow that killed the Agitator slowly.

"No," I said at last. "No, I don't think Halvar is a murderer. He saved me."

Legion stepped back and I wished at once his arms were around me again. "I hope you never have to kill again, but in New Timoran, the land is made of blood. You are a royal—there will come another time you may need to defend yourself. I have made a vow to defend you, but I must know you will also protect yourself. At all costs. Promise me."

Worry was in his voice, and it was strange, maybe a little

exciting. I lifted the hem of my skirt to show the knife sheathed to my shinbone. "I'll defend myself and anyone I care about."

"Good." He reached a hand inside his jacket. "And you should also have these."

On the table, Legion placed two thin books. Old, battered leather held the rough parchment in place.

"What are these?"

A crooked smile teased his mouth. "As promised. Old Ettan journals. One of strategy, the other I thought you might enjoy —Queen Lilianna's before the raid."

My mouth parted and traced the spines of the journals with a degree of reverence. "The Ettan queen?"

Legion nodded, notably pleased with my response.

"How . . . how did you ever come by these?"

He sighed and gently opened the one of war. "Not everyone who barters recognizes when they hold treasure in their hands. I still feel rather guilty. The cost of these totaled to a sack of bread and a half dozen silver shim. Poor bastard—I practically robbed him."

I chuckled and nodded. "Yes, I'd have to agree. I couldn't possibly—"

"I want you to take them," he said. "You can read old Ettan, can't you?"

I nodded. "I read it better than speak it."

"Good. Tor does not find my interest in history as amusing. In truth, I've felt connected to these journals and reread them more times than I can count. I've been looking forward to sharing them with another fool who reads too much. But I do intend to discuss them, for I have many opinions."

My insides soared until I was certain my feet lifted. "I shall talk your ears off, no doubt, *Herr* Grey."

"That is all I ask."

The door opened and Runa appeared with a lanky woman, the household healer. Wild hair like dry grass, teeth that jutted over her lower lip, but the woman could draw away pain like her touch held a bit of fury magic. I snatched the journals and held them behind my back.

"Pardon, but *Kvinna* Elise needs her dressing changed," Runa said with all the regality of a future queen. She didn't address Legion. In my sister's mind everyone ought to know they were being addressed without Runa needing to condescend and explain it.

Legion offered a slight bow to my sister, but his eyes never abandoned me. "I'll leave you, then."

"Yes," Runa said. "*Kvin* Lysander wishes to see you anyway."

Legion nodded his head once more, then left me with a searing glance that said too much and nothing all at once, before disappearing behind the door.

Later, when the healer had finished with me, when I'd endured a dull meal with my mother and sister, talking only of her upcoming vows with a repulsive prince, I hid away in my room with a queen I'd never met.

The first pages were worn the most. Lilianna's hand was gentle, neat, with delicate curves to her writing.

Arvad ascended the throne. Two days since his mother's funeral pyre and he wears the burden of the crown. He is a beacon of strength to our people. He will be remarkable. But how my heart burns for him when in the dimness of our bed he confesses his fears, his worries, to no one but me. The greatest lot in my life is being a strength, a confidant, a lover and helpmeet for an imperfect, magnificent king.

I beamed at the pages. Love.

So be it. I'd been wrong. The former king and queen of Etta had a great deal of love for each other. I'd be envious, but I reveled in her writing too much to even find a spark of jealousy.

THE NIGHT WAS TOO cold for the season. North winds whipped over the shore, stirring the black sand around my feet. Air, heady with brine, burned the back of my throat. The chill went into my blood, so I wrapped the borrowed woolen jacket tighter around my shoulders.

Only the lap of the water against the docks broke the silence. A silence that raised the hair on the back of my neck. Most nights, even in the early hours of the morning, folk out drinking, gambling, and visiting brothels could be heard. Tonight, it was only me and the shadows.

I scanned the docks for the skiff. With such little light, I nearly missed it tied to a narrow dock five down. My brow furrowed when I found the boat empty. I hadn't arrived all that early, and I expected the others who'd paid to go around the cove would be there.

A shudder raced up my arms. I hugged my body and abandoned the dock to seek out the others.

The first step off the dock, my boot splashed in something

hot, something sticky. My gaze drifted to the dark sand. I screamed and stumbled back, falling into a thick puddle. Heart racing, I staggered to my feet, hands coated in the dark, tangy scent.

Blood. It soaked the shore, bleeding up from the tide pools, from the docks. Rivers and rivers of blood surrounded me on all sides.

I tried to run. My feet wouldn't move.

Footsteps crunched over sand and shells and pebbles. I froze. The night stilled until I felt I could reach out and coil the tension around my fingers. The eyes of someone else pricked across my skin. Finding the will to lift my feet, I darted the way of the trees, but my bumbling steps would not take me far. A hand wrapped around my arm and wrenched me back.

I think I screamed, my throat was raw, but I didn't hear a thing over the blood pulsing in my skull.

Above me the red of his eyes glowed from beneath a black hood. The red mask covered his mouth, but the black, elongated fingernails—claws were more like it—dragged the cloth off his lips, his snarl revealed the whites of fangs. Wolvyn, or some mix of man and beast.

The Blood Wraith raised one of his cursed battle axes, his gaze filled with nothing but bloodlust and murder.

But when I looked again, the darkness of his face brightened, and my own countenance sneered back at me. Blood stained my hands. A wild frenzy lived in my eyes. A monster.

I didn't scream again before the axe held by my vicious doppelganger fell.

With a jolt, I snapped up in bed. My shoulders heaved in short, stilted gasps. Sweat pasted my hair to my brow, and my skin tingled like tiny flames danced across my body. How real the nightmare had been—I'd felt the Wraith's breath on my skin, seen the hate in his bloody eyes. Until it changed and the hate came from me.

I scrubbed my arms as if I could brush the feeling away.

My cheeks were wet with tears, throat raw. Bleeding hells, I hoped I hadn't screamed. Sometimes when the nightmares came, I woke the entire household, and they always brought too many questions.

A breeze came in from the crack in my window and I hurried to bolt the latch. Stars were quilted in the sky tonight. Those were real, not the empty pitch in my dream, I reminded myself. There weren't rivers of blood on the sand. I'd never made it to the shore, I'd been cornered in the forest, laughter and lanterns at the docks in my sights when the Wraith swung his blade. Truth be told, I'm not sure he even saw me, more like he attacked out of habit and my fingers simply got in the way.

But when blood spilled, he'd paused. I closed my eyes against the memory of the Wraith sniffing the air. Only then did he seem aware I'd survived, that he wasn't alone in the wood. I'd been helpless to move as he'd prowled like some creature made of shadows and blood.

A second shudder ran up my arms and I shook my head. No sense wondering what might have happened if the Guild of Shade hadn't dragged their Wraith back into the night. I survived.

A linen robe draped over one of the upholstered chairs near my bed. I dressed in it, discomposed by the way shadows filled the corners and crevices of my room. Childish perhaps, but I didn't want to stay in the room. At least not until my pulse slowed. I wouldn't sleep anyway.

Securing the belt of my robe, I left my room for the small sitting chamber. The space wasn't terribly grand, a few chairs, an ottoman covered in furs, and a bookshelf near the heating stove. Near the window, a tallow candle flickered golden light, and a grin broke over my mouth.

Legion, head propped on his fist, slept with a dagger across his lap.

In the light, his toasted brown skin looked more bronze, and his damp hair crossed his forehead, darker than the normal gold. For a moment I simply studied him. Dressed in a loose tunic, dark trousers, and sturdy leather boots, he looked more like a Ravenspire patrol than a tradesman.

It suited him.

But why was he here? I'd been too amused at the peace of his sleeping face I hadn't taken the time to wonder why he'd take up a spot in a small chair rather than enjoy his own bed.

I crossed the room and took a woven quilt from the back of a chaise. Perhaps I was more confident in my slyness than was true because as I laid out the quilt over Legion's body, he stirred. With a start he bolted from his chair, the dagger clattered on the floor, and he reached for me.

"Elise," he said, voice rough. "Are you . . . What are you doing awake?"

His grip curled around my palm; his skin chased away the last of my chill with its warmth. I returned the hold, lacing one or two fingers with his.

"I might ask you why you're in my chambers instead of in your own."

Legion cleared his throat. He didn't seem to notice—or mind—his hand was in mine. "I . . . I don't like the idea of you being alone."

My insides backflipped. "You go above your duty, *Herr*."

"Duty does not drive me in this, *Kvinna*." His gaze dropped to our hands and a rush of . . . something . . . heated my cheeks when he didn't let go. "After the raid on the camp this morning, Agitators took a manor near Mellanstrad. A noble house. They're growing bolder, and I'd rather not risk you to them."

"No one mentioned anything . . ." I paused. "Would you have told me about the attack if I'd not found you?"

Legion would not be the first man to keep a woman in the dark in the Lysander household. I hardly knew anything about what my father did on the days he felt well enough to leave his chambers, and even if he married the higher rank, my mother knew even less than me. Perhaps it was how she preferred things.

"I'm not afraid to tell you hard things, Elise," Legion said. "But I didn't see a need yet." He released my hand and crossed his arms over his chest. "Why are you awake, anyway?"

I fiddled with the belt of my robe and took a seat on the fur-covered chaise. "A nightmare, and like a bleeding child I didn't want to be in my dark room alone. I came out here to calm my nerves."

Legion scrutinized me for a long moment before he sat beside me, our shoulders touching. "I know a bit about the Marish demons and have been told if you invite them to the morning meal, they will not haunt you any longer."

I smiled but shook my head. "No fae demon cursed me tonight. The nightmare was a memory."

"A memory?" Legion squared his body to mine. "The Agitator?"

"No," I said, voice dry and hoarse. I'd never told anyone outside my family about the Blood Wraith, but now it was as if I needed to bite my tongue to hold back. Then I considered— why was I holding back? Already Legion Grey had proven a man of his word; he'd kept my secrets, weighed my desires. In truth, he seemed as disquieted about the betrothal negotiations as me. After everything, how would the tale of the Blood Wraith turn him away?

"I'm intrigued," he said when I went quiet. "You hesitate, and my curiosity has gotten the better of me. What frightens you into silence, Elise?"

My eyes lifted. I rubbed the missing tips of my fingers as if warmth might grow them again. Never one to point out the strange shape of my left hand, I was surprised when I lifted it and spread my fingers. "You asked once how I lost my fingertips."

If Legion had curiosity before, now he was wholly captivated. "What happened?"

"Some believe I mistook what happened and replaced it with a tale, so I don't speak of it often. Only my family knows, and I honestly don't know if they believe me."

Legion tipped his head, no smirk or grin or jest to be found in his expression. "I will believe you."

"Why?" I took his hand between mine. "Why do you say those things? Why are you so . . . kind to me? I should be a charge to you, a woman you must chaperone and assess, yet you treat me—"

"Treat you how?" he interrupted, his thumb drawing small circles on mine. "Like someone, instead of something?"

"Yes!" I said, strained. "No one but for serfs and a carpenter see past my title. Negotiators care little for the noble women they match. They care more for the prestige and *shim* the winning bidder gives them. Yet, you sit here with me because of a nightmare. You spar with me. You read with me. Why?"

Legion looked unsettled. He pulled back, faced forward, his mouth tight for too many breaths. "You were unexpected. Instead of a spoiled, arrogant princess, I was given you. Someone bold and daring and kind. What you have been dealt is . . . wrong. When these fools who come to me with coin, and promises, and threats, all for your hand, I see them as a strange kind of enemy. Forgive me, but it's the truth on how I feel."

I hardly believed he was saying these things, and that each word seemed true, almost as if Legion tried to fight them but simply couldn't. I bit my unease into my bottom lip. "You are unusual, Legion Grey." I smiled softly. "But against all my good senses, I trust you."

His body relaxed and the sly grin overtook his discomfort. "A poor choice, *Kvinna*."

I chuckled and stared at my fingertips. He'd been forthcoming, so could I. "My fingers, the cause of my recurring nightmares—" I took a long breath. "Nearly two turns ago, I bought passage on a skiff ride around the cove. I'd never sailed, and I couldn't resist. I snuck out when the moon was highest, but before I could even reach the water . . . I was ambushed."

Legion's brow wrinkled. "Ambushed? By whom?"

All gods, please believe me. I don't know how I would react

should he stare at me like I were a lunatic. "The Blood Wraith. He came from the shadows—there before I even knew it, and he struck at me. I've never seen eyes like his. Red, drained of humanity. I saw beneath his red mask and knew I'd die. No one ever sees behind the Wraith's mask and lives. And I would have fallen by his blade if the Guild of Shade had not pulled him back. I know they're said to be as ruthless, but only the Norns know why, they saved me."

It took a moment for me to look at Legion. Fear of his reaction more potent than anything. When my eyes found his in the dim light, he looked horrified. His fists clenched over his knees and his shoulders rose in sharp breaths.

"I know some believe he's a myth, but I saw him. The same as I saw him the other night."

"I believe you," he said in a rasp. "As I said I would." Legion's eyes fluttered and he cleared his throat, his body less stiff. "You are very lucky to be alive, Elise."

At that, he took my hand and kissed the ends of my missing fingertips, his eyes rolling up to meet mine.

A new sensation took hold in my body. The feeling of falling and spinning and drowning all at once. The heat of desire and need was raw, sharp, and heady as new wine. Legion's mouth on my skin sent my pulse racing like it would never stop, and truth be told, I didn't want it to.

I liked Legion Grey. He had, in fact, made me like him better than I'd ever liked anyone.

CHAPTER SEVENTEEN

Sol is a prince worth waiting for. The gods have answered our endless prayers. Dear Arvad, my resolute, loving king. How many times these long eight turns have I offered consorts, if only to give him the heir our people need? My king, I believe, was beginning to resent me for even considering it. Yet, each tearful time I told him to find another, he'd kiss my brow, and assure me the Norns would never bring him such a queen only for him to bed another. Palace healers believe I will bear no more children, but it does not matter. Sol—the Sun Prince—is born. And by the gods, does he have strong lungs . . .

"It's been too long since I've stepped inside the gates of Ravenspire. This fete will be one to remember," Runa said as she tucked rowan berries in her braids. "I can hardly wait."

I closed Lilianna's journal and looked at my sister. "It's disgusting."

My body was overheated with anger as Mavie tugged on

the laces of a new rose gown; ordered from the Ravenspire seamstresses after the three Agitators from the camp had been arrested.

"Do explain," said Runa.

"Having days of banquets celebrating executions," I snapped. "What are we supposed to do, eat and dance while we stare at their mangled bodies?"

Siv stared listlessly out the window, unlike herself for most of the day. Mavie sighed but said nothing. Not with Runa in the room.

My sister looked up from her place in front of the vanity mirror. "Hush, Elise. Agitators deserve what they are dealt. Why do you say these things when these men would've killed you without a thought? By the gods, it's as if you want the enemies of Timoran to drag us down to the hells."

I rolled my eyes. "No, but someday I would like peace. A way to negotiate a coexistence in this land without bloodshed."

Runa glared at me and stood. "Peace with traitors? They worship a dead prince, Elise. They will never accept us. Tell me you truly don't think this way, sister. Tell me you don't place value on anyone else but the strength of your own people."

Runa had not shown such a level of passion in turns. It was unsettling. "Runa, I dream of the day when Ettans, and fury, and Timorans are united as one. We'd be stronger for it."

My sister winced as though my words were a fist striking her jaw. Her discomposure lasted no more than a few breaths before she rolled back her shoulders, a sneer on her face. "Such a pity."

Without another word, Runa strode from the room, chin high.

I waved her exit away. For the next week I'd be expected to make merry with the high royals and high nobles of Lyx inside Castle Ravenspire. A spectacle. And I was the catalyst for such an event. We would leave for Castle Ravenspire in moments, and there, King Zyben had planned a feast of feasts, court entertainment, balls, and hunts. To honor his poor niece who survived the enemies of New Timoran. Then as a warning to all, the three Agitators would be executed and hung on the gates.

I had no desire to feast over such things.

"Try not to think of it," Mavie offered as she handed me a fur-lined cloak.

I took it grudgingly.

"You both look lovely," I said in more of a snarl.

"I've never worn something so fine," Mavie said as she smoothed out the silk pleats of her skirt. Siv gave a mere glance at her emerald dress. As my official maids they would be allowed into Ravenspire and were required to dress the part.

Together we made our way to the front entrance where the coaches were being loaded with our trunks. Our entourage would be stacked with four Ravenspire patrols for each carriage. My father insisted on bringing at least half a dozen of our serfs. Our travel party would have at least four coaches. We'd be noticed the moment we left the gates, and it boiled my temper even more. This was not a proud moment. I didn't understand why death—even an enemy's death—was a thing to celebrate. How many more centuries would pass before the people who claimed this land found peace amongst each other?

"Bevan," I greeted the old man as he awaited near my parents' coach. "I'm glad you'll be attending. It'll feel a little more like home."

He bowed his head. "I rarely pass up an opportunity to visit Castle Ravenspire."

"Nor an opportunity to see *De Hän* Odda," Mavie muttered.

Bevan glared, but in his weathered face was a hint of color. I snickered and patted Bevan's arm. Odda was one of Zyben's head cooks. If anyone were Night Folk, I'd guess Odda. The woman had the blackest eyes and something about her cooking left anyone who tasted feeling lighter than when they came.

The single bright moment came when Legion stood aside the coach I'd be using. He dressed all in black. Not the fine clothes of a tradesman, with polished shoes and trousers and sharp collars. Legion wore a thick, boiled leather belt around his waist, boots to his knees, and a tunic dark as night. Hardly discreet were the bone-sharp blades on his belt, his thighs. Even sheathed across the small of his back was a dagger with a silver hilt.

My fingers went numb. He was a sight, almost inhumanly beautiful. I stumbled on my hem when his dark gaze found me. The corner of his mouth curled as he approached us, one hand outstretched.

"*Kvinna* Elise," he said and pressed the top of my hand to his lips. "You steal the night's beauty with your own."

As he spoke, my father limped past with my mother reluctantly on his arm. Still, she heard Legion and nodded her approval. I snorted a laugh and leaned in. "Careful, or you will charm my mother's affections straight to you."

"I simply spoke the truth." He held out his arm, waiting until I took it. We would drive separately from my parents. Runa and her maids would remain at the head, and I was grateful to be away from my family for the evening.

Seated beside Halvar on the driver's bench, Tor was dressed much like Legion. Two Ravenspire guards bowed their heads and held open our doors. Mavie muttered declarations of excitement under her breath being treated much the same as me. She ran her fingers over the silver threads in the plush velvet seats. Siv huddled in the corner and pulled back the black shade, peering into the night. In a window basket was spiced red and apple wine with flutes, and the musk of sharp cheeses perfumed the air. Nothing but the grandest things for the king's guests.

"So, tell me, *Herr* Grey," I began as I settled on the bench. "Why are you dressed like our heavily armed escorts?"

"Fortunately for you, I am not playing the role of negotiator during our time in Ravenspire. I am, in fact, the *Kvinna's* personal guard." Legion sat close, and I fought the urge to lean into him. I kept my attraction to Legion Grey personal. Not even Mavie and Siv knew I was drawn to him in a way I didn't quite understand. "Which reminds me—" Legion leaned forward and pulled from his boot a slender knife with a row of emeralds embedded in the blade. He handed it to me. "You promised."

To defend myself. I recalled the moment he made me assure him I would not be afraid to strike again. I took the blade with a touch of caution but smiled. Again, the man did not treat me as something incapable or fragile.

"Are you trained to be a guard?" Mavie asked.

"I believe *Kvin* Lysander prefers that I'm not trained like Ravenspire patrols. Street waifs learn to fight by a different set of rules."

Mavie lifted her dark brows and pinched her lips. Siv closed her eyes as if she might be ill and turned toward the window again. A cinch tightened in the pit of my stomach. Whatever had happened between my friend and Legion was still there, and part of me believed neither had told the full truth about their confrontation. But I could not force them to give up the truth if they both refused.

We'd left Mellanstrad as the sun faded over the Fate's Ocean, and by the time we arrived at the outer gates of the royal city of Lyx, the black velvet sky gleamed with stars and the quarter moon. The ride smoothed over paved brick roads. Dozens of painted and polished gas lamps lined quaint streets with red twin homes and apartments with painted shutters. In Lyx, the air was different than the docks of Mellanstrad. Instead of mildew and brine, a perfume of flowers and cinnamon and freshly baked bread hovered at every corner.

Town folk waved colorful ribbons and kerchiefs as our caravan drove past. All celebrating the grandness of Castle Ravenspire, all shouting praises to the royal family for protecting New Timoran from Agitators, from Night Folk—from traitors.

I leaned back in my seat, refusing to look out again.

All my guilt over this execution, this celebration, was beginning to feel more like treason than empathy. Naturally I should want my people to dominate. I should be as Runa, filled with pride Timorans could crush the backs of the rest. But I could not deny the wretched desire for a different kind of change.

The Agitators' cry that my family were the imposters had embedded into my mind and would not let go.

At the top of a sharp incline, the coach rolled to a stop at the gates of Castle Ravenspire. My knee bounced and my stomach soured. Not long and I'd need to play a role I grew weary of playing. While Mavie and Siv both glanced out the window as the coach drove slowly into the royal grounds, Legion's hand covered mine in my lap.

"Something troubles you," he whispered.

Lanterns outside were the only light we had, but I could make out the profile of his strong jaw and the concern on his face. I slipped my fingers through his and tightened my grip. "I'm not suited for Timoran royalty. This entire ordeal feels . . . wrong."

Legion scrutinized me for a moment. "You don't believe Agitators need to pay?"

"Yes," I muttered. "Yes, of course. Anyone who tries to murder another should be punished, but I grow tired of the endless bloodshed. There once was a belief that dissent should be met with discussion and, if possible, compromise."

Legion raised his dark brows. "*Kvinna* Elise, are you quoting ideas from, dare I say, Ettan war journals?"

I flushed. "I read their decrees of war and law, perhaps. I might not agree with it all, but their laws boasted fairness and justice. All I'm saying is not once has anyone at Castle Ravenspire, even before Zyben, tried to hear them out, tried to understand their hatred." I shook my head, feeling foolish. "As I said, I'm not suited to be a royal."

Legion didn't assure me of anything. In truth, he seemed a little bewildered, and I wished I could read his thoughts. He squeezed my hand once, then released it as we pulled in front of the entrance of the fortress.

Castle Ravenspire was indeed a fortress.

Built behind a sphere of mounds and wooden fences, the inner dwellings were made of slate bricks and stone, of black oakwood and iron. The castle was divided into six main buildings, shaped as traditional longhouses on some, while others rose over the grounds with three levels. All were connected by covered cross halls or bridges; all had a tower with guards armed in axes and knives and arrows; all were large and exaggerated.

Castle Ravenspire was not bright or welcoming. Dark walls with flames in harsh iron sconces gave the formidable message to those visiting that Timoran warriors built the fortress, and Timoran warriors claimed it still.

Bits and pieces of the Ferus palace were still there, though.

I gazed at the white brick schoolhouse where the old royals of Etta would study their history, no doubt. Where they learned of their people, or fury, if they had it. Every few paces another bit of white brick, or gilded edges hinted this place was once a bright palace on a hill. Now Castle Ravenspire was a symbol of war.

"Three hells, I never . . ." Mavie said in a gasp, staring at the towers. "This is enormous."

"It is." I grinned. Now, when I visited Ravenspire, it didn't surprise me, but I was much the same as Mavie the first time I saw the labyrinth of corridors and walls and rooftops.

We fell into a formation once the other coaches were emptied. Runa and her maids at the lead—since she would be queen someday and would never let us forget—next my parents with Bevan and Inge, my mother's maid, and a few guards at their backs. Tor, Halvar, and Legion crowded around me and my friends. I'd not noticed back at home how Halvar looked less like a stable hand and more like an assassin with rows of knives on his belt and a black hood over his dark hair.

But his playful voice robbed him of viciousness. "By the gods they better have tarts in the kitchens." He'd muttered it to Tor, who nodded without changing his stony expression.

Legion spared me a quick glance and signaled for me to lead on.

Inside, Ravenspire transformed. Painted walls in pearly white with flecks of gold. Silver and gilded filagree on the moldings. Rows of hanging iron chandeliers with a hundred candles. Zyben used rich blue as his color, and every bit of floor was covered in long woven runners of blue and gold and black. Ravenspire's symbol: a raven holding a single arrow in its beak, and its talons gripping a spiked crown, was on every mantle, every banner, every rug.

The corridors burst with noble folk from Lyx, Mellanstrad, the south shores, and north cliffs. Gowns with crystal beads and fur bodices. Suitcoats hemmed in gold and silver. Gold watches, bangles, necklaces. The air was hot in meads and wines, and dining had not yet begun.

Being the second royal family, the crowds parted, even bowed, as we strode past. My pulse quickened. I kept my eyes on the beams in the ceiling. A hand on the small of my back turned me toward the banquet hall, but I wished he'd keep it there longer. Legion's touch was fast becoming an anchor, grounding me through the storm of this place, of this life.

Double doors parted and opened into the glittering hall. Chatter from a growing crowd echoed off the domed rooftop. A dozen tables were set and prepared, and in the center of the room was a platform. I closed my eyes. An executioner's block.

On a raised dais, Zyben and the queen sat. Calder stood stalwart beside them, until he saw Runa. As expected, he abandoned his position and took his future bride's hand, kissed it, and led her to a seat at the head of one table with him.

My stomach rumbled as I scanned the feast. Bread stuffed with dates. Honey glazes on poached salmon. Cold eel and stewed turnips. All of it reminded my insides I'd not eaten since this morning.

"*Kvinna* Elise."

I turned quickly, nearly ramming my head into Jarl's. "Oh, Jarl. I didn't see you."

Jarl was dressed in his blue captain's gambeson. He took my hand and pressed a kiss to the top. "I wonder if I might escort you from here." He pointed his stare at Legion. "That is if *Herr* Grey approves."

A muscle twitched in Legion's jaw, but I guessed I was the only one close enough to notice. Legion hid his disquiet beneath the signature slyness of his grin. "I don't speak for Elise. She has her own voice."

By the gods, the man knew how to set my pulse aflame.

I blinked my frenzy to Jarl, who seemed either perturbed or surprised at the response, and nodded my consent.

If I didn't take a few steps away from Legion, I might do something foolish . . . like kiss him.

CHAPTER EIGHTEEN

LEGION KEPT a distance of three strides. Jarl said nothing, but I could've sworn he grinned as we passed *Herr* Svart, who sat on a lower table. Svart narrowed his eyes into daggers. I wanted to disappear.

Inside, Mavie and Siv took a place against the wall with the other maids and stewards. Bevan stood with them, while Tor and Halvar exited the hall for the kitchens. They weren't needed and would not be permitted to stay.

At the table, I took the seat between Legion and Jarl. For sharing many of my sentiments on Timoran culture, the negotiator settled into the finer things of life like a second nature. He knew how to sit like a man who catered to no one; knew how to piously hold out a drinking horn for more ale or wine, then how to stroke the glass pride of surrounding nobles until they'd gone blue in the face from swallowing their self-importance.

Me, raised in this life, could hardly bury my resentment. As boorish conversation went on, even the way I shredded the wet eel skin screamed of discontent.

No one noticed if I was troubled, of course. No one but Legion.

"I'm well," I said at the hooded glance he gave me when my knife skidded over my plate. He didn't need to say anything, I knew what question danced on the tip of his tongue.

"I said nothing," he returned with a grin.

I tightened my mouth.

We sat at the king's table. I'd prefer if the ground swallowed me whole as prying eyes stole pitiful glances my way, their stares prickling my skin. Folk would stare and whisper about me, but never approach me.

I was surrounded by countless people, yet always, in some way, alone.

The whispers ceased when Zyben took Queen Annika's hand, and they claimed the two high seats at the table. Annika was a pasty woman, as though she'd never stepped outside, and her face was always twisted as if she smelled something putrid.

The queen sat, but Zyben remained on his feet. He lifted a polished goblet. "Welcome. You honor your King by being here, to celebrate a defeat of traitors." His icy eyes traveled the table. Bone beads threaded in the braids of his beard clapped together when he sneered. "Eat, drink, and enjoy yourselves during these days."

A murmur of approval rumbled through the crowds, and wait staff set to work serving the wealthiest, the noblest of Timoran.

I ignored most of the conversations, since most had to do

with the attack, or status, or troubles in the kingdom. But a lady to the side of Legion soon caught my attention, the way she giggled and leaned in close to him. His smile was polite. Perhaps he enjoyed the attention. I didn't know personal things about Legion Grey, who he entertained, the sort of affections he'd won in Mellanstrad. Only that he was desirable to many, and some talk hinted he was well known in other ways.

"You've been missed in town, *Herr* Grey," she said. I didn't know her name, but she was lovely. Shapely, poignant features. A diamond dangled from a hair chain to the center of her forehead. She was not without means.

"I highly doubt my company has been missed, *De Hän* Svensson." Legion leaned on one elbow, but it angled his body closer to me and further from her.

"Inez," she said. By the gods, she rested a hand on his chest. Bold of her. "How many times must I ask you to call me by my given name?" Legion didn't reply, simply grinned, and returned his attention to his plate. Inez frowned but leaned around him with a new determination. "*Kvinna* Elise. How does *Herr* Grey favor in negotiating betrothals? He has cleaned my brother's purse in the game halls many a time. I imagine he is rather sly. But perhaps we should ask *Herr* Magnus since he has placed his name in the bidding."

I flushed and dabbed my mouth with a linen cloth, even though I'd hardly eaten since I decimated my eel. The last thing I wanted to do was draw any kind of attention my way.

Jarl cleared his throat. "*Herr* Grey has handled everything with great respect for our *Kvinna*. In fact, I feel as though it will be her choice in the end, not his."

"It will be," Legion said without hesitation.

My heart jolted in my chest. I folded my hands in my lap beneath the table, closing my eyes when the heat from his hand was there to meet it. He rubbed his legs, then his fingertips brushed against my leg, a shudder of sensation strong enough to penetrate the folds of my skirt. I froze, a pillar of hot and cold, of tension and peace.

Inez chuckled. "Your pardon? Why are you there if you leave the choice up to her?"

"My thoughts exactly," Jarl said through his teeth.

I shifted in my seat, so my knees touched Legion's leg. The discomfort of the moment drew me to him. A place where I'd been safe before, where I could escape. In so short a time Legion had become such a place.

"*Kvinna* Elise will not ascend the throne, true," Legion said. "But she is of royal blood, a leader in Timoran. It is my belief, allowing her to choose the match who makes her stronger will be for the benefit of everyone."

"Most unusual," Inez muttered.

"Why?" I blurted out before I could stop myself. Both Jarl and Inez turned their confusion to me, but it was Legion who I looked to. "Why is it unusual to allow a bride an opinion on her husband?"

Inez snorted in her wine. "A love match, you mean?"

"Perhaps." Was it such a ridiculous notion?

"All respect, *Kvinna*, but that is what consorts are for."

"I disagree," Legion said softly, facing me. "If anyone should find a match that could be both lover and equal, it will —it *should*—be Elise."

My breath caught in my chest. Underneath the table his hand settled on my leg. The weight of it stirred my insides until

I could hardly hear the chatter through the pounding in my head; made worse when his thumb drew slow, seductive circles on my thigh. The way we sat, no one would realize how close we'd come.

"Is this what you're looking for, Elise?" Jarl pressed.

My mouth had gone sticky, like honey, and I couldn't form words. Swifter, more deliberate circles came from Legion's thumb. His other fingers stroked my inner leg gently. Unbidden, I parted my knees. Legion drew a long breath in through his nose, but never met my gaze as his hand drifted higher toward the apex of my thighs.

Gods, what were we doing?

My skirt was thin enough, each spark danced up my leg to my head. Like a hook in the center of my chest, I wanted to be nearer to him, wanted more of him. I shouldn't be allowing this to go on, but it would be more of a tragedy to make it stop.

I licked my lips and answered Jarl's question, but my attention was only on Legion. "Choosing someone who shares interests and ambitions while holding my heart is all I've ever wanted."

Legion's eyes simmered in a hot desire. All at once, his hand moved indecently high on my thigh, and I curled forward with a gasp. My pulse ran wild, my body a flurry of need and want and sensation. No longer did I want to leave to spare myself discomfort, I wanted to be free to find some seedy, dark corner and fill it with me and Legion Grey.

Through the fog in my head, Inez's mutterings about my oddities were heard, and I noted the way Jarl tipped the rest of his wine back, a frown pressed on his mouth.

I slipped my fingers into Legion's underneath the table,

unbothered if he sensed how sweaty my palms were, or if he saw the thud of my heartbeat in my neck. I held his open palm on my leg, silently encouraging him to never let go.

He didn't. Not until we were forced to retreat. For the whole of the first meal, Legion Grey claimed me with the firm grip beneath the royal table.

And I had let him. Without a second thought.

ONE OF THE longhouses nearest the king's villas was where the Lysander household would stay the whole of the week. Where once the houses were open, some built in a single, long room shared by many, now, were a honeycomb of hallways and arcades and chambers with private doors.

I praised the gods Runa would be at the opposite end as me. She'd grown more unbearable throughout the evening, even striking one of her maids for sloshing wine on the floor.

Most folk laughed.

Calder drunkenly praised the viciousness of his future bride, then took the moment further by ordering ten lashings for the maid.

I'd taken my leave then.

"Shall we send any tea to your room?" Mavie asked. "Are you still not feeling well?"

Truth be told, I'd lied through my teeth to escape the banquet. I shook my head and rested a hand on Mavie's arm. "No, thank you. I'll be fine. You both should rest."

Siv and Mavie shared a look, then bowed out across the

hallway. Each royal room was aligned with a small chamber of goose-down beds for the maids and stewards.

If I left, so did my maids. So did Legion and Tor and Halvar. All with more than one duty this week. The stable hand would drive the coach, and handle a bow, and be a lookout on the grounds. Tor would be a shadow on me and Siv and Mavie. A silent guard in the dark. I often speculated how my father learned of Legion's talent with a blade. Without Legion admitting to it, the way he was admired, I'd never have known he came from the cutthroat life of the streets. He must've disclosed the truth before being selected as negotiator.

One of his many surprises.

Not unlike his villainous hand at the banquet.

My heart still had not returned to its normal pace, and on the walk through the royal corridors, I'd stolen no less than a dozen glances at that hand. Imagined what other things it could do, then tried to shame such musings away without success.

"Tor," Legion said and pointed at my friends' doorway. "See to their room."

Siv pinched her lips but didn't speak. Doubtless she took great pains being treated like she could not watch her own back. And doubtless Legion was not the sort of man to argue with on such things.

She held her tongue and spared me a glance before following Tor and Mavie into the smaller chamber.

"Halvar," Legion said.

Halvar offered a lazy sort of salute. "Say no more. Consider thy outer doors scanned and searched and surveyed."

I bit my bottom lip through my smile as he sauntered with a touch of arrogance back the way we came.

My grin faded once I realized Legion and I were wholly alone.

I faced the arched wooden door guarding the royal suite. The hinges were made of black iron and appeared new, though this part of Ravenspire was built in the Ferus empire. Reaching for the door, Legion stopped me. His hand over mine on the latch.

"I'll go first," he said, his eyes telling me to stay back.

Legion tugged one of his daggers halfway free of the sheath on his waist and entered the room. The air was musty from disuse, but soon came the click of a latch, the slap of wood on stone, and a gust of coolness against my face.

"It's empty," Legion called.

Closing the door behind me, I stepped into the golden light of a newly lit lantern. Legion blew out the matchstick as I rounded the corner.

The room was grand, small as it was. A washroom with a gilded tub behind a diaphanous shade, and a covered bed with a fur duvet and oversized pillows. The wardrobe was already stocked with my gowns and a jar of rose oil was capped, awaiting me to perfume the rugs and threads.

I avoided Legion, both afraid of and yearning for his touch. Rounding to the opposite side of the bed, I leaned out the window, closed my eyes, and breathed in the silky night.

The burn of the negotiator's eyes distracted me from it all.

"What ailment shall I declare for you come morning?" Legion asked, a laugh in his voice.

"Am I so obvious?"

Legion's steps padded over the rugs. My breaths quickened once the warmth of his body came at my back, his breath on my neck. "To me."

I prayed he couldn't see the way my hands trembled as I closed the window, latching it, giving the privacy I wanted. Fog grew in my head as I puzzled over Legion's behavior. It would be presumptuous and embarrassing to question him on it. Perhaps he'd meant it all innocently, a sort of friendly reassurance. Assuming differently was only an overwrought trail of thought. Unnecessary to address . . .

His chest butted against my shoulders. I closed my eyes, my voice all wrong and hoarse.

"Why do you come so close to me?" I swallowed past the stickiness in my throat. "Why do you . . . touch me the way you do?"

With lips close to my ear, he said, "Would you like me to stop?"

I faced him, my eyes wide. "What are you doing?"

Legion retired any space between us. When I took a breath, my chest brushed his, the fabric of my bodice hardly able to dull the seductive flame swirling in my pulse.

"I want to learn about you," he said. "Learn of the things you truly want. Things we both know those crown chasers will never give you. You have so few choices they allow you to make, so I want to know—when I touch you like this . . ." Legion inched his fingertips lightly up the length of my arms. They claimed the shape of my wrists, my shoulders, they memorized the angle of my collarbone. My jaw. "Is this something you would like?"

I dug my fingernails into the meat of my palms. "Yes."

"And how would you want your match to hold you? Like this?" He altered course with his fingertips, and one arm encircled my waist, palm dragging down every divot of my spine. When he reached the small of my back, he flattened his hand, urging me against his firm body. "Is this right?"

My hands had nowhere to go but on him. Up his chest, resting over the steady beat of his heart. I nodded mutely.

Legion tilted his head, and the rough stubble of his face scratched my cheek. "If one came close to you, like this." His lips touched the round curve of my ear. He kissed me there. "Would you want it?"

"Yes," I said in a gasp.

With one graceful motion, Legion turned me, holding my back to his chest again. I was dazed enough, I hardly noticed until his palm splayed across my middle. Gentle strokes heated my center. He followed the curve of my waist, hand on my hip. I was undone.

The whisper of my hair leaving my neck, draping off the opposite shoulder, was followed by his lips on my skin. "What of this, *Kvinna*?" His rough voice came more like a demand than a question.

"Legion . . ." My hand cupped the back of his head as his palm explored the shape of my hips, the side of my leg, back up my ribs. Never had a touch had such power over me. A word, a command, a simple gesture, and I'd break. Bend to his bidding.

Bid me! I wanted to scream but with his arms encircled around me, words turned to ash. Worthless and unnecessary.

My body arched against his, no space between us, and yet not close enough. Legion snaked his hand alongside my bare neck, beneath the sleeve of my gown, pushing it aside until my shoulder was free. A groan escaped me, and heat flooded my face for I could not take it back. But when his mouth left a trail of kisses across the ridge of my shoulder, I'd groan again if it brought the same result.

"This," he said, voice raw. Legion's palm opened on my chest, over my furious heart. "This is what you should demand. Ragged breaths, fire in your blood, sweat on your brow." He kissed it away.

I sank against him, knees weakened as Legion slowly, methodically, gathered bunches of my skirt. Too soon, before my heart could prepare, his hand found the untouched skin of my thigh. Those wicked fingers left sparks of fire across my skin until the barest touch to my sensitive core had my legs trembling.

My skirt was lifted, if anyone strode past the window they would see my naked flesh, they'd see my dowry negotiator touching me. They'd see his fingers beginning to claim the wet heat of my center for himself.

None of it mattered.

I let my head fall against his shoulder, legs spread, and throat bared. I wanted more. Wanted everything.

A steady knock pounded at the door. "Legion. We're needed at our post."

Cursed gods! Leave, Tor. Be gone!

Legion's hand danced down my leg and released my skirts, so they gathered again around my ankles. He spun me to him, chest to chest. My eyes widened when he lifted the tips of his fingers to his lips. His tongue swiped out, tasting me on his skin. All hells, I'd never seen anything so provocative, so seductive.

A simmering heat roared in his dark eyes as he pinched my chin between his fingers. Leaning in, his lips feather soft on my cheek, he said, "All of this is what you deserve in a match. And I wish, *by the gods*, I wish I could be the one to give it to you."

He stepped back and I think I hated him for it. Legion pressed a chaste kiss to my palm.

"If you wish it then do not leave!" With Legion five paces away now, I used the bed to brace my failing legs.

His countenance shadowed. "I boast an honored position as your negotiator, but in truth we know I am nothing but a servant." He hesitated at the door. "Sleep well, Elise."

When the door closed, my legs were spent. I slumped to the floor, back to the bed. My skin on fire as the remnants of his touch burned in place.

By the skies . . . The thought was futile, rendered nothing.

How could I think of anything else but the memory of what we'd done, what we hadn't, and what I wished we would.

CHAPTER NINETEEN

FROM THE GRAY dawn to blue dusk debauchery rang in the halls of Castle Ravenspire. King Zyben promised celebration and he delivered mightily.

With Mavie and Siv on my flanks, we strode through the courtyards, the corridors, the banquet halls, lost in entertainers, open trade markets, tables of exotic fruits and meats, glazed breads, and ale. I laughed when we discovered the Eastern Kingdom's brän had been added and bid my friends to try some. Mavie required a horn of water to cease coughing.

While my friends laid out on the grass beside me, eating wild lingonberries, I read more excerpts of Queen Lilianna, imagining her walking these very grounds.

Two turns after Prince Sol's birth came the young Princess Herja. The healers called the child miraculous, wonderous, a blessing. But Lilianna had a dream she believed from the All Father of gods about another child. For three turns more she worked with Night Folk, drinking remedies and pungent herbs to help her conceive.

> *... the silver of moonvane blooms across Etta tonight. Another son is born. A boy of the night, Prince Valen Krigare Ferus ...*

I read of the prophecies from court poets and philosophers, of the mystical shrubs of moonvane blossoms the people believed were blessings from the gods at the new prince's birth. The corpses of the high shrubs, once believed to have healing powers, still stood across New Timoran. Dry and brittle and dead.

Moonvane had gone extinct with the Ferus line, I thought. An ache bloomed in my heart, but I still smiled reading Lilianna describe her dark-eyed babe when Mavie nudged me to move. Too many crowds were gathering to stay sprawled out on the lawns without being stepped on. I tucked Lilianna's journal away and joined them in the fading sun as revelers danced about the courtyard.

By dusk I caught the glimpse I'd longed for all day. Legion, across the courtyard. With the guards surrounding the whole of the courtyard, my uncle made it known that Legion wouldn't be forced to spend his waking hours following silly women. In fact, I thought King Zyben had begun to treat the negotiator more like a personal advisor than anything.

Drawn to him like a moth to its flame, its destruction, I looked. I watched. Through a band of minstrels flicking lutes and pipes and lyres. He wore a gray tunic, armed with knives, with a sword. A knight from fae lore.

Legion paused at a cart of whalebone jewelry. He studied a comb shaped into a silky winter blossom while Tor and Halvar watched a troop of acrobats bend, twist, and flip with ribbons and batons around a Foolish Storyteller. The fool wore a gilded mask and curled shoes with silver bells. His verse and limericks captivated his audience with a bawdy tale of the far north where a righteous princess tumbled with a rake.

"A wicked darling, make no mistake.

The highest born chose the lowest rake.

Such a cruel lovely tipped her crown and sang: Methinks tis time,

To bend the knee and toss 'til the ground doth quake."

The fool tossed handfuls of glitter powder at his audience and danced among the flailing ribbons of his troop, applause and laughter from the nobility encouraged more and more.

I'd stopped watching.

Across the spectacle, Legion abandoned the comb and caught me in his sights. Where I stepped, he mirrored.

No one noticed our furtive glances.

On the side of Legion, Tor seemed ready to pounce at any moment, his misery at being in such a crowd apparent in his scowl. Halvar laughed and drank up the whole of the festivities. Siv and Mavie were much the same. I faced a plate of spiced figs as Mavie indulged, giggling. Siv studied the gates, tracked the guards on watch in the towers. When I glanced again, Legion's grin said a thousand mischievous things.

A serf tapped his arm and reluctantly, Legion looked away.

My heart quickened when after the serf scurried out of sight, Legion and his posse crossed the courtyard, aimed at us.

"Oh, oh, Halvar, *Herr* Grey," Mavie said, unapologetically

unlike the serf girl from home. "You must try these." She held up a silver platter of the figs.

Legion gave a subtle bow to his head, as if Mavie had a title. I smiled, warmed by the respect. Mavie and Siv were dressed in gowns again and looked every bit as noble as the crowd.

"We would love nothing more," Legion promised. "But we've been summoned to *Kvin* Lysander inside."

"My father will run you ragged even from his bed," I said, a catch in my voice.

"Worried for me, *Kvinna*?"

"Very."

Our words were heavy with the storm we'd created last night. Legion grinned, bowed his farewell at us, but as we passed, our fingertips brushed, then curled around each other for a secret, forbidden moment. Not enough, yet satisfying in a way that when Halvar was my guard for the night, stating Legion was again occupied by my father and the king, I imagined the moment over and over again in my head until I fell asleep smiling.

The next day was much the same. Music and melodies were accompanied by performances and drink. Mavie convinced Siv to watch a girl, no taller than my hip, walk a rope tied from one tower to the next.

I was not so fortunate.

"*Kvinna*, I grow greedy for a moment of your time."

I didn't even fight the urge to groan when *Herr* Gurst and several of his advisors, all wearing the same worried look as if their heads might be lopped from their necks at the next word, barricaded my retreat.

"I cannot speak to your negotiator, always otherwise engaged, and it is tiresome fighting for a moment with you."

"*Herr* nothing good comes easily."

He grunted, affronted. "Well, that may be, but I desire a turn with you."

He held out his arm and the advisors adjusted, giving me no choice but to accept or deliberately deny him.

I trusted Legion would not pick this man for me, tradition and society demanded I had no power to deny him an audience during the process.

With a grimace, I took his arm.

Gurst let out a long, breathy sigh and sauntered slower than a frozen stream through the celebration. As though he wanted everyone to see who held his arm, as though he were a bleeding king.

"My estates boast grander . . ."

And I stopped listening, held my breath, and kept my attention on the bright colors and scents around me. My feet ached by the time we rounded the first courtyard. Gurst strolled so leisurely it gave folk time to accidently smash my toes more than once. I was offered murmured apologies from the advisors; Gurst never noticed.

As he guided me toward a second courtyard where dining tables were set with light foods for snacking, a tight grip took hold of my arm.

My heart flipped in my chest.

"Apologies, *Herr* Gurst," Legion said, coming from nowhere. His golden hair had been braided on the sides, holding it off his brow and the shadow in his eyes seemed brighter. "But *Kvinna* Lysander is needed by her mother."

Gurst protested, until a meeting with Legion Grey became more pressing. "*Herr* Grey, permit me to discuss—"

"Apologies, again," Legion said as he tugged me away. "I am to speak with *Kvin* Lysander, and as we both know, I am at his bidding."

We disappeared around the corner and into a narrow alcove in one of the stone walls. A laugh burst from my throat. Legion's smile went wide, and he tried to muffle his own amusement.

"Three hells, I'm not sure I would've survived another moment with that man. Many thanks for rescuing me," I whispered. The size of our dark space was small enough we were forced to stand against each other.

Legion's smile faded into something more or less than that. A challenge.

"I am here to be of service," he said.

My ability to breathe was stilted when his hands ran up my waist again, until he caressed the curve of one breast, teasing the shape of me.

By the gods, my head spun in a beautiful haze.

"Legion." I ran my palms over his chest.

"I'll get the rack for this," he said, pressing gentle kisses against the curve of my neck.

"Then, we ought to stop." I wanted his lips on mine but understood the hesitation. I could not speak for Legion, but should I begin, I doubted I'd stop.

Out in the open was too great a risk.

He smiled, but kept his head tilted, his face buried in my hair. "I'm not sure what would cause more pain."

I closed my eyes and let my hands explore the muscle on his

shoulders, his back, simply being close. He hesitated for a moment, then emboldened, palmed my whole breast in his grip.

The sigh of pleasure from my throat drew a grin across his face. Legion began to tug at the neckline of my dress. All gods, to feel the rough touch of his hand on my bare chest was a dream I'd not realized I needed.

Until our choice to stay like this the rest of the afternoon was robbed.

"Legion," Halvar hissed beyond the alcove. "All gods, where the hells is he?"

Legion lifted his head, slowly dropped his hand, and stepped aside.

I sighed. "Gods, I thought I liked him until now."

A demure gleam lit in Legion's gaze. A simple moment and still my chest rose and fell in sharp gasps. I could not stop this, a feeling of rushing toward the edge, where below, destruction awaited. This would not be allowed, no matter the praise for Legion's abilities. Never mind I knew little of him, never mind his sole duty was to find me a husband, then step out of my life. Still, I could not deny a need to be near him had bloomed within and I could not dull it.

Legion lifted my knuckles to his lips and left them with a kiss. "I must go."

"I'll leave after you're gone," I assured him.

"In my absence, do wise up and avoid crown chasers, *Kvinna*."

I rolled my eyes, and when I looked again, Legion was gone, at the mercy of the royals and nobility. Why was he constantly summoned? Had he caught the eye of the king and now my uncle desired to have him in his employ? Though, it would be an advantageous move for the tradesman in Legion Grey, I wanted to shout that he could not be taken from Mellanstrad.

After all this ended, I still had grand plans to escape to the game halls, steal sights of the handsome trader, and perhaps steal a few more private moments.

CHAPTER TWENTY

Even with summer heat in the valleys, the river at Ravenspire had bits of ice at the surface from the northern falls. This close to the peaks it was no surprise. Beyond those mountains was the tundra of Old Timoran. The ice seemed a fitting reminder of what our people had won through blood and bone.

I tugged the fox fur mantel tighter around my shoulders as men gathered near the river's edge, mounting steeds and swift cabriolets. Some held curved longswords and sickles, most checked the give and pull of bowstrings, checked the points of their arrows.

Runa grinned with a wash of smugness as Calder trotted past on his royal charge. The prince gave his betrothed a nod of recognition, but more a greedy look shot between them. A power madness that would anchor the two together. Had Runa never mentioned how their ambitions for a greater Timoran aligned, I might've missed it. They would rule in fantastic brutality, no doubt.

Behind the prince, Captain Magnus and a gaggle of mightily armed officers followed on stallions draped in bright Ravenspire sashes and tassels on the manes. Jarl nodded his head and grinned. "I shall catch you a fine fur, *Kvinna*."

Was I supposed to swoon? I had plenty of furs. By the hells, I grew weary of this constant battering of overconfident men with a need to conquer. No mistake, when a wedding was over, their ambition to win me body and soul would end, and I would become a tarnished prize they tucked up in the cupboard and promptly forgot.

Mavie snorted once Jarl and the prince were at the bridge. "He'll be hunting, all right. For *Herr* Grey. Serfs of all the suitors have gone on about how they plan to get close to the negotiator the whole of the day."

"I wish them the best of luck. Legion will do all he can to avoid them."

"It is his duty to speak with them, to choose a match for you," Siv snapped. "We all would do well to remember it. They are not our friends."

Together, Mavie and I gave her similar looks of confusion.

Then, my chest tightened with frustration. I lifted my chin and watched the procession of hunters cross the bridge toward the forest. "Forgive me if I relish the idea that my negotiator holds as much disdain for this process as me, Siverie."

She blanched. "I didn't mean anything by it, Elise. I simply don't want you to wind up hurt when the crown assigns *Herr* Grey elsewhere once this is over. They favor him. No doubt he will have plenty of offers across the kingdom."

Had she witnessed something between us? One of the hidden touches in passing, or how Legion stood close, how sometimes we disappeared together? So what if she had? Her point had merit. Legion would leave and if I did not defend my heart, it would be an agonizing blow when it happened, indeed.

"I'm aware," was the only reply I could give.

Admittedly, it had been a disappointment when this morning my father had summoned me to his side at the morning meal and informed me Legion and Tor would be called to the royal hunt with the king. I caught Legion's gaze before he'd smiled and queried about me.

"Gods, boy," my father had said through a wretched cough. His skin gray as death. "This is a bleeding fortress. What sort of trouble do you think will befall women at tea when an army of royal patrols mark every corner? You will hunt. Be free of women's gossip for a time."

He'd drawn laughter at that. Zyben sneered at his queen who had planned a grand gathering of all the women while the men hunted—but in truth the queen's tea was more to slight her husband's consorts who were not invited to attend.

Legion never lost his composure, simply accepted the invitation, and drank to it. But his eyes had found me over the rim of the cup and held tight.

"Elise," Mavie snapped. "The king."

My stomach dropped as the crowds around me lowered to their knees in a wave. I being the lone person standing. As Zyben came forward, I skinned my knees I dropped so quickly.

The king drew his horse to a halt. "Niece," his voice like the ice in the river.

I lifted my eyes. "My King."

Zyben tilted his head, a smug curl on his lips. "How have you enjoyed the festivals thus far?"

"Greatly, Uncle. You have my thanks."

Fondle Zyben's ego and you win favor. You keep his healers for your father.

It seemed to work since he puffed out his chest, his voice with less of an edge. "They remain in your name. This will end in honor for you. I've spoken with your negotiator and insisted by week's end, you shall have your match." Zyben grinned, pleased with himself. I wanted the ground to devour me. "Even from terror, Niece, good can come. No doubt you and your match will bring glory to our line."

With that, Zyben kicked the belly of his horse and trotted ahead. Zyben's two younger sons followed with their guards. Next, Legion. Hooded, his horse packed with a longbow. Beneath the shadows of his cowl, I noted the pinched look of his mouth, the flex of the pulse in his jaw.

He was angry.

Then it was true. The sting of tears took me off guard. I thought I'd have more time, but the truth was in the way Legion did not look at me, the way he hurried his horse after the king, as though speed were the only way to satiate rage.

In two nights, Legion would be forced to end the bid. He'd bring my free life to an end.

"It is a pity, Niece," Queen Annika said as she returned a painted cup to a matching plate. I looked up, my tea and honey cakes hardly touched. "All you've been through. How ever do you walk around without fear?"

I straightened in my seat when I realized Annika was speaking to me.

Back in the banquet hall, gowns, beringed fingers, and flower petal perfumes spun around the room. Select ladies were called in to join the queen in a capricious tea where we all praised and offered veiled insults to one another until we were bloodied to a pulp by words and arrogance.

I kept my voice meek. Annika despised her husband, no doubt, and put on a good show of affection for our family. I believed showing submission was the way to her kinder graces. "I am rarely alone, My Queen."

"Dear Aunt, *Kvinna* Elise has been paired with a negotiator who knows a blade as well as his trade. He's the reason she sits here with us instead of at the bloody end of an Agitator's sword," Runa said boldly.

Addressing Annika so informally would not be accepted by anyone but her. Annika was not Calder's mother, not Runa's aunt exactly, and I deduced it made Annika despise her even more. Annika's son was made of a weak disposition and was passed over to be future king. Pallid and rail thin, he'd been married to a plump woman who demanded fatted food in the hopes the first prince would thicken. As far as I knew, my cousin lived in his estates in the North, eating and giving his wife children. Nothing more of note.

Still, Annika feigned an affectionate smile. "Ah, yes. The king is quite impressed with the cunning of *Herr* Grey. I hear he has . . . quite a reputation in Mellanstrad." Inez who sat amongst a feckless group of noble ladies from town giggled.

Queen Annika was buoyed and widened her grin. "So, tell us Elise. Has such a rake tempted you?"

By the gods, yes. I folded my hands in my lap to hide the moisture on my palms. "*Herr* Grey has only treated me with the utmost respect."

Annika snorted into her tea. "Well, that tells us nothing." The queen lowered her voice. "Dear girl, though not publicly stated for women, there is nothing wrong with taking consorts after vows. With a face as his, I might be tempted myself."

"Oh, Your Majesty," Inez said. "You would not be alone in such a desire."

More giggling rose and Annika drove on about Legion, other soldiers, other merchants, faces many of the ladies would favor as their lovers.

I took a sip of tea, face hot. The idea of taking vows with a man I cared nothing for, then taking many lovers after—it sickened me. My heart had known a furious beat, my skin had endured passion, and my body had survived a gentle touch. It could never want anything but the same again and again.

But time was running short with the hand which had awakened the need.

Could I ask Legion such a thing? An official, though hidden, consort to a second niece of the king? Surely more prestige awaited a man as him. A truer love. He'd spoken once of Ettan folk, how devoted they were to their partners. A bit of admiration was in his voice then. It would be selfish of me to deny him the chance to find something similar by tethering him to me, a woman he could never truly claim as his.

From the back of the hall the doors swept open, and a quartet of guards stepped in, boxing in a woman dressed in white robes and a stern knot behind her head. She reminded me of my old duenna who'd shout at me when I slouched at the table. Behind the terse woman, was a girl. My heart skipped. It was the same veiled child from the ball at my manor. Now dressed in lavender robes, the girl remained hidden behind the filigreed veil.

"Ah," said Annika. "My husband's little pet is finally here."

"Forgiveness, My Queen," said the nurse. "The witch dallied."

Annika sneered. "As always. Such a disobedient little monster." The queen faced her guests. "It can be no secret fury is wretched and dangerous against Timoran blood, the reason our king promptly places true Night Folk to death. But I will give my husband credit for finding the most curious descendants of the fae for entertainment. Traded from a gods awful blight of a kingdom somewhere in the West.

"We call her Fate's Daughter. Not entirely fae, but with a curious little talent of twisting destiny we simply cannot ignore. Come here, my wicked little darling. Show our guests what you can do. Entertain us. Tell us a bit of our destinies."

The nursemaid ushered the girl forward. I expected the child to tremble in fear under such a bitter gaze from a queen, but even with her veil I could tell she lifted her chin in a bit of defiance.

"As I've told you, Queenie," said the child, "it does not work like that."

The soft, warning voice from before was harsh and snappy. A child with a bone to pick. When the nurse swatted at her backside, I wanted to run with the girl. She was not free here.

Queen Annika laughed, seemingly amused by the girl's bite.

"I've seen you tell many a story. Now, do I need to force it, or shall you do it on your own accord?" Queen Annika held up a woven band with clear spikes sewn into the threads. "Remember, I know when you are putting me on."

The girl's defiance waned. Her shoulders curled forward.

"That's better," the queen said when the veiled child came to her side. "Now, tell us something fate has in store."

Impossible. Fury couldn't read the Norn's plans. Could it? I'd not heard of fae doing such a thing—then again, the queen had called her not entirely fae, a sort of witch. Curiosity rivaled my sympathy for the child when the girl sighed, and from a pouch tied to her leg she withdrew a bit of rough parchment and a charcoal pen. No burst of power, no gust of wind, she simply began to write. Then, she rolled the scroll up in her hand.

"Who shall I anger Fate with first?"

The queen harrumphed but turned her sights on Runa. "*Kvinna* Runa, our future queen."

No one would miss the bridled disdain in the queen's voice. Runa made no indication she was bothered. Why did it matter? One day she'd take Annika's place. She didn't need to give the queen the same level of respect as the rest of us.

The girl faced my sister. She did nothing. Stared—or so it seemed since we couldn't see her eyes. Then she began to write on a new roll of parchment. "Your game of crowns begins. In your eyes you will be victorious."

The words made a bit of sense to me, particularly if the girl were intentionally drawing attention to the reality that Runa would be queen. It could be a kind of game between her future crown and the one Annika wore. The queen watched with seething anger as the girl tied off the scroll with a bit of twine and handed it to Runa.

"What am I to do with this?" asked my sister.

"Eat it, burn it, does not matter. The line of fate has been cast and cannot be undone. Cannot be avoided," the child replied.

"As I explained, Runa," Annika said. "The girl is called Fate's Daughter for when she writes a story, eerily her little missives come to pass. Enjoy your games, dear Niece. Doubtless a great many formidable opponents will be there to meet you."

Runa grinned down at her scroll. "How delightful. I do love to rise as a victor, *Aunt*."

My stomach squirmed, while the other oblivious women found a great deal of delight in the back and forth. Nothing like a vicious crown to spur the inner warrior in Timoran folk. The balance between blood and peace is where my people thrived.

"Be warned," the girl said as she moved along the table. "Though it is written, Fate does not always deliver the way we expect. Words can mean many things."

"Me! Little witch, me next," shouted Inez.

The girl repeated her silent stare, her eerie writing. Then, she handed the sealed scroll to Inez who tore into it, her face alight for a moment before her grin fell. "Watch the window? What in the three hells is this supposed to mean?"

The girl shrugged, moving down the line to anxiously awaiting ladies. "A missive of Fate. I write what the words demand. The rest is up to the fickle Norns who sit on their plump asses at the tree of the gods."

She spoke of old lore, and it was both frightening and intriguing such a child believed in such power.

Annika passed the girl around, delivering missives. Some dull, some with promises of excitement in the future. I didn't want the child to deliver anything for me. No doubt the fates had nothing bright instore for my future. But the girl came to me at long last.

I kept my gaze on the untouched cakes on my plate.

The child didn't move. For too many moments she stood at my side, she had not even reached for the pouch on her leg.

When my tongue began to stick to the top of my mouth from nerves, I glanced at the child.

"A troubled heart," she said. The room went silent. The girl stepped closer. "Release the past and trust those undeserving of it."

She repeated the same strange warning as the night of the ball. I yearned to look away but couldn't.

"What your heart desires, there your fate lies." She lowered her voice to a rough whisper. "When you see the beast within, let him in to let him go. Only then will he bring the change you seek."

A different ending to the strange declaration, but at the ball the guards had been shoving me away. The change—I wanted change. Peace and unity. I wanted Ettan, Night Folk, and Timorans to walk shoulder to shoulder, work fields together, defend our land as one. The change I wanted bordered on treason.

And I was supposed to believe a beast would bring it about.

I shook my head and looked away, a little disappointed. This girl was putting us all on. Clearly, she hated the royalty of

Timoran. True, she might have some gift of twisting words, but this was madness.

"Why are you not writing it down?" Inez whined. "*Kvinna* Elise got such a longer one than the rest."

The girl didn't budge, not even a flinch ruffled her veil. "This path is not written in stone. It must be chosen."

Queen Annika looked annoyed. She waved her fingers at the nurse. "That will be enough. I grow tired of riddles from a child.

The nurse came for the girl, but before she left, once more as she did at my manor, the girl gripped my wrist. A steady thrum of heat pulsed along my skin. "The tomb. Open it. *Change* it all."

The nurse muttered a few hurried apologies and peeled the child's fingers off my wrist, practically dragging the child away.

Laughter returned. Led by the queen, taunts at the mad, wicked darling of a witch. The table droned on about their odd little notes. Some had promises of fortune, others were simple like Inez's—watch the knives, watch the gardens, don't dine with a back to the door. Foolish, meaningless things.

But I could not draw the simplest of smiles. The final touch of the girl still hummed in my blood. Fury. I'd never truly felt fae magic, but this girl had blasted me with something and now it swirled within like a new part of me.

What beast? What tomb?

And what—by the hells—was about to change?

CHAPTER TWENTY-ONE

Sol is rather jealous of the new babe and fled to his father's horses this morning, a pack across his little shoulders, demanding the hunters take him on the Wild Hunt. Arvad, one always amused with his young ones, treated the boy with dignity. His compromise: should Sol mount his own horse, hold his own bow, then he'd be welcome on the days' long hunt.

Gods bless the first prince, he mightily tried. Alas, when the boy failed, the king placed his hands atop his shoulders and vowed he was needed here. For how else was the princess and second prince to learn how to behave and misbehave as children ought without the guidance of their brother?

My king assured him it was never too early to begin mischief.

A new light has lived in the boy's eyes since the hunting party took leave, and he has at last visited the new Night

Prince. Even touched the points of young Valen's ears and asked how his father's Night Folk blood got into his brother.

Ah, the hours spent telling tales on the fury in Arvad's blood, and how Night Folk of the trees helped bless us with his new brother, are some I shall cherish. The babe will have strong fury, no doubt, but sweet Sol will make a wonderous king.

I CLOSED Queen Lilianna's journal and hugged the tattered pages to my heart. She seemed so . . . kind. An enemy queen, and I desperately wanted to know her. Desperately wished she had not been killed so viciously. A mother who loved her children and her king. As Legion promised, the Ettan royalty vowed for a great deal more than advantage.

I desired the same. I would not receive it.

Rolling onto my side in my bed, I tucked the journal beneath my pillow. After the tea, I'd asked to be alone and hoped Mavie and Siv were finding some sort of enjoyment at the revelry still going on in the courtyards. I could not shake the witch girl's words. Foolish and ridiculous as they were, they burrowed deep in my heart and mind and unnerved every last stitch keeping me together.

A frenzied screech rang down the corridor of the longhouse. I bolted off my bed. A clatter rang out, and I snatched my robe, slinging it around my shoulders, then hurried into the corridor. Some of our serfs and patrols sped past my door, barking commands as they darted outside.

Mavie and Siv both poked their heads out of their chamber.

"What's happened?" I asked.

Siv shook her head. "We don't know."

I turned back into my room, snatched up the knife Legion had given me, and returned to the corridor. Siv had her dagger, and Mavie held a wooden rod—I didn't question where she'd found it, simply followed the rush of frantic people outside.

Across the lawns Ravenspire guards stood in steady rows, blocking all entrances of the gates, all houses, all towers. My father hunched over a cane, a fur robe around his bony shoulders. A scowl deepened the shadows on his face. My mother stood at his side, hand over her mouth.

Something had gone terribly wrong for the guards to descend upon us like this. I rushed to my father.

"What's happened?" I asked, breathless.

My father had been muttering something to my mother and paused. He glanced over my shoulder as Runa slowly sauntered up the hillside, as though nothing chaotic were happening all around us.

"Whatever has happened?" she sang.

I gritted my teeth. My sister cared for nothing but herself and I wanted to hit something.

"An attempt was made on the king. An assassination," rasped my father.

I covered my mouth. Terrible as Zyben was, to be attacked so close to Ravenspire was unheard of. When the king traveled, then he had cause for worry.

"Bleeding Agitators," my father went on. "They're a plague."

"Was anyone harmed?" I asked.

I wasn't thinking of the king.

"No," he said. "No, I heard it was a poor shot. The guards are still scouring the wood for the assassin."

If Agitators were attacking again, then they must have enough of a following not to fear retaliation as much. Two royal attacks in less than two weeks. My stomach clenched. They'd see us dead or die trying themselves.

"Those bastards will be executed tomorrow. No more delay," Father went on. "The king made vows that their screams would be heard throughout all the kingdoms of the Fate's Ocean. Hurry, now. No one is to be out of doors tonight."

My family turned toward the longhouse. Runa seemed perturbed her sleep had been interrupted at all, but I couldn't stomach the idea of being in my room. Burdensome thoughts battered my skull. Questions about why the Agitators were striking now. How they'd come so close to Castle Ravenspire. What they wanted. It made no sense to me. They'd never gone for the king, truth be told; I'd been the first royal they'd attacked to my knowledge.

Agitators stirred contention, true. Ravenspire hated them because of it, but most attacks had been thieving—food carts, textiles—the sort of thieving done when folk couldn't feed themselves. They had never stooped to such violence.

True they were zealots who worshiped a dead prince. The fae boy prince Lilianna loved so much, but the Ferus royals were dead and gone. It was the only thing I once feared about Agitators. If they worshipped a ghost, could they be reasoned with?

Now I feared them because they had altered course to murder and assassination.

I doubted a bloody, merciless execution would solve

anything. More likely, it would stir Agitator hearts to anger even more.

"Come," Mavie said. "We should get inside."

I bit the inside of my cheek and tied my knife to my waist with my dressing robe belt. "I need air."

"Elise," Siv warned. "We shouldn't—"

"I didn't say we," I went on. "Please. I can't be in that room."

Siv narrowed her eyes. "Then, we're coming with you."

I shook my head. "You'll be noticed missing more than me. You know our serfs enjoy ratting others out. Give me this. I have but a few nights alone remaining before I'm promised to another."

Siv opened her mouth to protest, but Mavie stopped her with a gesture. "There is an old schoolhouse from the Ferus era. It's away from the walls, so we won't worry about anyone slipping by the guards, but it's covered in a bower, so you'll have privacy. By the north tower."

I grinned. "I won't be long. You have my word."

Siv pouted as Mavie dragged her toward the longhouse, but she didn't fight me. They knew how afraid I was to take vows. They knew I believed to my core it would be the death of my freedom. Perhaps I overexaggerated, but I could not help the way I felt.

Enough of a crowd remained that I traveled the length of the courtyard without drawing attention from the guards. They demanded folk return to their dwellings, demanded patrols at every door. I ducked into the trimmed gardens of rowan and wolfsbane and ferns.

Light on my feet, another twenty paces, I reached the bower covering the schoolhouse and slipped inside.

A heavy scent of dust and old parchment burned my nose, but I assumed this place was rarely used. A podium with tallow candles was at the head of the rounded room. A table with nothing but a thick book and a copper plate engraved with the symbol of the gods' tree. A few pews made of black oak lined the center, and the lancet windows were painted in scenes from folklore. Night Folk blessing the trees. Sea snakes and monsters churning the tides. Fury drawing shadows, breaking the soil, healing. So many things I'd not heard fury accomplish. Then again, I didn't know all there was on fury.

Different lands, different powers.

Little by little the night quieted. An occasional footstep would go by, a few murmured voices, but no one bothered my solitude. I remained in the frontmost bench, thinking of what the veiled girl told me, how she spoke of change, how I longed for it, and how I'd lost faith in it.

I didn't know the tears were there until a drop splashed on my hand.

Tomorrow I'd watch brutality. I should be glad for it, but my stomach burned as I imagined the way Timorans would cheer, how they'd rage as Ettan Agitators were tortured and flayed.

"Elise."

I startled and sucked in a sharp gasp. The door closed, and Legion locked it before he lifted his eyes to me once more.

I wiped at my face, embarrassed. "What . . . what are you doing here?"

"I bribed Mavie to give up where you'd gone," he said with a grin. "She has a true love for figs."

I laughed softly and turned around again. My heart pounded in time with his steps over the floor; a trill shivered down my spine when he sat beside me on the bench. He'd replaced his longbow with two knives, and his skin looked recently scrubbed.

He said nothing.

As if he sensed I needed quiet, Legion sat beside me, studying the glass in the windows.

I wasn't certain how long we sat in silence, but it sounded foreign when I spoke. "I'm grateful you were unharmed during the hunt. Did you see anything? The attempt on the king?"

Legion shook his head and leaned his elbows over his knees. "No. I wasn't close at the time, but I'm not convinced it was an Agitator."

"Why?"

He let out a sigh. "Too perfect a shot. The arrow ended in a small notch on a tree, perfectly level, deep in the trunk. A clearly aimed shot. As if intending to miss. An Agitator bold enough to kill the king wouldn't try to miss. They might not succeed, but they'd shoot to kill."

"Then who?"

"I don't know, and I don't like not knowing."

I smiled softly and rested my hand on his forearm. Legion studied my touch before he covered my hand with his own. Another breath and he brought my palm to his lips, a signature mark from him I was coming to love.

"I feared for you," he said. The admission was soft, as though he considered not speaking at all. "When you weren't in your chamber. It took me from behind, this fear deep in my chest, and for a moment I could not think straight. I would've torn the longhouse to pieces had Mavie not seen me."

His words lifted me from the sorrow of my thoughts, eased my burdens, set fire to my heart. A few nights. Freedom for a few nights. I had no wish to waste them, no desire to spend them parted from Legion. Swallowing the last of my nerves, I scooted against him. My palm stroked the far side of his face, drawing him to look at me. I was lost in the silky black of his eyes. The woodsy hint on his tanned skin.

"What brings your tears, Elise?"

My chin quivered. I turned away, embarrassed, but Legion used his fingers to guide my face back to him.

"Everything," I admitted. "Tomorrow traitors to my king will die, and I cry for them. I'm the weakest kind of Timoran. I hate that I feel this torment inside, how I love my people and hate them all at once. How I love Ettans but stand above them. How I'm fascinated by fae but fear them. The weight of it is crushing, and tomorrow I will be expected to sneer, to shout, to hate.

"The king will execute them not only in his name, but mine. What if he asks me to speak? How can I look condemned men in the eyes, who were not to blame for what happened to me, who fight for their land that was stolen from them? How do I look at them and feel nothing?" I pressed a hand to my chest, killing a sob before it burst out.

"You steal my words," he said, eyes on the ground. "Timoran is a land that has not been terribly kind to me for most of my life. I find myself disenchanted by the whole of society most days, but these weeks with you have stirred something within me and I hardly know how to make sense of it. Your love of this land and its people—it's *original* people—I don't know why I care, but you've made it so. There are no words for you."

"You make me too grand a thing."

"Not possible."

"I sound cowardly. Hiding in here, crying. When I should either use my voice, or not, then stand by my choice without faltering this way."

Legion scoffed and straightened. "True. You could be bold and sure on every choice, but then I would fear you might not be human."

I laughed, not a pretty sound, more a gurgle in my throat mingled with tears.

Legion chuckled and went on. "I was told once, each decision we wrestle in our minds, each consequence we weigh, is how we gain faith in our final choices. We take time to decide who we are and when we choose, as you said, we stand by those choices fiercely."

"Who told you that? I like it."

A furrow gathered over his brow. "Actually, now that I think of it, I don't remember."

I sighed and pointed my eyes at the domed beams above us. "In truth, I am brought to tears for more than executions and Agitators and cruel kings. Call me a fool, for I knew it would happen, but being matched leaves me feeling like my choices, good or bad, will no longer be my own."

"So, you do know the king has ordered me to select a match," he said, voice hoarse.

"Yes. He told me before the hunt."

"It was not supposed to come so quickly. How am I to do it?"

The burden was heavy in his voice. A touch of sympathy reached out for Legion, though it would not make his lot easier if I could not hold my tears. I forced a wry smile. "Well, how did you plan to do it when you first came?"

"The answer to that isn't simple anymore. Nothing is like it was when I first came."

"Oh," I said, grinning through the heat in my cheeks. "Has so much changed?"

He returned my smile, then curled his hand around the back of my neck. I wasn't fooling him by playing coy. Legion leaned his face closer. Our brows touched. He paused and ran his fingers through my hair. "I ask how I am to give you to some fool because I do not know how. How am I to accomplish anything I set out to do here when my heart *burns* to have you for myself?"

I started to speak; there weren't words, but the moment demanded a reply.

He pressed a finger to my mouth, silencing any more attempts. His eyes broke me, put me at his mercy. There was enough time to pull away, enough time to stop this, and enough to admit I'd never stop this even if I should.

Legion kissed me.

He claimed my lips with a passionate tug on the back of my head, drawing me in, so I never wished to be set free.

I gasped and he took it for his own with the sly glide of his mouth on mine. Legion canted his head, parted my lips; teeth and tongues collided as desire grew. He tasted like rain and honey.

My arms curled around his neck, needing him closer. Legion's hands went to my waist, his body pressed against mine. I tilted back, fingers digging into his shoulders, and pulled him over me.

Echoes of his knives on the wood, of our greedy breaths filled the old schoolhouse. His weapon belt dug into me, and when I winced, he made quick work to be rid of it.

I thanked him through touch. Legion groaned into my mouth when my hands slipped beneath his tunic to his skin, tracing the lines and sinews of his chest. I didn't know if there was a delicate way to remove my night robe, certainly I didn't find it as I tangled my arms in linen, trying to keep him as close as I could.

Legion hovered above me, eyes dark with desire. His fingers ran the length of my neck to my chemise and tugged it off my shoulder.

Exposed in such a way, I expected to feel a bit of embarrassment, but Legion's eyes gleamed in a greedy want.

I arched into him.

He pressed a kiss at the swell of one breast; his tongue dragged across the peak, heating my skin. "This is dangerous."

"Yes," I said. Forbidden to touch another during the bidding, not to mention how a negotiator touching his charge would set the town aflame in scandal should anyone discover the truth.

None of it mattered.

Another graceful motion and the tunic was gone over his head. I marveled at his strength, the scars on his skin from street fights, I assumed. A pretty, black stone hung from a chain around his neck, like a bit of the night sky he carried with him always.

I kissed the place over his heart. He dragged his callused fingertips up the sensitive skin of my inner thigh, slipping between my legs to my throbbing center once again.

I drew in a sharp breath, and he kissed me until the bright shock of sensation faded into pleasure.

The roughness raised my skin, reaching for more. His kiss was a flame, his clever fingers a fog. Like spinning until the mind couldn't focus, like power you couldn't control, the kind that robbed you of wits.

His gaze met mine, unblinking, watching me as I melted beneath his touch, as I bit my lip to keep from making humiliating sounds and failed. His fingers thrust and flicked and tormented.

Words burned up in sensation.

Our hands explored each other, but there was still a wall between us. He could not have me fully. I did not know how I knew it, perhaps the look in his eyes, the desire he couldn't truly take, but there was a hideous line I knew he would not cross.

Still, I planned to lavish his body as long as I could. With trembling fingers, I unclasped the buckle of his belt and slipped one palm below the waistline of his trousers. I gripped the warmth of his length in my hands and stroked.

He gasped. A furrow gathered between his brows as my touch drew him to a delightful madness much the same as he'd done to me. His face grew flushed. I lost my ability to speak when his thumb circled the swollen apex of my entrance.

Legion brought me to the precipice. I writhed under him,

panting his name, then spilled over the ledge in a collision of heat and need.

When I cracked my eyes, Legion's face was close. A sly sort of smirk teased the corner of his mouth, but his eyes were black with sensual greed.

We weren't finished.

I didn't look away and curled one arm around his waist, urging his body closer. Through short gasps, my body still alight in the fading heat in my core, I tightened my grip on Legion's length.

He burrowed his face against my neck, my name on his tongue like a soft vow.

"Elise, gods . . ." He lost his words when my thumb dragged over the sensitive tip. Legion rocked his hips faster, deeper. "Dammit, I'm . . ."

He didn't finish before the hot, burst of his own release spilled over my fingers, my belly. His body jerked in my arms until he slumped over me, breathless.

For a drawn pause we held each other, unwilling to move. At long last, Legion lifted his head.

He pressed another needy kiss to my neck. "Gods, Elise. This . . . *you* mean everything."

Legion's teeth scraped down my neck, my ear. He kissed me until I could think no more, until all I could do was *feel*.

CHAPTER TWENTY-TWO

MAVIE RATTLED ON. Something to do with Bevan and Odda in the kitchen and their glances and grins.

"He gets redder than a rose when she walks in," Mavie said as she finished with the laces on her bodice. Her dark hair hung in curls around her shoulders, and she seemed alive. Like she ought to be, I thought. She was born Ettan, but she should not be damned to servitude for it.

Perhaps someday I would find the fierceness in my desire like Legion described.

The very thought of him sent my heart to my throat. All day I'd floated about, catching glimpses of him here and there, but my uncle had taken his time as those in the hunt were questioned, then cleared and assigned to the assassin hunt. I tried not to think of what we did last night, of the sweet taste of his mouth, or the gasps my touch drew from him. I thought of what we'd done in the schoolhouse and what it would mean at the end of the celebrations.

We both could not be free of the vow negotiations. But perhaps knowing he felt the same, I might dare mention a life of love in the shadows. Destined to be half a husband and half a wife, but if we were favored the slightest by fate, maybe it would be enough.

"Elise." Mavie lifted her brows.

I'd dazed off as I braided my hair. "Yes."

"When did you return to your room?"

I swallowed a scratch back down. "I'm, I'm not sure."

Mavie smirked and shot Siv a knowing look that wasn't returned. "I assume you were escorted back by *Herr* Grey."

The curl to my lips sent my friend into a fit of giggles that reminded me of when we were younger girls watching the dock men toss sacks onto their barges.

"Enough," I said, my face red in the mirror.

"I agree," Siv grumbled and slid a knife into her ankle boot.

Mavie balked. "Always the sour one." My friend began twirling my braid into a crown around my head, but Siv swatted her away.

"I'll finish. Your turn to see that the guards are ready to take the *Kvinna* to the main hall."

Mavie muttered curses for Siv's snarly mood, but handed the last of my braid over to my other friend, who'd yet to smile today.

Silence was at times welcome, but in this moment, it was unfortunate and thick and a nuisance.

"Elise," Siv finally said. "I might be out of turn, but I want you to be careful with Legion Grey."

I studied her in the mirror. She'd expertly hidden herself behind my head as she pinned my braid, so I couldn't see her expression. I folded my hands in my lap. "Why do you say this, Siv? Speak plainly. We've always been honest with each other, haven't we?"

She didn't answer, but finally met my eyes in our reflection. "I don't think you should trust him."

My stomach twisted in a harsh knot. "Again, why do you say this? I must have a reason."

"I just . . . I just think he's dangerous."

I thought I might be understanding, but instead I was angry. A fast, burning kind. "Then he certainly is bad at being the villain. When he had his mouth to my neck last night, he could've easily slit my throat. I made certain he had all the access he wanted."

Siv blinked and let out a long sigh. "I don't wish to upset you, but . . ."

"What happened, Siv?" I snapped and spun around in my seat. "Between the two of you at the bell tower. There is something you've left out. He told me he approached you aggressively but corrected the mistake. I'm not upset you use your voice; I'm upset you don't trust my judgment. I, who has spent the most time with Legion, who pressed him and questioned him, until trust came as naturally as it did for you and Mavie."

Siv finished pinning my coiled braid and stepped back. "I wish you had more people around you that you could truly trust."

I had no idea what she meant, but a knock interrupted us. Tor stepped into the room. "*Kvinna* Elise, it's time to go."

"Right." My insides clenched again, but not from anger or seduction. The execution was beginning. With a layered glance at Siv, I lifted my hem and followed Tor into the corridor.

"It's off tonight," Halvar was saying when I left the room.

My pulse raced when Legion smacked Halvar's chest, shutting him up, and stepped to me. Siv hurried past us and took her place by Mavie. I didn't mean to, but I followed her with a glare, and it didn't go unnoticed.

"What is it?" Legion whispered.

"Oh. Nothing." I saw no point in telling him about Siv's request. She was wrong, and I believed my point to be valid. In the time I'd known him, Legion had ample opportunity to do me in if he held malice toward me. I hurried to paint my discomfort with a smile as I wrapped my hand around his arm. Never was I so grateful thoughts couldn't be read, for if he could see into my mind as we walked so near each other, he'd likely go red in the face.

The courtyard outside the king's main dwelling was the finest of them all. Private hedges with blooming flowers and a regal fountain in the shape of a raven in flight. Tonight, the courtyard was ugly. The podiums were set, each with a rack where the three Agitators were placed on their knees. Their wrists were bound, then tied above their heads by posts. From the look of them, I doubted they'd had anything to eat and little to drink throughout their imprisonment. One was missing an eye, another bled severely from his mouth. I wasn't positive the third was even alive still, the way he slumped forward, only his bound arms keeping him upright.

Legion followed my stare to the broken men. He dropped his arm and took my hand instead. I held fast, cutting off blood by squeezing, but he never released me until we found our places beside my parents.

"Where is Runa?" I asked my mother.

"She had other worries," my mother said lazily. "No need to bother her with this sort of thing when she is the future queen."

By the hells, everyone acted as though Runa were preparing to take the throne tomorrow.

My fingertips went numb when Zyben rose from his throne and stepped to the edge of his dais. His voice boomed like a god across the yard. "Traitors to the crown belong in the third hell with the most wretched, the most despised in life. You deserve to suffer," he seethed at the podium of broken men. "But we are not without mercy. Denounce your beliefs, give up your fellow Agitators, and you will be granted a swift death."

One of the executioners kicked the lead prisoner. His head flopped forward, but he mumbled a few, sluggish words. "Hail . . . the N-N-Night Prince." The man chuckled and spat blood at the king, though he was too far.

Zyben's glare darkened. "So be it. You've been tried and found guilty of treason. For your crimes—you die by pain for the suffering you have caused Timoran, by blood for the blood you have spilled, and by cries for the tears of the people you have harmed." Zyben waved his hand and returned to his throne.

In one step, three executioners were at the backs of the Agitators. My father chuckled. Ill as he was, his eyes were alive now, as if torture thrilled him. I clenched my eyes and squeezed Legion's hand. He urged me against his side, disguising it as a mere comfort for a princess with a weak disposition.

First came the barbed whips.

I jolted at each lash. Each roar of agony from broken men.

The third was not dead, but on the verge. He whimpered under the whip, while his companions wailed.

Bile rose in my throat. I swallowed it down.

The whips ceased, but next would come knives, carving runes into the skin, slitting gaping holes in their flesh, watching them bleed.

I shuddered. "This is wrong."

"Hush, Elise," my mother snapped.

I shook my head. "It's wrong," I whispered to no one.

"Change takes time," Legion said against my ear. "It takes time, but if you desire it, you can make it happen. I have every faith in you."

"But . . . these men—"

"Have committed crimes in the name of a dead royal," Legion said logically.

No. They were suffering for dead men. The Agitators who'd attacked us in the clearing were not these men. This punishment did not fit their crimes. Something burned inside me, from the soil through my feet and legs, as if the earth mourned with me.

"My King!" I croaked before I could stop myself.

"Elise," Legion begged and pulled me against him again, trying to tear me back. But it was too late.

Zyben held up a hand to hold.

"*Kvinna* Elise Lysander," he said. "My niece, the one who has suffered more than us at the hands of traitors. Do you wish to speak, Niece? Do you wish to deliver a lash? Say it and it is yours."

I melted beneath every hungry, bloody stare. Legion's arms were frozen around me, holding me against him. I felt the hammer of his pulse, could sense the way his mind reeled, desperate to save me from my foolish mouth.

"I . . . I only wish—" What did I wish? For this to end, to find a better way for justice? What crimes did these men truly commit? Had we turned so savage that we kill due to association?

"Elise, please," Legion muttered.

Whatever power urged me to speak before, loosened my tongue again. Doubtless the power of stupidity.

"King Zyben, these men have suffered well enough for their crimes."

An audible gasp raced through the crowd. My father seared me with his gaze. Were we not in public, Leif Lysander would lift his weakened hand and strike at my mouth until I could not speak.

My uncle tilted his head, a cruel expression on his face. "Suffered enough, you say?"

"My daughter suffers from the trauma, Majesty. She doesn't know what she's saying," my mother insisted. What little affection Zyben had for his sister might work in my favor.

"These men were not the ones who attacked me, My King. Those men died for their crimes. These men have their punishment, have learned your wrath."

Zyben's eyes were like blue ice; even at this distance, I noted the hatred in them.

"Tor, stand ready," Legion hissed at my back. Ready for what? Would he take up arms against a king for me? What had I done?

"Agitators are traitors, Niece. As a royal in my household, I expect you would know this, but I see you stand against it.

What would you have us do, *Kvinna* Elise? Welcome them who have slaughtered my people? Women and children? Is this the sort of weak-boned leadership my sister's house has bred?"

"No," my mother insisted. She shot to her feet. "Our first daughter is strong and will prove formidable to our foes, brother. Have mercy on Elise, I beg of you. She is not right, has not been right since the attack."

Zyben scoffed. I hadn't noticed, but during the venomous discussion, Legion had positioned himself in front of me. Mavie and Siv huddled close together, Siv with her blade in her hand, Mavie praying to silent gods. Three hells, I'd placed everyone I cared about in harm's way. I deserved to be on the rack for my brainless tongue.

My uncle spread his arms wide, a wicked sneer across his mouth. "I am not without mercy . . ."

I held my breath, waiting for his capriciousness to deliver a painful blow.

I wouldn't get my answer. A swift *ffft, ffft, ffft* broke the stunned silence. A scream. A gasp. A wet cough. An arrow pierced through the king's throat, his middle, his chest. Blood stained his woolen doublet and fur cloak. Then, the king stumbled forward, face down in his own blood.

Dead.

CHAPTER TWENTY-THREE

WHAT CAME NEXT WAS A BLUR.

For at least two heartbeats no one moved, stunned into horrified silence at the sight of Zyben soaking in his own blood on the dais. Then another scream came. It was close. I had a moment to wonder if it was my mother's cry.

The sound was drowned by roars at the gates. From every direction Ravenspire patrols flung arrows, axes, and maces at darkly clad intruders. They scaled the gates like web spinners on their silken threads.

The next that I remember was a pair of sturdy arms pulling me away, toward the inner palace. Out of range. Out of sight. Legion held my hand in his, a blade in his other. Tor and Halvar flanked Mavie and Siv, and as a unit we darted into Castle Ravenspire as the hot reek of blood filled the night.

My knees buckled. Legion caught me before I fell.

I clung to his arm as he shoved through the heavy doors. "My parents!"

"They ran," he said briskly.

"Legion, where do we go?" Tor asked, his tone an even keel, as though moments as this were where he thrived.

"Somewhere out of sight until we can figure our next steps. Move fast, stay low, stay in the shadows."

Mavie crouched at once, her hands over her head. The corridors were packed with fleeing serfs, maids, and stewards. A few wayward nobles fumbled out of royal rooms, half-dressed, drunken, or well loved. Most in a daze. Until they listened to the roar of voices rising outside.

"All hail the dead king!"

"Death to false kings! Death to false queens!"

The sight of Ravenspire patrols, rushing into the fray with weapons at the ready, it didn't take much thought to piece together what had happened. Soon the inner corridors racked in screams and terror the same as the lawns.

"This way," Legion boomed, ushering us through a hall door. It would take us through a stairwell, into the sitting rooms. There we could cross into the banquet halls, down into the kitchens.

I suffocated my skirts in my grip, keeping close to Legion's back. Much too late, the warrior in me sparked to life and I recalled the knife I now kept tucked on my leg. Lifting my gown indecently high, I ripped the blade from its sheath. My grip no longer trembling. There would be time to fear later.

Legion stared at me, then the knife, face as stone.

"I promised," I said in a rough breath.

"You did." He clutched my wrist above my blade. "Do *not* hesitate should you need to use it."

We hurried down the cross hall and spilled into the wide

stairwell. Windows lined the space, open to the night. Halvar demanded we get low, notched a dart in a tricky crossbow I'd not seen before, then gave us cover.

I breathed only once we descended the final stair. The main house shuddered in chaos. Whimpers of those attempting to hide beneath a chaise here, a table there. Brainlessly terrified people lunged through us, knocking Mavie to the ground. Legion hardly paused as he reached down and dragged her back to her feet.

He moved like a shadow. Slipping from one place to the next. Halvar and Tor moved much the same. If we lived through this, I told myself, I'd ask more details of his life in the gutters. Had he thieved? Joined a corner gang? Murdered? None of it mattered now, but my mind was spinning, desperate to grab onto anything outside this reality. The reality that the fortress of Timoran, that Castle Ravenspire was under attack.

"Stop!" Legion commanded all at once.

We obeyed and slammed our backs against the wall as he cautiously peered out a window overlooking the bloody courtyard.

Legion clicked his tongue and Tor responded. He was at his side. "They have the Agitators from the execution," Tor reported. "They're cheering, taking them to safety."

"They're Agitators," Halvar snarled.

The obvious attackers. Vengeance for slaughtering their family camp, for taking their men.

A door burst open from another cross hall and a frantic woman tripped over her gowns. Her eyes lifted and found me. "Elise! Thank the gods. Elise!"

"Inez," I said in a hushed whisper. The fool would draw their attention straight to us if she kept shouting.

"Elise," she sobbed and rushed across the hallway, halting in the center of the window. "Oh, Elise! They've taken the north tower, the queen—"

Inez let out a gurgled moan. Mavie screamed and collapsed back against the wall. A dart much like Halvar's had pierced Inez on the side of her skull. She wobbled on her feet. Then another black dart whizzed through open window, striking her in the shoulder.

She fell forward. Tor caught her and let her down gently.

Mavie wailed and hugged my neck. Inez's lifeless eyes stared at the ceiling, blood staining her porcelain face. My blood turned to ice. I couldn't take my eyes away. Inez, foolish Inez. We'd been crouched, hiding out of sight, and she'd just stood there. Panicked. An open target at the window.

A memory stirred. My chest squeezed painfully.

"Watch the window," I said under my breath. Bleeding hells. *Watch the window.*

The witch girl's omen to Inez. She was real, and if a window brought death for poor, stupid, and innocent Inez, then I had no idea what lay in store for me.

Trust the undeserving, was mine.

When I see the beast within . . .

One thing was certain, if I remained frozen and unmoving, then death would come here. "Get up, Mavie. We must go."

"There," Legion demanded, pointing to one of the empty rooms near the banquet hall. We obeyed and sprinted to the small room. Maps and books and desks were at each wall. The royal scribes would direct their missives here. It was abandoned, and not long ago by the smoke still flurrying from a hastily discarded herb roll.

Tor slammed the door at our backs, then with Halvar, barricaded the door with a desk.

"Away from the window," Legion said, but what came next rattled me to my bones. Legion's lips curled and he pointed at Siv. "Grab her."

Siv tried to bolt away, but Halvar hooked his elbow around her shoulders and held her against his body. "Nah, nah, little one," he crooned. "You'll stay right close to us."

"Legion!" I shouted, forgetting for a moment, we were under attack. "What are you doing?"

Either he did not hear me, or he ignored me. I watched in horror how Siv buckled beneath his glare, she shook her head, tears in her eyes as Legion grabbed a tuft of her hair. "Anything to confess before I cut out your eyes?"

This was not the man who whispered in my ear last night. A man with a gentle, loving touch. Red flashed in his eyes, hatred on his face. I grabbed his arm, pulling him away, but it did little good.

"P-Please," Siv whimpered. "I knew n-n-nothing. I promise."

"Stop!" Mavie cried.

"Legion!" I pounded on his shoulder. Once, three times. His sleek dagger was aimed at Siv's throat. "Stop this! Stop!"

At last, he faced me, a wild rage in his eyes. "She's an Agitator, Elise!"

He might as well have slapped me. My breath sucked out of my lungs, and I simply gaped like a fool. "What?" Real tears dripped down Siv's cheeks. I shook my head. "No. She's a serf—a maid. She's . . . my friend."

"Think well, Elise," he snapped. "How long has she been with you?" Not quite a turn. I didn't say it out loud. Legion didn't wait anyway. "At age twenty, don't you suppose she would've been a serf before now? She befriended you quickly, did she not?"

Siv reached for me. "Elise . . . I—"

"Not your turn to talk, lovely," Halvar taunted and tightened his grip on her.

"There is no time to explain it all, Elise," Legion went on. "But at the sparring night, the way she pinned Tor is an Agitator's move. It is how they're trained. Think of the attack, how the man had pinned you down. It was the same. We threatened her, learned the truth. She'd been planted at the manor to assassinate *you*."

I was going to be sick. "No."

A pathetic response, but it was all I could muster.

"Pick off the royals from the bottom up," Tor said, his glare on Siv.

"Elise, I . . . I'm sorry," Siv said through her tears. And that was all I needed. The truth. My friend the Agitator. "I changed . . . I got to know you. I left my clan, betrayed *them*, because we . . . we became friends. You must believe me."

I took an unsteady step back. Mavie's arms curled around me. I wanted to look away, but I couldn't peel my eyes from the honey golden gleam. Siverie. She'd defended me, worried for me. Secretly, she cared for Mattis, though she'd never admit it. She knew the blade . . . I coughed, clutching my neck. She *knew* the blade nearly as well as Legion.

Had I wanted friendship so desperately, I missed the signs?

"You were right, Siv," I whispered. "I wish I had more people I could trust around me, too."

Then, I left her to Legion. Betrayal a new knife in my heart.

"Who told you they'd come tonight?" Legion pressed.

"I'm telling the truth," Siv cried. "I left my clan. I abandoned them. Out in the open like this, I will die should they find me. I gave up the plan months ago, as I told you at the bell tower."

"You knew," I whispered. "And left me alone with her."

Legion glanced over his shoulder. "She knows what would've happened should she put a finger on you. I do not hold back on details."

"Better to keep your enemies close, *Kvinna*," Halvar said as if this were all a game.

Legion studied Siv's face, but eventually sheathed his blade. "She comes with us. We might have use for her should we need to make a trade."

"Agitators would not attack Castle Ravenspire," Siv insisted as Halvar adjusted his grip to run with her in his hand. "You must believe me—something is amiss here."

"I must believe nothing," Legion said, but he tilted his head. "Nevertheless, we keep on our toes. We don't know what is happening here tonight."

"Do we go forward?" Tor said, but the tone came out with underlying meaning. Something the rest of us didn't understand.

Legion shot his eyes to me, mouth tight. After a few somber moments, he nodded to Tor. "Yes. There is no better choice."

I held tightly to Mavie who trembled and fought bravely not to cry.

"Right, then," Halvar said. "Where is he?"

Legion dug into his tunic and removed the black, polished stone from around his neck. His thumb rubbed over the surface, and he peered at it. Like looking at a reflection. Nothing happened, and I wondered if the stone was a totem of sorts, something to help him think, until at last he said, "He's made it to the kitchens. Hurry now, if we want to keep our heads, we're running short on time."

Legion allowed no time to question him before he guided us back into the corridors.

Screams rattled in my skull, though somewhere in my mind I knew they were dying. Steel against steel rang in the dark. A battle still raged, but hardly. It was ending. Someone, soon, would be victorious.

Had Ravenspire fallen? Had the Agitators overtaken the guards? In the terror of the night, it was hard to know.

Mavie clung to my skirts as we ran. Siv struggled to keep pace with Halvar. I thought she might be crying. I didn't care. Yet I did all at once.

Fear burned for . . . everything.

My parents. Runa. As distant as we were, they were my family, and I did not want them to die. But they were clever. I had to believe they'd find a way to escape or fight back and survive.

"Elise," Siv said.

"Hush," Halvar demanded.

She ignored him. "Elise, you must listen to me. They cannot be trusted either. Something is strange about them, they—"

"I said hush." Halvar paused long enough to grip Siv's jaw and frighten her back into silence.

Mavie hiccupped at my side and took hold of my hand. "Eli," she whispered, her voice small and raw. "I did not like you at first."

I shot her a furtive glance, unsure where she was going with this. "I remember."

Mavie had come to the manor when we were both around thirteen. She would serve me, then stick her tongue out when she thought I couldn't see.

"But . . ." Mavie went on, gasping, "you are my friend. Believe that I am who I say. Titles do not matter. We are friends."

Tears stung behind my eyes. Sweet Mavie. We ran for our lives, but she claimed the moment to remind me I was not truly alone, there remained some people I could trust.

We rounded the corner into the banquet hall. Legion went first, then wheeled back behind the wall. A knife had aimed for his heart. He let out a growl, then threw one back.

I lifted my blade, ready to fight those beyond the wall, but was knocked off balance when Mavie fell against me.

I caught her and saw.

In her stomach the knife aimed at Legion had burrowed deep. She let out a gasp, eyes wide with fear.

My stun robbed me of breath. "Mavs. *Mavs!*"

I shouted at nothing and everything. It drew Legion's attention, then Tor. Siv sobbed and crumbled against Halvar who, for once, seemed unsure of what to do. Mavie's eyes spun to me. I wrapped her in my arms and tumbled to the ground with her when her body went limp. Ragged breaths broke from her lungs. The smell of blood filled the corridor.

"El-Eli," she whispered. "I d-d-don't want to die."

I hugged her head to my chest, my cheek on her brow, my tears in her hair. "No, you won't. You won't, Mavs."

Legion kneeled on the side with the knife, inspected the place of it. His eyes lifted and said what I already knew. I shook my head, desperate to scream and rage.

"Elise . . ." he began.

"No!" I shook my head, angry at him for giving up. "No."

In my arms, Mavie shuddered, her grip on my wrist went slack.

"Mavie," I said when her breathing quieted. I shook her. Harder the longer I went unanswered. "Mavie! Wake up, Mavs!"

I kept saying it, over and over. No response came.

It never would.

CHAPTER TWENTY-FOUR

I SCREAMED HER NAME, tears on my face. Hands peeled me away from her. No! I couldn't leave her. I refused. She needed help. Needed healing. I fought as arms embraced me. My fists swung. I wanted to lash out, strike anything. Kill everything.

The arms tightened. My head fell to a chest. I breathed in a shuddering gasp. Rain and spice. Legion had me in his arms, keeping me still, the beat of his heart a ballast in the agony. His hand rested on the back of my head.

I trembled and wrapped my arms around his waist.

No one said anything for a few moments. Mavie was gone and it was too cruel a truth to accept. Too wretched to understand.

"We must keep going," Tor's voice broke through the heavy cloud settling in my chest. "They're coming."

Legion's arms tightened around me. "Elise, we can't stay here."

Like a spark of a flame, anger latched in my heart. The one

who'd killed her was kept from me by a mere wall. I wrenched out of Legion's arms, knife in hand, and turned the corner. Only a man, sprawled out on the floor, Legion's knife in his heart, remained.

"You killed him," I muttered, grateful and disappointed all at once. This time, the thought of killing didn't frighten me. I'd wanted to be the one to end the man responsible for taking Mavie's goodness from this bleeding kingdom.

"You drew blood," Halvar said, a panic in his voice. "The night is—"

"I do not need reminding!" Legion returned, a coarseness to his voice, a temper that was almost frightening.

"Go," Tor suddenly snapped. "Go now. We cannot wait any longer."

In my head, I knew it. If we did not want to meet the same fate as Mavie, we needed to move. The thought of abandoning her here burned like a thousand knives. My feet moved me away, but a piece of my heart would always remain there in the hall of Castle Ravenspire.

"The swiftest route is through the banquet hall," Legion said. He entered the space where Mavie's murderer lay dead and retrieved his knife, pausing for a moment to inspect the blood on the blade before he cleaned the edge on the dead man's chest.

I was as ice. Cold and hardened. I hardly heard his instruction, simply followed. Still in Halvar's grip, Siv cried silent tears. She looked at me, searching, perhaps, for a bit of comfort. I gave her nothing. She'd lied and tricked both Mavie and me. Siv didn't lose a friend tonight. In my mind, she could not claim the word.

We crept down the corridor, leery of windows, and shadows. Legion rounded into a narrow passageway, and I recognized the spot as the entrance to the king's throne room. Light spilled from the open doorway, and a voice rose in cries, chants, and cheers. Legion held up a fist and peered into the doorway. I leaned around him, gaining a sliver of sight in the room.

The throne room was packed with darkly dressed people, armed in blades and bows. The insurrectionists. But among them were a spattering of Ravenspire guards. Their blue cloaks with gold threads bright in the sea of pitch. Why did the guards stand among their enemies?

My eyes lifted to the dais with the king and queen's seats. My hands went numb. Calder stood at the front, Zyben's bloody circlet of briars on his brow. But there at his side stood Runa. She had a silver tiara atop her head and the queen's gilded cloak on her shoulders.

Three hells! Kneeled before them were my parents and Queen Annika. The guards . . . pointed their weapons at them!

Legion tugged me back, out of sight. Though I couldn't see, each word spoken in the room sank into me. Memories never to be forgotten.

"Dear Annika," Calder said, mockingly. "Pledge, like Mara. Surely your husband's sister is enough to give you confidence. Pledge your fealty and you will live."

I curled against Legion. For comfort through what I knew would come, but in a way, I needed him to keep me from barging into the room, screaming, fighting, and no mistake, dying. My mother pledged loyalty to Calder, naturally. With Zyben dead, he was the heir apparent. But why did the queen resist? A better question—why had the attackers crowded around the new king?

Annika's cutting voice rose above the murmurs in the crowd. "Death to traitors," she seethed. "You sent the attack at the hunt."

"Well, we couldn't have tonight simply come out of nowhere," Calder replied with a laugh. "Alas, my queen and I have found our families difficult to kill."

Runa snickered. "Yes, I thought for sure at least my father would go when we allowed the cursed ones onto Lysander land."

I coughed against Legion's body and clapped a hand to my mouth. Runa had breached our gates. The cursed ones? All I saw was the black in their eyes, their mouths. Did my sister use the Blood Wraith, too? I'd been right, though, something had been wrong with those men and women that night.

"You kill your father, steal the throne," Annika went on. "You are no king. You are a coward!"

I gasped, and now Legion's hand covered my mouth.

Calder laughed. "Strong words, Annika. But they mean nothing since you are there, on your knees, and I am . . . here. Last chance."

Annika was not kind. She was brutal like her husband had been. But she did not falter. "I will never bow to false kings and the whore who dares call herself a queen."

It happened almost instantly. The slice of a blade, the thud of a body hitting the floor. Calder sighed dramatically. "Well, now we have that done with. Well fought, my people!"

The crowd roared.

"Hells," I muttered. Calder—he'd called the siege. He'd—

no, he and Runa—they'd taken the throne by force. Those moments of Runa's wicked passion about change and new order, of her disappointment when I did not comply. Her lack of respect for Annika, her disinterest in Zyben. She'd been plotting this all along.

"The last loose end will be to find Queen Runa's wayward sister."

"She is not loyal."

My heart shuddered hearing my sister's voice mark me for death, the same as Annika.

"Be that as it were," Calder said. "We find Elise, find anyone who has yet to pick their lot in this new era."

His band of killers grunted and shouted their approval.

I was dragged away in a flurry. Legion's grip tightened on my wrist, and he hurried me behind Tor and Halvar with Siv into the banquet hall. I was a fugitive amongst my own family. My sister's hatred left a brand on my soul. I knew she did not think much of me; but to spew such venom, to want to be rid of me? It unlocked a poisonous anger of my own, a pain that dissolved any love once had between sisters.

Another death in this bloody night.

A stairwell was built into the wall just before the banquet room. Tor wrenched it open, waving us inside. We'd escape through the kitchens. Thieves in the night. And then? Where would we go? When the crown wanted you for its own, where could anyone hide?

At the first step, Legion doubled over. His eyes clenched and he pounded a fist against the wall.

"Legion." My hands went to him. His body was hot to the touch.

"I'm fine, go," he grunted as he straightened. Beads of sweat coated his brow.

"Where are you hit?" I asked. Hells, I refused to lose anyone else tonight.

"I'm not," he insisted. "I'm fine."

"Elise, in the kitchens is something we can use to help," Halvar explained.

My next thought recalled those days after Legion's ailment. His red, haggard eyes. His pale skin. *Cursed gods.* Now was not the time for our strongest to fall ill by a damn disease!

I braced my hands on his back on the remaining stairs. His steps more rigid, his fists clenched. The veins in his hands and neck bulged with too much blood. I fought the urge to beg his assurance he was all right; speaking seemed more effort for him by the time we slammed, one after another, into the wide, stone-walled kitchens.

No death here, no tang of blood, only steam in stew pots, savory bread, honey icing, and . . .

"Bevan?"

The old steward wheeled around from a syrup he boiled on the open flame. His eyes were black as midnight, and there was a strangeness on his expression. One of power, not submission, and he didn't look to me long. His eyes flashed to Legion who breathed heavily, leaning against the wall.

"You drew blood!" Bevan shouted. He stormed to Legion and—*hells*—the old man smacked the back of Legion Grey's head. "You bleeding fool. Not enough time has passed since the last incident, so it will be much worse."

"Careful old man," Legion said in a kind of growl. Then, he

blinked, and his voice softened. "Hardly avoidable when the bleeding castle is under attack."

"No need for you to fear a blade," Bevan retorted. "You could've let them strike you."

Legion's jaw tightened. "But it was not me on the line."

His red, glassy eyes lifted to me. Bevan seemed to remember I was there and softened his face at once. He reached a knobby hand for mine. "*Kvinna*, are you harmed?"

I was wordless for too long. My eyes darted between my old steward and Legion—two men who seemed to know each other a great deal more than I thought. "I . . . I'm fine, but Mavie . . ." I couldn't finish.

Bevan winced, understanding, and tapped his head. "May the Otherworld embrace you."

The prayer of the dead did nothing to ease the blow, more drove the agony deeper knowing she needed the prayer to begin with.

"Bevan!" Tor shouted. "Do you have the elixir or not?"

The old steward snapped into action and gathered the syrup concoction from the stove. "It's just finished brewing, but it will likely only hold through the night. He'll need to take another dose in the morning and the next day to return him back to the normal cycle."

"Fine," Tor said with a bit of exasperation. "Just hurry."

Legion groaned and dug the heel of his hand into his forehead. I hurried to his side. Confused as I was, I hated seeing him in pain. Legion tried to turn from me, but I slipped my hand in his and he squeezed through the next moan.

Bevan poured the pungent syrup into a waterskin, then looked at me. "Elise, you calm him."

"What is this ailment? I've never seen such a thing."

"No one has," Bevan said softly and held the skin beneath Legion's nose. Legion swatted at the concoction, snarling.

He was losing himself in agony. He couldn't think straight. I reached for his face. Legion's eyes pooled blood red, his skin drenched in sweat. I blinked through the tears. Watching his body attack him was terrifying and heartbreaking.

I stroked his hot, damp cheek, voice low and calm. "Legion, this will help. Take it."

I didn't know if the concoction would improve him. Bleeding hells, I didn't know what this sickness was, but Tor and Halvar seemed to believe this smelly potion would help. Bevan, too. Legion clenched his eyes, pressed a fist to his head again, but shot out a hand for the waterskin. Bevan handed him the elixir and watched, ensuring Legion swallowed at least three times.

"That'll be good," Bevan said and took it away. "Two more doses. Do not skip them."

Already, Legion's breathing slowed. His eyes were clearer, and he was able to stand straight again. I kept one arm around his waist and beamed at the old steward. "Bevan, I never knew you to be such a healer."

His face contorted and he lowered his gaze. "I'm not a healer, Elise. I'm what is called an Elixist."

"I've never heard the term."

"No, you wouldn't. Not here. It is what folk in the Eastern Kingdom call those who can make otherworldly things with alchemy and potions and spells."

My jaw dropped. "You have fury?"

"Mesmer is what we call it in the East, but our magic is

from the body, not the earth. I am what is called an Alver, my *Kind* is an Elixist. There are different Kinds of Alvers in the East, and I suppose you could say we're cousins of Night Folk. Each kingdom calls us what they wish: fae, sorcerer, Alver, demon. And each kingdom finds ways to abuse us all."

Bevan had . . . fury. Or mesmer, or whatever he'd called it. I would have a thousand questions later, no doubt, but for now I could simply be grateful he healed Legion.

"Bevan has been spoon feeding me for turns," Legion said gruffly.

"Why did you not say you knew each other?"

"There isn't time to explain, Elise," Bevan said. "You must leave now. They will come for you. Already, Captain Magnus has been here seeking you out."

"Jarl!" My eyes widened. "He's on Calder's side?" They didn't need to tell me. I was a fool, thinking Jarl wanted change, the same as me, when really, he'd been plotting a coup with my sister. "Three hells, he told me he wanted to use fury for the sake of Timoran. I think they're going to turn Night Folk into slaves."

"More like experiments," Bevan said. "They will hunt them across the kingdoms. In the east, Alvers are already traded and bartered. With the strength of new Timoran and the fury in this soil, it will grow tenfold. The south accepts fae and mystics, but they will close their walls, defend their folk. Nowhere will be safe, and Timoran will be an unshakeable force. They may well turn their raids to other kingdoms. How many will die, Elise?"

Bevan's voice choked off. He shook his head. "I've seen war. I fled my own kingdom, sought refuge here with my brother's family, lived the life of an Ettan, simply to stay out of sight. But

I've seen enough to know peace is possible, my girl. If the true leaders of this land could unite all the powers, be it spell casting, fury, or mesmer, then lives could be saved, and the power of every land would flourish."

"True leaders?"

A rumble in a nearby corridor silenced us. Legion drew his dagger, Halvar raised the crossbow. Even Siv went for the blade that was no longer there.

"Bevan," Legion said. "We can't wait any longer."

The old steward bounced his gaze between us. "These things take time, there must be choice. She must be willing and loyal. As you must be."

Legion's jaw pulsed. His clear, dark eyes found me, and my heart fluttered. "I cannot speak for Elise, but for me—I am ready."

"Ready for what?" I reached for Legion's hand, needing balance in this chaos. He took it and held fast.

"Elise," Bevan said. "Do you believe in fate?"

"Yes," I said cautiously.

"Then, trust that fate has a part to play in all this. You have a desire to heal this land, but you may also heal another. I knew the moment we first met you could be the one to help Legion."

"Help Legion? How?"

"It can't be said, it must be shown, and now is not the time or place. You must get somewhere safe, and you must choose him. Choose to leave down this path with him."

"Bevan, I don't know what you're talking about." I glanced over my shoulder at Legion. His gaze was on the ground. "I would gladly help him be free of this ailment; is that what you're asking? But I don't have fury or . . . mesmer. How can I help?"

"By choosing him. That is the first step. By trusting him and offering your loyalty. The rest will come the more you know."

"The choice is yours," Legion muttered. "You do not know everything about me, Elise. But I swear to you, what you have seen has been sincere."

This was strange. Pressure gathered in my chest. What secrets did Legion Grey keep? Would I regret trusting him once I discovered them? Possibly, but the trouble was, I did trust him. I cared for him. Deeply. He'd saved me, empowered me. He showed me what true passion and what love could be. In time, secrets could come forward and we could weather them.

I swallowed with effort and tightened my hold on Legion's hand but spoke to Bevan. "I will do anything I can to help him."

Bevan nodded and dug into a cupboard in the corner. He removed a satchel, stuffed with what I assumed might be supplies. Then, took out another vial of a murky sort of liquid. He tossed the satchels at the men. Legion met my eye, a look of trepidation in his expression, but he led me to the center of the kitchen.

"This will bind you to him," Bevan explained. "His strength will be yours; you will not be harmed so long as he's breathing. The bond of loyalty will last through the night."

"Why just through the night?" I was certain, for all he'd done, I would be loyal to Legion Grey until I took my last breath.

Legion answered instead. "It is to ensure your safety as we travel. My strength is yours."

"Yes, but if you're harmed—"

"Elise," he said, as though embarrassed. "I cannot be harmed. I cannot die. Nor can Tor or Halvar. We will not bond with the Agitator because we do not trust her, and this only works with trust."

Siv lowered her gaze to the ground.

"What do you mean you can't die?" My voice was shriller than before.

Shouting in the corridors caused us all to jump. Bevan took my hand, his slate eyes desperate. "Time runs out, *Kvinna*. Make your choice."

The hair raised on the back of my neck. I spared a glance at Siv. She wouldn't look at me. I didn't blame her for not speaking, doubtless she knew none of us would listen. Not after she'd lost our trust so brutally.

Back to Legion, I nodded, but felt more confused than before.

"Take his hand," Bevan instructed.

He passed the vial to Legion who tipped the potion in his mouth. He winced but handed it to me. I followed suit. The taste was harsh. Like peppered spices and vinegar, but I managed to choke down the entire swallow. In the pit of my stomach something warm spread, heating fiercely between my palm and Legion's.

Bevan patted our joined hands. "It must be sealed with a vow."

Legion nodded and cleared his throat. "Elise Lysander. For this night I bind myself, my loyalty, and my protection to you."

My forearm prickled as the power from the potion traveled to my heart. Bevan gave me an encouraging nod.

"Legion Grey, I . . . bind myself and my loyalty to you until the sunrise."

I drew in a swift gasp when the heat bloomed over my skin. An unquenchable desire to follow Legion overwhelmed me, as if stepping too far from him would cause sickening anguish.

"It's done. Now get out of here before you're seen." Bevan rested a hand on Legion's shoulder, a sad smile curled over his lips. "This will be the end of it. I feel it in these old bones."

Legion gave a curt nod, but then looked to me. "We will travel off the roads, Elise. Where we are accustomed, but it isn't easy terrain. Stay close to us and we'll take you to a place that is safe."

I hugged my middle as Legion, Halvar, and Tor dug into their satchels. Siv slumped against the wall, a look of fright on her face. She feared whatever was to become of her, and a pang of sympathy pierced my heart. She'd lied, but as she accused Legion of nefarious intentions, Siv had plenty of opportunity to harm me, yet didn't.

I faced Legion again. He'd slipped a cowl over his shoulders, and a black hood shrouded his head.

"Elise," Legion said, voice rough. He took my hand. "With what comes next, remember what I told you. I meant every word."

My stomach tightened. Foreboding took hold as Legion released me and gathered something from his satchel. He rose from his haunches, red fabric in his hands. His dark eyes narrowed, but there was pleading in them. Legion took the red fabric and used it to mask the lower half of his face.

A red mask that looked . . .

The truth came like a rod to the skull, a slice at the gut. I fumbled back as Legion took the final piece of his puzzle from Bevan. My sweet, Bevan. He held out the two black axes, at ease, as though they were sacred and not deadly.

Weapons cursed by the hells. Weapons I knew too well.

I stumbled to the ground.

Bevan caught me around my waist and told me to hush.

Legion Grey had disappeared, and in his place stood the man of my nightmares.

Legion was the Blood Wraith.

CHAPTER TWENTY-FIVE

He held my stare as though no one else but us stood in the Ravenspire kitchens. Fiery pain shot up my arm. A phantom pain from the cut of one of those axes. I'd cowered beneath the bloodlust of this man.

I'd had his mouth on mine.

The Wraith turned to Halvar and Tor. My stomach turned viciously. Not Halvar and Tor, the Guild of Shade. They'd covered their faces in the black masks I'd seen the same night. The two killers who'd ripped Legion—the Blood Wraith—away from slaughtering me.

"Halvar, keep the Agitator with you. We take the briar roads and—"

"I'm not going with them." The words spilled out in a frenzy, a breathless panic. "I'm not going with you. I'm not."

I backed away.

The Wraith turned over his shoulder. The terrible red glow

of his eyes missing. Legion's beautiful, glossy black eyes were all I saw. It was a sickening twist of fate. It broke my heart.

"You don't have a choice." His voice was low and dark and still belonged to the man who'd held me so sweetly hours before.

"You bonded with him, Elise," Bevan's voice added to the suffocating panic in my chest.

"You knew!" I shrieked. "You knew what he was and still you—"

"I know there are things you do not understand," the steward replied sharply. "Now go. Your life is in his hands tonight, and he will keep it safe."

"No," I shook my head, ignoring the tug of whatever fury Bevan had linked between us. An undeniable urge to go with the Blood Wraith, to stand at his side.

Tor, behind his awful mask, groaned. "No time."

The Wraith wore a weary look. Bevan's hands gripped my shoulders. "Forgive me, Elise. This is for your own good."

A harsh taste of burning grass and smoke coated the back of my throat. Beneath my nose an open vial wafted fumes down my throat and into my lungs. My legs buckled. Arms scooped me up. Red. Black. Colors of those moments as the sunset meets the night blurred in my mind. I was inches from the mask, the Blood Wraith's mask, and hood. He had me in his arms. I ought to fight, ought to scream.

My head curled against the beat of his heart. The steady thud. Legion's heart. On my next breath, the kitchen, the faces, everything faded into syrupy black.

THERE WERE times in my life when I thought I'd never wade through the haunting memories of the night on the beach. Times when it was too much to bear; the feeling of being so lost even the light in the heavens faded into gray. This moment doubled the despair from anything I'd felt before.

Missing pieces of the night made my head throb. I leaned over my knees, massaging my skull, and tried to make sense of what happened.

The taste of fire and smoke. I'd fallen and I think the Wraith caught me. There were moments when the night air had kissed my face, stirring me from sleep. We rode horses. Where did we get horses? I'd breathed in spice, rain. Breathed in leather. My body was pressed to Legion's chest and . . .

No, the Blood Wraith. I smacked my palm three times on my head. The Blood Wraith. Legion Grey was the Blood Wraith. A liar. A killer. A fiend.

He'd tricked me. Bevan tricked me. Siv tricked me.

The one person I could trust was dead.

I shook away the thought of Mavie's last breath and stared at my hands. In the haze, I had bits and pieces of being lifted off the horse. The moon had still been high. The reek from ale and unwashed bodies had struck me like a hot wall of filth.

We'd entered an alehouse.

"Get away!" I'd screamed at the Wraith when I stood on my own two feet. He'd complied without protest and turned me over to the Guild of Shade. They weren't any better.

Silent and stewing.

Tor had slammed a horn of ale under my nose. Halvar tried to breeze about the journey here, laughing, and poking fun at the way Tor rode a horse, as if he were not terrifying.

I'd never admit his laughter beneath the black mask helped slow the race of my heart.

They'd sent me to freshen up if I'd wanted, and now, I sat with hands still shaking, bonded to a man I feared. I'd been duped into it, no doubt. He knew if I learned the truth of him, I'd have turned and ran. Fury was powerful. With this bond between us, I'd never have been able to leave his side even if I wanted to.

The washroom was dingy, and a reek of feet and mildew perfumed the space. Still, the small room had become a sort of refuge from what awaited me beyond the door.

"Did you need to bite me?" I blinked my gaze up at Siv. She rinsed the mark on her hand in the basin of cool water. "I wasn't going to hurt you; I was helping you walk in here."

I narrowed my eyes. "And I should just believe you? *Agitator.*"

Siv sighed. "Elise, I will never stop asking for your forgiveness. You're right, I lied to you when I first arrived. I was there to get close to the second princess—"

"And who would kill my sister? My parents? Once you finished me off, that is?"

She simply shook her head. "I know I lied, but it changed. And quickly. You befriended me straightaway." Siv leaned her back on the wall. "I'd spent months training for abuse from Timoran royals, but do you remember the first thing you said to me?"

I didn't, so I pinched my mouth and turned away.

"You asked me if I liked iced milk cakes." Siv chuckled, a sad grin on her face. "First thing. You offered me a delicacy off your plate—a royal's plate—because you didn't like goat milk."

"Well," I began slowly. "It's too sour."

Siv's eyes lifted, and she tried to smile, but it was more a trembling grimace. "Then, you'd laughed with Mavie, teasing about my surprise. I tried all night to get the truth from . . . from Mavs, tried to hear her tell me the brutal stories of your beatings or harsh words. She got so irritated she blurted out that you were . . ." Siv hiccupped a sob. "That you were her truest friend and had been since you were girls. A serf and a royal."

I wiped away the tears. I wanted Mavie here now. I wanted her to complain about the sticky stains in the washroom, the hint of piss that followed us everywhere. I wanted her to tell me the bright side of this night. But she wasn't here. She supped with gods tonight.

"You may never forgive me," Siv went on. "But I swear to you, I have not been an Agitator for months. I've been your friend and I hope . . . I hope you will one day be mine again."

"You knew he was the Blood Wraith."

She shook her head. "I didn't. I knew he was dangerous. Saw it when he cornered me. He was not who he said he was, that was all I knew, and I didn't know how to tell you without—"

"Without giving up your lies, too."

Siv tucked her russet hair behind her ear and looked to the ground. "Yes. I know you don't want me, but I will not leave you now."

"I need to escape."

"You can't. I felt the fury bond. He is yours for the night."

I shot to my feet. He robbed me of my choice by a trick. There had to be rules about that. "If you stand with me, then you'll help me do this."

Siv blinked, fought against what she truly wanted to say, then nodded. "All right."

Convinced Siv wouldn't stop me, I faced the washbasin. Why did the Wraith want me? Why had he come into my life? Bevan said I could help him—from what? The strange sickness? Was that even real? I nodded to myself. I'd seen the way he'd nearly crumbled in the kitchens. Something ailed him, but I saw no clear way I could help.

Why, then, was I here?

Too many gruesome thoughts pummeled my skull. I hunched over the stained, smelly wash basin afraid I might vomit.

I cupped yellowed water in my hands and scrubbed my cheeks. A tarnished silver platter served as a mirror. There were too many streaks on the surface and my reflection bent and warped. Distorted, but I noted the blood splatters on my face, the dirt and grime from fleeing through the forest. My hair fell in matted tresses around my face. Dirty as the water was, it refreshed my skin once most of the sweat, tears, and blood was washed away.

Siv kept quiet as I curled my fingers around the handle of the door and peeked into the alehouse. My stomach back-flipped. Across the room, the Shade huddled around a table with the Wraith, drinking and muttering in low voices.

There were no windows in the washroom, but also no one standing watch. Now was my chance. I whispered to Siv to keep watch then slid through the narrow crack in the door. I lowered to my knees and crept along the wall, below the line of tables. A musty breeze blew in, the door was a mere twenty paces away. A stickiness on the floor caused dust and grime to cling to my palms. The scars on my left hand from my missing fingers throbbed with pressure and being stretched, but I didn't stop. When I made it out of the ale room into the front of the house, I scrambled to my feet, making a mad dash for the door.

Hands out, inches away. I could taste the outdoors.

A shadow stepped out of nowhere and blocked my escape.

I tumbled backward, landing in a heap on my back. "Cursed hells!"

Halvar had abandoned the signature half mask, his smile wickedly bright and mischievous.

"Now just where do you think you're going?" He reached beneath my arms and tugged me back to standing. Face close, he said, "You go a step further and it'll be the worst pain you can imagine."

"From you?" I croaked.

"I'm hurt, *Kvinna*," Halvar said as he dragged me back. "I'd not lay a finger on such a lovely head as yours. Nay, my dear princess, the pain will come from your vow to be loyal until sunrise. I promise at the dawn you may become a thorn in our sides. In fact, I welcome it. Life will be more interesting, but until then—stay, talk. Drink. Whatever you please."

My knees threatened to give out. The aleman stood behind a long counter, scrubbing foggy glasses. I reached for him. "Please, help me!"

Halvar chuckled and looked to the man. "Sven, another round."

The aleman ignored my pleas entirely and jutted his chin at Halvar in a jerky sort of nod.

I was on my own.

Back in the aleroom, Siv stood off to the side of the table where Tor sat with the Wraith, still wearing his red mask. He watched me fumble on my feet. His eyes were Legion's but harder. Angry I'd tried to run, maybe.

"Sit." His command sent an icy ripple down my spine.

My body trembled, but I lifted my chin, daring to meet his eye. *I mean this, Elise.* He'd whispered it against my ear, then left kisses on my neck, my lips. He knew this would happen. Knew his identity would be revealed eventually. My heart cinched because part of me wanted to believe it was real, the other part could not see beyond that bleeding mask.

"Sit, Elise."

I swallowed my fear and obeyed. "Take off your mask." I closed my eyes, feeling weak and pitiful. "I beg of you."

The Wraith drummed his fingertips over the table, studying me. His scrutiny peeled back my skin until he could undoubt-edly see every emotion, every thought I kept hidden. But after a moment, he complied, and removed the mask; he tossed back his hood. Legion Grey stared back at me.

"Ask," he said.

"Ask what?"

The arrogant smirk curled his lips and I wanted to cry again. Wanted to go back to softer moments and pretend this horrid truth didn't live between us anymore.

"Anything, Elise. But like it or not, eventually you will need to speak to me again."

"I don't need to do anything."

He tapped his fingers again, almost grinning. "No. I've learned enough about you. It is utterly frustrating trying to force you to do anything."

I frowned. I didn't want to talk about how he knew intimate thoughts of mine. Tonight, I'd build a wall between us and refuse to let it break. "You want me to ask you a question?"

"I want to have communication between us. We will need it."

"Fine. May I have my fingers back?" His eyes widened. Good. He deserved to be taken off guard at least once. I tilted my head smugly. "What? You think I haven't recalled every bleeding moment from the night you tried to butcher me since you put on that damn mask?"

"What is she talking about?" Tor grumbled.

I rose to my feet, anger buoying me. "Did you recognize me when you came? Did you return to finish the job, torturing me slowly, allowing me to believe . . ." My voice cracked.

Legion, or the Wraith, or whoever, was on his feet, too. He towered over me. "I have no memory of that night. Nor the attack at your manor. Only what you have told me."

"Ah," I said wryly. "You kill so much you don't remember faces."

"No," he said, discomfited. Strange to see the Blood Wraith uneasy when my memories remember him vastly determined and deadly. "You don't understand—"

"Stop," Tor snapped. "Have you met before all this?"

"The docks," Legion said through his teeth. "The Mellanstrad docks. You told me how I nearly . . ." He glared at his Shade. "Do you remember?"

Tor's eyes went wide, and he looked to me. I wanted to

scream at him to speak everything running in his head. I needed to know it all. But in Tor fashion, he pinched his lips and went silent.

Halvar was different. He chuckled nervously. "This just got more uncomfortable, didn't it?"

Uncomfortable was one word for it. Exhaustion, betrayal, all of it cut me at the knees and I slumped back in the chair. "Release me. Let me go. I don't want to be here, not with you."

Legion tried to keep his expression unmoved, but his eyes gave away the truth. I'd cut him the same as he'd cut me. "The bond will fade by morning. Until then you may as well ask your questions."

I wanted to be free of him. The bite of memories of the way he made my heart soar, my breaths catch, kept colliding with the brutality I'd suffered at his hand, and so many others. There was a reason he was called the Blood Wraith. He'd earned the title, earned the tales of his lust for death. A thousand sweet kisses couldn't wipe it away.

"I have nothing to ask you." I had a thousand things to ask. "Release me."

Legion shook his head, sighing. "You chose me."

"I chose Legion Grey, not a murderer."

"He and I are one and the same. You trusted him or the bond would not have worked. Trust me now."

"You have an obsession with trust when you do nothing to earn it."

Trust those undeserving of it.

I shook my head, chasing away the little witch's words. They had no place here. I would not trust this man.

Legion leaned onto his elbows, dragging his fingers

through his dark golden hair. It seemed to be darkening even more. I scoffed—it wasn't real. He didn't have golden, Timoran hair. No. I had no doubt in a few days the false color would fade and I'd see him plainly. The deliberateness of his deceit hurt worse than the actual lies.

"What do you want with me?"

"I need your help."

"With what?"

"It's difficult to explain."

I sneered. "Because it isn't a lie? It seems you only know how to speak in falsehoods."

"I would tell you everything should you only ask," he said softly and looked away.

Right then, I almost believed he hurt as much as me, but doubtless it was all a ruse. Everything had been a chance to get close to me, to use me. Truth be told, in all the pain racking my body, I didn't even care to know the reason.

"I opened my heart to you," I whispered, voice trembling. "And you deceived me."

I stood from the table, finished talking. When his hand curled around my wrist, I gasped. My insides fluttered and I cursed my body for betraying me.

"Stay, Elise. Build trust again. I never lied."

"You never told the truth either, Blood Wraith."

He closed his eyes, gaze to the floor. The name bothered him, and I didn't care.

No mistake, I wanted to believe him. Even as the Wraith, I wanted to believe he had not tormented my heart for nothing. But there was no sufficient reason to make up for his omission.

Like Siv, he'd infiltrated my life for some selfish need and in turn had turned my world on its head.

"The bond lasts until sunrise and then the choice is once more mine, true?" I asked.

"There is more to explain."

"Will I have the choice to leave?" I said again.

"You need to understand what your choice will mean," Halvar said. For the first time his voice came out in a dark threat. "Listen to us."

"No." I said, hiding my agony behind a carefully placed wall. I turned back to Legion. "You want me to choose to stay, don't you?"

"Yes," he said without hesitation.

"Trust and choice mean a great deal to you."

"They mean everything. Nothing can change if you do not choose it."

I took a deep breath and stepped back. Hot tears blurred my sight. "Understand something: I will never choose you again."

CHAPTER TWENTY-SIX

THE ALEHOUSE WAS TUCKED FAR BACK in the trees. In the stuffy garret, between boxes and crates and old pelts, I'd opened a box to an old hand drawn map of New Timoran. It was missing a few towns and farms, but it would be enough to orient myself. Enough to begin finding a way out.

From an upper window, in the ashy dawn, it wasn't easy. Trees here bore damp like they bore the weight of their leaves. A constant mist hovered in the air. After too many moments pretending I knew what I was doing, I found a distant cliffside in the gilded morning which mirrored the map.

"Three hells," I cursed under my breath and held up the map to the new sun, comparing the landmarks. If I was right, then we were near the Cliffside Falls, in the east. A solid day's walk from the Ribbon Lakes and my family's land. It'd be a gods-granted miracle if I made it away from here, through the tangle of forests and thickets, across the trade roads, and to the west side of the kingdom before Legion Grey found me again.

But I couldn't stay here.

All night terrible sounds kept me awake. The kind I felt to my bones. Shrieks, shouts, wails—as if a war raged outside. But in the light of the dawn, nothing seemed amiss.

Night creatures were part of the fae, and this far into the trees perhaps Night Folk had come out to play under the moon. Thoughts wandered to water nyks, to the wolf Fenrir haunting the trees. But the sun chased them away.

Morning. A new day. No foolish bond of loyalty. The loyalty I had was to myself alone.

"Don't do this," Siv whispered at my back.

"I have the choice to leave. You ought to do the same."

She shook her head. "I have nowhere to go. I leave, the Guild of Shade and Agitators hunt me. I stay, well, at least they have not killed me yet."

I wanted her to leave. The Guild of Shade might retaliate against her, but I wouldn't fight to convince her to choose differently, either. Friends were enemies now, and none of us had any business trying to alter the course of anyone else.

When the first hints of dawn came through the window, the aleman had poked his head in to ensure I hadn't slit my own throat or something. I pretended to sleep as he wheezed and repeated, "Young miss" in the doorway five times before he gave up. How could a man who seemed so ordinary be in league with the Blood Wraith? How could he stand for the mistreatment of an innocent woman? I didn't think the aleman was Timoran, but neither was he Ettan. Perhaps he held no loyalty to any people here.

I didn't want to see Legion, or his guild. They'd rescind their offer to let me choose, no doubt, and I couldn't stomach his face again. Not when I still had a desire to feel safe in his arms when those arms had also tried to kill me once.

When the corridors and immediate area outside my door were quiet, I set to work.

The window was cheap, bubbled glass with a narrow latch. Easily broken. I shot praises to the All Father when I peeked outside the window to three vine-covered trellises on my side of the building. Questionable, perhaps, in their stability, but risking a fall was more favorable than remaining.

I wasn't one to sit around and wait for death.

I used a scrap of linen to tie my hair off my neck and bunched the rough pillows in the center of the bed, shaping them to look like a body was tucked beneath the quilt. If the aleman decided to look in again, at least I'd buy myself some time.

"Good luck, Elise," Siv whispered.

I paused, then turned over my shoulder. "And you."

At the window, I held my breath, clutched the sill, and leveraged one leg over the edge. My boot kicked around, searching for the rung on the trellis. I tested the give of the wood, and when I was confident it would hold, I pulled my other leg over the window's ledge.

The vines were littered in thorns. "Damn the skies," I cursed when my thumb stuck against a harsh thorn and blood coursed down the meat of my palm.

I gritted my teeth and went on, carefully selecting each spot to place my feet.

Ten paces from the ground, I lodged my boot on a rung of the trellis and before I could get my foothold, my stomach lurched into my throat. The snap of wood, the scrape of leaves on skin, the tug of my hair getting tangled in the thorns. All of it collided as I plummeted.

I hit the ground with a grunt. Breath ripped from my lungs and my body shuddered as a painful ripple danced up and down my spine. I coughed and rolled onto my side. My ankle throbbed from twisting, but I didn't think I broke any bones.

The window was open, twenty paces above me, and no calls for my capture came from the alehouse. A cautious smile spread over my lips. Legion Grey was wholly arrogant to underestimate me, to manipulate me into staying.

Before my run of good luck changed, I limped into the dark tree line and didn't look back.

The ground sloped and bent and caused my ankle to scream its protests. I didn't stop. If I didn't orient myself soon, I'd be wandering the trees into nightfall, and those haunting screams would be mine to deal with. I wasn't sure how long I'd wandered away from the alehouse, but when the trees thickened, I cursed my stupidity for leaving without a blade, or at least something to hold water.

My leg went numb, my limp had worsened to the point my strong leg burned, and my skin raised in gooseflesh even though sweat dripped off my brow. I almost considered returning to the alehouse and pleading for my life when at long last I found a road sign. The wood pallet was covered in thick brush, and the road was so overgrown it could hardly be called a road.

I fell to my knees, beaming in relief.

One direction led to the Southern docks, the other to the Ribbon Lakes. My manor was maybe a two length walk from the Ribbon Lakes township. I didn't plan to return there, not with Calder and Runa seeking me out, but at least I could find my way to Mattis. He'd help me without question.

I almost smiled imagining Mattis's face when I told him the truth about Legion Grey. I believed he'd come to admire the vow negotiator, and now Legion's skill with sparring would make much more sense.

A child waif. I puffed out my lips. He said he never lied. Legion knew a blade because he was the Blood Wraith, not because he was orphaned.

I sat on a fallen log and stripped the tattered jacket I'd stolen. The threads burned in old sweat and dust from the storage trunks. I stared at the road sign, as if it might offer some enlightenment. If I recalled my maps and my geography lessons well enough, there would be at least three small townships on the way to Ribbon Lakes. Already the chills and what felt a bit like fever settled in my head. I didn't have time to be ill. The trauma of the night would need to wait until I could find a safe place to crumble.

I rose and began the trek into the trees again.

By the time the flicker of lanterns in the windows of quaint little homes came into view, my knees quivered holding my weight. The Ribbon Lakes were in sight, and the memory of spending time there with Legion, being attacked there, stirred my emotions into a tightly woven knot. Hells, everything reminded me of Legion Grey. I shamed my bleeding mind to remember he was a wretch and liar and killer.

And sometimes all of it didn't matter. What sort of person did that make me?

I shook out my hands, shook out the worries, and focused

on pressing forward. My hair stuck to my clammy forehead, and my breaths were harsh, labored.

Not long now. Not long and I'd be home.

I kept to the backs of buildings, avoiding the main roads. The sun hung low in the sky, not yet sunset, but dusk wasn't far off. My throat yearned for something cool to drink, ached for a bed to curl against. How foolish of me to think I could make such a journey in such a pitiful state. I should've eaten. Should've taken medicines or blankets for the night. I should've looked the Wraith in his eye and told him I was leaving.

Silent tears carved lines through the sweat on my face as I struggled up an incline on the backroad. I'd die here. How ironic that I had escaped to avoid death, and here I would die, alone and in the open for wolves to gnaw my bones.

At the top of the incline, what little feeling I had left in my body abandoned me. A line of Ravenspire patrols blocked all roads leading to Mellanstrad.

A watch row, it was called. Impossible to breech on the best days, but in my haggard state, I wouldn't be able to take a single step without being seen.

"Captain! At the ridge!" A patrolman shouted.

My pulse pounded in my head. I used what energy I had left to turn to make a run back toward the cold forest, but two hands grabbed me on either side.

I cried out as the guard tossed me to the ground. Facedown in the wet grass, a boot pressed between my shoulders. Steps rustled through the weeds until polished boots stopped in front of my face. A man sniffed, then crouched, using his fingertips to tilt my chin so I might see his face.

"Elise, my love," Jarl said, a touch of arrogance and hatred bled through each word. "You've come home."

I struggled beneath the boot, panic clouding my thoughts. I couldn't breathe. Couldn't think.

"No, shh," Jarl said, reaching out and stroking my hair. "No need for that. I had hoped you'd return. I'd hoped to see you again. So much has changed, you see."

"Yes," I said, face in the dirt. "You committed regicide. How noble of you."

Jarl chuckled. "Ah, Elise this is the new order I spoke of. I thought we could share it together. We still can, we can still help bring about a new rule, a stronger Timoran. All our king and queen need is your loyalty. Though, I must admit, your sister is not especially hopeful you'll join."

"Tell Runa she will never be my queen. She's too ill read for my liking."

The bitterness in Jarl's laugh sent a shiver down my back. He whistled and the patrol removed his foot, but soon the hands that pinned me forced me to my feet again.

"Bring her," he commanded.

The guards dragged me forward, uncaring if I had solid footing or not.

"Jarl . . ." I started, but lost strength to even plead for my life.

"Look, Elise," Jarl said through a strange chuckle. "Just look."

The patrolmen stopped once the path curved to the drive of my manor. One lifted my chin, squeezing my jaw too tightly.

Perhaps it was good the patrols were holding onto me, or I would have fallen straightaway. A choked kind of sob burst from my throat as I stared at the charred ruins of what had once been my home. The white marble walls were broken, crumbling. Smoke and ash perfumed the air. My mother's wolfsbane and rowan bushes were nothing but briars and dead twigs.

Jarl yanked back on my braid. He whirled me around and held me against his broad chest, his lips against my ear.

"This," he whispered, voice harsh, "this is what happens when you cross me, Elise. When you cross the king and his queen."

"Where are they?" the words burst out of my throat, raw and desperate. "Where are our serfs, our . . . people!"

I felt Jarl smile against my cheek, felt his fingernails dig deeper into my back. "Dead."

One word had power.

One word had the strength to break me.

"I know you had such affection for so many gutter rats," Jarl went on and tossed me into the hands of the patrols.

I knew little else of what was happening for the next moments. I hardly realized the patrolmen were dragging me forward again. I cried silently as they led me into the skeleton of my home, forced me to soak in the blackened walls. I gagged on a scream when a burned form was sprawled out in the corridor. Rotting. Who was it? A servant? Three hells, was it Bevan? Had the old man returned to the manor from Ravenspire, or remained at the castle with my parents, who cowered beneath their vicious daughter?

"Take her to the master room," Jarl demanded.

The deeper we went into the home I realized the lower floor was the worst of the flames. The staircase was intact for the most part; one missing step caused me to fumble, but it held our weight. Upstairs, filmy smoke had stained the walls and portraits. It reeked of flesh and ash, but the doors were still closed on the floors.

The patrolmen tossed open my parents' suite. I blinked through the tears. The master bed was made up, untouched. A new suit for my father was still being tailored. My mother's hairbrushes were still aligned in perfection on the white vanity. A ghostly sight. The space was as if they'd simply disappeared. But they hadn't disappeared, no. They had left those who'd depended on them to slaughter.

"Restrain her," Jarl commanded the patrols. "By the looks of her I doubt it'll take much to keep her down."

Two guards shared a laugh at my expense. I struggled to lift my chin. Let them mock me, I would not rise to the occasion. The patrolmen forced me onto my back, tethered my ankles, then wrists to the bedposts.

The hiss of the wooden vanity seat scraped across the floorboards. Jarl settled in the cushion with a sigh. "Elise, my dear, we have been searching for you through the night. I'd nearly given up hope that we'd see you alive."

"Glad I could oblige," I snapped.

"Do you think being witty when I have your hands bound is the wisest choice, Elise?"

"Are you asking if I'm pleased to injure your pride by not groveling for my life at your feet? Yes, absolutely."

Jarl's smile faded and he leaned over his knees. "Do not be a fool, Elise. I am authorized to cause pain to traitors of Timoran."

I turned away, refusing to allow the tears to fall. My heart was in shambles. I knew I'd die. Jarl had placed me in a completely vulnerable state, and as his true nature bled out, I was certain he'd make me suffer as much as he could.

"I found your dead maid," Jarl said. I clenched my eyes. "We heard you left with Legion Grey. Abandoned your new king. So, this is how King Calder answered your disloyalty. Do you suppose he would allow the estate of a traitor to stand?"

"They had nothing to do with it!" I screamed.

My lack of control drew out a vicious smile on Jarl's face. "Our king does not care in the least."

Air ripped free of my lungs. I bit the inside of my cheek until I tasted blood. When I closed my eyes, I saw our serfs. The faces of Cook, of little Ellis. Mothers, children, fathers. Their screams boiled in my brain.

"Kill me," I said. On the verge of pleading.

"Not yet," Jarl said. "I would like to know where Legion Grey has gone. Castle Ravenspire has use for him. I hear he is quite skilled with a blade—quite the tracker, too."

"I don't know where he is." Not a lie. Not entirely the truth, but why was I defending him anyway? The Blood Wraith could slaughter Jarl without question. Maybe I ought to lead Jarl right to him.

"I swear to you, Elise, if you serve the Crown, you will have position. We can wed and bring about change in this land."

"You will enslave Night Folk. Use their fury for your benefit."

"The gods led us here and we are entitled to the powers of the land. King Zyben wasted fury. We can study it, make it our own. There are more powers out there being wasted by mystics hiding in the shadows. If the gods gave us this land, then they want us to use their gifts."

I thought of Bevan and the Alvers he spoke of. How many kingdoms had different magically inclined? Like the witch girl at the castle. Where had she come from? They'd all be taken, used. Studied. My jaw tightened. "If the gods wanted you to have fury you would have been born with it. I will not stand by and watch you torture and dissect the innocent simply because of their gifts. I want unity, to work with fury the way Ettans did once."

Jarl's arrogance dissolved, replaced by darkness. "Now you sound like an Agitator. The ones who worship a dead bloodline."

I chuckled because I would die. There was no reason to hold back. "Maybe they were on to something. I'd rather be classed with Agitators than cowards like you and a false king and queen."

Jarl's eyes turned to black slits. He rose from the edge of the bed and stripped his captain's coat, then his belt with his sword.

"What are you doing?" I asked, heart racing.

Jarl kneeled on the edge of the ash-soaked bed. He crawled to my side and scoffed. "You don't expect me to let you die without having you?"

Blood drained from my face, and he took pleasure in it.

"I tried so hard to find favor with you and *Herr* Grey, after all," he rambled on. Jarl placed a hand on my leg, lifting the hem of my dirty gown until he could see my exposed skin beneath it. He clicked his tongue, grinning. "Lovely."

"Bastard." I tried to kick him off.

He released my dress, but left the skirt too high on my thighs. Jarl touched my calf, skating his hand up my knee. "I'll take our vows now. It is all arranged. The deeds to the second royal house, the fortunes will be mine by law and by the order of the king. But, you know, such a thing must be consummated between a husband and his wife. I'll have you now. As long as I want, as many times as I want. Then, I'll grant you a swift death out of thanks."

"You won't lay a hand on me," I spat, disgusted.

Jarl trapped my chin in his hand. "Perhaps you do not understand the duties of a wife?"

His hand traced the line of my waist. I tried to roll away, but the fetters kept me in place. He curled his fingers around the laces of my bodice.

"Bring in the officiator," Jarl said to the guards who'd remained in the room. "I'll vow with the bitch, then leave her to the men to kill."

"Too cowardly to kill me yourself?" I shouted. What use was it to hide my hatred now?

Jarl gripped my chin and clambered over my body, straddling my hips. One hand pinched my skin along my thigh, a sneer grew on his face as he tried to frighten me during my last moments. "I'm wearing my best uniform, Elise. I'd hate to soil it," he whispered against my lips. "But trust me—I'll watch."

Jarl slid off me and adjusted his gambeson. The door opened and a stoic clergyman entered, draped in his red marital robes. A man of the gods, of the All Father, or so he said. Yet, he would vow a monster to a woman bound on a bed.

"*Skam vara din! Smärta från eld!*" I shouted my curse of his shame in the old language. No doubt the man understood. For the first time, I was grateful my mother had insisted I become fluent. I rolled as best I could onto my shoulder and spat at his feet.

I took a bit of pleasure in the way he ruffled at the insult.

"Get started, holy man," Jarl commanded.

The clergyman sniffed in disgust and opened the thick leather book of sagas and poems that were traditionally read in Timoran wedding ceremonies.

As the clergyman opened his mouth, the bones of my family home shuddered as someone pounded into the lower entrances.

Jarl held up a hand. Silence entombed us in the smoky room. I held my breath, confused, too frightened to admit.

From outside shouts rose through the hush. Another shudder rocked as footsteps pounded below us. Shouts bled into screams, into the glide of steel on steel.

Jarl withdrew his blade as heavy footsteps smashed up the stairs, down the hallway, until the bedroom door smacked against the wall. A tall patrolman tumbled into the room clutching his middle, fresh blood on his hands. "They . . . the . . . Blood Wraith."

The guard fell forward and the next breath he took was his last.

CHAPTER TWENTY-SEVEN

JARL STIFFENED. Fear flashed in his eyes, but he fought mightily hard to bury it beneath commands. "Go, you bastards! Stop them!"

Three of the patrolmen in the room rushed into the bones of my ruined house, knocking the holy man as they went. The wicked clergyman whimpered and slid into the corner, praying to the father of the gods for protection.

"*Långsom död!*" Slow death. I spat again at the clergyman. He had no business praying to the gods. If they were even watching, doubtless they'd like what they saw.

Jarl snapped his fingers at one of three remaining guards in the room. One patrolman blinked away from his fallen brother and looked to his captain.

"Get her feet," Jarl commanded.

I thrashed and kicked. Jarl slapped me across the face twice. Coppery blood soaked my tongue, and my skin glistened in heat from the blow. My skirts had gathered around my thighs from the tussle and from Jarl's wandering hands. A few more nicks and bruises stained my skin after he'd pinched and tormented me.

Glass shattered and a black arrow pierced the window, thudding into the patrolman's chest. Jarl startled back as the guard dropped with a wet gasp. His limp body tumbled over the bed, pinning me back onto the mattress. I shouted out in fear and desperation. His heavy form made it hard to breathe, while his blood dripped in hot, sticky veins down my neck, into my unlaced bodice.

Jarl stared at the scene with horror, then tightened his jaw, and darted for the door to the room.

"Coward!" I cried out, tears of rage on my face. I arched back, desperate to be free of the dead guard, his weight gaining with each moment. My ribs ached; my chest pitted.

Cursed gods! I'd suffocate beneath a dead man before anyone reached me.

The clergyman whimpered through tears and scrambled on hands and knees toward the door. He wouldn't get far. A cry of pain answered him when the door smashed open. The holy man clutched his skull, a line of blood trickled down his face.

Jarl froze, three paces from the door as it fell off its hinges.

The room went still as death. Not even my panic beneath the body could survive the tenuous pressure that came when the Blood Wraith appeared in the broken doorway.

The clergyman sobbed, begging for mercy. Legion noticed him first, then his slow gaze found Jarl, next me, tied to the bed. When the scene clicked, it was a frighteningly, perfect moment. Though, I ran from him, I could not deny I reveled in what his gaze told me would happen next.

I'd seen the bloodlust in the Wraith's eyes. Red, glowing, inhuman. This look was different. Black, simmering rage. The look of a mortal man defending what was his with his life.

He took out the twin battle axes. The strength of his grip curled villainously around the weight of the iron. A metallic tang in the air sent a wave of nausea through my insides.

The way his eyes gleamed, I imagined the vicious curl to his lip beneath the cursed red mask. He kicked at the clergyman, forcing the fool back into the room. The man held up his book of sagas as if it might protect him.

"You're outnumbered, Wraith!" Jarl sounded pathetically weak. He backed up to the broken window, then signaled to the two remaining Ravenspire guards to raise their blades.

They wrung their hands around their weapons nervously.

Legion hardly paid them any mind and kept his eyes on Jarl. His voice was low, a rumble of darkness. Not the voice of Legion Grey. "Ah, you can count."

It happened in a blur.

Legion drew in a fast breath, raised an axe over his head, and slammed the curved edges deep into the back of the dead guard on my body. I screamed with what little air was left in my lungs. With a great heave, the axe serving as a kind of hook in the corpse, Legion dragged the body off me, then set to his bloody work. One guard rushed him. Legion opened the Ravenspire seal on his gambeson, deep and swift. He stepped on the guard's face once the patrolman fell in his own blood.

The second struck, less sure, almost accepting this was his final moment.

If the Blood Wraith had mercy in killing, he showed it on the young guard. A swift slice to the throat and the guard fell.

Legion's shoulders rose in sharp breaths. For a moment he studied me on the bed, saw the state of my dress, my tethered limbs. He pointed a bloody axe at Jarl. "Who touched her?"

"They arranged forced marital vows!" I blurted out. Hells, no denying I wanted them to suffer.

To my surprise, Legion pointed his fury at the clergyman at his feet. His eyes were hot embers now. He swung his punishment into the holy man's neck. I jolted at the sound of the man dying.

Despicable he may be, but death was still sickening.

At the doorway, Halvar and Tor rushed in, masked and bloody. But Siv followed, a dagger in her hand. When she saw me, her eyes widened. She'd come for me. They all had. Even after I'd abandoned them. I still didn't understand why. Legion needed something, so perhaps a selfish motivation, but I could admit in this moment I'd never been more relieved.

Jarl straightened at the window. Alone and at a precipice of fight or die. Hatred boiled in his eyes for me, but he slid his sword free from its sheath. "She is mine to take. But let me live, and you may have a piece first."

Halvar chuckled, lifted his crossbow, and gave a little nod at Legion. "Wrong thing to say to the likes of him."

Jarl sneered. "You want her, Wraith? Interesting."

I saw Jarl's sword before I heard my scream. He swung it to kill me.

A hiss of air and a dart flew over my middle. Jarl cursed, clutching his gut, and staggered back. His sword dropped out of his grip.

Time slowed, and the captain's sword kept falling, aimed at my body. The Guild of Shade chased after Jarl, who leapt, dart still in him, from the open window. Siv came to me. The burn of the cutting edge of Jarl's blade struck my exposed thigh before it clattered on the floor. A graze, but deep enough to draw a swift rush of blood.

Another breath and Legion was there, kicking the sword across the floorboards.

I winced when his hand pressed on the gash. Siv hacked the fetters off my wrists and ankles. The moment I was free, I grappled for Legion's shoulders on instinct, forgetting the truth of who he was for the smallest moment. He pulled me to him and adjusted my gown, so my legs were once more covered.

With a swipe of his hand, he tossed back his hood and tugged on the red half-mask. "Did he touch you?"

"S-Some." I couldn't stop trembling now that it had ended.

"Halvar, Tor!" The Blood Wraith's voice had returned. "Get after him. Bring him to me. I will give him the ending he deserves."

Then, Legion jolted. His shoulders curled around me with quickening breaths. He shook his head, the red in his black eyes brightening.

Tor cursed. "He lives another day, Legion. You're out of time. We need to go. Now."

Legion met my gaze with more ferocity than I'd yet seen. I held my breath. His arms tightened around me, but I was unsure if he planned to gut me like he'd done the rest, or if his intensity meant something more.

"You will come without incident," he snarled.

Stay and meet my fate with Jarl and Ravenspire, or return with the Blood Wraith and the Guild of Shade; the ones who frightened me and kept me safe in the same breath.

"Dammit, Elise," Tor hissed. "Choose. He cannot force you, but we are out of time."

Legion winced, a kind of growl tore from his throat, and he curled forward again.

"What's happening to him?"

"If you want to survive, we leave now," Tor said, his finger in my face.

I nodded in the same moment Legion straightened. His jaw was clenched, and he clearly tried to keep his breaths even as he took my arm and lifted me off the bed. At once, he abandoned me, and staggered with a quick step from the room.

More than in the kitchens of Ravenspire, something was happening to Legion, and I had a hungry need to make it stop.

"Halvar, keep Elise and Siverie with you." Tor was already at the door, his expression pained. "I'll ride ahead with him. If I give the signal—"

"I know," Halvar said somberly. "Run."

CHAPTER TWENTY-EIGHT

THE GUILD of Shade brought the horses taken from Ravenspire previously. Between the three of them and Siv, the guards from Jarl's unit were nothing but meat and blood as we abandoned the shell of the Lysander manor. Siv took her own horse, but Halvar placed me in front of him.

Legion and Tor had already disappeared into the night.

Halvar sped us at a difficult pace. My body ached, but I said nothing. I'd not complain when they'd risked life and limb to save me.

"What's happening to him?" I shouted against the wind. "Halvar. What is wrong with him?"

"He's changing. Once he found you missing and when Siv told him you'd returned to Mellanstrad, he didn't take the dose he needed. Just left."

"Needed for what?"

Bevan said he needed the potion, that he could not skip a

single dose, and he'd abandoned it to chase after me. To save my neck from my own recklessness.

"I pray to the gods you don't need to find out." Halvar kicked the flanks of the horse and picked up the pace.

I closed my eyes, braced, and didn't say anything more. When fear should be there, all I could think of were moments when the Wraith was Legion. When he sat quietly and read with me in the library. When he kissed my missing fingertips after I told him how I lost them—the pain in his eyes. How it made sense now.

I feared him, true, but whatever was destroying him made me ache for him more.

The ride was endless. Branches pummeled my skin as Halvar pounded the horse through briar-tangled roads, on uneven paths, overgrown with roots and rocks. And every moment he needed to pull back and slow our pace. I cursed the delay.

He took us to the same alehouse, the trellis I'd used on the side of the house still broken, and only a few lanterns flickered in the windows. The instant the horse came to a stop, Halvar kicked his leg over and dropped to the ground. He said nothing before darting inside, a knife in his hand.

My heart had grown so violent it felt like it might break out. Siv's horse snorted behind me, gasping from the strenuous ride. Though my body protested and had molded and stiffened to the shape of the withers of the horse, I forced my leg to swing around.

Something smashed inside the alehouse. Wood snapping, I thought. Then a roar of pain that shook birds from the trees.

My palms quaked as I tethered the horse to a post near a trough.

Another cry of pain and I snatched Siv's hand when she came to my side.

Both of us, wide eyed, stared at the open door of the alehouse. I heard men shouting. Halvar cursed.

Legion needed help, but at my first step, Siv pulled back. "Elise, no. We . . . we don't know what's happening."

"He's suffering!" What more did she need to know? I tried to shake off her hand, giving her the choice to stay outside, but she didn't let go. Together we stepped into the alehouse.

A grisly scene played out.

The aleman had a two-pronged fork in his hand and kept jabbing the air at the Guild of Shade—no—at Legion.

With a fist, Legion knocked another table, cried out, and doubled over as if he had no control over his own body. Tor wrestled with him and used his knife to cut off Legion's tunic until his bare back showed. "A little longer. Hang on a little longer."

Legion shouted hatred and pain and fear in reply. Halvar had gathered rope and chains and danced around when more furniture reeled across the room.

A hand went to my mouth as Halvar lunged and wrapped one of the chains around Legion's neck. The Blood Wraith roared his rage and swung at his Shade, but Halvar tugged on the chain, so Legion was wrenched to his back. Both Tor and Halvar leapt on his arms and pulled them out to his sides, then tied the rope around his wrists and secured him to the ale counter. Dark veins coated Legion's skin. Like wicked, gnarled roots sprouting up his neck and face, they reached for his blood-red eyes.

Halvar shackled Legion's neck, choking him. Hurting him.

"Leave him be!" I screamed.

The distraction lifted Tor's gaze, loosened his grip on the rope to Legion's arm, and earned a strike to the face from the Wraith. Tor spit blood.

"Damn you!" Tor raged, using the chains to pin down Legion's throbbing arms. The muscle seemed too swollen for his skin. Sweat and trails of blood drenched Legion's face, his mouth. Even the beds of his nails looked black and bloody. "Sven! Take them away!"

For a somber man, Tor shouted a great deal now.

The aleman dug his fingers into my arm, then Siv's, and dragged us—stronger than he looked—to the stairs. As I passed, I caught Legion's gaze. The glow of the Wraith's eyes, hells red, black veins around the sockets, his mouth, and his temples.

When he locked on me, he sneered. He snapped his teeth. An animalistic desire in his eyes. No mistake, he'd *devour* me should I step any closer.

Stunned, taking me to the garret proved easier for Sven. Below, the battle waged and the aleman practically threw us into the room.

"No matter whatcha hear," he grumbled. "You don't leave this room. If you want to keep your heads, you don't leave. Not until the sun."

At that he turned and slammed the door. Over the roars of agony, the bolt clicked.

Rogue Agitator and shamed princess clung to each other in

the darkened attic room. Shivering, jumping at every shriek, groan, and snarl.

"What is he?" Siv breathed out.

"I don't know."

An ailment. This was no ailment.

This was a bleeding curse.

FOR HOURS I listened to Legion's raspy curses at his guild. Glass broke. Tables crashed.

I tried to visualize what was happening below me, but every imagining didn't match the sounds. The havoc was inconceivable.

Siv wrapped herself in a quilt. She shuddered and closed her eyes at each crash and cry. Torture enough to hear it, I let tears fall for Legion who was enduring it.

Then, the cries shifted. Not his voice exactly, something rough and brisk and deadly, but buried in it all was his deep timbre.

"Please," he begged. "No more. Please."

A piercing, guttural sound followed.

I swatted at the new wave of tears and bolted to my feet. Why would they hurt him? He was begging them to stop. When would it end? Couldn't they see it was enough!

"Please!" His broken voice shattered me.

I was out the door in an instant. Siv hissing my name at my back. They wouldn't torture him, not anymore. He couldn't bear it—selfishly, part of the truth was I couldn't bear it.

In the aleroom, Sven nursed a gash on his wrist, and Halvar leaned, exhausted, over the back of a chair. Only Tor remained standing, and he slashed a knife back and forth. It glistened in blood.

Bile jumped to my mouth. By the gods he was carving Legion's back, his arms, his shoulders. On his knees, arms flayed and in chains, Legion could not fight him. He simply had to endure the ruthless jabs of a blade in his body.

Blood pooled around his knees, his boots, his skin . . . everywhere.

"Stop! Stop it!" I cried and made a mad dash to him.

Halvar jumped in my path, his arms around me, but he wasn't the one who stopped me. Legion whipped his head around and I turned to stone. My blood went cold and heavy. Teeth, the size of my thumbs, curved over Legion's lips. A ring of yellow swallowed up part of the glowing red in his gaze. His fingernails, on those hands that loved gently, were jagged, pointed, and an ugly, rotted black.

Fear pierced me when instead of the cries of pain and pleas to stop, this face, this creature, grinned a vicious kind and laughed. The rumble of it shook me to my soul.

"Elise you must leave," Halvar begged. I'd never heard him beg and it shook me to hear him so desperate and pained. Blood had dried in his fingernails, his hands pink and dark with the stains of Legion's wounds.

"Why do you do this to him?" I sobbed.

The lips of the creature curled at my pain, like it reveled in it.

"Get her away," Tor said without looking at me.

Halvar dragged me away when the beast who'd taken hold

of Legion's body tried to rip the chains from the hooks that held him fast and in place. He shouted for me to return, shouted terrible things in words I could hardly understand. He wanted to shred me apart. The creature yearned for blood and begged for it until the pathetic pleading returned, drowned out as Halvar pulled me back up the stairs.

"Halvar," I said and ripped my hand away. "What are you doing to him?"

"He is cursed with bloodlust," Halvar said breathlessly. "He must have blood when the change happens. If we do not do this and control how much blood spills, then he will tear himself apart, or . . . others. Go. Please. It will end at the sun."

I didn't argue with Halvar. I was too sickened, too discomposed to imagine seeing Legion in such a state ever again. It *was* a curse. A vicious, cruel curse. He relived it, told me he did. Each last moon, he'd said. Every twenty-two days, Legion would succumb to this, and my heart cracked. But what drew it out before the last moon?

I didn't enter the room, not yet. He was chained and controlled, so I slid down the wall and hugged my knees to my chest.

If I had any brains, I'd run. When his mind went right again, I doubt he'd pursue me. Logically I knew I couldn't help him. How could anyone without fury save him from this curse?

But to leave him would mean leaving a piece of me behind.

It had happened outside my control, but I cared about Legion Grey. Not the monster downstairs, but the man inside it. The man I knew.

He lived each day knowing this horror would take him again and again, yet when he'd been with me, he smiled, he teased, he comforted. I shuddered and let my face burrow in the tops of my knees. He could be violent and vicious, but even if he'd been pretending, the entire time he served as my vow negotiator he fought for my needs and wants.

A good man lived underneath the lies.

This beast was not him; this beast was what he'd sought me out to help him with. My stomach dropped. *When you see the beast within, let him in to let him go.*

The tips of my fingers prickled with a rush of blood. The witch girl. She'd said it twice, she'd never written it. By the gods, she'd mentioned choice the same as everyone else. Choose Legion, the Blood Wraith, a beast.

Let him in to let him go.

Curses were things of legend, certainly I didn't have any knowledge how they were undone, but could it be so simple?

Choose him . . .

To free him.

CHAPTER TWENTY-NINE

SOFT LIGHT STIRRED me from haunting dreams of pain and blood. Dried tears hooked my lashes together and left a film of crust in the corners of my eyes. I rubbed a fist to chase what little sleep I'd gotten away. With a groan I sat straight. I'd fallen asleep outside the door of the garret, and someone had placed a quilt over my body during the early hours.

The alehouse was strikingly quiet. A quiet I could taste.

I brushed my sloppy braid off my shoulder and slowly inched my way into standing. Joints and bones ached. Siv had wrapped my injured leg, and Sven had proffered an herb to help with the pain. My lips were cracked and sticky. Inside my mouth tasted sour. With a sinking feeling in my stomach, I took a careful step down the staircase. The wood groaned under my weight. I held my breath. Nothing came, so I kept my steps light and descended into the aleroom.

I coughed at the harsh scent. Wet blood soaked the floor-boards, and it reeked of sweat and innards. Carnage, as though war had been fought here. Father always told us how most folk pissed themselves as they died. A natural response to a failing body. This was how I imagined a battlefield might look and smell.

"He's outside."

I turned to meet the raspy, throaty voice.

Tor sat on a window bench, swirling ale in a horn. Swollen lumps had grown under his eyes. The whites were red and dry. His hair was matted in blood and dried sweat. He looked like a man who'd gone to battle.

"Is he . . ."

Tor shook his head. "He's him now. The morning air helps the healing."

I took a moment and rinsed my mouth with mint powders in the water closet behind the counter, then returned and sat across from Tor. He didn't look at me.

"How did he change so swiftly? I thought this only happened on the last moon."

Tor flicked his eyes to me. "Or when he draws blood from someone. In that case he takes Bevan's potion. It dulls the change and keeps him on the proper schedule. He killed that man at Ravenspire, then missed a dose, then killed more at your manor. It was a violent change this time. He'll have maybe eight nights until the true cycle starts again."

I winced. "Only eight days. What does . . . what does that do to him, being so close?"

"It gets more difficult for him to break out of the call to blood and violence," Tor said.

"Halvar said . . . he said you must hurt him."

"Took a long time to figure it out. A curse of bloodlust," he said bitterly. Tor swirled the drink in his horn. "Meant to make him a monster for the use of vicious men. But it turned him uncontrollable. If he could not find something to break, he'd break himself. Do you know what it's like to watch a man who is like a brother murder himself over and over, but never die? But he'd do it if it meant saving someone else's life."

My stomach lurched. I closed my eyes against the images of it all.

"If we draw the blood, then we can control it. Satiate the curse's need, and save him some pain, at least."

"How long has he lived with this?"

"Too long," was all Tor said.

I stroked the end of my braid and let him drink in silence for a stretched pause. "Thank you, Tor."

He lifted his weary gaze. "For what?"

I held out my hand, so he dropped his gaze to my fingertips. "For saving me. You and Halvar, it was you who pulled him away."

"He didn't know," Tor said defensively. "He slipped us that night. Understand, he can't think during the change. He won't recognize anyone. Not us, not you. Only blood."

I rested a hand on his arm. "I know. I don't hate him for what happened. After seeing what he becomes, I can see it isn't him."

Tor took another drink. "Thought you'd be gone this morning, if I'm honest."

"I considered it," I admitted. "But I made a different choice."

"You want to help him?"

"I don't know how I can, but the idea of him suffering through that again . . ."

Tor looked at his hands, a twitch in the corner of his lips. "You're not so bad, you know. For a royal."

I scoffed with a grin. "You're not so bad for a Shade."

"No, I mean it. You're different. Something about you calls to him. Even when the curse takes hold. When the fury changed those people, the ones who attacked your manor a week ago, he slipped me again."

"So, it was fury."

"Dark fury, to be sure. But Legion, he ran after them. Almost as if he was running to you. Like some deeper instinct knew you needed help."

I picked at a sliver on the table, trying to mute the tears threatening to fall. "I knew I saw him."

"I don't understand it," Tor said shaking his head. "I've never given fate much credit, but he is different with you. He should've changed before we reached the alehouse last night. He was able to keep his head until we arrived. I am starting to believe you do have a role to play in all this."

"May I . . . see him?" There were questions to be asked and answers hopefully to be had.

Tor nodded. "He'll be weak, but I have no doubt he'll talk for you."

Guilt stacked heavy in my stomach. He'd talk with me when I'd caused last night in a way. If I'd given him a chance to speak to me yesterday instead of bolting into the forest, he would've taken Bevan's potion. He wouldn't have suffered last night.

I rose and left Tor in his cups.

The alehouse was fenced in the back. A little plot of dry grass was home to a few evergreen trees and three mangy goats. To one side, where the sunrise was brightest, Legion was shirtless and facedown on a thin linen sheet.

He rested his head on his forearms and appeared to be sleeping. Beside him was a table with a wooden bowl and folded linens. Across his back the angry gashes were pink and swollen, some covered in the linen. Healed swifter than typical wounds to be sure, but still painful looking.

My stomach turned when I recalled the welts I'd seen after he'd left for his 'ailment' before. Had I known they were endless stab wounds I would have done all I could to break this curse then and saved him this pain.

It could begin now.

I worried my bottom lip between my teeth and strode across the lawn. He didn't move as I approached, and his steady breathing hinted that he was asleep. I hesitated, ready to let him rest, but beneath the dried linen a bit of blood had started to run. With care, I took a new cloth and dipped it in the water—ripe with a spice of crushed yarrow and honey. I gently peeled back the old linen, careful not to catch on any skin.

He flinched and his eyes fluttered open. The inky black of his pupils were strangely constricted, so the bits of gold were in bright rings around the center. When he focused on my face, he tried to sit up. "Elise, you shouldn't—"

"No," I insisted, a hand on his shoulder, gently easing him back down. Truth be told, it didn't take much. "Let me."

His muscles were taut, but he complied and rested his cheek over the tops of his hands. I splashed some of the herb water over the angriest wounds, then unfolded the cloth and rested it on his back so it soaked into the open skin.

"You saw?" His voice was coarse and raw. Beneath it was shame.

Convinced the cloth would do its duty for a time, I curled onto my side, facing him. "You truly don't remember?"

I know what Tor had said, but it was strange to think his vicious night was utterly blank in his mind.

"Oh, gods," he groaned. "Did I attack you? Tell me—"

"No," I said. "You didn't attack me, but you looked straight at me. Like you knew me or hated me. I couldn't tell."

"Probably both, I wouldn't know. All I recall is madness." He stared at the fading bruises on his fingernails. "It is like I'm out of myself and only the scent of blood will keep the pain away. A pain that drives me to do anything, to anyone, all to be free of it."

A tear dripped onto my cheek, and he studied it with a level of distress, as though he misunderstood the reason. I wanted to touch him, but held back, unsure how to do any of this.

"You told me when we first came here, I could ask questions," I said. "Do you have the strength to hear some now?"

"I will force the strength if I don't."

I smiled because he was not a beast, not the Blood Wraith, in this moment he was Legion Grey. "I'm serious," I insisted. "If you need to rest, I can come back."

"But would you? Come back, I mean."

Would I choose him. The true question he was asking. With one finger I brushed a piece of his hair off his brow. He stared at me, surprised, but I answered with a smile. "I would. Now, is that a nudge to leave you be, or . . ."

"Stay," he said. He relaxed his face back onto his hands. "Ask anything and I will try to answer."

In my head I organized the questions. There were so many, but a few were more pressing. "Why were you cursed?"

"The first question, and I don't know the answer." He let out a sigh. "I remember the curse, remember it was ordered by a Timoran king, though I don't know which one."

I lifted one brow. "Which one? You are younger than Zyben."

"Am I? I don't know. Elise, I don't know my real name. Halvar named me."

"Your pardon? Halvar did what?"

He grinned—sort of—and nodded. "Tor and Halvar know their first names, but after the curse took hold, not one of us remembered mine, nor who any of us were before. Halvar insisted on Legion for the strength of it, so, Legion it became."

I dabbed the cloth around his back, my fingers gently pressing the herbs into the gnarled skin. He was warm and calm, and I wanted him to stay like this. To never endure another night of such gore again. "I don't understand, though. You told me of the waif house, of childhood, so surely you must know your age or something about who you were before. Unless it wasn't the truth."

"I never lied to you about my past. I do remember a waif house, but I don't know if it's a true memory. If I lied, then it is because the memory might be false. Tor does not have the same memory. In fact, he has no childhood at all. And Halvar insists we sailed as children on the Fate's Ocean. Which one is true?"

"How is that possible?"

"What we take from it is the curse prevents us from knowing exactly who we are, simply that we three have always been together."

I flashed him a bemused smirk and moved the towel to a different place on his shoulder, inching closer so my knees touched his side. "You must be someone who would be a danger to the throne."

"Who is to say? Perhaps I was wicked and a killer before. Perhaps the curse magnified evil."

I snorted a laugh. "I don't mean to make light of this, but I don't believe you were evil. Not a chance."

The barest of grins played at his mouth. "Oh, so sure?"

"Yes," I said lightly. "No evil man would sit and read books with a silly girl for hours, or offend wealthy, powerful suitors every time they met. I don't think *Herr* Gurst will ever forgive you for putting all the choice in my hands."

Legion chuckled, then groaned, fists clenched when his skin pulled wrong. "Well," he said through his teeth. "He is more boar than man."

I smiled and drizzled more water over his wounds. This time I used my hands to gently massage the herbs. His breathing softened. "Do you remember how you were cursed?"

"Yes." He lifted his head and looked to me. "I call her the enchantress. I can see her in my head, but not her face. I hear her voice casting the spell, the terms of what would become of me." He dug his hand beneath his chest and tugged on the black stone he kept around his neck. "She gave me this seer stone. It's filled with strange fury. I suppose to help me figure how to end the curse. But it does not give up secrets easily. Still, it's led me this far in this game."

"A game?"

"To me this has always been a game with the throne of New Timoran. A hunt for answers, and at the end we will see if I succeed or remain a beast, the bane of this land."

I rubbed the sides of my head when my skull ached. Legion winced but rolled onto his side and faced me. We were close, a single pace from each other. He looked so much like the man I'd kissed in the schoolhouse; I could hardly believe the things that had happened since. "And you know how to end the curse, now?"

He lowered his face back to his hands, a burden in his eyes. "Yes. Turns ago we learned a way out."

"You said I could help. I'm part of this discovery, I presume."

"Yes."

"Why did you infiltrate my life?" I finally asked the looming question between us.

He looked down and clutched the seer stone again. "This. For the most part I'm shown writings, or books, or Night Folk spells to help me understand how to break the curse. Slowly, we learned of a place, said to have all the lore, the sagas, the fury to undo *any* magic. Even the sort from different kingdoms. But we can't reach it."

"Why not?"

He picked at the dry blades of grass. "Only a certain royal can open the gates. It is part of the fury that guards the place and keeps it hidden. It is called the Black Tomb."

I thought of the child witch and how she mentioned a tomb when the queen put her on display. The eerie omen struck me, and now my heart raced, wondering if she could've meant this place. I didn't tell Legion, unwilling to lift his spirits when really, I knew nothing about this.

"So, you picked me because I'm royal."

"There is a catch," he explained, a heaviness in his voice. "The royal must be willing to open the tomb and use nothing for themselves."

He shifted onto his side, his hand coming to rest in the center of us. I thought to take it, but wondered if it might hurt the healing from those razor-sharp claws.

"There's something you're not saying."

He cleared his throat and rubbed one of the red marks on his arm. "There is another piece. Trust, choice, and devotion must be given in equal measure from the royal to me, and me to them. To help must be their choice. You can imagine it is not easy finding a Timoran in the royal house who would care enough to free a monster with formidable fury, yet use none of it to make themselves more powerful."

"You didn't know I would, though. Why me?"

He held up the seer stone. "I saw the Lysander manor. I don't mean to hurt you, but it didn't take long to find the one who might be the most compassionate in your household."

Heat filled my cheeks. It was almost laughable to think of my parents or Runa caring about anyone outside of noble Timoran enough to abandon power for themselves. I studied Legion as he studied the grass. Did I care . . . I didn't even need to finish the thought. I cared. Enough I'd seen him as a cursed creature and still wanted to be here. With him.

"And so you planned everything to get us close to each other."

He nodded. "I made myself a name in Mellanstrad. I

believed more than ever fate played a role when it was clear the second daughter would need a dowry negotiator. I made certain it was me. But the things I said, I never lied, Elise. I thought I would. I thought I would despise you. Truth be told, I was hopeless this would ever work because how could I ever give devotion or trust to a Timoran royal, when a royal is who caused this?"

"But you believe you have?" My voice came out in a barely controlled whisper.

His eyes pierced me. "When I told Bevan I was ready in the kitchens—it meant I chose you. That I could honestly give all my loyalty, my devotion, and trust. The protection bond would not have worked otherwise."

I bit the inside of my cheek and curled my legs beneath me. "This has been . . . so much. I trusted you with everything. But you kept secrets from me, made me believe you . . . wanted things for different reasons."

He never looked away and I wished he would. There were unsaid things, and I didn't know if I dared drag them out, or if the truth would hurt worse. Truths that perhaps he did not feel the same things as me or did not want the same things.

"You didn't tell me you were the Blood Wraith," I finished.

"Because that is not a name I use. It is a name given to me," he said angrily. "In moments when I've had no control, I was called a Blood Wraith. Fitting, perhaps, but I despise it. I don't want to be *him*, Elise." Fingers still stained in blood, he carefully reached for my hand. His thumb dragged over the two missing tips. "When you told me this, hells I could hardly breathe. I don't know how you're still here, still with me."

I curled my fingers with his and a weight lifted off my shoulders.

"I won't deny I was terrified at first." A shy grin played over my lips. "But I'd already given my trust, my devotion, my compassion to Legion Grey. Behind the mask, isn't that who you are?"

His eyes smoldered in heat. "Yes."

I swallowed the dryness in my throat, my thumb traced his knuckles. "Well then. There you have it."

Legion slipped his fingers through mine, pressed the back of my hand to his lips. "You don't have to do anything more, Elise. After all of it, I see what a disruption this is, how selfish I've been—"

"Selfish? This was done to you by Timoran; the least a Timoran can do to make amends is break it."

"What are you saying?"

That I cannot bear to let you suffer again. Never again. "I plan to finish this. Do you know where the Black Tomb is?"

"Elise—"

"Three hells, what do you want? You slip into my life, drag me to this smelly place, and now you are denying me my sole duty in all this?"

His teeth showed when he smiled. All gods, it was good to see his smile again.

"I would not dream of denying you anything, *Kvinna*. I've no doubt you'd be terrifying should I try."

"I would be," I said, hoping he did not see the way my heart raced. "So, what do we do?"

A furrow nestled between his brows. "You're sure you want to do this? I don't know what we'll find once we're there."

"Then it will be another adventure."

The gold faded as more of his smoldering black darkened his eyes. He shook his head and squeezed my hand. "I am forever changed knowing you."

I dragged out a bit of the bold warrior blood, nestled back on my side, and scooted across the space between us. Our bodies aligned, Legion rested an arm over my waist, and me, a palm on his cheek. His hooded eyes struggled to stay open. I grinned and whispered, "I hope soon you will simply be forever changed into who you once were."

I rested my head to his damp brow and stayed there until he closed his eyes and at last, slept.

CHAPTER THIRTY

The Sun Prince and Night Prince fight much like the day battles the dusk. Poor Valen, such a fighter's temperament, but no match for the cunning of his brother. Sol, gods help me, the boy will be the scheming king of history. If he sets another trap for his brother, I don't know if Valen will live to see ten turns.

The poor boy was found only this eve, sobbing, and when he laid eyes on me, he covered his ears and cried harder. Distressed, I asked the child why he feared me. His response: Dear elder brother, along with children of the gentry, convinced Valen he was not true Night Folk, and in fact, Arvad and I had stretched the curves of his ears into points because we hung him by fishing hooks as a babe.

Gods deliver me from my silver-tongued first son.

Arvad spent time in the sagas with Valen, showing the boy what Night Folk can do. Reminding his second son that he, too, had a taper at his ear. After—such a thing happened—Valen shifted rock.

The first inkling to a gift with bending the earth. While other children of the gentry have shown fire, air, and water fury, my heart soars thinking at long last fury to bend the soil might show itself. So many generations have passed since the last Bender.

Arvad bolstered the boy and went on, explaining how our line is fully blessed with fury, but it chose to present in his blood, in his new gift, and yes, his fae ears.

And gods deliver me from my husband. Next, Arvad pierced the child's ears right then. A way to show off his uniqueness and boast about his faeish features. If Sol keeps up his schemes, if Herja continues her desire for knighthood—by the father of gods—I will not survive my own strong-willed, thick headed, beloved family.

I THOUGHT Queen Lilianna might give us answers. But she simply left me wishing for Arvad and her rule once more.

Doubtless, the Ettan king and queen would not have cursed someone. Would not have tortured another with fury.

I closed the journal, a delivery from Bevan just this morning. I'd cried and embraced him, wholly relieved he hadn't been the scorched body at my family's home.

The old man had scoured through my room at Ravenspire and brought them to the alehouse with some elixir for Legion, and an added note: Calder's hunt for Night Folk, to dissect them and steal fury for Timorans, had already begun.

Legion's curse had something to do with the Timoran crown, and I could only hope once it was broken, we could work together to stop the new king and his foolish queen.

"HALVAR, ARE YOU ALL RIGHT?" I asked.

Halvar lifted his head off his hands, a look of astonishment written on his face. "We're really going? We're doing this?" He raked his fingers through his dark curls and faced Tor. "When you discover I am a bleeding king or something, I expect you to bend the knee and kiss my hairy—"

Tor punched him in the shoulder, hard, sending Halvar laughing and moaning at the same time.

I shared a smile with Legion; even Siv grinned.

"Do ya even know how to get into the bleeding tomb?" Sven asked as he passed around horns of sharp ale.

This was the piece that had Legion unsettled. He didn't like knowing I might have more tasks that could catch us unaware. But what choice was there? How could I walk away knowing they suffered? I had feared them—sometimes I still did—but the truth was Halvar had saved me; Tor had protected us all with his watchful eye. And Legion, he had brought me to life in more than one way.

"We will approach each step with caution," I said after a pause. "We take this in strides."

"Agreed," Legion said. "Any unnecessary risks arise, though, and we change plans. We think of a different way."

"What about her?" Tor asked, nodding at Siv.

I considered for hours after speaking with Legion about how to handle Siverie. I might be a fool, but tonight we needed all the help we could manage. "She is an Agitator but has had ample chances to kill me and she didn't. For now, that trust will need to be enough. We could use an extra fighter."

The others agreed. After another round of silence, Halvar slapped the table. "Right then. We meet the old man at the high moon, so until then I plan to drink until I'm singing delightful sonnets that will woo you all into maddening love with me."

Tor muttered about brainless half-wits, but it only brought out more laughs from his companion. Siv rose from the table and headed for the stairs. "I might rest, if you don't need anything."

"Siv, you aren't my serf. Not anymore."

She nodded and left me alone with Legion in the empty, pungent aleroom.

"You've been quiet," I said. During the discussions with the others, Legion had said very little; only offering a few explanations, or thoughts on what he knew about the Black Tomb and how to find it.

Still a little weary from the lingering effects of the curse, he lifted his gaze to me and held out a hand. "Walk with me?"

I took his hand and went back to the yard. The moon was rising, and the first calls of night birds filled the treetops. Legion didn't release my hand and stood with me at the edge of the yard, his eyes at the first stars.

"I want to give you another chance to turn from this, Elise."

"Thank you," I said flatly. "You've given your chance and I won't hear of it again. I'm staying."

He kept his eyes on the sky, but even in the dimness the smile was visible. We stayed shoulder to shoulder for a long moment, breathing in the night, maybe breathing in each other.

I nestled closer. "Are you afraid of discovering who you are?"

"Yes," he said with great deliberateness. "I don't know who else to be but Legion Grey."

I'd thought the whole of the day about who Legion could be. A disgraced Timoran noble. An experiment much like Calder planned to do with fury. Perhaps an Ettan warrior; a Night Folk rogue. I considered he could be from the Ferus line, but they died nearly two hundred turns before. Still, there was talk they lived on. Even Agitators worshiped the Night Prince. I'd happily return Lilianna and Arvad to the throne, but I had seen the grave markers. Arvad in a rocky quarry, murdered in front of his sons. Lilianna and Herja, slaughtered after they refused to be consorts to the first king of New Timoran.

"Now it is you who has gone quiet," Legion said, glancing sideways at me.

"I was thinking of what happens after." I had too many thoughts all at once and picked one. "I am not welcome in Timoran courts for I will not give my fealty to Calder. Ever."

Legion shifted on his feet. "I want to promise you protection, but I don't know what will happen if we succeed. But I do swear to you, as long as I am able, I will keep you safe, Elise. You did not abandon me when you rightly should have, and I will not abandon you."

As long as he was able.

What if the curse ended *everything*?

I shuddered. No. The idea of losing him sent sharp, prickly pains into my middle. I tightened my hold on his hand and he allowed it. He drew me in against him. We'd go in a few short clock tolls, and I wanted to forget about what we would face. Wanted to pretend nothing had changed between us, and we could be the insignificant second daughter, and the handsome tradesman from the Mellanstrad docks.

"Legion." My stomach spun and coiled and jumped, my hands were damp. I met his eye. "Kiss me again. Once more, before everything changes."

A spark of need lit his eyes. His hands trapped the sides of my face and urged me closer. He grinned against my lips. "It will always be my pleasure, *Kvinna*."

He claimed my mouth with his. Slow at first, gentle and warm. My palms traveled around his waist, holding him close, and it unlocked what we'd held back before.

Legion kissed me deep and raw. He parted my lips with his and groaned when my tongue teased his bottom lip. A kiss of give and take. One of hidden things we wouldn't say, or were too afraid to say. We kissed with hope for a new dawn, and with the dread of the end.

I kissed him. Kept kissing him, touching him, holding him until the moon raised to its highest point and the time to face our fate arrived.

THERE WEREN'T enough horses for me, but this time I chose to ride with Legion. Held in the space of his arms, my back to his chest. I could almost pretend my body did not protest to the rough ride.

He'd dressed like the Blood Wraith, black axes on his waist, red mask over his mouth. I told him if we all lived through this, I'd be getting him a new color, so I didn't startle every time I saw it. He laughed, pulled the mask down, and kissed me quickly. And I wanted to stay, to not leave into an unknown direction.

But the hope in the eyes of Legion and the Guild of Shade couldn't be ignored.

This night could be their liberty.

Warm air off the shore hinted at a storm approaching. The forest was alight with sounds of creatures, and in the foothills of Castle Ravenspire the sweet spices of Lyx perfumed the air.

Legion rode into a narrow clearing in the forest beyond the gates. He abandoned the horse but helped me slide off with his hands on my waist. Sven had stocked his alehouse with clothes, and I'd come to understand most were for the Guild of Shade. A refuge over the turns where Legion could transform and be kept chained and beaten and bloodied without killing anyone. I'd first thought the old aleman a sort of saint, until I learned the hefty sum Legion Grey paid him to keep his mouth shut.

Sven was more businessman than friend, but I was glad he had a tunic and hose I could use tonight instead of a tattered gown.

Seated on a fallen log in the clearing, an oil lantern in hand, Bevan stood and grinned as we approached. He wore a traveler's jacket, a sea swab knit cap, and had a knapsack on the ground.

"Bevan, are you leaving?" I asked.

He glanced at his supplies and nodded. "It's time to return

home. Calder has devised a way to test for different mystics. Unfortunately, we Alvers, if you cut us our blood is quite pungent. It will be easy to figure me out, and I've lived too bleeding long to be a rat in a cage, being poked and prodded."

"But you said they trade Alvers in the East," I protested.

"Still true," he said. "But in Skítkast, my old region, there are rings of Alver smugglers who know how to stay hidden. I will survive, *Kvinna*. If you find my foolish nephew, do keep him in line." He tapped my nose and lowered his voice. "You chose this?"

"I did," I whispered. "He doesn't deserve this anymore."

"He doesn't. And I knew you'd be the one to help. The moment he mentioned the Lysander manor, I knew. You are a different Timoran, Elise Lysander, and I believe fate has a grand plan in store for you."

"Bevan," Tor interrupted.

The old steward gave me a final smile and approached the Guild of Shade. From the knapsack, Bevan removed a leather pouch, tied in string. He handed it to Halvar. "Can you handle this without dropping it?"

Halvar balked. "Dear Bevan, why the constant interrogation on my responsibility? I am the obvious choice to bear something gravely important."

"It is a powdered elixir," Bevan explained. "Use it at the markers and it will reveal anything fury-hidden like—"

"A tomb," Tor said.

"Yes." The old man looked to Legion, a fatherly sort of pride in his eyes. "You helped this old man once turns ago, and it has been an honor to help you since. I believe fate led us together. Led all of us together. This is the end of it, and I know you will have a part to play in healing this kingdom. In all the kingdoms."

Legion took Bevan's forearm, a warrior's farewell.

We didn't have long. I wanted to spend more time with Bevan, tell him I worried for him on the tides. Ask him how we'd know if he made it to his smuggling ring in one piece, but we parted with final goodbyes and left on foot through the far thicket behind Castle Ravenspire.

"You helped Bevan?" I asked Legion softly.

"He'd been ambushed in the trees, we intervened."

"As Legion or the Blood Wraith."

He chuckled. "They do not flee from Legion Grey, *Kvinna*."

At the base of a slope, dead shrubs were stacked in a far-reaching archway. "Moonvane," I whispered. Dead, brittle. A reminder of the fae prince who'd died and took power away from this land. I'd heard more than once the land resisted us, and in a way, I believed it did. Loyalty, good intentions, compassion—all of it was needed to break this curse, and if I had to guess I'd say fury thrived in good intentions. Not that it didn't work for the wicked, but potential was unlocked for the genuine.

At least, I hoped.

"This is the marker," Legion said as he broke off one of the dry moonvane branches. He stepped back as Halvar took a rather grandiose step to the front.

"Ready?"

"Been ready," Tor grumbled.

Siv settled behind me, silent and observant. We had hardly spoken in all this, but I felt a bit of gladness she was here and willing to help end this. When this was over, I'd tell her. If I could forgive Legion his secrets, I could forgive Siv hers.

Halvar opened the leather pouch and dumped a bit of silvery powder into his hand. "Oh, it sort of tingles." He faced the arch of dead moonvane and tossed the dry elixir.

I held my breath and waited for a marvelous rush of wind as a magical place appeared.

There was no wind, but a smoky kind of haze wrapped around the space, and when it lifted it was as if the ground had extended. A great space that had not been there before. The courtyard was surrounded by a hip-high stone wall. Statues of the gods—the father of gods with his ravens, the goddess of love, even the god of tricks and schemes. The statues protected what looked to be a cluster of mausoleums. Simply built from wood and wattle and sod. The mounds were reserved for burial chambers of warriors and royalty.

To see it appear from air left me breathless.

"This is it," Halvar whispered, entirely serious now.

"Which one?" Siv asked. "You said the help to end this will be in the Black Tomb, but there are several mounds."

"We'll search all of them if we must," said Tor as he withdrew a slender short blade from his hip. "Keep low and keep alert. Let's go."

CHAPTER THIRTY-ONE

T̲he̲ ̲ni̲g̲ht̲ ̲wa̲s̲ ̲ee̲ri̲l̲y ̲s̲t̲il̲l̲. Once we stepped through the archway it seemed we were cut off from the rest of the world. I could no longer see the lights at Castle Ravenspire, nor smell the cinnamon from Lyx, only this place with its musty earth and damp grass.

I gawked as we passed beneath the legs of an ancient *jotunn* giant made of dark granite. The symbols were beautiful and heady with old beliefs. Night Folk were honored here. Amongst the gods were different folk carved from stone. Some with curled horns on their brows, others with round eyes and triple jointed fingers. Some with delicate wings. I touched the pointed ear of a pixie girl staring into the basin of a stone fountain. A sense of despondency tightened in my chest.

Old Etta must've been wonderous. Night Folk, Ettans, maybe even the gods, walked among each other.

How far we'd come from it all.

"Elise," Legion said, interrupting my thoughts. "We will stand watch. But if royal blood is needed to open the way . . ."

I glanced at the burial mounds and nodded. "I'll start going through them."

He kept me locked in his sights. "Be careful."

"Promise me the same."

A quirk at his eyes led me to think he'd grinned beneath his mask. I looked to Halvar and Tor, but they'd already slunk into the night, searching for trouble.

"Siv," I whispered. "Stay safe."

She drew in a sharp breath and tightened her grip on the dagger the Shade had returned to her once we arrived. "I will. You, too."

I didn't waste any more time and rushed toward the first knoll. The doorway was sealed. No knob or latch. A heavy slab of stone, too heavy to move. But at the door there was a stand with a gilded chalice on top. Tethered to the chalice was a stiletto knife. I frowned, but soon understood.

Royal blood was needed.

Thank the gods it seemed only a small amount would be asked. I'd never thought of spilling my blood intentionally.

I gritted my teeth and lifted the knife. Like a frightened child I let the point hover over my palm for a few heartbeats before I sliced the pad of my palm. I winced but squeezed my hand until the drops started to fall into the chalice.

At once, a scrape of stone on stone echoed into the night and the slab moved aside, only enough to slip through. The idea that I might be trapped inside crossed my mind only once before I hurried through the gap into the dark.

When the slab didn't move, I breathed easier. The only light came from the moonlight in the courtyard, but the smell was enough to know this was indeed a burial chamber. And I'd disturbed it. There were five wooden boxes in the tomb, each with a blade at rest over the top.

I kneeled and pressed a hand to my heart. A warrior's respect. Whomever was laid to rest here, had fought with honor and would be revered by the throne. I stood and peeked at one of the blades briefly—curiosity too much to resist. A vine of thorns was etched down the center of the blade with an eclipse of the sun and moon in the center. This was old Ettan. So, these would be honored Ettan warriors.

I bowed my head once more and left the tomb. The moment I stepped outside the slab grumbled back into place. There was half a dozen more, but as I studied them, trying to find which one might hold more than death, one stood out among the others—a center tomb with dead moonvane shrubs.

I took a step on the path that would lead to the center tomb and the silence of the night tilted. A wretched, gnarled shriek sprang from the dark. My heart leapt to my throat. I drew my knife, eyes wild and wide. Tor's roar sounded the loudest and the first. I whipped around, scanning the darkness.

Next, Legion shouted, and the clang of steel followed.

A bitter cold wrapped around the night, and on the slope, I caught sight of Siv. She was fleeing and fighting in the same breath. Fighting what? Then, a glimmer of something gold came into view. Three hells—shadows surrounded her, but when she turned and fought, they took shape. A human form painted in night held a glittering sword. Though the shadow was made of mist, the blade was not.

Legion came up behind Siv's shadow and ripped an axe

through the back of the . . . ghost, an apparition? I didn't know what to call them, but it dissolved.

Another was there to meet them both.

"Elise!" Legion shouted. "They're fury guardians. Go! Hurry!"

His voice deepened. The rage of battle seemed to draw out the voice of the beast within. Though these shadow guardians never bled, the desire to kill them would be alive. The creature cursed inside him might be spurred to life all the same.

I rushed toward the tomb. Otherworldly screams followed me at my back. I shouldn't have looked, but one glance over my shoulder and three phantom shadows rushed at me. Halvar blasted a dart into one and it burst into drops of dew. Tor took the others with a swing of his sword. Another shadow warrior appeared at his back and swung its fiery gold blade.

The third spectral still chased me.

I bolted for the moonvane tomb, hands trembling. The hair on the back of my neck stood as I reached for the stiletto blade. My fingers shook. The cut ended more jagged than the first.

Behind me the shadow shrieked. It lifted its blade that seemed made of embers. I screamed and smashed my hand over the chalice. When the first smear of blood touched the edge, the heavy slab slid away, I swung the tomb's knife at the phantom and caught the shadow on what might be its shoulder. It burst into thousands of bits of night.

I leaned back to catch my breath against the tomb. Easy enough to kill but when one died, more appeared. An endless amount of darkness that could rise up in arms against us. The others would fatigue before they were victorious.

I hurried into the tomb.

This was vastly different than the last. Musty damp soaked the walls, but it was absent the scent of death. And in here there were oil lamps in each corner for light. This was not a place of burial, but more a prison. Bars walled off artifacts and books and scrolls and . . .

My eyes widened when bright green eyes locked on me in the dimness. A skinny girl peered out through the bars. She was dressed in a white frock and had hair that hung to the small of her back in long russet waves.

At the sight of me, she backed away.

"Who are you?" I asked. Was she fae? Who would lock a child in a tomb? My eyes widened. "All gods, are you the witch?"

The girl narrowed her eyes. "That's not a nice word. Story-teller, thank you very much. It has a better ring to it, don't you think?"

By the gods! I rushed to her cell, searching out any kind of lock and key. She chuckled bitterly. Such a small, underfed girl. Her eyes were a little sunken and her cheeks were hollow.

"You won't find anything," she said. "Only a certain key can unlock me and the king's fae must do it."

"The king's fae?"

She snorted. "You don't think the wretches up in the palace don't use some dark fae from time to time? They say they slit 'em across the throat, but they have their uses, like tossing me in here when I misbehave. Out of sight in a tomb they can't even see. Pleasant, right?"

I stared at her bewildered.

She spoke strangely. Rough and accented, but rife with bitterness.

The girl studied me again, and a smug grin spread on her face. "Wait. I know you. The kind heart." A bit of thrill brightened her eyes. "He's here, isn't he?"

I curled my fists around the bars. "Tell me what you know! Please, help us. There are shadows and—"

"Oh, yes," she said with a scoff. "They're worse than fleas." She clapped her hands rapidly. "Pop, pop, pop. Always there. Those fire swords they've got—they hurt like the hells before they kill you."

"Then it's a good thing he can't die."

She chuckled, but I thought it came more from nerves than humor. "Outside the tomb, maybe. But in here, power like that doesn't work."

"Girl!" I shouted, a new rise of panic in my chest. "Then help us! You knew this would happen, you predicted it. Tell me what you know."

She looked wholly like a child once I raised my voice and a bit of guilt sped through me when she pointed at the cage beside her. "It's a crest, like a symbol or something. It was made by a Night Folk smithy and is the key."

"A crest?"

"It's what you want."

I ran to the next cage and rattled the bars but could find no lock again.

"Blood, kind heart," she said. "You're a royal, aren't you? Willing, royal blood opens it."

I fumbled for my knife and opened one of the marks on my

palm again, then gripped the bars. The rattle of metal rang in my head, but the cage opened for me. Inside were stacks of books and scrolls. I tossed them aside in a flurry of paper and parchment.

"Hurry, kind heart," she said, apparently unaware of my true name. "You'll lose him. The guardians will bring out the beast and make it stay."

"If you'd tell me what I'm looking for exactly this might go much—" I stopped. A scroll fell back and hidden beneath it was a slender box.

I tore into the box and let out a maddened kind of laugh. On a velvet cushion was an iron crest of runes.

The girl clapped ironically. "Well done."

"But now what?" I said, irritated. "How is this done? How does the curse end?"

Her face contorted and I was reminded of her youth. She looked ready to cry. "Unraveling a new path of fate is more than speaking the words. It takes a hells lot of sacrifice."

"I don't know what you're talking about. Did you put this curse on him?"

"No!" she said a crack in her voice. "But . . . someone like me did. She wrote him a new fate. That's what I do beyond telling stupid bits of fortune. I rewrite destiny."

The ground tilted in my haze. "You wrote him into the curse. Wrote the terms. Made it so his fate was to transform."

"I told you I didn't! I am the fifth Storyteller to be dragged into this cell. And the first four—dead. Once they got a taste of our fate spells, though, these kings have hunted us ever since. Made sure their plans were fated to happen."

My eyes widened. "The coup. Did you—"

"No. That stupid ghoul of a prince has his own fae to do tricky, bloody things. But I've been forced to write other things for other folk. Things that make folk powerful and dangerous."

"But how did you know about the curse?"

She gestured at some of the stacks of parchment and books. "I wasn't always in a cage. I read about it."

"No," I said shaking my head. "You know more. What part have you played? You knew me right away."

She hesitated. "I knew he'd be important—your beast. Sometimes I get these feelings, these things I just know. He'd be the one to help me, so I helped him."

"What did you do?" I repeated.

"Understand, he needed to get into your house somehow. So, I thought it out. Sorry your father got sick, but it had to be done."

My eyes widened. "You . . . you're the reason my father is ill?"

She grimaced and her eyes went glassy. "I don't like hurting people, but I needed to write a path to you and the rest would be up to him."

"But why me?"

"Because the last Storyteller called the king's niece a kind heart!" she shouted. "Right before they cut her into the Otherworld. Well, I sure as hells wasn't going out the same way. I decided to do something about it. Fate wanted a way to get willing royal blood, by the gods, I'm wise enough to know it'd take a kind heart. Like any good story there is always an end, so I wrote one, a simple one—the beast would find love and be set free."

The wind knocked free of my lungs. "Love is his way out?"

She shrugged. "Or something like it. You had to care enough to be here. He had to care enough to give you the choice. Good enough for me."

"Why would you help him find the answer?"

"I told you. I know—have *seen*—if he is free, it will begin a change that will heal lands beyond this one. It might give me freedom, or my brother. They took me from him and . . . all I want is to see him again. But we aren't free. Always hiding. This could start something, could change the world. Small and simple things can bring about greatness."

"You wrote that."

"Saw it. Like a glimpse into the eye of fate. Call it a curse or blessing, but I saw it and know it. So, I moved things along as best I could without getting caught. It's a good thing the dead king didn't know what the beast in the curse of crowns looked like, or the role I played, or I would've been more than a trick at fetes."

"The curse of crowns?"

She shrugged again. "It's what the first storyteller titled it. Not that catchy if you ask me."

I didn't care if she was a child, there was no time! My heart in a frenzy, I slammed my fists against the bars of her cage. "How do I break it?"

She recoiled, eyes wide. "Sacrifice! I told you! There is a seal of the original royals, it faces east, just beyond this tomb. They are called the true heirs of this land's magic. That's where it must be done. The crest must be placed in the center, it's all very symbolic and vain, but I don't make the rules of this land and their fury. Once it's placed, you make the sacrifice."

"More blood?"

"No, kind heart," she said softly. "It's more. Life must be given for a life."

CHAPTER THIRTY-TWO

A LIFE FOR A LIFE. Me for Legion, for his freedom. Could I? Did I even dare? The girl stared at me as though I might burst into flames.

"You—" I cleared away the fear. "You said when he is free, he will be the force that could change things for fury and magic-folk?"

She hesitated. "It will begin *something*. I don't know how because you must remember, kind heart, fate is not always interpreted correctly. Each word could mean something differ-ent. I saw change. Not all at once, but a spark that will begin it all. I don't know how it will be done, though."

I closed my eyes and tears fell down my cheeks. One life for a life, but if she was to be believed this was one life for poten-tially many. Legion—who he was before—could be a force for change in Timoran, the sort I'd always wanted. Timorans might walk the streets with Ettans. Night Folk could emerge from the trees, from wherever they hide. But she spoke of a fire catching across the Fate's Ocean, to different kingdoms. Bevan might not live out his days with smugglers. His sort of folk could be free.

I didn't know anything about other kingdoms or their fury, or mesmer, or magic, but if it made a more peaceful world wasn't it worth it?

I forced a grin, clutching the crest to my heart. "At least they'll write a saga about me."

The girl's eyes grew wet. "Be sure you want to take this step. The guardians will do all they can to stop you. It is the nature of this cursed place, to keep it hidden."

I nodded. In truth, I didn't want to do this, but if it was the only way—if this is why royal blood was needed—then it would fall to me or no one. Certainly, no Timoran royals I knew would even consider it. Legion would be trapped, never dying. Timoran would dissect and destroy fury for their gain.

"Tell him," I started, "if you see him when this is over, tell him I wanted it to be different. I wanted to bring the change at his side."

She blinked, and as brisk as the child witch tried to be, she felt a great deal and tried not to show it.

"Will you be freed from this?"

She shrugged. "I don't know. I hope."

"But still, you sacrificed, too. You wrote this path for someone else."

"I told you," she whispered, "I know what it's like to be a prisoner. And maybe I was a little bored."

I laughed. What a strange girl. "I hope you will be free to find your brother."

She winced and looked at the ground. "Gods be with you, kind heart."

"I'm Elise. What's your name?"

She blinked her gaze to me. "Calista."

I nodded with a smile, offered her a final look, prayed she'd get free, and turned back to the entrance. Once I stepped out there, my decision would be made, and I would be targeted by the guardians. We'd come this far. I sent a prayer to the sky that we wouldn't be undone by some aggravating shadows with swords.

Holding my breath, clinging to the dagger, I ran.

Tears stung in the cold night. I kept my head down, my intent focused. All around, the cries of my friends, Tor, Halvar, Siv, echoed around the swirl of shadows as they battled the guardians.

"She's out!" Halvar cheered. "Elise! What—"

"Elise!" Legion's shout was haggard. He battled the curse, even here.

I couldn't look at him.

"Elise, stop!"

No. A slope to the courtyard was before me. Twenty paces, ten. I sprinted until my legs throbbed. A shattering cry shook the courtyard. From the corner of my eye, shadows gathered in coagulated mass of night. My heart quickened, and I forced my feet faster up the hillside. Wails and shrieks gained behind me as the guardians rushed to stop me. I didn't know how fury worked, but somehow, they knew my intent, and their instinct was to attack.

At the top of the hillside, I fumbled over a lip of rock. My knees skidded over the rough surface, peeling off a layer of skin.

I winced but kept limping to the center. It was a symbol of briars and coiled serpents on the hilt of a blade.

"Elise! Stop! What are you doing?" Legion was chasing the cloud of shadow guardians.

I curled over my bloodied knees, gasping, but spared a final, longing glance. His eyes were lined in red again, but he was still him. Still there. Still good.

He would be the good in this world.

I smiled, turned away, and placed the crest in a divot at the center of the symbol. A raised circle that seemed to be missing a piece. A spark of heat shuddered under the symbol once it was placed. I raised my knife over my heart. One breath. One more heartbeat. One plunge. I let out a long breath and pulled back the blade for momentum and—

The knife knocked out free of my hand. Legion glared at me furiously, scooping me in his arms.

"No!" I screamed. The guardians loomed at the base of the hillside. "No, you don't understand this is the only way to end it!"

"No!" he shouted back. "Not like this. I would rather live a thousand more turns with this curse."

I touched his face, tears blurring the sharp lines and edges. But I held onto them. "Forgive me."

With all I had I shoved Legion back, so he fell over the uneven ground. "Elise!"

The guardians shrieked. I fumbled for the knife and dropped it more than once. I screamed at the glint of gold as a guardian raised its sword over my head. No, I couldn't die. Not yet! I needed to do this!

The instant I circled my hand around the hilt of the knife, an angry hiss broke from the shadow guardian.

I turned.

My head refused to accept what I was seeing.

Hunched over me, like a sort of shield, Legion blinked in stun. He stumbled to his knees and slowly, together, our eyes traveled to the center of his chest.

A fiery gold sword had torn through his heart.

"Legion!" No! This wasn't the way it was supposed to be. Blood dripped over his lips, down his chin. Blood from his chest splattered onto the stone seal beneath us. I patted his shoulders, afraid to touch him anywhere that might cause him pain. It didn't matter, after another moment, another hiss of wind, the sword faded with the shadow guardians into the mist. I didn't care where they'd gone or why, nothing mattered. Not now.

Legion fell back; I caught him and rested his head in my lap. I stroked my fingers through his damp hair. He coughed and more blood stained his teeth. My tears fell in heavy drops onto his cheeks. "Why did you do that?"

I choked on a sob. He could die here. He was dying.

"I couldn't . . . let you."

I pressed a kiss to his forehead, holding my lips there. "It had to be me. Willing, royal blood, Legion. It had to be me."

His warm palm covered my cheek. I covered it with mine and met his eyes. They were too glassy, too faded. "You set me free."

A shudder ran through his body and his hand went limp. The thud of my pulse in my skull was deafening. A deep crack built down the center of me. I couldn't think, couldn't even breathe. I pressed his hand against my face, desperate to feel him hold it there himself. My fingers anxiously tangled in his hair.

"Legion," I cried. "Legion, please."

He was silent.

As best I could, I hugged his shoulders to my body and buried my face in his neck and cried. Vaguely, I sensed the others had come closer. Siv sniffled. If Tor and Halvar had words in their heads, they didn't say them.

Silently, I begged Legion to return. But I knew he wouldn't.

Through my clenched eyes a white glow shone, blinding me.

"What the hells?" Halvar muttered.

I peeked and startled. The patches of Legion's blood had started swirling in an incoherent pattern. Lining the curve of the serpent's coils, the points of the thorns. Everywhere it touched, a bright glow burst from the pattern. Legion's body was surrounded. I released him and scrambled back.

Tor and Halvar cried out at the same moment. They crumbled, and like Legion were swallowed by the glow of light.

I sprinted to Siv, and we scurried away. Dumbfounded, I stared at the dome of light. It burst everywhere across the stone seal, chasing away the shadows in the trees, the darkness of the tombs. It burned like a star, then faded back into the earth, leaving us blinded to the darkness.

I blinked and rubbed at my eyes until they adjusted once again in the night.

Groans and painful shouts replaced the ethereal glow. On the stone, Halvar staggered to his feet first, then he helped gather Tor.

"Halvar," I whispered.

He faced me. His eyes were piercingly black, his dark curls longer than before. Halvar stared at me strangely, seemed to recognize me, but said nothing. Tor was more changed. His body leaner, but with more divots in his muscle. His russet hair was dark as a raven's wing now. His skin the brown of the trees.

He rubbed his forehead. "By the gods . . . I know . . . everything."

Siv and I had frozen in place, entwined together, simply watching it all unfold.

But my knees knocked when at the place Legion had fallen, his body arched; he staggered to his hands and knees.

A grin, deliriously happy, spread over my face as I watched him stand. His back was to me, but he'd changed, too. His hair no longer the washed golden color. It was midnight blue, so dark it almost looked solid black, and struck his shoulders in messy waves.

He was alive.

Beaming, I took a step forward, but stopped when Halvar and Tor reacted too strangely not to be distracted.

The Guild of Shade stared in astonishment at Legion's back, then they each bent a knee. They *kneeled* and *bowed* their heads.

Legion's shoulders rose heavily as he caught his breath. His fists clenched at his sides, and I jumped back when he shouted rage at the sky. It wasn't only the shout I felt. The earth shuddered with him. Stone trembled. Trees groaned and bent. A fissure snapped through the soil.

Siv and I hurried back again.

Legion grabbed his head. Doubtless all the memories he'd forgotten were rushing back. I was terrified, amazed, unsteady.

Should I reach out to him, should I run? Hells, would he even remember me?

"Sol!" Legion roared. "Herja! By the gods, they killed them. Everyone."

Tor's body trembled with unmanaged anger. "Give us the order and we'll see vengeance is had. It's long overdue."

I held my breath when Legion turned around. Part of me didn't want to see differences, but the greater part could hardly wait for answers.

His black eyes remained, the strength of his jaw the same. His lips were curled into a snarl. Siv noticed before me. She dropped to her knees, muttering prayers. Then, I noticed his ears. They were the change. Instead of rounded, Legion's ears came to a slight point. Fae ears.

Legion was Night Folk.

My mind reeled.

He was fae.

Cursed because he mattered.

He'd called out the name of the Sun Prince, of the Ettan princess. His anger, it had moved the earth. I felt my jaw drop when he locked me in his black gaze.

Oh, hells.

"My Prince," Halvar said in a kind of growl. "What would you have us do?"

He didn't answer Halvar. Didn't acknowledge him. He came to me; his eyes sending waves of fear and need to my stomach.

No longer Legion Grey.

I had helped free Valen Ferus. The Night Prince.

CHAPTER THIRTY-THREE

HE TILTED his head to one side as if seeing me for the first time. Tears stung in my eyes at the idea of him not remembering. The dead Ettan prince or not, I wanted him to know me.

"Elise," he said. "Elise Lysander."

My chin quivered and I dropped my head, embarrassed by the flood of relief in my gaze. He used his knuckle to tilt my chin up.

"How ... how is this possible?" I said in a breath.

"Willing royal blood. Isn't that what you said?"

It struck me like a fist to my jaw. As the girl in the tomb said, fate played tricks and often didn't turn out as expected. He'd died for me, willingly. Royal blood was needed, and he was Valen Ferus. His own blood had broken his own curse.

I lifted my shaky hands and rested them against his chest. He didn't pull away, so I gripped his tunic. "I worried you wouldn't know me."

"Do you know me?"

I nodded shakily. "Valen, th-the Night Prince."

Siv beamed. "We knew he was alive. The true heir of Etta."

I swallowed. Valen was the last Ferus heir. He'd be king.

"Unexpected, I admit," he said.

"Impossible," I added. "You were born a lifetime ago."

"In Etta, lives were long before the raiders came. Before they *slaughtered* my people. My family."

His voice was lined in venom, his eyes bright coals. I lowered my hands. "And Tor and Halvar?"

Valen grinned at his two companions. "Torsten Bror, a pyre fae, my brother's consort, and most loyal friend. Then Halvar Atra, an air fae, and son of the first knight of the Ettan court."

Tor hardly flinched. Halvar winked as though this had not changed everything.

"So . . . you were cursed for being fae, then."

"Timorans have a wretched fear of fury, but also want it for themselves. They killed my father for his, my brother."

Sol had fury? I didn't ask. Too many questions pounded my skull. "Which king saw the curse through?"

"The first false king. Eli Lysander," he said.

I swallowed. My damn namesake had destroyed his life.

"A prophecy frightened him after he'd killed everyone else," Valen went on. "Should I be killed by his hand, this land would be the wasteland he left behind unless he *earned* the crown. The crown of Etta chooses its kings and queens. He would need to be chosen, but I'm certain he knew he could not stand against a son of Etta, of fury. So, he cursed me. Kept me alive, but without memories, so I would never stand against him. And Etta has lived in a stagnant state where this land resists his people but does not die."

Each word ripped from his throat. As if he hated knowing the truth, or perhaps hated me because the man who'd ruined him was my bloodline after all.

I lifted my chin. Cruel and vicious as Timorans were, we were warriors. And I would not cower if the man I wanted to sacrifice everything for wanted me dead. "What becomes of me, then?"

His brow furrowed. My resilience cracked when Valen touched his fingertips to the line of my top lip. "What are you asking?"

"I am Timoran, Night Prince. Your enemy. A royal. If you plan to execute me, then I ask it to be done swiftly."

"Execute you?" he said, a little astonished. "I may know my name, but I have yet to question for whom my heart beats." Blood rushed to my head. His finger pinched my chin and drew me closer. I didn't resist in the slightest. His lips hovered over mine. "I've not forgotten, nor will I ever forget any part of you and your sacrifice."

I lifted a hand, touched the new point of his ear, traced the lines of his neck. He closed his eyes for a slow breath but set his mouth in a tight line when he opened them again.

"Even still," he went on. "This is where we must part, Elise."

"What? No. No, we talked of change. You promised you'd be here. With me. Valen, we can change things. Together. Two sides united."

"My name from your lips is a new pleasure I didn't know I wanted to hear." He grinned and my insides melted. "I promised as long as I am able, I would keep you safe. I have no plans to break that promise. But I also have made vows to my family, my people."

"You'll take the throne?"

"No," he said, surprising me. "Something simpler than that. Revenge."

"Please don't—"

"I will avenge my family," he interrupted. "My mother, father. My brother. A sister who was gentle, but fierce. Their blood is in this soil, and it has been silent for too long. I will not drag you to the places I will go."

He stepped back, and I felt him withdrawing from me.

"I know they deserve it. I know they do. But Valen, you can unite this kingdom. Heal it."

He smiled sadly. "Perhaps someday I will learn how to forgive like you."

"Prince Valen," Tor shouted. "Castle Ravenspire! The flares."

We all turned our heads toward the fortress. At each tower fires roared. A warning that something wrong has gone on. Doubtless the brilliant flash of light from the seal and the shuddering earth alerted Calder of a shift in his stolen kingdom.

"The guards will be here soon," Halvar said. "What do we do?"

He took out his crossbow, a little too hopeful.

"You must go, Elise," Valen said. "They won't show you mercy."

"Stand against them," I snapped. "Claim what is yours and heal this place."

"I plan to stand against them but have no plans to reveal

myself. The Night Prince is dead." Valen closed the space between us, an arm curled around my waist. "I *must* avenge the past."

Hells, I understood. I couldn't imagine knowing my family was gone, my life had been robbed and cursed. But he could have his vengeance by taking the throne back. He would be just. I'd seen his heart, held it in my hands for a time, and it was a wonderous thing. Vengeance would blacken the goodness I knew was inside.

"I can't stay quiet, Valen. I won't deny you."

He tucked a wild lock of hair behind my ear and nodded. "I know. Your loyalty is astounding." Valen pressed a gentle kiss to my lips, then pulled back enough to speak. "You will not speak my name to anyone but those present."

Something tickled the back of my skull. A light breeze rushed my veins, made me feel light, lifted my spirit. I shook it away. "What did you do?"

"Fury," he said against my lips.

I narrowed my eyes. "You compelled me?"

Night Folk could mystify a mind to do their bidding. And I hated him a little for it.

"I promised to keep you safe and speaking of me will not allow that." He looked to Siv. "You will not speak my name to anyone who is not currently present."

She swallowed, clearly disappointed. Valen, whom the Agitators had fought for all this time, if anyone wanted him to take his place it was them.

"The ravens come," Tor said.

Valen stepped back. "You trusted me, cared for me. You set me free, and I will forever be in your debt."

"But you do not care enough to stay."

"Quite the opposite. I care for you, *want* you, more than I care to breathe. But this will end in your blood. And I will not do that. Not to you."

Panic rose in my chest. He was pulling away, leaving. "Don't hide from what you were born to do."

A frown deepened on his face. "I was not born for the crown. My brother was. I was trained to fight for him. And that is what I plan to do." He narrowed his eyes again at Siv. "Keep her safe."

She bowed her head.

In the distance the thunder of hooves approached as a Ravenspire cavalry sped toward the revealed courtyard. I hadn't noticed how it had all become unguarded. The curse had broken, perhaps the fury guarding the tomb had lifted with it.

"You'll need to drag me away," I shouted, planting my feet. "I'm not leaving you. Not after everything."

His face was burdened. "Then I hope you will forgive me, yet again."

The Night Prince lifted his hands. The earth shook. When he closed his fists, Siv and I rolled with the soil and were shoved backward by some unseen force. Like giants bursting from the bedrock, jagged slabs of rock barred us away from the Black Tomb. From the approaching soldiers. From Valen.

He made his choice. And I wasn't it.

CHAPTER THIRTY-FOUR

WE WERE FORCED to keep to the trees, and it took another day before we reached the alehouse. I'd almost dared hope the Guild of Shade and their prince might be there.

I was left disappointed.

Sven asked about Valen—Legion—but we couldn't tell him the truth. We were compelled to keep quiet. We told him he was alive and then went his own way. The curse was broken.

The aleman seemed a little agitated Legion Grey had not returned himself to share the news. I understood the feeling.

"You're from Mellanstrad, right?" Sven asked as he wiped down one of the tables.

"Yes," I said, swirling some spiced red in a horn, absently.

"Well, did you know Ravenspire raided the town? Said it was in search of you and Legion. Word must've got out about what happened at your old manor."

My stomach lurched. "Ravenspire attacked its own people?"

"Went mad, from what I hear. A lot of folk fled to Ruskig. Mostly the half-Ettans. Ravenspire is determined to make this land all Timoran. I wouldn't be surprised if serfs wound up missing. These days are mighty strange."

I scrubbed my face as he walked away. Calder had attacked Mellanstrad because of me. What had become of Mattis? The game hall used on respite eve? I couldn't stay here and do nothing. Up in the garret I gathered what few supplies we'd left behind. Mostly journals—Lilianna's especially. Valen was in them, and strange as it was to read about his childhood, it helped me feel close to him in a way.

Outside, Siv had saddled her horse and mine. She no longer looked like a serf, but a fighter in a mottled tunic and knee-high boots.

"Elise, I miss Mavie," she blurted out. "I loved her as a friend and I know you don't believe it, but I plan to stick together, you and me. I didn't want anything bad to happen to either of you."

I secured my satchel, chest tight. "I know, Siv. Perhaps we can put the past behind us and go forward from here."

She grinned. "Good, because I think I know where we can go until we figure out our next steps."

"Where?"

Siv handed me a bit of the roasted squirrel meat Sven had cooked this morning. "I'm taking you to my clan."

"You would turn me over to the Agitators?"

"No," she said and wrung her fingers together. "But I don't know where else to go. They will be angrier with me than you, but if I tell them how you stood with Ettans and how you've been kind to me, that you aren't loyal to the crown, they might give us refuge. We're very good at hiding."

I didn't want to hide. Too much was changing. I needed to speak with Prince Valen Ferus again. Give him a piece of my mind, then maybe kiss him before demanding he come to his senses all over again.

He'd broken my heart. A heady pain I carried hour after hour. Day after day. But by the gods I loved him. A brutal, funny, irritating, passionate dead prince.

"We have nowhere else to go, Elise," Siv said. "Trust me, it is my last resort, but it could give us time to plan how to reunite with the Night Prince."

My mouth tugged into a grin. "Ah, so you have plans to tell a prince he's wrong, too?"

Siv chuckled and mounted her horse. She adjusted the bridle in her hand and guided the mare toward the trees. "Not a prince, Elise. I plan to tell a king he's wrong."

I didn't argue. Where could we hide from Ravenspire? I would not wait for Valen to change this land. Not when I knew my sister and my cousin did not belong on the throne. He'd either join with us or be forced to tolerate us being outspoken and putting our necks on the line for his family in our own way.

I'd see him again. I was too stubborn—so was he—to let this matter lie.

As we darted into the trees to seek Agitators, who would either kill us or welcome us, a silky scent of vanilla and honey and a little hint of rain wafted from the bushes. As we galloped past, I grinned at the satin blossoms of silver. A new sight to me. Big and bold on vines of black leaves, tangled into a towering shrub.

Moonvane was alive once again. The land had already begun to welcome back its prince.

FOR THREE NIGHTS we kept to the thickets and briars lining the roads. Too many ravens rode back and forth between townships.

In alehouses we bought bits and pieces of what had happened in Mellanstrad. Blood. Attacks. Imprisonment. Chaos.

By the third night, I slouched beside a miserable fire, tugging a thin woolen mantle around my shoulders. I couldn't know for certain, but if I had to guess, Mattis was gone. Imprisoned. Or worse—dead. If my sister had become as vicious as I assumed, I had few doubts my known friendship with the carpenter would be his downfall.

Siv had said little today. I didn't press. What was there to say? The Night Prince lived but would not take the throne. Mattis was gone. Our land, our people, would soon be at war, and we were fugitives.

"We will be crossing into Ruskig territory tomorrow," she said once the fire died down.

I nodded and gathered a tattered quilt Sven had supplied us. Tomorrow would be the day we earned the loyalty of the Agitator clans, or it'd be the day we die. Either way, I was nearly too exhausted to care.

"Do you—"

I didn't finish the question. Branches snapped. Stones

scraped on stone, as if a large creature stalked the darkness in the trees. Siv had a knife in her grip. I was less prepared but fumbled swiftly through our packs until I secured the dagger Valen—when he was Legion Grey—had given me.

My heart pounded in my chest with such rage I thought it might split its way out. Night thickened. I was ashamed how my hand trembled on the dagger.

Too soon the branches parted, and our meager campsite was filled with hooded figures. Most stood tall and broad. Furs and pelts and cowls enrobed their shoulders. I focused more on the glint of steel on their waists. Each man bore a battle axe, or knife, or dagger sharp enough to cut bone.

They said nothing.

Silence tortured.

I licked my bottom lip and held my dagger as firmly as I could. The blood pounded in my ears as the dark crowd of men divided and a man without his hood appeared in the moonlight. His skin was toasted brown, eyes like tilled soil, but his hair reminded me of harvest wheat. Golden brown. I pointed the tip of my dagger toward his chest once I noted the tapered point of his ears.

"Night Folk," I said in a rocky rasp. "Stand back. We are not your enemy."

He laughed, revealing his white smile. "I believe we've found the right woman, brothers."

My eyes flicked to the men in the shadows. Laughter rumbled through them. I faced the leader once more. "Who are you?"

"First, answer me this: are you Elise Lysander, the second *Kvinna* of Mellanstrad?"

"I don't need to answer anything to—"

"If you wish to keep your tongue you'll answer," he said, grinning.

"I have been threatened worse than that. You'll need to do better." I lifted the dagger, so the hilt touched the side of my cheek.

The fae man beamed, a gleam of thrill in his dark eyes. "I think we will get along nicely, *Kvinna* Elise."

"I never said my name."

"Ah, but I have heard too many tales of your strange bravery and disloyalty." He made a gesture to my wrist. "And there is that, too."

I glanced down at the raven head bracelet on my wrist. My stomach backflipped. The hot tang of bile soured my tongue. I was a fool. My arms dropped to my sides, and I let out a long sigh. "What do you want with me?"

He tilted his head. "I believe you've been looking for us?"

Siv perked to attention. "They're part of the clans, Elise."

"Yes. You call us Agitators. It's rather offensive, really. Perhaps it is the Timorans who are the agitators. But no matter, we know you've been looking for the refuge we can offer."

I nodded, desperate now for them to accept us. "We are not your enemies. By now we are enemies of the crown."

Dark murmurs hissed through the men.

"Forgive them," said the fae. "They prefer the Timoran royals to be called the false royals."

I didn't care. "Will you help us? We wish to fight against the false king and his queen."

"Your sister?"

It bit, sharp and harsh, but I nodded. "Yes."

The fae paused for a long moment. "We will give you refuge, Elise Lysander. If you do something for us. Odds are you won't survive, but it is the price we require for taking you in, what with you being such a risk. Do you agree?"

"Without knowing what the task is?"

He grinned with a touch of wickedness. "Your choice."

I glanced at Siv. She shrugged, but worry lived in her eyes. What choice did we have? We were alone out here with the entire guard of Ravenspire breathing down our necks.

"Fine. Agreed."

"Very well." He turned to retreat into the shadows again.

I quickened my step to jog by his side. "Wait, what is your name?"

"Ari Sekundär."

"And you lead the Agi . . . the clans?"

More laughter rose behind me, but Ari simply stopped walking and looked to me. "We have held out hope for true royals to rise. But, alas, we fae have accepted our hopes were misplaced. They are dead. A new line has begun."

"What are you talking about?" The Agitators worshiped Valen.

"Ari brought life back," said a man in a hood. He palmed a silver bud of moonvane.

I furrowed my brow. "You . . . you think you brought back the vines?"

"I do not think. I know." Ari shrugged, a smug grin on his face. "Fate is fickle."

But he didn't bring back life to this land. Valen was alive. I wanted to scream it at the top of my lungs, but his damn fury kept me silent. How dare they abandon him; how dare he hide from them. Clearly, the Night Prince was needed more than ever. I bit words through my teeth. "So, what? You're now taking control?"

Ari bowed his head and pressed a cold kiss to the top of my hand. "Yes. My folk have claimed me as their new, very alive, king. And I swear to you Timoran *Kvinna*, I will take back what my people lost. By any means necessary."

He grinned, a wicked kind. I thought he might be trying to frighten me, but it sent a thrill running up and down my spine.

These were the people of Etta. At the moment they accepted another king, true. But in heart they were Valen's people. They were loyal to him and would be again.

My smile widened.

They would be the way back to him.

I knew it like I knew to breathe. Fate led me here, and in all her games and tricks, she would lead me back to the Night Prince of a new, rising Etta.

WANT MORE?

Scan the QR code for two sexy bonus scenes from Legion Grey's POV

COURT OF ICE AND ASH
SNEEK PEAK
THE ROGUE PRINCESS

"It's *Kvinna* Elise," the guard said once he pulled back my hair and studied my face. His grin sent a shudder dancing up my arms. "The little traitorous princess. There can be no doubt what side you've taken now." He spit on my boot. "You stand against your folk. I'd do the king a service by slitting your throat now."

He whistled and three guards surrounded me, all placed their hands on my arms, holding me with unyielding strength.

I dropped. They dragged me. I kicked. A guard slapped me.

Outside smoke from the battle burned my throat. In the corner of my eye some of the Agitators fought. I didn't know who, but they would be my chance. Halvar and Siv were likely deep in the trees by now. By the time my absence drew them back, I'd be on my way to Castle Ravenspire.

There, Calder would humiliate me. Runa would torture me. Then, they'd kill me.

"Ari!" I screamed, desperate for anyone to hear me. "Ari!"

"Shut your mouth," a guard snapped. He hit the back of my head with his fist.

"*Kvinna*! No!"

I let out a rattling breath. *Ari*. He saw me. He sounded distressed. But would he take the risk and come after me? Halvar, maybe. Siv and Mattis, yes. But what could they do against the whole of Ravenspire?

The guard tried to shove me in the back of the coach. I struggled against him, earning another strike to my mouth.

"Get inside you stupid—" The guard let out a sick grunt. At once his grip loosened and his fellow ravens scattered.

A scream caught in the back of my throat.

In the center of his forehead a black battle axe split his skull. I stumbled against the coach when another person leapt from the top and splattered the blood of another guard.

My throat tightened. He was here.

Hells, I wanted to reach for him, to fight with him. The Blood Wraith ripped his axe out of the guard's head and turned on the driver and two remaining guards. They slashed bronze swords at him, but he sliced their legs at the thighs, or the weak points under their arms.

The driver weaseled his way out of the bloodshed after taking a strike to the arm. He crawled on hands and knees toward the front of the coach.

I took a raven's blade off the ground and met the driver at the front, jabbing the point against his throat.

"Get up," I said, dark and low.

With his hands overhead, the driver came from under the

coach, but in another breath, he shoved me and tried to take the sword from my grip. I kicked at his ankle. He fell forward, but took me down with him.

The driver tried to roll on top of me, but I managed to leverage the sword between us. I thrust the blade up until a strangled gasp ripped from his throat. Out the back of him, the point of the sword gleamed bloody and wet in the dim light. I'd skewered the man over me; his blood dripped on my face. My grip on the sword faltered and dropped his dead weight on me.

Until different hands tore him off.

Valen, masked beneath his hood, pulled me to my feet.

"Valen," I whispered. Three hells, it felt as if turns had gone by since seeing those dark eyes. "You're here."

I didn't know what to expect. His eyes gave away his anger. He might turn away and disappear. Would he ask about Halvar?

All at once, I forgot to breathe when he dropped one of his axes and pressed his palm to my cheek.

Blood and bone surrounded us. But for a moment, I could be still.

"Elise." His voice was soft, a hint of desperation underneath it all. Then, he stiffened. "What have you done? Why are you here?"

Ari needed the Blood Wraith. And I agreed. But, no doubt, he'd be coerced. Ari and his folk wanted this fight badly enough he would threaten and use me against him. Perhaps he'd use Halvar, too, now that I'd delivered the Shade into the Agitators' hands.

I gripped his arms. "Valen, the Agitators attacked, but they came for you. They knew of Halvar, so they planned to break him out, but only to get to you."

His eyes narrowed. My heart sunk in my chest when he stepped back. "You told them of me."

"I cannot. You made it so."

"You will not stop until I stand in a fight I do not want."

"No, I am telling you so you may go before they see you. Halvar is safe, Siv and I got him out. Leave, Valen. I see it in your eyes that you do not want to stay here. Go, then. We will take back this land without you."

So many words were being left unsaid. I wanted to plead for him to stay, to fight, to be here with me. All gods, I was furious with him. My heart ached for him.

I turned away. By the cheers ringing from the clans, I guessed the battle was ending. They'd been victorious and it would be over soon.

"Elise."

I winced but didn't turn around. If I looked at him again, I would not leave him a second time.

"Elise! Down!" Valen's hands gripped my arms and yanked me to the mud. His body covered mine. Shouts broke out, something about an archer on eaves.

I stopped listening when Valen didn't get off.

His breaths were ragged, sharp, and shallow. I adjusted, so I could sit up. "What hap—no! Valen, no!"

He met my eye, blinking rapidly. In his lower back an arrow had pierced deep into his body. Blood pooled around the wound.

The stakes are higher, the passion is fiercer, scan the QR code below to continue with Valen and Elise.

ACKNOWLEDGMENTS

I'm so grateful to everyone who helped with this book. First to my family for rocking out to Viking battle music all day with me during lockdown. Your support is everything.

Thank you to Moonpress Design for the beautiful covers. I'm so grateful for your stunning work. Thank you to Eric Bunnell of the chapter header art, it's beautiful.

Thank you to my editors, Jennifer and Sara. I so appreciate your help in smoothing out the edges of this book.

Thank you to my readers. I wouldn't be here without you. I'm so grateful for your love of Legion and Elise and these delicious fae Vikings.

Here is to many more adventures. Thank you for going on this journey with me.

All the best,

LJ

Milton Keynes UK
Ingram Content Group UK Ltd.
UKHW010833230424
441593UK00018B/416/J